The Runaway

The Runaway

by

Albertine Sarrazin

Translated by
Charles Lam Markmann

Grove Press, Inc.
New York

to my one-sixteenth of a mother
Doctor Gogois-Myquel

Part One

(1)

I am really done up for my entrance into prison tonight: opossum and slacks.

The fur remains in the property room: it may run the risk of feeding the moths for a few seasons, true enough; but no prison authority is willing to be responsible for the possibility of its being swapped and going up in cigarette smoke.

I also have to take off the slacks: wearing them is bad for the health, and, though they might make it easier to climb up onto the examining table (known as "the camel") for the specimen routine, on the other hand they would make it harder to get the speculum in. If you are due for incarceration one of these days, be sure you are always bare-assed or else have a suitcase full of underwear close at hand.

So here I am—I, who had expected to be able to cross that underworld equator, the summer solstice, in freedom—safely sheltered from sunstroke and moonstroke, and left defenseless against getting chewed out and having the blues for a horribly definite period.

Several years, in fact.

The police have very carefully deposited me at the admissions office: the goods have been delivered. Once my money has been counted, recorded, and put in a safe place with the ice and the transistor, and my history has been taken down and my morale been lowered, I follow the matron, the night one, since I'm a late arrival: it is at least seven in the evening. At least I think it is, since my watch has been sequestered in the police station with the other evidence of the crime, duly ticketed with a label resembling a railway shipping tag which lists descriptions of everything down to the smallest detail, the special markings, etc. Granted, when some millions of francs in jewels vanish through a broken wall in the course of a night when you just happen to be sleeping in your car in a peaceful parking lot a few yards away; when the cops checking license plates wake you up without apologies to find out what the hell you're up to; when they decide to go through the whole thing again in the morning and ask you so many questions that you take off like a shot just to be able to finish your nap a few miles away; when the same cops, resolutely determined to deprive you of sleep, turn up a few days later and go through everything in your pad just as you were domestically doing the breakfast dishes in your robe, before you'd even gotten washed yourself, and offer you a ride in their 2CV Citroën—I detest that model—promising to have you back home in time for cocktails, taking you away just long enough for a calm chat with good company to explain how the devil it is that *your* jewels look exactly like *those* jewels, etc.—well, you have to admit it would be silly to think of taking along your toothbrush.

That morning was yesterday, and now I'm beginning to feel a bit tired of being dragged about, searched, questioned, jostled, with no relief but some butts, some Vittel-Délice soda and some coffee—there is one cop detailed to running errands, and with dough everything is possible. Oh, excuse me, we had been given a few hours out during the night. Sleeping on benches, it seems, is good for the vertebrae. We'd just come

10

out of the hospital, Zizi and I—a long story of broken bones, smashed ribs, and fractured skulls, as well as involuntary manslaughter and the whole works: it couldn't have come at a better time.

Nevertheless I ask the matron about the chances of cleaning up soon, which got me an outraged: "You certainly aren't thinking of washing tonight?"

I give it up, and keep an eye on my keeper while she burrows in my luggage—handbag and wallet—deciding what I may or may not bring in with me. "Hey, take it easy," she protests when I grab as many photographs as I can, my bosom naked and my unhooked stockings drooping down over my slippers, for hearing the hallowed: "Get undressed," I had lost no time in obeying: since yesterday morning I had begun to forget what that word meant.

Finally, in the business of unpacking, I manage to rescue my stationery and to palm my eyebrow tweezers. Feeling quite a bit better, I go into the fitting room.

But where in the world are the jails of my youth?

Here there is no sign of those orderly shelves proffering the weary, dirty customer heaps of coarse cotton prison dresses, coarse cotton prison coats, dozens of T-shirts, jewel bags, hand towels, kitchen towels, sanitary napkins; no inventory catalogue and hence no signature to be given. They are satisfied to hold out to me, at arm's length, two rough denim dresses that come down over my ankles—"Tiny, aren't you?"—a matching belt, with nothing to hook it, a pair of grayish sheets, three blankets, and that's that. I agree that indeed I need nothing more, and, preceding my guide, start back up the stairs.

The railing clings to my fingers and I cling to the railing.

The matron's footsteps behind me, sometimes crowding me on, sometimes lagging resignedly behind, would make me ashamed of my slowness if I could still feel shame at anything.

At the top floor the last door is unlocked: two locks, top and bottom, and, in the middle, the huge pass key to this wing of the prison.

Before I waltz in, I have just enough time to get a glimpse of a patch of dusk through the leaded skylight.

Ugh! just my luck: the prison is a collective, for there's the dormitory, which implies the workroom tomorrow. Rather unrealistic to imagine that you'll sleep in a group and then be left to yourself by day. Besides, I'm much too sleepy to imagine anything at all, and the only thing that catches my attention is the empty bed with its inviting mattress over by the window.

All the other times, however, I've been lucky enough to have an individual cell, and I feel rather like a first-timer in front of these girls, all of them lying in bed and observing me over the bit of fabric or paper they were working on when I came in.

The first thing to do is to show them I'm hip by making my sack up exactly right. A first-timer even if she's a chambermaid on the outside, won't come off so well as an old hand whose bed is always made for her outside (why not? having nothing here doesn't mean you're a nothing outside). The right corners on the sheets, the pillow . . . no real pillow here, a rolled-up blanket has to do the trick. The other two blankets doubled: it's always freezing in these god-forsaken establishments.

Since there are no closets, no shelves, no chairs, no stools, I put my writing kit and my smokes on the floor.

I have had the errand boy get me a supply of Gitanes so I won't go out of my mind waiting for the canteen to open.

One of the girls turns over in bed and pulls at her neighbor's sheet: "Say, doll, you didn't bring up any water with you, did you? I'm dying of thirst."

An orange is very useful in unpleasant surroundings: hospitals and detention places. I offer one of the two that I still have. The girl thanks me; she looks very much the angel with her one thick braid, her pastel nightgown. Right away everything is quite cozy: I get undressed and snuggle down under the sheet, my back very comfortable but my toe on guard: if you ever stick a toe through one of these damned holes. . . .

The angel addresses me: "Tell me, *mademoiselle* . . . or are you *madame*?"

"Anick."

"All right; Anick. Mona's my name. Been in before?"

"Not here. But I've been in other pens."

I mention some of them, and we chew the fat for a while. Now that I've made port, getting some rest there has become less urgent. Then bit by bit the place is silent once again— a silence that is beginning to sigh and snore now.

I try to get my bearings: the dormitory is a rooftop dovecote, because I climbed forever just now, and the tops of the trees come nowhere near the windows. These are real windows—set high up and barred, certainly, but they don't block all the outdoor scents of the season like transoms in country jails. The wall is stained and blistered: have to watch out for the paint, there are black spots above the beds where heads have leaned back against it at night as the girls read or sew.

My bed is under the window, at right angles to the others: probably a kind of test-bed. In the beginning the girls keep a closer watch on you than the matrons do. Luckily, in prison or anywhere else, I make it a point not to demand or offer explanations, and I despise pointless chatter and bullshit.

The girls seem reassured: apparently I don't look like a stool pigeon.

"May I climb up?" Mauricette looks like a boy descended from the Maid of Orléans: very straight hair, very blue eyes, very flowered pajamas. When she comes over to my bed I expect the worst, but I say *yes* anyhow. The kid walks over my legs, springs up, grabs hold of the bars and hoists herself up

13

to the window sill. Once she's settled herself, she begins to whistle *The Little Ship,* takes a spool of crocheting thread out of her belt, and begins to pay the thread out the window as soon as she hears the chorus of the song whistled back to her from below. It is then explained to me that, in order to keep in touch with pals downstairs, everyone take turns sending messages this way. If I like, they'll find a pen pal for me.

Mauricette jumps down, her thread weighted down with a packet of notes. She goes from bed to bed, playing postman: "One for you . . . One for you . . . Sorry, doll, nothing tonight. . . ."

When will a letter come for me?

On what kind of paper, with what kind of stamp?

When will I get the first "darling" after our *so long* a few hours ago in the paddy wagon just before I saw those iron doors close at his back?

His broken back, which frightened me so—the croakers yelling: "You could end up paralyzed!"—and the cries of pain whenever I gave him the prescribed massages.

I left all that in the property room tonight.

I know you never leave your Self for long, never long enough, in the property room, and you get it back without the superintendent's permission.

But something's on fire in the joint!

No, it's just Mauricette burning the "telegrams" on the floor, once they've been read; after which she brushes the ashes, with the help of an unbelievably bald broom, into the john.

Oh, yes, there are toilets here; they're doubtless more practical than buckets—for the guy inside. Oh, nothing complicated with a handle and a flush tank, no indeed. Once one's intimate desires have been fulfilled, it's enough to step on the pedals in front of the platform: a panel slides back and everything tumbles down into the cesspool. The strong

14

odor of ammonia takes the place of smelling salts when you feel faint.

I get rid of a vague wish for chow with what's left from this noon's buttered sausage sandwich. I make orange stains on my only handkerchief; tomorrow there would be canteen coffee, java, nigger-sweat whose taste I can predict without any risk of error—it's the same everywhere.

After which, my head and my legs absolutely empty, all my mental images tamped down behind my eyes, I too dive into the springtime blackness of the sky.

(2)

That crack-up with the heap put one of my wrists out of action, I've just come out of the cast, and it's still damned stiff.

You'll tell me that it's not so bad, since it was my left arm, that I can write with either hand, that all I need my wrist for when I read is to turn the pages, and that in stir the literary ration is the one I like best.

Granted, but literature is not what's going to help me make my bed. Because I am ambidextrous only with the ball-point Bic and a lefty for everything else, and this sack . . .

Here there's no hope of throwing the bed together with all your night things rolled into a ball under the pillow—that is the rush-hour sack job—nor of a muscular setting-up exercise with your man on the other side of the bed helping to tuck in the sheets—that is the nuptial bed.

No, here it's the regulation sack.

First, chuck everything on the floor, right down to the mattress, which is too hard to turn, so I leave it as it lies.

Then you throw on all your wardrobe, except the bra, which you've already gotten into under the covers, out of modesty, before jumping into your shoes. The same goes for

16

panties, unless you've kept them on from the day or the week before—or unless you never wear them: it all depends on what personal standards of cleanliness you aspire to. Then each horse blanket is folded in four and then in eight, until it looks exactly as it should, and the same thing with the sheets; the whole lot is then piled in a neat rectangle at the foot of the bed, after which you simply flop back on the bare mattress to sneak in a short nap.

Mauricette, in top form, takes a swipe with the broom at all the cigarette butts, candy wrappers, and matches that were left over from the night's orgies.

Time for the door to be unlocked! We parade before the matron, I don't know her, I don't say "good morning," my eyes are glued closed, my rough denim chafes my bare legs, I stumble at the rear of the squadron; stairway, corridor.

"The workroom," Mona, who is showing me the ropes, explains.

The least that can be said is that for our preservation Justice does not boggle at the most modern techniques: here it must have resorted to hibernation.

What a fridge this room is!

On the window sills, in rows, are onions, empty Nescafé tins, bottles of Dop shampoo with the last bubbles clinging inside; between the windows and dangling down the walls, between the closets and brushing against our heads, are garlands of plaited cotton with blackish clothespins holding up very dirty rags, slightly less dirty napkins; and among the least dirty of the least dirty, are the occasional panties that the esthetes hang up to dry every night.

Other Nescafé tins, side by side with all kinds of beat-up shoes, crown the two yellow closets that match the wall. The full tins are inside, on the shelves, half a shelf per person. Since I have no goodies to store, I am assigned to the Mona-Aliette shelf; I stash my glass, above theirs, along with my plate

17

and my spoon, which have already been allocated "for the new girl," but the mess-tin has been forgotten, I'll have it right away, for sure. No knife. I'll find an old corset stay; once it's been sharpened on the stones of the exercise yard, it'll make a first-class blade.

The girls are going through their vanity cases while they wait for the coffee, which is late. In other days I used to bitch if I didn't see the attendant trailing the morning matron with a great steaming bowl and a ladle, a big quarter-liter one. But that was in another life: here coffee has to be earned. A place to sit is also hard to come by: every girl has already thrown a leg over her bench and flopped into place at the row of planks on trestles that takes the place of a table; I remain standing, my arms dangling awkwardly.

"Make a little room for her, Marie-France," Aliette says.

Marie-France professes to be an Egyptian; she must have had a touch of the tar brush. Oh, mother, those Mediterranean coasts, and now this heavy, musty cold! Since Marie-France doesn't move a muscle, something of a fight starts, but I look so trampy and tired that it gives me a kind of priority and in the end I get a place to sit.

Aliette puts a spoonful of Nes and two sugars into my glass; I protest, but then I give in, saying I have dough and will pay her back as soon as the canteen service comes around.

With a magnificent gesture Aliette rejects my offers. On the way down from the dormitory, one of the girls sneaked into the medical room to fill a messtin at the hot-water tap; the water is already only lukewarm, and George, the oldest inmate, loses no time lighting the stove in order to heat the water at the same time as the room in general. The smoke burns my eyes, and George's constant poking at the fire sets my ears as well as my teeth on edge.

The stove is just behind me, if I turn around I can toast my legs all day long.

Stagnation and not wanting, in short.

I drink the Nes without feeling bad about it; I have a hundred and twenty bills in the office, I'll have no difficulty holding out until the money orders begin to arrive. Besides, the girls like you much better when they can help you than when you're the one who helps them fill their guts: this way they know whether it's to their advantage to go on liking you or not.

The Nes drinkers take no part in the grand rush set in motion by the inviting announcement of the matron: "Coffee's here!" as she opens the door again. Today being Sunday, there's also milk: I offer my share round, it makes me look good and besides I hate milk.

Now the chatter has begun: "What is there to do here on Sundays?"

"Same as any other day: it bores the shit out of you. There's mass, if you want to go. But tell me, *madame*—"

"Anick's the name. Never mind the *madame* bit, don't ask me to tell the story of my life, and tell me what the fuck there is to do. Aside from going to mass."

"Nothing, I tell you. The office bell doesn't ring the whole day because there's no visiting hours. The ones waiting for trial have visitors the other six days, the rest on Thursdays and Saturdays."

"You know how to play belote?" Mado interrupts.

What a question! Since I'm an insider, I'm allowed to admire the cards custom-made in the establishment. The eight of clubs is a regular flotilla under a sky embellished with clouds drawn in with a ball-point; the trump looks like a business letter, and the little cassino could be taken for a minor obstacle: no one is afraid of paradoxes.

"If you bring me sixteen packs of Gitanes—empty, of course, I don't draw for money—I'll make a new set for you," I said, to make an impression on my fellow inmates.

My informant goes on: "No lawyers, no mail, no volunteer

workers, no social workers—really nothing. Except for the canteen, the lousy meat with the rotted salad, and, of course, the string bags. Are you going to make any?"

"What kind of bags are they?"

String bags are to this place what tags are to La Roquette: badly paid busywork, real exploitation of the proles. Prison being the only form of factory that I've ever set foot in, I want to hear more about it. Mona is the forewoman: she'll be glad to show me how to do the work, but at the moment there's no extra crochet hook to be had. In one corner there are huge cartons filled with spools of thread, white, red, blue, green, and string shopping bags not yet put together, tied up in groups of ten: at last a little color! Yes, I'll be glad to do them. But I have something else to do first.

As far as crocheting is concerned, I have to unravel the net in which I'm caught and crochet a cord that will get me out of here.

Who to contact? Friends and relatives who are still on the outside; the prosecutor, the 1 . . . of course, I don't have a lawyer. My usual champion lives far from here, I prefer to take on a local substitute, someone who knows the local angles: a mouthpiece who'll be around at least through the arraignment, those few hours that sum up whole years of past and future in a couple of words, the code words of the verdict.

"You could ask the bar association to assign you somebody."

"But I don't want a public defender, I'll pay."

General amazement: I must really look down on my luck. Finally I decide on the guy who has the most clients in the place: his fees may be big but it costs nothing to get in touch with him. I set up my writing kit among the crumbs, everyone is jealous of my unruled stationery, I give away a few lined envelopes and begin to scrawl.

In stir, the Bic is my piece.

Reappearance of the matron: "Time to wash!"

20

Washing is done downstairs. In a corner of the workroom there is another table, also on trestles, which supports (shakily) a family of basins: the big fat mother basin, in which the dishes are washed, and little chipped enamel basins, individual ones, for washing yourself from head to foot. The toothbrush glasses are mostly empty Nes tins.

In the bathroom the water is fed into iron troughs through a row of separate faucets controlled by a master tap. The girl assigned to the tap has her hands full:

"Turn it on!"

"Shit, not so hard, it's splashing all over!"

"Hell, are you paying the water bill here?"

Every prison has its own little amenities: here, if you're fast enough, you can wash your ass with hot water. One public-spirited citizen splits out and goes to the laundry to fill two buckets. The matron slams the door on her: for the rest of the washing period there won't be one more drop of water, whether there are five or twenty-five of us. So you have to struggle into line, basin in hand, and try to sneak up enough places so as to get there before the buckets run out. Otherwise . . . brr . . . the heart and all the other organs shrink at the thought of what it'll be like with cold water.

The news that the new girl has plenty of bread, and the consequent deference, make it possible for me to get everything I want: a bath glove from this one, a towel from that one, and that fucking basin of hot water. I much prefer the open drains of toilets to flooded cubicles, and make myself forget that I also possess nostrils. I get jammed into a corner, and have to twist three-quarters of the way around to get washed.

Wring out the gloves, twist the arms to reach the shoulder blades, spread the legs, juggle the breasts.

Clean at last! I gulp down a water cocktail and go to wait for food.

The menu: tuna fish with mayonnaise, chicken, peas, cakes.

As I silently welcome the reappearance of the Nes tins—
I have eaten too much—I wonder: "How do they still manage
to have money to canteen with on the twenty-third of the
month? As a rule chicken disappears from the order list after
the second Sunday." Let's not try to understand. Let's charge
the first items on our brand-new canteen account: "How is the
canteening done here? Is there one big list, or do you each
order separately?"

Good, there are individual orders and they are collected
every evening; this is a good break. Girls hurry over to
give me a form and show me the list of food, sundries, newspapers. "If you like mild cigarettes, they have Baltos."

Two years in stir on Baltos, when I was a juvenile in
Fresnes, were enough for me: this time I'll treat myself to a
sentence on Gitanes. Mado also is a *gitane,* a gypsy with
dyed blond hair with the black beginning to show again at the
roots. She is fat, healthy, flabby, and chubby, with a golden
smile and small plump hands. I yawn and look around absent-
mindedly, still studying the pile of order forms.

"Well, what's with you? Don't you know what the bells
are for?"

I jump; quite so, I'm not yet on to things.

In this soft end-of-April day, not one square of blue lights
the windows: the sky heavy with gray, the prison without
color, the stir of bodies young and old, this one doing her
hair, that one disappearing into the john, the other one spread-
ing a piece of bread with margarine—one of the two basic
elements, the other being Nes—the ten-times-multiplied image
of the Eternal Feminine.

Bedtime is an hour earlier on Sundays, that is, the matron
brings dinner at four in the afternoon, and at five-thirty, with
all her charges locked in, she can go off to tea in town. Just
as we are going to bed, in short, the sun comes out: it brightens
the whole dormitory. Tonight I shall sleep with a sunbeam.

The Runaway

My man once gave me a snapshot folder with two identification photos: he had the female version, since we had had the pictures taken together for the phony identity cards that described us as husband and wife.

How else could Zizi have married me?

I bawl into the hollow of my hands where the plastic folder lies wide open.

(3)

It seems to me that the joint has become quite active in the past few days. I'm not the one who is stirring it up, I'm rolled up in a ball in my corner: always best to play dead at first, right? But the courts are going back into session, people out on bail are coming back in on the night before their hearings, as the law prescribes; others are leaving for other prisons; there are arrivals and departures . . . The whole workroom, busily crocheting, discusses all the gossip passed on to the girl at the observation post by the girls assigned to general duty who have permission to go into the exercise yard. Everyone takes turns at the observation post: in these soft early spring evenings everybody has the urge to climb. A chair in front of the high window, somebody fat to sit in it and hold it steady, and there's our ladder. Once you're up, you sling your ass over the sill and spread your toes out toward the sunshine . . . As soon as you see or hear something, you're supposed to report it at once, and in detail. The crap that comes from these trusties outside is worth exactly what it costs, but when there's nothing else to do. . . . We can even find out what's going on with the men: these dames pull yards and yards of lies through keyholes and pass them on with a few embroideries of their own. We repeat them, we make wreaths for those who are sentenced to death, we reconstruct the whole ritual of the big trials: a click of the crochet hook, a click of the tongue, a click of a click, as Nadine says.

"What do you think of this place, Anick?"

I would have preferred to keep my mouth shut, or talk about something besides prison, but they all keep asking questions, perhaps because my glasses and my kind of gab make them think I'm an intellectual.

"There was a guy guillotined the other day," Gina says, "and you know what? There was ab-so-lute-ly no proof, and he denied it right to the end."

"Then he didn't do it," I say.

"You were in on it, maybe? What do you know about it?"

"Not a thing, obviously."

I have no way of explaining to Gina that in my opinion, if you take the trouble to deny a crime long enough, you eventually exonerate yourself, disassociate yourself from it; and that changes everything. Sure, you get your head cut off just the same, which certainly proves that the death penalty is ridiculous, an example that no one pays any attention to, and one that has to be repeated over and over.

"Look, if I had a choice, I'd prefer that to life . . ."

Suddenly I think of Caryl Chessman, knocked off in the springtime, in the lovely California June that he'd been done out of, big-mouth Chess who had had to shut up all the same in the end.

"It's better for everybody, you cut out and other people don't hear another word out of you."

"I don't know whether you've seen many stiffs," Gina said, "but . . ."

Her voice trails off, to make us believe that she's seen plenty of them, and by no means in the best of shape. We all shut up, ashamed: all we can produce is proper corpses, all cleaned up and lying on beds of petals with rosaries in their mitts. We've never seen even our brave heroes killed in Algeria; we haven't seen anything, even those of us who are in for murder: Gina is contemptuous of our miserable corpses, she's contemptuous of everything, and big talk is her department.

"In the life you don't need the executioner or the fuzz to get rid of people, you settle your own accounts."

"You're wrong then: you should leave that to the experts."

The moment of silence that follows makes me hope that the subject has been exhausted. Why talk about the death penalty when you're condemned to go on living, living without a respite, shackled to life like a punishment, a festering sore?

The girl at the observation post is wriggling on her perch. "Shut up, girls."

For once nobody was saying a word!

"They say Zorah's back. Somebody saw her downstairs . . ."

Zorah! I've heard so much about her, here or elsewhere, I can't remember. She's been in and out of stir so often that she's worn a path; what's more, she's a mulatto, a dame to lose plenty of nights' sleep over.

Bang! The outside door slams shut, four feet are making the stairs creak as they climb up toward us . . . Holy Mother! A half-second glance, averted at once, is enough for me to take in the vision in its entirety: cloaked in all her black splendor, the Virgin of the Basilica of Algiers is bearing down on us.

The murmur that follows, however, is less deferential than disappointed: this isn't Zorah, nobody knows this girl. But to all of us more or less pure-blooded Frenchwomen, as soon as it's a question of an Arab, a Berber, a Targuih, or even a gypsy when summer is over, as soon as we see braids and a

26

dark complexion, it's an Algerian. This is an Algerian: whether she's Zorah or someone else no longer matters.

She's wearing a bright green cardigan, a transparent plaid bandana that shows her very black hair; some kind of mysterious little red plastic bag is hanging from her ear on a gold pin; a kind of clip like a small cluster of grapes is shoved up her right nostril—at first I thought it was some flourishing excrescence; in each eye socket, beneath the blue lid, there is an opaque carbuncle that must be an eye; there are not six square inches of her visible skin area that are not covered with tattoos; and, finally, the inevitable portable kit—in this case, an Arab hut—is slung over her arm. She explains in her odd lingo that she has been transferred here from a prison in the south. Even before she asks what the name of this town is, she asks for hot water—not for washing, for coffee. She has a bag of ground coffee, the real stuff, it is allowed down there, as well as Méta burners and fuel capsules. She's going to ask the matron to let her have hers back, on the pretext of cleaning it before it's put away to be reclaimed on her release.

"Just watch," Mona whispers; "she'll get it, too; her kind always get away with everything."

But meanwhile . . . it is exactly coffee-break time; but, in these troubled days, terror of the terrorists makes it impossible to Nes ourselves in front of one of them without cutting her in; on the other hand, the same terror makes it impossible to have the slightest truck with the rebel side. The hassle between the races continues in stir on the level of political parties, if not political understanding.

In any case, our attitude would annoy the President of the Republic: we absolutely refuse to fraternize. We answer the Algerian's loud complaints with evasive gestures and "we don't know anything about that, you'll have to ask the screw."

"You know, the underwear in her bundle of stuff seems pretty clean . . ."

27

"There's nothing cleaner than a clean Algerian, everybody knows that!"

What does create some confusion, however, is the handle she goes by, a pisspot full of names that are not easy to pronounce or to remember: Ben Sidi something, something that sounds like "dump truck."

Prophylaxis is the order of the day, the word is whispered from one to another: "Because they're all sick, you know . . . Watch out for the lice . . ."

Though I can't swallow all that racist stuff, it is undeniable that the woman has gone to the toilet three times even though she arrived barely an hour ago; and it is no use for Solange, who was nearest to her while she was in there, to insist that all she's heard her do is spit, we all think immediately of dysentery. Not to mention that with those fucking carbuncle eyes she is sure as hell going to put the hex on all of us. Might as well keep on the good side of her.

She's managed to squeeze in at the table on the other side of the stove, which we called "the tramps' table"; I have my back to it. Since she's just sitting there, everybody goes back to their conversations, their string bags, or their card games, but no one forgets the Algerian for a moment.

"They're a tricky lot, she'll jump up unexpectedly and slam you one . . ."

Gina smiles and waves the fan of her cards scornfully. "Balls! Algerian or not, I'll beat her up; I'll kill her before she sticks a knife in my back two days later. And besides . . ."

"With a knife from the canteen! If I'd known, I'd have hung on to my dough, I can't even cut my meat . . . The stuff must come from Bilbao . . ."

"You and your gripes about the food! Look, she may not be so bad."

"You talking about the meat?"

28

"God, no. Wait a second, I'm going to get the scoop on those tattoos."

Gina goes over to the tramps' table, speaks very carefully, as if she were trying to make friends with an animal, shows her own shoulder tattooed with a heart and the name *Tony,* and in half an hour she has conquered Algeria.

"Oh, you're really something, you are," the woman said; "yes, doll, you are."

Good: she won't start anything with Gina, and Gina is us, she's our mouthpiece, our shield.

An incident does take place, however, at chow time, over a bowl of potatoes. The Algerian offers her share to the crowd. Someone near her takes half, then holds up the bowl like a monstrance: "Who else wants some?"

Solange, who has her back to them, turns her head: "Me."

"They're O.K., you know: she hasn't touched them."

"Oh, are they hers? I don't want any, then."

The Algerian has taken in the whole scene and is hopping mad. Her potatoes are as edible as ours, after all, since they're all the same. But Gina has every intention of maintaining her monopoly of the soapbox: she yells at Solange: "All you had to do was take them instead of turning your nose up at a plate of spuds!" Then she adds under her breath: "You could have thrown them out afterward, quietly." She turns to the Algerian: "No, darling, she didn't do it to make you mad, it was just that she thought you'd put Harissa in them. What do you expect, we can't all like Harissa."

There is more whispering at bedtime: some are about to ask that the woman be segregated, or put with her compatriots, etc. I protest, nonviolently but strongly: "You know damn well there's no single cell. Otherwise I'd have been put in it, or anyone else as sick as I am . . . We're all sick, and I guess that's why they put us all in together. No, seriously, if you raise hell, all that'll happen will be that they'll set up two workrooms, one for the girls who haven't been tried and the other for those who have. Since this woman's in both classes, she'll have to be shoved into one workroom one day and the other the next, and . . ."

"And when she's finally been tried," Aliette, who still has a year to go, interrupts, "I'll stuff her ass. I sure as hell will!"

All this makes the guillotined man a totally dead issue.

(4)

"Wanted in the office!"

I climb off the bench I've been sitting on all morning, wallowing in my thoughts, and, without the "What for, ma'am?" that she obviously expects and is just waiting to answer with "I have no idea," I limp off behind the matron to the main office. The assistant director who had taken custody of my worldly goods the other night is standing there, freshly uniformed and less freshly shaved, his hand over a document, which I immediately try to read upside down and between his fingers to get some idea of what it's about. "Urgent—Prisoner": the official stamp on communications from the Justice Ministry.

The warden has noticed my impatience: "The examining magistrate has ordered—the papers just arrived—" here he tapped his knuckles against "Urgent" "—that your account be blocked."

"What do you mean, blocked?"

I don't get it.

"The money you had with you when you came in," he explains to me with sly patience, "has been seized."

I imagine he's enjoying this moment. Ever since my arrival, I have showered the office with letters demanding explanations

—for delays in the delivery of canteen orders or mail, or the reasons why I have not yet been notified what my account number is; in other words, I haven't let them get away with a thing. "Now they'll really make me pay for my gall," I think; and immediately I realize that three minutes ago I was stripped of the means of paying for anything.

"But some margin must have been allowed me? None? What about postage stamps? What about money to pay my lawyer?"

I see Sainte-Anne Asylum in my future.

"You can ask the judge the reasons and apply for whatever permission you may need to take care of things like that. As far as we're concerned, we're under orders to block whatever you have or whatever may be sent to you. Naturally, this doesn't apply to what you earn making string bags."

Those string bags! I don't even know how to hold a crochet hook. I've seen no reason so far to make a start on them, because the inroads made on my funds by the support of a crew of girls who are strapped and myself are still relatively trivial. But now everything is going down the drain at once.

I go back to the workroom without reacting. I am struck dumb, I must be pale, the girls look at me, none of them dares to ask the first question, which would set off a flood of others. Finally Aliette takes the risk: "Something get fucked up?"

I simply nod gloomily. I must not break down, I must . . . but suddenly, at the sight of all that stuff on the table—packs of butts, food, newspapers—at the thought that I don't have even the price of a stamp, and if there ever was a time to write to people, this was it!—at the thought that I was going to have to let all my parasites die and instead try to keep myself alive on their loot, the shit hits the fan and I break down for real.

The girls forget that each one's place is hers and hers alone,

and make me lie down with a whole bench to myself, pouring
water on my head, which feels like a boiling kettle, propping
up my back, which hurts like hell, as it did when I came out of
the coma. Somewhere, quite close, I hear a familiar sound: a
spoon prying off the lid of a tin of Nes. "You take two sugars,
don't you, deary?"

These women know right off what must be done in such
cases: glug, glug, glug, the sound of boiling water, plink,
plink, plink, the sound of the spoon stirring.

My problems revive with my spirits: will any more Nescafés
be offered to me so generously? I have not yet established the
nature of the beast . . . I may know a lot about jails, but I
didn't know much about jailbirds: this is my first time in a
"collective." In the Central Prison, after a day in the workroom, you have the whole night in your own cell to recuperate,
so that doesn't count. As suspicious and sharp as I am, there
still must also be dirty deals that I can only guess at until I've
had them . . . Since whispering anything to anyone in this
place is the equivalent of using a public-address system, I say
as much to the girl nearest me on the bench; and in fact in
half an hour the whole atmosphere changes: it is protective
and reassuring. If only it'll stay that way!

"You're not in any big jam. That happens to almost everybody who's hit for breaking and entering: you know, as far as
the judge is concerned, any dough that's suspicious is crooked
dough. But all you have to do is talk to your lawyer, and he'll
get it unblocked for you right away. At least you can prove
how you got it, can't you?"

"Sure I can! Isn't that what they put me here for?" I can
joke now, but I feel lost, lost, lost. As long as there was bread,
there was hope; the hundred bills in the account was a hunk
of money, edible money, but no matter, I'll eat something else.
What is less amusing is the thought of all the money that is

lying about in the bank and elsewhere and will probably go
down the same road.

The judge will refuse to approve any money orders except
those from my mother, and my mother will cut off all the cash,
as she always does every time I'm sent up, saying my guy
should take care of me and if he's inside she doesn't want to
know about it, but in any case I will always have her moral
support . . . And anyway whatever anyone does send me will
all go to build up the kitty for getting back on my feet when
I get out.

As for what was at hand now, let's see: in the clothing
room, in my wallet, I still have a few books of stamps which I
had completely forgotten about in my shock. All I have to do
is to get hold of them and swap them off little by little, because
here it is possible to stamp your own letters and get stamps
from the canteen. Furthermore, I have all the broads on my
side:

"We'll manage something, don't worry. And things will
turn out all right for you too . . ."

"Yeah, sure, and my husband will be let out and we'll be
happy and we'll have dozens of kids. I know all about that,
thank you."

"Oh, well, if you're going to take it that way . . ."

"Come on, let her alone, you can see she's in the shit, can't
you?"

I cut them all off: "Is there a dentist in the house?"

General amazement. This business with the account must
have sent me completely off my rocker. I explain: "You know
I lost two fillings Thursday; I have two cavities to be filled and
they were being taken care of when they picked me up . . ."

"Oh, sure, and I inherited . . ."

I gesture to Mado to shut up: there'll be an accessory rap
for her if she yacks too much.

Yes, the other Thursday I was sitting in the torture chair

in the medical department, with the worse than primitive drill hanging over my kisser like the sword of Damocles. Before he went to work on me the jerk had asked me how far I'd gotten with the treatment, whether I had had temporary fillings, etc. I interrupted him: "Yes, there are nerves in two teeth to be killed. I've had a root canal job, but since there's some arthritis from pressure as well . . ."

Absolutely stunned, the jerk hadn't opened his jaws—his, not mine—until, in the midst of digging away at my molar, he suddenly shouted: "Oh, shit, I forgot them in the men's prison." And he tore out of the treatment room without explaining what he had forgotten. I did not pursue the subject: I jumped out of the chair. In cases like that it's worth-while getting the lead out.

When I had made sure that the matron was busy letting him out by the ground-floor door, I did a quick once-over of all the stairs to be sure that no general-duty girl was loafing about. The risk was minimal: at meal time no one is hanging about anywhere; there are more important things to do. No one, that is, except the old hog-butcher of a dentist, once a week, and that walking corpse, the general nurse, every day more or less, so that, if you have business with both of them and are still hungry afterward, you have to mix the dental cement, the sedative, and the restorative potato in the same mouth at the same time. This time, at any rate, we had been spared the nurse, and I was completely alone.

Unfortunately, the cupboards in the treatment room were all locked, and I didn't have my vanadium screwdriver. Otherwise I should certainly have found something among all the supplies in them to drink, or to make a drink from: a lousy bit of ninety-proof alcohol stretched out with sugar and a few scraps of apple and left to age a week, and our thirsty taste buds would have quite a powerful imitation cognac. I therefore fell back on the goodies in the surgical kit, but no luck there either . . . when the jerk came back, all I had been able to cop was a little bottle of stuff to deaden the gums.

What's more, the junk didn't do me a bit of good: I could stand the effects of the drill, and my bra, the only one I owned, was beginning to stink of the loot at a hundred yards. Those leak-proof bottles aren't worth a fuck! I was going to throw it into the john, but Mado intercepted me: "Let me have it, I can always use it. I have the most frightful neuralgias!"

Something always ails Mado somewhere, everyone knew that. And, really, I was not so keen on doping myself: once you've started . . . to my way of thinking, getting doped up should be, and should remain, deliberate. Even when I was broken in a dozen pieces and twisted every which way, after the accident, I kept away from it. So I gave the thing to Mado, on the express condition that she be careful about getting rid of it, and above all not let it fall into the hands of the screws.

"Oh, Anick! There aren't any cops among us gypsies."

But let me get back to today. I go on: ". . . and you know how it is, no dough, no dentist." Oh, blessed Central Prisons! Central Prisons with your major and minor attentions, where every jaw, regardless of whether it's covered by social security or not, from the moment it arrives, is systematically examined, measured, treated, manipulated; where, for gums forming scar tissue while they wait for their dentures, there is always a pot of soup on one corner of the stove. Here in this provincial house of detention, you have to supply your own gold, in the form of a bridge or in the shape of bank notes, or else have a mouth filled with thirty-two stinking cavities. Oh, sure, when a jaw swollen to ten times its normal size and a temperature of a hundred and four leave no further doubt as to the character and the progress of the infection, it may be possible, if it is absolutely necessary, to see whether there is not some way of letting you have some sort of credit; but as far as I'm concerned there's not a hope along this line: I'm healthy, dis-

gracefully so, there's no sign of an abscess, my fillings are not
going to crumble and I'll have them forever, until I kick off,
until I rot.

It's really something to shoot yourself for.

But wait a sec: an idea I've been kicking around for several
days begins to take hold: medical parole.

My mother, as I expected, has continued to be fond of me
but has withdrawn her financial support; through the mouthpiece I sent word to my friends that they shouldn't make a
move or send me anything; what Zizi kept telling me is absolutely true: "every one of us is all alone, baby. All alone."

But I would like to be even more alone in order to have the
peace I need to draw up my request to the examining magistrate for a medical examination. . . .

Mado spends the whole evening imitating Aznavour, it's
almost as bad as the original, everything drums on my nerves
and my ears: ears tired of everything, everything tired of
everything, with sometimes a brief respite punctuated only by
the noise of turning pages and the periodic glare of the re-
volving searchlight: "Lights out in three minutes," the matron
calls through the peephole, "put your things away."

Sighs; someone grinding her teeth; someone weeping, and
alone at last and exhausted, I dream on, not making a sound
except for a moan when I have to change position: *aïe, aïe,*
and the chorus answering in unison, with sometimes a solo
from a snorer, who prevents me from closing an eye the whole
night because of her nasal emanations, but mutters for my
benefit that people should get a sedative from the nurse if they
have to howl like that when others are asleep. Sedative! Seda-
tives have to be swallowed in the nurse's presence, which
drives me to all kinds of digital acrobatics to palm them while
I keep her concentrated on the glug-glug of my glass of water.
There are days when I lose my touch and my clumsiness forces
me to really put them in my mouth; nevertheless I never go

37

so far as to swallow them, but when they're so chewed up and half melted, they lose all their trading value.

In stir even sleep can be traded in.

You trade, you whisper, you lie. It is an atmosphere of perpetual plotting, of secrets that everyone knows and discusses, without interrupting the incessant murmured vow not to tell, sworn on the heads of children, husbands, or dogs. Not to mention the fact that inevitably there are two or three stoolies, to make the proper contact between the said secrets and the penal administration or even the judiciary.

Aside from my "case," a forbidden subject, and my newspapers, that I keep my eye on at all times, lest they disappear in the john before they've been read, I have damned little to keep to myself: I don't correspond with the broads downstairs and my guy has been forbidden to write to me.

Tonight I don't take advantage of the three-minute grace to go on writing to the judge: that's two pages thrown away. Perhaps it is my new sack that makes me feel homeless: Aliette has suggested in a motherly way that I give up the test-bed and take the vacant one next to hers.

Yes, I've already adapted to being broke.

Jammed in between Aliette and the wall, facing the john, I can't smell another thing. Aliette is a good kid, at least she was today; strange, because on the whole she's strictly out for herself. Herself! it's obvious from the interest she takes in other people's plates and the way she listens to the canteen orders when the matron reads them off while the girl on duty doles out the items; sometimes, when desire gets the better of her, Aliette whines: "Oh, gee, I really love that!" in a voice turned suddenly childlike and silly—somewhat of a shock coming out of a hulk like her.

Aliette, who hides her used sanitary napkins in a carton that her dear girl friends discreetly point out to the matrons, too disgusted even to touch it, while she is downstairs with a visitor.

Hell, I like Aliette. There are charges against her whichever way she turns—she's doing time for some, accused of others, held as a witness in still others: all fraud raps, and this is dazzling to me, for I'm only a poor little provincial burglar.

The lights have not been out two minutes when several taps on the wall bring me back to my surroundings with a start. Gina gets up, runs into the john, listens, and comes back out. "Aliette, it's for you." Aliette groans, she had just started to snore. Others nag at her: "Get the lead out, shithead. It's for you."

Finally she condescends to go into the john, shuffling along in her slippers. According to what she told me earlier tonight —delighted at having a neighbor, she had never stopped talking—she has a co-defendant in the workroom downstairs who sleeps in the next dormitory. Theoretically the walls are soundproof; if two colleagues want to confer, for the sole purpose of ascertaining whose fault it was that the other is in stir with her, let them wash their dirty linen in front of the judge. After all, that's probably the only washing Aliette knows how to do: look at the carton.

Blood on the courtroom floor, O.K.; but the management doesn't want any here. This floor is sticky enough without that.

Nevertheless, the two ladies seem to be on the best of terms in the john, and this is no figure of speech. Tucked away in there, Aliette is conversing with the Invisible.

My recently repaired head, the darkness and the heavy smell of tobacco and the breath of ten fellow inmates in the dormitory, boredom, worry—all this makes me want to cork off, but the nearness of this speaking-tube is a major obstacle. Oh, lord, tomorrow night I'll go back to my old sack.

I wonder whether it's really necessary, in order to hear clearly, for Aliette to shove her face right into the hole or whether it may not be enough for her to stand there with uplifted head, like a certain Virgin. No matter: in my opinion people's business should not be shouted from rooftops, still less in the john.

And besides: didn't even the cleverest liar get her story mixed up when her voice was made so gloomy and deep, the position was so uncomfortable, and the place smelled so bad?

It doesn't take long for Aliette to admit defeat. But she's accustomed to telephoning this way almost every evening. Completely out of breath, she throws herself on the foot of my bed: "I'm sick of it. Tomorrow I'll have somebody say I'm asleep. There's no getting round the fact that it's all her fault, she . . ."

"But, Aliette, I thought just now I heard you calling her *darling*."

"I can't just break it off, I'll get rid of her gently, don't you see?"

Regally Aliette goes back to her own bed, and five minutes later her nasal Diesel engine is running.

And now in the silence of the window I have my other friend, the night rain. It wakens the soothing scent of washed earth and trees and carries it up to us. Pour out the bitter herb tea, Anick, and rinse your glass in rain.

One thing sure, things are going badly: if my account has been blocked by the judge, it's because he's trying to pin the robbery of the jewelry shop on us. Might as well try then to serve part of my time awaiting sentence in the sunshine, because it is going to be a long haul.

I feel certain that the whole thing began with that damned car. We had just traded in the old one, our friend, our accomplice, so beautifully broken in to our hands and our habits; the new one was too pretty, too respectable, too heavy; it had never acquiesced to being driven by two hoodlums drunk on weariness or alcohol and being used as a bar, a restaurant, and a bedroom. Craftily, it had bided its time. What a nasty crash it must have been! Lucky I went out like a light. And then the cops on our necks, and now here.

Well, for God's sake, why not reverse gears and try now to use the whole thing as an argument for getting out?

Medical parole . . .

That beat-up heap, that mess of metal rusting away some-where, might yet be able to lug me to the gate.

(5)

What the hell, I'll go to mass once, anyway; Sunday is especially dead, and this will kill an hour.

The extra-religious George is unbeatable in the field of devotions, she has a first-name relation with every saint who takes particular interest in jailbirds, she knows the right prayer to be offered to each of them and the itinerary of all the holy places where she'll light candles when she gets out.

When getting out comes into the question, no one is a heathen. Whenever a girl in the workroom is called to a hearing, or to a little session with the *Police Judiciaire,* George calls a prayer meeting, leading the psalms with the chorus of virgins chiming in. Only the ill-bred go on working on their string bags or setting their hair! As a rule, the service is concluded with the ritual appeal, "Saint Expédite, speed her way," and though this Expédite has nothing to do with my case, I wonder whether he may make up his mind to speak one of these days.

We are *ad hoc,* fetishistic believers.

This morning George asked us all to go to the chapel, it is the birthday of one of her kids, and, even though she murdered the other one, she wants to pin a medal on this one to assure her a long life, O God of justice, preserve us from eternal oblivion.

And lead us into the men's wing!

We take our places in our stall to the accompaniment of a ragged *Tantum Ergo* brayed by the male prisoners: as long as they bawl out something . . . Our dusty stall, full of shadow and stale air, overhangs the driveway; the altar has been set up on the roof of the sentry box in the middle; through its windows we can see the keeper's desk and his hand, which, devoid of respect for the deity tramping about over his head, is crumbling cigarette butts. There is also a veil for this temple: four pieces of brown cloth, sewed together by machine and hung from a rod. They are probably sheets swiped from the prison stores.

The matron has come through the veil, tangling herself in its threads, just before our harem took its place in the stall; so that the only food for their souls that the men got out of it was the shuffling of soles, the clack of heels, and the rustling of skirts in the gymnastics of settling ourselves on the benches. The matron settles herself in her chair, drops her keys into her lap with a warning clink, and gives our assembled heads a once-over: good, they are all in line, everything is nice and hermetic, and the Holy of Holies, without lips or fingers, can start grinding out the Mass of the Angels.

How to fill the time until the *Ite*? The missal is the same as in other prisons; you know the psalter; you don't want to know your neighbors.

Oh, if only I were not so pious—and above all if I had known that this stall was so badly lighted, I would have brought a book, or a pencil stub and a crossword puzzle, or a match to clean my nails with. Oh, well . . . remembering my boarding-school, I stand up in all the right places in the mass, and take a gander over the railing, making sure that my nose doesn't stick out farther than the others; below us, behind the line of bars, a man with a shovel and a broom has stopped still, on his way to clean up the slops; and there he stands, parked in his heavy boots, his face rapt, without moving.

What vision froze the guy in his tracks? And will he be used to season the grub if it turns out that he has been turned to a pillar of salt there, Sodom and Gomorrah style?

Sure as hell one of our shoes must be sticking out, or a bit of nylon must be peeking out from under a skirt; in mixed company made up of people under lock and key, everything is important and a reason for kicking up your heels; at mass no one pays any attention to the priest; at the monthly film the screen always seems too bright.

The matron fingers her keys.

I resume my piously bovine expression, I bow my vertebrae gratefully, and soon a legion of angels is doing invisible battle with the little demon perched on my shoulder.

On the outside, I used to sleep late on Sundays to make up for balling all night; my man puttered around the joint, anxious for the new week to begin. Here I'm going to take advantage of the day to do a little writing. Writing as a sacrifice and a favor to the damned brain, which must be force-fed because it has no appetite and yet refuses to die.

The girls have gotten into their best clothes and are preparing to stuff themselves: "Hey, doll, did you at least canteen some string beans to go with the roast beef?"

"Not worth the trouble; there's usually mashed potatoes, and they'll be good with the gravy. They've stuck us in here, they can damn well feed us then; I'm not kidding."

The singing, the humming, and the whistling that took the place of the organ made me feel half like wallowing, half like going spiritual. Sleeping is forbidden: I have to write; and not sleeping is forbidden: I must not wake up, because of the stupid automatic tears that might irrigate the first yawn. I dream, sucking the end of my Bic: why not order dreams from the canteen list, or simply sit up all night over a bottle of nothingness?

My mind is really vacant. I've slept too much, which is as bad as a night without sleep: I feel dirty, dried-out, weightless. The bed is too narrow, and yet I'm not big enough for it: for this bed I would turn myself into a river, a river of tears washing away all the shit of the dormitory. I have hardly bawled at all, however, since our arrest.

The last time I wept on the outside was during the last night with Zizi, just before dawn: the gasoline gauge was on zero, and I had parked the beast next to a wall, waiting for the man on the pumps at the Esso station next door to get moving. We had just sat there an hour or two, dumb with weariness, half asleep; then a sudden sharp thrust in both of us at the same time hurled us together; and that passionate, dog-tired kiss, almost a bite, somehow made me weep. . . .

The next day, when the *Police Judiciaire* arrived, we still had done nothing but sleep and eat; and only this kiss remains, as cruel as pure snow.

That was how we loved each other, forgetting to make love, robbers, hallucinators, prowling through the night with death at our heels . . . What could fill that bitter void, what future dawn, what cup of canteen coffee grown cold?

An empty minute breathes boundless eternities.

Mado is singing, but no one wants any more of Aznavour: what we need is the newspapers and the canteen. Even if the roast beef comes at three o'clock, what the hell, we'll eat the regulation slop at noon and enjoy ourselves all the more in the evening; but, to kill the afternoon, we have to have *Confidential* and *Festival*. I'll explain the hard words—there are some, even in these rags—and in return they'll leave the singing words of the crossword puzzles for their expert and the family puzzle page. "Just be careful, doll," Gina said: "don't tear the pages, I've got to lend them to the workroom downstairs later. Might as well lend them all in one piece, if we want them to give us theirs."

"Oh, knock it off; books—these especially—are sacred."

Ah! there came the hand-out: newspapers, canteen, lunch; except for the roast beef everything comes at once. "You order roast beef?" the matron asks, looking vague. "Well, just wait a while, the kitchen hasn't sent it up yet."

"But what are we going to eat, then? That's pretty damn lousy, we pay and then we get fucked. Every Sunday it's the same racket with cooked food."

Resignedly, Aliette goes to work on her cold platter: she has made one big mess of the meat like shoe leather, the salad, the usual gravy, and the regulation noodles that Nadine can no longer bear even to look at but that she always takes anyway so as to salvage their bit of margarine: you can always remove the little cube placed in the center of the noodles before any of it has melted, although a trace of oily flour shows that some effort has been made to warm them.

Having thus made certain of her margarine for tomorrow's breakfast, Nadine joins me over my crossword puzzle. Holding the paper between us, armed with pencils and pieces of bread, we rack our brains while Aliette gorges herself, we don't open our mouths except when it's necessary to feed our faces; our hair mingles, our knees stick together; suddenly there is osmosis and at the same moment we both cry *Eureka.*

Distracted from their *True Confessions,* the girls look at us reproachfully; and we are pleased to feel our two think-machines firing together, courtesy of crossword puzzles and publishers; we soar above the *Festival* slop and will not come down to earth again until the roast beef appears.

A Latin and a barbarian, I revel in fruits and meat; I am already savoring that red meat, the red tomatoes that perhaps will come with it, the Sunday-night potatoes, wormy but smooth and delicately golden. I make myself not look at my fellow-revelers: otherwise all these fountains of strength will turn into purgatives, masticating, and belly rumbling.

"Is it good, doll?" the *grande dame* of the day asks.

"Wonderful, doll, and all the more for having to wait for it. Incidentally, I think the beef had to wait a while too, wouldn't you say?"

The roast is like a pale shoe sole. Sawing painfully away at it, I reflect that it is cruel to kill the steer and wrong to eat nature unless one intends thereby to become partly the fruit, partly the animal.

"Oh, darling, the ramified chemistry of transubstantiation—"

"Eat," says Nadine, whom the sight of the midday noodles has not been able to discourage.

(6)

Going downstairs from the dormitory the first morning, I was still in my glory, I was full of arrogance and self-satisfaction, in spite of the denim and the two days' dirt.

It was my time of splendor purely and simply because I had dough.

I dashed off one letter after another to the Superintendent, casting doubt on the qualifications of his staff, the accuracy of his records, and the soundness of his mind; every flourish of my handwriting expressed my most whole-hearted contempt.

One after the other, I requested the release of various documents required for my defense that were held with my clothes, and photographs of my old mother; I demanded the social worker, and reimbursement for a pot of yogurt that had borne an expired date; in a word, in my time of glory, I indulged in all kinds of caprices.

As my debts went up my morale went down.

If the office is still getting petitions written in my hand, they are those that I draw up on behalf of my illiterate companions; I slink along the walls, I look humble and drag-assed, I have nothing left, I am no longer anything, until I get my dough back.

The Runaway

No chance of suggesting some other means of exchange here: you'd look great if you began to yak about the intellectual and artistic stuff you can do. Much better to pass the pack of butts round, even if it comes back three-quarters empty. What's more, it's better still to show your ass instead of your pack of butts.

Anyway, since the writ of sequestration arrived several weeks after I did, I had time to stock up on toothpaste, notepaper, cigarette paper, and enough garlic for a year: there are a lot of things you can cook up with garlic on the stove.

But all the same, it doesn't do to treat to chicken or roast beef one or two Sundays when you know perfectly well that you won't be able to do it again the following Sunday and all the other Sundays as long as you're in stir. To win forgiveness for all the damage done to me by those shit-assed account blockers, I give the very best of the little of myself that's left.

For instance, I make the hot water for the Nes.

The tap in the medical department is broken; in spite of the matron's explanations about a particular porcelain cylinder that is unobtainable, her pleas for calm, and the assurance that everything will be right and hot water will come through the pipes again before the end of the week, we went without water from that source until Sunday; another week has gone by, and the tap is now relegated to the category of the good old days.

The stove also departed, to the storage room, until cold weather returned. Without heat, without water, we resolved to do what is done in every prison in the world: bring back the age of fire.

It was a good chance for me to earn free java without too much injury to my pride: I offered myself as the officiating vestal.

I gathered together all the old newspapers, old cheese packets, cartons, little boxes, and tore or broke everything into small pieces; I set two empty Nes tins on the platform of the john, flanking the hole, and at all hours of the day I was busy lighting this improvised barbecue, keeping it going with paper torches, one lighted from the other as it was on the point of collapsing into the hole. I kept the cardboard boxes for the days when pride got the better of me and I had my belly full of begging them for their old newspapers.

And when the makeshift pot standing on the Nes tins began to boil all I had to do was to grab it by its ears with a couple of old rags as potholders, lower it to its trivet—a sardine tin— and sing out like a hash-house waiter: "The ladies' hot water is ready!"

I also have my postage stamps; when we were on the outside, it was my job to answer all the letters that my man and I received, to send the money orders to friends in Algeria or the *Santé* prison, and to keep the household accounts, so I always carted about a really commercial quantity of forms, note-paper, and stamps; in this way, when I had to wait in the car or in some hang-out while Zizi kept his innumerable and frighteningly complicated appointments, I didn't waste too much time.

I have buttered up the chief matron, sweet-talking her and explaining a situation that she understands as well as I do, since she enjoys the pillow confidence of God the Father—in a word, I bullshitted her to the point where she unblocked a few books of stamps on the promise that I would be discreet, adding that I could ask her for more when I had eaten them up "in correspondence or whatever." This amounted to a direct invitation to engage in a limited black-market trade. Hence the workroom sometimes was filled with remarks that would have horrified a philatelist:

"Hey, sweetie, would you canteen me some lard for a stamped envelope?"

All the same, it seemed a bit too much like petty-cash accounting.

I have had enough of knocking my brains out all week long on the problem of "physical survival," of being grateful for whatever bone is thrown to me, of playing up to the girls in order to stay on their good side. I'll drink the Nes that I've earned, yes, because playing stoker in the john isn't a soft job; I'll smoke as little as possible, and, as for the rest . . .

NO MORE CHOW.

Please note that this is a phrase that is heard periodically.

After each month's weigh-in on the scales, no one eats. If you're rich, you set up your line of defense on a supply of crackers, and, if you are penniless, as I have become, it's just dry bread. But, inasmuch as concern for your figure is rather frivolous in such penitential precincts, you begin in a week to pass up the privilege of going hungry.

In order to refuse any offers with a flair, and because I can not allege any excess fat on my bones, I stop eating because "I'm waiting for my experts." MY experts, mine, yours, hers: the court always sends the same two to everyone who asks for them, but each girl takes possession of the guys and refuses to share them.

What does one have to do to con a medical expert?

First, look bad. Essential. An end to doing the hair and rubbing the lips with red paper: the hair should be dull and brittle, and worn in a severe style; a touch of lead pencil on the eyebrows, a bit more on the circles under the eyes, just enough to look like death warmed over, not enough to be attractive.

The experts can neither be corrupted nor vamped.

Next?

Symptoms of advanced anemia: loss of weight, hypertension, dizzy spells. In order to be labeled "unfit to withstand imprisonment," there is hardly any choice but anemia, we think, not being lucky enough to have spots on our lungs or cyanosis.

As for me, I have: several very badly knit fractures, myopia corrected quite well by excellent eyeglasses, and two teeth three-quarters filled.

And with all that would you expect me to eat, yet?

Soup is served downstairs, by two beauties armed with ladles and busy attacking two giant pots, soup and a stinking stew, backed up on meat days by a receptacle like a picnic thermos jug, in which the meat or fish rations float lazily in a pallid, watery sauce. The minute the doors open, at eleven and again at five, the race is on, everybody with their plates in their hands: first come, first (and best) served. The servers had put their own food under ours "to keep it warm," but "sure, we want to feed you ladies, but it's something else again to hand over the best to you and go without ourselves" . . .

I don't see why I should go on risking my life twice a day. It's enough that I have to walk a mile to the toilet, the lawyer, the office, etc. Let's save our strength. Not to mention the fact that the ting-a-ling announcing the arrival of my experts may come just at that moment and I won't have time to make sure of the circles under my eyes.

But the girls may think I'm pulling the loner act so as to go through their things or swipe something while they're downstairs; the matron may think I've started a hunger strike to get her in a jam; and the experts, coming at chow time like everyone else, may wonder where I am. For no one aside from me looks ill.

When the doors open, then, I pretend to mingle with the crowd; I hang back in the passageway, so that I'm the last; when they're all on the stairs, I cut out and wait for the line of them to turn the corner of the stairs. I offer to carry a plate for one of the girls, so that the matron won't see me empty-handed and, if she ever takes it into her head to ask me what has been served, I'll be able to tell her.

Tonight I un-fasted.

The arrival of my first expert deserves to be celebrated with a small revel. True, the fish is raw, and no one has to be coaxed out of it. I don't like begging people; their haste to dump theirs into my plate suits me perfectly.

I know by now that the phosphorus content of the body doesn't get into the medical report: and besides, between now and the session with the second son of Aesculapius—they usually space their visits about ten days apart—I'll have plenty of time to re-de-phosphorize myself.

I describe the session to the girls who are bursting with curiosity as they watch me spit out the fishbones. I'm lucky.

"Just think, I've had my lawyer ask for an exam three times already . . ."

"Oh, shut up, if your judge is as busy as mine . . ."

"You don't give a fuck, you're going to get the charges dismissed when you get into court, your case is a big laugh . . ."

So what? if hers isn't, why the big hurry? Certainly she doesn't think she'll get out on a medical, the way she looks? . . .

"Don't kid yourselves," I say. "Naturally, with the croaker they have here, you forget what a session with a doctor really is. But I swear, to con that one! . . ."

"But what did he do to you? Did he make you strip completely?"

Looking very important, I nod. "He didn't leave out a thing, from childhood diseases on up to this very moment."

"But . . . did he write it all down?"

"Of course, he made a complete report, all the details. He gave my wrist the works with a dynamometer . . ."

"A dyna-what?"

I explain. I explain whatever they ask. "I got a quick look at the report: it was one of those big Ministry forms, with my request for the examination clipped to it. One of the things it said was: 'Re: medical release or transfer to Fresnes.' "

This time there is deferential silence: let a girl go, all right, but send her to Fresnes! God! I must be a mean customer . . . or stinking smart.

As for me, I can already picture myself there. I close my eyes and see the Fresnes of my adolescence, I see the face of the jerk who examined me just now, the list of my miseries, and, having weighed everything, I decide to be an optimist.

After a few words of medical jargon that I had offered to open the proceedings, we had got on like colleagues, so to speak. After the stethoscopic examination, which turned up my butts and matches in my bra, he offered me a Pall Mall.

My blood pressure was just right too: I couldn't believe it, I had a confederate in my very arteries. What was more, the further the consultation went, the more my whole organism got into the game: my back, as soon as it was bared, curved to such a degree that the cervicals, brought into play by this, made the guy mention scoliosis; my stomach, which until then felt as if it had sunk down to my ankles, suddenly climbed up toward my cheeks, with which it shared its hollowness; and meanwhile my whole body, turning blue and shivering in the cold, made itself so miserable that I could no longer hold back the tears and just threw myself back in the chair, sobbing: "Doctor, please, please, I can't go on any more, do something . . ."

He promised to do something.

But what?

(7)

I recognized her dog-tired walk, her gentle way of smiling, of putting her few little night things in order on top of the carton. It was as if she had always slept there, in the next bed, the head of which touches the head of mine.

It was a good idea to desert Aliette and her telephone: a second bed has been set up under the window, and Maria will sleep in it.

I had seen her fleetingly in the corridors, but I had never seen so much of her as I have tonight. I should point out that there is no contact with the girls in the other workroom except by thread telegram or Aliette-type telephone or by tapping the wall. The Office has switched Maria to our workroom.

The girl is quiet and self-effacing, but there is nothing humble or slovenly about her; indeed, she likes her comfort. The proof of that is the fact .that she's scrounged a second mattress from an empty bed in her former dormitory and jockeyed it into ours to put on top of the pancake that's enough for the rest of us. I made her a Nescafé by way of welcome, and then we jabbered late into the night, as if we had always known each other.

In the workroom the next day Maria sits opposite me. That

55

way, my eyes, even when they are concentrated on my writing kit, my plate, or my drawings—I was drawing masses of roses to decorate my letters—hardly left her. It's a shame that I have to sleep, or I would look at her all the time.

Why this sudden attraction?

It's not because I have any idea of going back to being a lesbian or of getting myself kept, even though I'm in the direst need of fattening. No, I've set up my scheme of love once and for all, and, as far as sustenance is concerned, even though Maria seems to be well fixed for canteening and completely open-hearted, I'm trying to take care of myself on my own.

But from the first we shared the same sort of bad luck: her dough, like mine, was blocked. And her mother's money orders, as well as those from friends whom she hasn't had the chance to notify, and her various assets on the outside, have all gone down the drain to the treasury. Both of us have had the good luck, too, to know only the genuine side of life in a communal prison, for we both knew damned well that anyone who smiles at us is smiling at us and not at our cash. And we aren't dying; no one refuses a match to a dog, the girls aren't dogs and gladly buy whatever junk we have to sell. Little by little, all my rags are going up in cigarette smoke.

Maria doesn't have a broken left arm, or even a broken right arm, and she could make a mountain of string bags as fast as anything; it took my breath away to watch her go at it like that.

Aside from those lousy string bags, all she has to keep her alive is a few photos: a wonderful *bambino* all shining eyes, dimples, and black curls; they were allowed to stay together for the regulation eighteen months after he was born, just long enough for Maria to learn to play mama. Now she can see her child only in visiting hours; as a special favor, they meet in the room set aside for talking to lawyers, and spend the time kissing, *baci, baci.* Afterward Maria comes back to us, to her crochet hooks, to her card game. Or she sings, which I enjoy very much.

"Maria, you're driving me nuts. Cut it out for a while." That's my way of asking for more.

I like Maria's silences, her impromptu songs, her quick, soft glances, the surprising contrast between the attractive things she wears—eyeglasses in Italian frames, chased wedding ring—and her rather sparse hair, her more or less unmatched clothes: oh, yes, the greater part of her wardrobe too has been sequestered. She's been wearing one of my summer skirts and I like seeing my skirt on Maria as if in a mirror.

We whisper together over the dirty dishes, the kitchenette in the corner is where it's quietest, and anyway I like to get my chow out of clean plates. That's why I wash everyone's, and at the same time make a show of what a good girl I am to have around.

I stumble my way through what little Italian I remember from school. Maria corrects my mistakes; behind us, the others are uneasy: when people shut themselves off, especially in a foreign language, it must be only to be nasty.

Maria has been waiting two years to stand trial. Anyone would be justified in having his belly full of that, but as for her she carries it off with distinction; her weariness comes out in the way she drags around, in her constant straightening of the curve in her back, which is something I do too. And then there are those damned glasses, which look like mine.

Nevertheless, I know very well that the set of the shoulders and wearing glasses don't mean a thing; I've always heard people say that you should never trust the Latin mentality: "You never know where you are with those wops, either they yak all the time and you can't shut them up or they don't say a thing and do plenty behind your back."

What do I have to lose here if I treat myself to a little

Italian vacation? The idea of the trip is attractive, but first
I must take a look at my *Guide Michelin.*

Why has Maria been put into our workroom? That's the
first leg of the trip to be studied. Gina, who has friends downstairs and all kinds of confused ties with everyone in the place,
prisoners, matrons, and social workers, would appear to be
an acceptable guide.

One afternoon I manage to have a confidential chat with
her: as you walk about the exercise yard in twos or threes,
changing your tone of voice and the subject of conversation
every time you come across two or three other girls who are
also conspiring among themselves, you can talk more freely
than you can in the workroom.

"Why did they put her in here with us? You really don't
know?"

"You know I'm not up on all the latest gossip, and besides
I just . . ."

"That's right, you never send notes. But everyone's talked
about it just the same. Look: they sent her upstairs after she
got herself into a mess trying to make a break. She's real tight
with a mess of dagos on the outside, they say she was getting
herself some hacksaw blades smuggled in and someone got
on to it—everybody knows everything here with these broads,
there's no way of making them keep anything to themselves."

And on and on. By the time we get back up to the workroom, I know all I need to. For me, all these runaways in all
directions, wild horses, phantom steeds that no one ever gets
a leg over, are things to dream over. But Gina, by contrast,
has her feet solidly on the ground: since I trumpeted all over,
when I arrived, that I was up for a big rap, the kind that
probably meant at least five years, Gina figures that it would
be logical for my mind to turn to a jail break. All the more
so because my John is in too: when both of you fall into the

shit, it's each one's duty to climb out so that he can help the other, if not pull him out too.

"Like me and Tony, see: he pulled a real fast one on them, otherwise . . ."

"Heard anything from him?"

Gina looks condescendingly at me and goes off again into the details of his and her mix-ups with the cops, Interpol, and all the rest. I look pretty sick next to such an outfit, with my gang that amounted to nothing but one lousy little burglar, and my lousy little record of only fifteen years in stir, but that's a thing of the past, a tiny sentence hanging over me like a dull, obsolete sword of Damocles, and besides there's this smile, this friendliness, this warm blondness . . .

Tonight Gina is telling about her own jailbreak, for, like everyone else, she once tried to take a powder:

"I was in the downstairs workroom too, with Liliane and Josette (her co-defendants: I think the three of them had knocked over a ladies'-model safe), on the ground floor, the workroom has a French door that opens right out onto the yard. Last year the matron left the door open and went off to the office—a whole hour alone like that, you can imagine . . . I hadn't even been arraigned, I'd only been there about two weeks, it was sure worth the try. Those fucking string bags gave us an idea. We made rails for ladders out of spools, and for the rungs we braided and braided miles of thread, the whole contraption took us . . ."

"Gee," I say, "it must have been quite a sight . . ."

"To make a long story short, the ladder was finished in three days; and we'd made a gangplank too, to go from one outside wall to the next. All we needed was a hook to hang the ladder on the first wall."

I interrupt her: "How far is it between the walls?"

"Five feet," Gina replies at once.

When I got on my horse, then—even in fantasy I am methodical—I would eliminate the gangplank and simply jump from one wall to the other. Another question: "What did you do about the hook?"

"I was just going to tell you: we managed to get a bar out of the john window, it was a hell of a job, and then we got it red-hot on the stove and bent it . . . No, you can't imagine what a job it was."

It was impossible, I must be dreaming!

Nevertheless I've heard before about this attempted break and the ladder, I know there's some truth in the story Gina's telling; but that three dames on the order of Gina—the two others couldn't have been any better, she was the brains—could have managed to put a whole room full of women in their pockets in just two weeks of being together is a little too much for me.

I begin to wonder whether she is as stupid as she seems. I can no longer believe that she's really snowing us: on the day they'd set, when all the matrons were out of sight, the ladder was brought out from under the pile of cartons and old clothes where it had been hidden; they took it into the courtyard and tried to hook it on to the top of the wall, throwing it up twice. Finally it caught.

Gina climbed up, straddled the wall and called in a low voice for the gangplank; Liliane got busy with it while Josette was joining Gina. But once she got up there the idiot got a fit of the giggles.

We are all hanging as desperately on Gina's story as the hook was on the wall; Aliette, panting all over, is halfway out of her bedclothes; Nadine is stretched out flat, motionless with suspense. I have a great deal in common with Nadine, or, to be more precise, we both have a common interest in crossword puzzles; only she really likes Gina, and that spoils everything, including Nadine.

". . . and there she was laughing her fool head off, and Liliane standing down below with her gangplank, and me beginning to become edgy. And it was almost time for visiting hours . . ."

A visiting period that will never know what it fucked up, an hour of chit-chat that had screwed up years of freedom. Hearing the first visitor ring the bell, they completely lost their heads. Gina somehow got down again and called the other girls; they all came out and hung on the ladder, shaking it every which way, and finally they got it down just as the matron was about to appear on the scene.

The ladder was thrown into the john like a turd: once the right moment was gone, there was no right moment any more. But there were repercussions a few weeks later, when the men came to clean the cesspool: in their haste, the escapees had forgotten to cut the ladder into small pieces.

"Talk about a mess! The Superintendent called us all in and grilled us, one after the other. But nobody had the gall to squeal on me, and since after all the authorities were in a bad spot—the matrons are supposed to be there when it's exercise period—the Super decided to forget the whole thing. They say he's still got the ladder and has showed it off to all the screws in the men's wing."

"I hope he had it cleaned first?"

Gina doesn't answer that, and goes on: "So they switched me out of the workroom too. They left the two other girls together, but the office knows it has nothing to worry about, those two can't do anything without me. They talk big, but when it comes to lifting a finger . . . I've done almost a year now, they've reduced the charges on the business with the safe . . . I don't really feel bad about any of it: I'm still in stir, but the stuff I'll come up with at my hearing will get my man out. I can still hold my head up when I'm back in the street."

Aside from the rare bird that caged me as I caged him, I have seldom found any of these people with brains that I've been looking for for centuries. I look up full of hope: perhaps Gina . . .

I take my walks under the linden trees with her for several afternoons in a row. For I have gotten it into my head that she's still hot to go on the lam and that, if I keep after her enough, we'll find a way of pulling off something really great, an act of charity that will satisfy the inclinations of all our fellow inmates.

I am still uncertain as to my own plans: the charges against me may be reduced, the lawyer is taking steps in that direction; I may get out on parole; in the evenings, when the tops of the plane trees, bent by the wind, seem to touch the bars, I dream; I dream of a tremendous disappearing act which no one will catch us at, of course, and of the empty prison, and of my return to life.

(8)

Now and then some girl comes back from an interrogation and tells me that she's seen her John or her husband, who is in the same wing as Zizi, and who has been entrusted by him with all kinds of "good wishes" for me. This is just about all that he can send me through third persons, but I am able to translate them and to feel their presence on my lips, in my head, and in my heart, bridging all the absence and the distance.

That's enough for me. I'm leaving it to him to try to get permission to write to me. Permission for what? to write what? Let's divide the work: he'll try to write to me, I'll try to make a break.

We have nothing to say to each other: in its own time, like everything else, the right to gab and ball with nobody to stop us will be ours once again. You keep on asking, baby; I'm tired, I've cracked my skull with scribbling, writing to the whole world and playing public stenographer to half the workroom.

And yet there is concern at my silence, there are reproaches for my laziness . . . The mail service is murder: five days for a letter to a lawyer and about three weeks for any other kind, both going and coming.

I limit myself to answering the letters that I receive, with machine-like punctuality. All the rest is silence, except for my bones that groan and creak from time to time. Mechanically again, I shut them up; I let my own gloom come up with the sun, I close my lazy eyelids, the day is just too long for anything to fill it, I let it stay empty.

I laugh when the girls put on a circus, I sympathize with the others when they're down, and I share their joys, I still am indulgent toward everything they do, even if it goes wrong or makes me sick. There are a few lesbians, too, mostly butches out of necessity—wives and mothers—but then that too helps to kill the time. Mona still has eight years to go, her transfer to the Central Women's Prison is due any day: if she's going the dike route, it is by way of preparing herself for the future.

I explained to Mona what life in the Central is like, my manner learned and irrefutable like that of all old hands; I do little things for her constantly, I confect bizarre upswept hairdos for her long hair, I slick her up with beauty care and other delicate touches, and every week, with my ball-point Bic, I make decorations of roses and pansies for the letter that she laboriously and sighingly puts together for her husband, her husband in Fresnes.

Then there is a call for me: what and who? Let it be a surprise, let's not ask questions. It's sure to be the lawyer, the verbal cocktail: the supper pots are rattling, it's lawyer time.

Seeming extremely annoyed, the matron takes me down to the consultation room. After all, what need is there for us to try to better our situation or for these gentlemen who don't look at all like our kind to come and see us?

But the guy who is pacing up and down in front of the glass-paned office as he waits for me looks nothing like what I was hoping for: he has bulging eyes, a tight-lipped mouth, and an unfathomably evil look about him.

He asks me to sit down.

After all, couldn't this guy be a legal eagle too?

He wastes no time in proving as much: suddenly becoming talkative, he introduces himself: "Inspector X, *Police Judiciaire.*"

It was only then that I became aware that there was something out of the ordinary in the office, a kind of silent harmony that the presence of the cop was not enough in itself to explain but that had some relation to it. I look round the room, and on the table I see a familiar object: my transistor. That's funny, I'm sure I left it in the property room when I arrived.

"Yes, you guessed right," the law says, having followed my own gaze.

I answer that, on the contrary, I am becoming more and more bewildered; but, between what I say and what I'm thinking at the same time, there is a gap as broad as that between indifference and panic: panic hits me so hard that I'm dizzy, it streams out of every one of my pores, while I try my best not to turn white, not to move a finger, and to go right on with the bewilderment bit until the interrogation has ended. Nevertheless, I had caught on.

I see at once that we're not going to get out on parole, neither a medical one, nor any other kind; as far as freedom is concerned, since we'll come up for sentencing and the authorities will then be in a position to treat us as husband and wife (*concubines* is their word for it), it will be the dreadful idyll of lovers who are jailbirds, with the paper kisses and wild, censored, sterile dreams, the dreams that I've had a bellyful of.

I ABSOLUTELY must get out.

The whole workroom already knows that I was in conference with The Man from headquarters, and, when I get back, the silence is heavy and uneasy: I stink of fuzz. It's so bad that I feel obliged to burst out in the loudest and filthiest of all jail songs to bring them out of it; my repertory was repeated in the dormitory, my crossword puzzles stay in my vanity case, for several evenings in a row I sing and yell in order to drown out that other, secret music, Zizi's voice tirelessly murmuring into my ears "Remember, baby, everybody's all alone in this world." I run away from that voice, I tell myself that Zi is 'way off, no one is as alone as all that; shit, the gods may come down to earth, no, will come down to earth and give me a hand.

But to lam out solo, from a collective prison, is no picnic.

Oh, sure, down there in the transistor department, I was told about a perfectly charming little prison, one with private cells; ah, those delightful provincial residences, with darling flowerbeds all around, and, in the back, the chicken-run and the Superintendent's vegetable garden; prisons as quiet and serene as Verlaine's vision of life, and so soul-satisfying to haul ass out of at night. . . .

The real story: unquestionably the prosecutor's office in that district will go on with its investigation by sending people here to take depositions, and then very soon it will give that up and let the law here take over, in order to simplify the whole thing and save on travel costs; and, in any event, these formalities will be slow, extremely slow.

Putting me by myself here is out of the question: minors are segregated, for their safety or for ours, but, once you're over twenty-one, you can be a dike, a troublemaker or a would-be suicide, and it makes no difference, it's the workroom for all of them. As for the infirmary, no one has ever been in it; or, more accurately, no one has ever come back from it.

Besides, it's all very well to make yourself absolutely inconspicuous in order to control the situation and to keep to yourself in order to make a break, but even so it is essential to be with it; and until now the only chances that I've had to take a look at the prison without the matron's taking a look at me are those that arise out of the normal daily routine. Nor is there anyone being released who can smuggle out a letter; there's nothing in the mail or in the view between the bars to indicate that anyone outside takes any interest in us; nothing but that endless passage through the prison postal system, where letters sit around for weeks or else vanish into the official files, where every package not marked "Clothing" is returned to the sender, where cash and money orders are turned over to the court, where confiscated drawings are turned over to the court, where reports and smuggled messages are turned over to the court—the court is the prison's catch basin.

The guiding rule of superior beings is that great undertakings are carried out in solitude. And that of burglars is that they are done at night. I combine both classes in myself and I am proud of it, and here I am in this sack of mine, tossing back and forth not only because I have metaphysical concerns but also because I have a carcass that is exhausted from doing nothing.

Do a disappearing act over the wall, do in a vice cop, do it with Zizi, do anything, but don't keep on turning back and forth this way like a steak on a grill.

As long as I have to find a connection among the girls, I may as well try them all. To hell with Maria and her hacksaw blades made of the same stuff as dreams, to hell with Gina's hook, I'll saw the bars with my bare hands if I have to, just the same as Madame Piaf, and I'll fly off above the walls and the trees. At this point reality takes hold of me again and one night I begin sounding off:

"Look, girls, I've got to get out. I'm not going to go into the Assises again . . . yes, I'm going to try to split."

Naturally, everyone asks how at the same time: The silence that follows is like the silence that envelops the model housewife when she is about to disclose the secret of her creamed duck.

How can I tarnish my glory by admitting to them that I don't have the faintest idea? Bursting out with whims like that sounds a bit like a pregnant woman. So I assume my Mona Lisa manner:

"There's no need to go into details: I'm simply putting you wise, not so you can help me but just to ask you to keep your pretty little traps shut and sleep like logs the day—I mean the night—that I do the job."

These girls are better than they look, just the same. Who would have guessed that I would lam, all on my own, just like that, simply because I had made up my mind to?

I reassure them, I'll still be there in my lousy bed tomorrow morning, I promise no one runs out on friends that way, I'll let them know beforehand.

Only Gina seems somewhat disturbed. Big talk, even if it's wild, fine; but the moment that something serious is said, you've got her on your tail. And Gina doesn't like feeling out of it at all, no matter what *it* might be.

"Take it easy, take it easy," she insists. "You know damn well I have connections. But wait for tomorrow's exercise period. You—Jesus, either you don't open your trap or you run off at the mouth and nobody can stop you."

I reply that we're all among friends here and that there's no law against talking.

"Wait till tomorrow, I tell you."

All right, all right, all right! I pretend to be suddenly dead tired, I wish everyone a relieved and conspiratorial *good night* and turn to the wall, where my runaway steed will be tethered until I wake up.

(9)

True to her promise, Gina descends on me the moment we're turned out to exercise.

Yes, I am still determined; yes, I know how I'll go about it; yes, I think I can make it.

In the back of my mind, as I answer Gina, I'm thinking of putting some questions to her; but she talks so much, how can I get a word in? You don't even get to answer her; it's a one-way conversation.

What I want to know is the whereabouts of that hook from last year—only the rope ladder has been gotten rid of, it seems that the hook wouldn't go through the pipe—and whether there is any way of getting my hands on it; but I suspect that Gina will want to get her hands on my plan first.

One problem keeps rattling round in my head for a while, I play with the idea of pretending to get them all into the boat with me in order to see which members of the crew will stick with it and which won't; but no, this is MY break, and I'm not going to fool around choosing ways and means.

"All alone," Gina says. "Hmm . . ."

Every point of view is of course worth listening to, and Gina, whatever she may say, is quite respectful and probably her hustler of a Tony is a good pimp. But that's beside the point. I'm not asking her for her life, or even for her money.

She is still going over the names of the girls who might be able to give me a hand. The list includes the whole workroom—come on, that's enough. In the end I explode:

"Why not get all of us to sign a petition to the Prisons Administration to give us back our rope ladder? No, Gina, you're just making the thing too cumbersome. As a matter of fact, you haven't said a word about Maria."

"Maria? Oh, yes, the one with the hacksaws. Go ahead and talk to her if you like; at this point . . ."

We call her, the three of us walk up and down together a few times, and then Gina disappears on her daily tour of gossip.

Even though my first glance at Maria spoke volumes, I force myself to be reserved and limit my conversation to small talk: how beautiful Italy is in summer, stars, both astral and terrestrial, and "outside" in general, that tenderest of sore subjects. Having got to that point, I hint at possibilities, test the ground, feel my way . . .

By the time we have finished our *passeggiata,* we are back from the end of the world, and, as Maria climbs the stairs, her eyes are glazed and her feet faltering. It's a good sign.

The next day I return to my delicate hammering on the iron that I am heating in the southern sun; the sparks fly from my forge. Her odd accent is hard on your ears, but who would have wanted to interrupt the flow of precious words, even if it did sound a little like the roar of the Po in flood?

The question of the hacksaws . . . Maria explains the means by which they get smuggled inside to saw the bars. It's like Columbus' egg: by the Bar: "Lawyers are paid to do what clients tell them . . ."

But, strangely, Maria's lawyer vehemently refuses to bring her her toys, just as he now refuses her request to trade my postage stamps for cigarettes, and I have more important requests to make to my own lawyer; in a word, Maria has just trampled down, with none of her usual gentleness, the last fragments of my illusions.

She looks at me point-blank with those pupils of glass and velvet and says: "As far as Gina's concerned, she wouldn't think of leaving any of her little pals downstairs behind. She can talk all she wants about all the ways they've screwed her up, she still wants to hang on to them. Now, you take me: I'd be willing to try a break with just one person. You, for instance."

(Oh, Maria, I am overwhelmed! but . . .)

I have a bit more confidence in the girl's common sense; I thought she was much closer to Gina. But in all this herd of runaways that gallop in every direction and cut across one another's paths without ever getting anywhere, in this junk-yard of bars and saws and hooks, I am emerging somewhat from my solitude, I am moving toward Maria and forever bumping against Gina, Gina who is everywhere, Gina who is getting in my hair.

How can I know exactly what her intelligence, her bold-ness, her promises amount to, and, if they're worth nothing, as I believe, how can I make this clear to Maria without stirring up trouble, without hurting her, without pulling a dirty deal? It's not easy to shut out one of the girls when she was forever being the big shot with Maria and all of us with her "baby," her "hey, I'll buy you a coffee," when she has plenty of dough and the rest of us are broke, when I have just arrived and she has all the connections and has known Maria more than a year.

God, I'm turning gabby and jealous, I would have done better to keep on listening to Zizi. I've announced now that I'm going to escape, and, instead of helping me, or even letting me lam on my own in peace, they're all hanging on to me so that I'll take them along. Mind you, if I had said nothing, they wouldn't have let me go even so.

Therefore let's let my plan remain in shadow, blurred and out of focus, and since they're all so absolutely insistent, let's go back to the boat bit. It's a tremendous boat, in which I'll take as many people as possible; I'll be careful to jump ashore as soon as it's launched, and, when the boat has labored days and days through brackish shallows and wound up pitiably at its point of departure, I'll be there on the bank, laughing.

A good laugh, especially if it rinses out your brains and clears the road, is as worth-while as a game of belote or a gossip column. I begin that very night.

"It's one thing or the other (I had attacked in the 'comrades' style, addressing Gina, Nadine, and Maria, all clustered with me round Aliette's bed, sitting on a blanket, Nes and butts at our finger tips): either I split all alone and come back for the rest of you, or else I work out a plan for everyone—anyway, the ones who want to, you, Gina, you, Maria, for instance—to come with me. Obviously, we aren't going to start a gang, or take an apartment together: just the opposite, we'll have a drink together and then each of us will go off wherever she has to. Because our reason for doing it isn't just 'being free'—that's a crock of shit; we have other reasons, real ones: our guys, Gina; our trials; the prisoner's duty to escape; in other words, the strongest possible reasons."

I go on in the same vein for a while. I need a different kind of Nes to refresh me, I've talked so much tonight. When I finally stop, Maria would have followed me to the end of the world, Gina is interested, and Nadine looks like a kindly Mona Lisa. Aliette is snoring like a machine. It's time for the opposition to speak.

"That's all very logical and very nice, just as you say. But where exactly has your big brain got to with this great idea, this mass break?"

"Figured out like clockwork," I answer confidently. "I'll give you all the details. But . . . if it makes sense to you, you'll come in on it, of course?"

And I get exactly what I want: Gina suddenly finds a pile of reasons for staying in stir. Her testimony will be useful to the other people indicted in her case, etc. She throws in a number of extremely threatening anecdotes, she believes in justice here and now, some people would be well advised to reverse their engines between now and their hearings if they don't want their run-out to get them into a worse mess. Anyway, the investigation of her own case is winding up, she can hold out that long. And then the good will be lifted up, the evil . . .

"But don't you want to see Tony again? Sure you do. So what difference can a court's decision make, since he'll only come up for trial by default? And since in any case . . ." I was going to say "you aren't going to see him again all that soon," but mine was a logical plan, remember. So I go on: ". . . certainly you HAVE to see each other, don't you?"

"Oh yes, baby, we have to . . . but if I walk, I mean really walk, even if Tony cops five or ten, I swear to you he won't do the time."

"I know, people who aren't around are always in the wrong, especially there . . ."

"Are you going to let me talk or not? It's the lawyers' job to get him, but I'm going to walk, and I'm going to build up a terrific defense to get him off, I'm going to get the brightest guy in Paris, Floriot, no first Floriot then Jaccoud—I trust him more. I'll pay a million, two million, I'll grease everybody —with dough, you know?—or even get the whole case thrown out . . ."

Staggering a little under this avalanche of millions, I pull myself together with an effort. "Great, Gina, you've got guts. But look—my man is inside, and, as much as I like all of you,

I have to think about him. In this place I'm just a big nothing. Anyway, if any of you has any job you want me to do—deliver a letter, make a phone call, go see someone—don't be backward." If I make them a deal, perhaps they'll give me a hand.

But Gina gets mad. "You forget Nadine's getting out soon, and Nadine's *my* friend. She'll do all my errands. With everything I've told her in confidence, she could hang Tony: that shows you how much I trust her."

Nadine has not dropped her Récamier pose. She is wearing a filmy nylon nightgown, which serves no purpose since she has it pulled up to her navel; with those long gams of hers stretched out one over the other, she creates an atmosphere of regal detachment, an impression of tranquillity and serenity that clashes with the seething in our heads; she merely nods her head from time to time, to indicate the statements that she especially approves of. Especially what Gina says.

That was that. I go on to explain my clear methodical casing of the joint. "I've noticed that the safety lock on the door of the trusties' dormitory is left open all day, I've checked every time we've gone out for exercise: all there is is the ordinary bolts, and anyone can open them. Downstairs, it's the same with the washroom doors, the one to the courtyard and the one to the corridor."

That means that if we go into the washrooms as if we were doing a washing or shampooing our hair, we can get up to the second floor, and get into the trusties' dormitory, where the window opens out onto the exercise yard and is at the same height as the first outside wall, and about a yard away.

I point out to my audience that beyond this point I am about to embark on pure hypothesis, the plan itself, in fact. Therefore I begin this part of the discourse as a hypothesis.

"Let's assume that, the night or nights before the escape, we make a rope out of the cotton for the string bags, strips of bedclothes—in a word, a decent rope. Preferably in one night, so we don't have to hide it. The next morning we take it downstairs with us, say inside dirty sheets—they'll be changed soon, I hope . . ."

"I hope so too, one of mine has such a tear in it that soon I'll have three sheets instead of two."

"Anyway, we could always say we'd stained them. All right, we hide the rope behind the cartons, or under the pile of string bags; with all the crap there is in that workroom it won't be a problem."

"What if the matron decides to look around?"

"Too much work for her!"

"But suppose there's a general search?" Nadine objected.

"There are only two ways that'll happen. One: the search will be ordered from the main office, and that never happens except when somebody's been singing. Now, there are only we four in on this, and . . ."

And the chorus of virgins chimes in: ". . . and we're all girls who are on the ball."

"Or two: it would be ordered by the Sanitary Commission, and you know damn well they never get that far . . ."

"The stink gets 'em at the door . . ."

"All right, then, we stash the rope in the workroom. Then what?"

"It stays there until the exercise period. It has a slip-knot at one end, I forgot to tell you that. One of us—Maria, let's say—sneaks back inside through the washrooms, runs into the workroom, gets the rope and ties it to the bars on the trusties' dormitory window. There's not so much as a fart to be heard that time of day, the matron's always yacking with us and there isn't a soul in the halls.

"The courtyard is in the form of a large L. At one end there's this window, I've marked it F; at the other, the corner where matron sucks up with us. Where the two sides of the

L join, there's a stone bench; of course it can happen that the matron gets smart and goes to sit there so she can keep her peepers on both sides at the same time; or certain stool-pigeons or big-mouths might see what we're up to and start to sound off."

All disorderly shouting, singing and yelling are prohibited. But the poster citing this regulation is tacked up six feet above the pavement, and it is so yellowed and dirtied with the years that no one can expect the prisoners to know it by heart. In my opinion, furthermore, stool pigeons don't have any guts.

"Wait until winter, they'll slip all over the yard . . ."

". . . and, while they're all running back and forth, we'll clear out."

"All joking aside," Gina says (she can't bear to have anyone making light of the dangers on the road—the fresh little bitches, trying to take the wheel away from her!), "I think that's pretty good. If you wanted, I could always fake being sick, or having a . . . a sunstroke, the matron would have me carried in and send for spirits of ammonia . . ."

We spend a little time discussing the best means of keeping the matron busy; after having noted that she's always busy, even if she's only busy watching us, we decide to wait until she's free. From there we continue.

"Fine, no one around: Maria sneaks the rope to me . . . I'm down here, ready to grab it and then climb up . . ."

"But aren't you going to take anything with you?"

"What things? If I split, I do it just to be rid of everything for a few days. I'll connect again when I feel like it, maybe after a train trip to Cannes and back. I'm not going to lose any more time than it takes for . . ."

". . . for some lousy lawyer to condescend to come."

"Take it easy! (I have an old residuum of middle-class upbringing that irritates me at times.) The lousy lawyer is the only pal we have here, and don't forget it."

"Oh, hell, everybody knows you've got a crush on him."

Everyone starts making jokes about the gentlemen of the Bar, and the runaway mare stands champing at the bit.

"Let's assume that I reach the window: from there, I throw a leg over the sill and get to the wall. Then I jump to the second wall . . ."

"Good Christ," Gina said, "who can follow you? How do you think you're going to jump that? It's at least six feet."

I point out to her that, at the time of her own attempt to split, the space between the walls, according to her own statements, was four and a half feet.

"It amounts to the same thing. You'll break your neck on the pavement between them."

"I've thought of that too. The rope will still be tied to the dormitory bars with the slip-knot: as soon as I'm on the first wall, I'll pull up the free end and drop it over the other side. When I jump, I'll keep hold of it, just in case. That way, if I miss the jump, I can climb back up the rope and try again."

Gina is worried. To her I seem really too clever, she is losing the thread and my rope is too fragile: "Your rope can't take all that. The cotton for the string bags isn't bad, but it has to be reinforced with pieces of bedclothes, with plenty of knots all along it."

"Why knots?"

"So you can hold on while you climb, you take a chance of slipping . . . because that bad hand of yours might make it tougher for you than for somebody else; excuse me, baby, I'm not saying it to make you sore, but . . ."

I explain that I have taken minutely detailed account of my deficiencies and that from time to time I indulge myself in a bit of Gurdjef—a super-effort, if she wants to know. Swedish gymnastics over the years in a cell leave traces as identifiable as those of fractures.

Maria listens in rapture, floating the wall in ecstasy by the miracle of the rope; she's like a yokel watching a dervish. I don't have the heart to leave her there, caught between heaven and earth. "Maria, you run right back down to the exercise yard and climb up after me."

The thought of going upstairs all alone to fasten that thick rope, the danger of being caught at it, even the idea of climbing the wall is not what frightens Maria: from the little that she's told me, she must have seen and done much more. No, it's the jumping. She's not supple, she doesn't have terribly long legs, that one . . . I reassure her: I'll jump first, she'll throw the rope to me, and I'll return the favor. "It'll be a change from appealing refusals of parole."

Then we'll proceed over the branches of the trees, like two nice little swallows that have eaten their fill of horse-turds. And then we'll come back to earth at last in the park that we can see from our windows, which no one ever enters, whose gate is always open; from there, we'll go on to Italy, or Belgium, or anywhere at all.

Yes, we shall soon be through with sleeping in this rotten stable, we'll be with our husbands; and, if they can't join us, well, then, we'll have them lead the lives of princes in their cells—big money and big lawyers overnight.

I feel a twinge of remorse. Because I know very well that all that was my own invention, invented in order to brighten my own smile. But then it gives us something to whisper about on our walks.

When Maria and I have our plot all worked out, we sit down against the wall, our knees drawn up to our chests, our arms round our knees, our eyes at rest under their lids; the stone is hard on our bottoms, and the passing legs of the girls and the matron walking up and down, along with the clothes-lines, create a new curtain of bars.

Sometimes there is a caress of sunshine during these end-of-

summer walks. I rest my head on my arms. "Do you hear it,
Maria? It's the prelude to autumn."

In this prison without music voices pass by, percussion and
rests in turn, the Platters doing *September in the Rain,* and
the tinkle of fortunes devoured coin by coin by the juke boxes.
But the rain has not yet come back, and the soft warmth continues to make us drowse. September, when I was born, the
Virgin's month and mine.

"Maria, let me have the newest photograph of your son and
I'll copy it for you, O.K.?"

(After more than twenty years, mother, do these heavy
suns still make you feel the heavier weight inside you? I think
of your youth of those days, mother, little sister, you who were
not even as old as Maria; under your dress, under your skin,
I was warm too, and you carried me like one of those summer
fruits you craved . . . oh, mother, how I adore you for having
remained unknown!)

"I'm getting old, Maria . . . Soon it will be my birthday; I
hope I won't have to spend it in stir!"

"Oh, hell, we'll canteen some beer, three bottles, ahead of
time, and we'll stash it away to get drunk."

Get drunk! Mother, let me have fifteen years more and
spend them drinking and loving, and then let me die if from
the love that I carry only love has been born! Everything will
be forgotten, like these impressions that I allow to fade away,
the warmth of evenings, the freshness of the corridors, the
waning prison light when autumn is near—I will not see any
of them again.

Where will I be next September? The judge is going to say
here, but the beat of my heart is already on the run.

Nowhere will I have better savored the broken fragrance
of the lime trees on the lips of the wind than within these
walls, four walls with a ceiling of sky; in this well of forgotten-

ness where we lie, our heads full of "standing on our own two feet."

The matron permits us to acquire a tan, provided that we don't lift or lower our clothes beyond the limits imposed by the decencies of prison.

"Did you bring down any Nivea? I want to be black for my next hearing."

"Are you out of your mind? If the judge sees you like that, he'll say to himself *well, she couldn't care less* and it'll be marked down against you in his report."

"Balls, give me your cream anyway, you old skinflint."

At the other end of the courtyard there is a triangle of sorry-looking grass; Gina is lying there, having herself massaged by her followers. Sometimes I like to squat on the laundry steps, where the rivulets of soap and dirty water gather in a moldy coldness; motionless, slightly bent over, my head leaning toward my shoulder, I open my mouth a little and feel the breeze vibrating through my cheeks, like a cool breath of air through a harmonica; and, a little higher up, the sun explodes lightly on my eyelids and roots me in the earth, through the rotting stones and the bubbles of laundry water; sudden joy pours out of the sky and swirls round my legs, while without changing position I move forward, with a slight effort, as against a tide.

Step by step, between the glassed cases of our limitless recollections, we move forward. We tirelessly imagine the end of the labyrinth, at once entrance and exit.

"My head is full of jewels."

Yes, paved and walled with jewels, no bullet can enter.

I think too of those summer wanderings with Zizi, when it was too hot to make love and we made love just the same; I can't really remember, I don't believe it; to think that being together, with nothing but the strength of our two carcasses, could be enough to send us soaring up there into the blue!

The Runaway

At this point I make a slight leap, and in an instant I have transcended time, scenes rise and close round me . . . For example, the spacious room in the inn where we had stopped for a ravenous meal; there were stains, true, on the wallpaper; and there was an electric clock whose big hand moved every minute, with a jerk, filling the silence with its suffering, while the bright brushes of headlights glided and danced over the balcony curtains, the mirrors, the ceiling—the world was parading down the highway, and we were sleeping.

Or, rather, I was cradling myself in Zizi's sleep; I wanted neither to sleep too much nor to think too much about the day; nights, riotous nights with Zizi, O Zizi, my night, and that frail delight . . .

"Time to go in, baby," Maria said.

That's right, Maria, and heat the water for the java, and play belote and wait for the cold sheets.

Come on, Maria, let's rub out the dream and stretch out our carcasses, the day has died.

Tomorrow, as soon as we have awakened, the flesh will steal the shards of strength that the spirit has accumulated and immediately adorn itself with them, forgetful of its surrenders in the night.

(10)

Like a fat shrew fixed in her habits, the prison yawns, howls, eats, and sacks out every day at the same hours.

Except that sometimes it suffers an attack of stomach pains, and then its internal organism is beset by disruptions as unforeseeable as they are disastrous. A girl makes a break, during her transfer to another prison or while she's in detention, or even after being sentenced, but in any event some of the shit always sticks to her shoes. Others, shadows, take her place; it doesn't really make a great deal of difference to us. No one comes here to make friends, but rather to do her time. That, in fact, is why the idea of a prescribed penalty has always seemed illogical to me: that rather archaic sliding scale of the courts, combined with the arbitrary freedom of juries to render verdicts, doesn't please me.

Any more than solid citizens are pleased by the surprises they have when they awaken after one of our visits. The scales are in balance.

I am neither logical nor balanced, nor am I the sociable type, and I have no hope of becoming so; I feel quite uncomfortable among my little sisters in stir, who have their own way of reshaping society.

The Runaway

Like every other inmate with any self-respect, I should make it a practice to read aloud every letter from a friend, carry my beloved's photograph in my bra, show it at the slightest pretext, while my eyes grow nostalgic and damp; or, when things become clannish, show my letters, with a slight pout, to whoever is my best friend at the moment. But I prefer to have some respect for my mail.

This savage part of me is compensated for by my nice qualities, artistic talent, good spelling, a fortune in postage stamps. Oh, I could do very nicely without drawing tulips on their letters, writing letters for them, and then stamping them. It's only that, since I can't do without smoking and drinking Nes, I have to pay my way. So I curse my perpetually being broke and the paths that have led me to it.

I am at the end of my rope, what could possibly make things worse? There are little irritations where my vanity is concerned, more clearly defined anguishes of heart and body, but my private little star shines on without pain. And, in the end, laughs can always triumph over everything.

And how is it possible not to laugh? There are times when you're compelled to wear the clown's suit yourself and be the funny clown, the sad clown.

After the dishes are washed, I go to empty the dirty water: holding the huge, greasy, overflowing basin in both hands, I have to stick my toe in the john door, open it the rest of the way with one shoulder, and then, with vast relief, dump the lot. Generally I get my feet soaked. I have an engraved wedding ring of platinum and a few stones, rather worn but I love it very much because I have never seen another like it except on my man's finger and because it came from a very old jeweler's shop somewhere in France. Not having been made to my measure, this ring is a bit large, and I didn't want to pay much more than it had cost me to have it made smaller.

Consequently, whenever I wash the dishes or myself, I put

it on a different finger; but on the middle finger this wedding ring loses all the charm of a slightly over-sized piece of platinum sliding up and down and round the symbolic finger, and I always put it back on the symbolic one as soon as I'm dry. One morning I must have plugged myself into the wrong circuit, my automatic switch failed to function: the clink of the wedding ring on the seat of the john, repeated as the ring tumbled down through the plumbing, was a terrible shock. In a flash I was back at the door of the workroom, banging away with the broom handle, banging and hammering hard enough to break the locks.

The girls, thinking it was an outbreak of some shameful and insane malady that I had kept secret from them, refused to turn a head or lift a hand: in cases like that it is dangerous to irritate the lunatic; after the crisis a good slug in the kisser will take care of everything.

The matron came running almost immediately, which proved that the silence that ordinarily followed our drumming on doors or floors was absolutely deliberate on her part: the matrons don't answer because they're too lazy to climb the stairs, but, if one throws a scare into them by pounding just a little harder than usual, then they'll come.

I explained what had happened. The matron threw up her hands in irritation and helplessness: but good God, I wasn't pointing a gun at her. I didn't even ask her to go head first into the shit-pipes, as normally I would have wanted to do. No, I simply asked her for my ring, and that was all. Suddenly that hunk of metal had acquired infinite size and importance: it was a barrel of jewelry, a universe of jewelry in which I had lived until that morning, stuffed with love and dishwater, and from which I had suddenly been thrown out; I, who never open my mouth to a matron unless I absolutely have to, would have kissed this one's feet if it would have persuaded her to allow me to go shovel through all the shit in the cess-pool.

I didn't have to go so far as that: she was really touched, and she led me right downstairs, opened the courtyard door and let me out on my own.

I located the cesspool that was fed by the workroom johns; desperation made me so strong that I yanked off the stone cover as if it had been a feather, and, kneeling on the very edge of the pit, my torso dangerously bent over the edge, I looked. Obviously, it wasn't going to do me a bit of good to look . . .

Then the tears splashed out, irresistibly, and a river of them rolling down my cheeks and plunging down below mingled with the shit in a miserable blend, while the matron kept tugging at my denim sleeve and ordering me to scram out of there. I went back to the workroom with my running eyes and my naked fingers and went right to work on a feverish letter to the Superintendent, asking him to send an emergency alert to the cleaning force and recover at all costs the precious object that I had so tragically lost. All this "because of the monetary as well as the sentimental value" that it had for me, and so on. Somewhat calmer now, I reread the letter, taking particular pleasure in the part that contained the reference to the monetary value: that should really scare the shit out of him, the way the shit is always scared out of all of them by any accusations of errors in accounting, requests for transfers of money, any letter mailed with more than one stamp and accompanied by a return receipt—in short, by anything that raises the question of the prison's financial responsibility. But on the other hand I knew something about the speed of the complaint procedure—and at lunch, at eleven o'clock, I had seen my letter lying on the ground-floor table with others of lesser urgency—and so I decided to take direct action: during our afternoon exercise I got some of the girls to help me move the stone (in my panic in the morning I had pinched my hand and now I could not move a finger), and every one shoved her face in the hole, in relays, each one yelling whenever she saw anything shiny. It is unbelievable what one can see in a cess-pool, especially when there are fifteen dames above it! Tons of food, first of all, both food that had been prepared and food never eaten: bread, peelings, yogurt jars, jam jars, all kinds of containers; rags, dishcloths, napkins, dish towels, and so on . . .

It was little Mauricette who spotted it.

Yes, there is a good God: there it was, on the surface be-tween a yogurt jar and a banana peel, miraculously saved from the greasy water that we had poured down by the bucket all morning in the hope of flushing it out: my wedding ring, spared and radiant.

I leaped for the broom, tore a yard of wire off the clothes-line, fastened it to the broom handle, and made a hook at the other end; then, kneeling as comfortably as I could and aiming with as much precision as possible, in order not to knock the ring into the muck, I managed to fish it out in triumph while the whole courtyard and garden rang with cheers.

The only false note came from the matron: feeling cheated out of her part in the salvage operation, she threatened to deliver my letter to the administration anyway. As calmly as I could, I pointed out to her that, in order to be logical, she should at the same time deliver a second letter canceling the first: "If you will take me back up to the workroom, I'll write it right away."

She shrugged and went away, after having reminded us to put everything back as it had been. I put back the stone and the wire, but I kept the ring.

On another occasion, I had heard that a new bookkeeper had been hired and I had tried to canteen, in the hope that he would not have his records in order yet and would not know what funds could be freed and what should remain blocked. Since my order slips didn't come back, I really thought that this was going to work, and so I repeated it two days more.

The order and the delivery were separated by three days of suspense.

"What kind of soap do you think we'll get this week? Cadum? Palmolive?"

"I wonder what view of Paris there'll be in the biscuit boxes." (Would it be the gloomy Chaillot, or the gay Trocadéro?)

The suspense finally ended and lightning struck: the matron, undoubtedly furious because she had had to straighten things out with the office, rushed in waving my order slips and called my name as if she had caught me in the midst of blowing the establishment's safe: "Don't you know as well as I do that you're blocked?"

I argued weakly that "I didn't think I'd spent all my pay from the string bags yet," and, "since I use my own stamps for my letters, I thought perhaps I could spend the three hundred bills that are usually put aside for postage . . ."

It was a little clumsy, even to try on a matron: any one of my orders would have cost enough to cover postage for the whole workroom; I had figured that, as long as I was going to try . . .

N.F. (no funds), A.B. (account blocked)—the initials are different in each jail when an inmate has to be reminded that she is broke. But in all of them the order slips come back annotated and crossed out with a kind of joyful cruelty.

Altogether, out of the whole consignment that I had ordered, I had laid hands on one little tart, which represented the sum of the funds at my disposal: a tart delivered to me one morning, all pink with quivering cherries, and I took it upstairs to share it with Mauricette, because she was the youngest and she loved sweets.

It was marvelous, piling all the crumbs of my half of the tart together on the pillow and licking my fingers and my lips; I had forgotten that cherries existed. But careful! I had to watch my figure, riding runaway mares means you can't carry much weight.

I like nice respectable trips, however, with a bank account, ready cash, identification papers with my name on them, whether borrowed or forged. Dough and documents, after all, especially the documents that prove one's existence, are the *sine qua non* of a life of freedom, especially when you can't walk much and have to get about, as a result, on crutches with wheels.

Before I buy even a lipstick, I'll get wheels. I can do my lips later, in the rearview mirror. I'll get a driver's license too . . . But, as a matter of fact, I can make a much better start with a real one: when the angels in uniform stop you, they are not carrying the whole WANTED list in their noodles, and your mug is unrecognizable under the make-up, so it satisfies them just as much as the insurance card, and, if you have the real thing in documents, you have a good chance of getting out of it.

So I'll have to get back my papers, taking advantage of my next trip to the property office for more of my postage stamps. I'll have to brace the chief matron in the morning, while she's still dry. The more you drink, the clearer your mind becomes!

I approach her very politely, and tell her that I've been doing a great deal of "writing" lately, I renew my promise not to barter my stamps, at any rate not to extremes. If the poor bitch only knew, beer alone was costing me two stamps a day!

I go with her to the Holy of Holies. Then a disappointment: she won't allow me into the clothing department; instead she asks me to tell her exactly where my wallet is. "The bottom shelf, ma'am," I sigh, "in the suitcase in the middle," and I wait there at the door, leaning against the wall with arms crossed and eyes staring up in resignation at the window. The chief matron burrows about for a moment, and finally comes back with the thing held in the ends of her fingers, away from her body, as if it may contain a plastic bomb; she sets it down cautiously on the stand in the corridor that is used for canteen trays and pots, and she begins being the functionary.

I see that I am off to a bad start: every move I made was controlled to the thousandth of a second, based on the topography of the room, which my mind had photographed when I first came, for there is always something that one has to swipe out of the property room while one is inside, and an eyebrow-tweezer is not the panacea for all one's lacks: just imagine showing your eyebrow-tweezer to a cop on a motorcycle!

My wallet is lying open on the stand, and way inside I can see the collection of cards that represents everything I covet.

The chief, with the dexterity of an old hand, has already taken out my books of stamps, she separates the twenty that she'll let me have and at the same time she is watching me out of the corner of her eye: if I jump her, who'll help her? Everyone is locked away at this time of the day, and, as for the door from the other wing, whence help might come—well, she has locked that herself and put the key in her pocket, and the workroom lock is on the outside.

Each of us is giving the other a real pain in the ass.

The sound of the telephone brings us out of this bad dream. Automatically, the chief starts to run toward the end of the floor, where the phone is ringing and ringing . . . the sound of that bell, and thirty feet to cover before she can reach it: the two factors canceled each other, and the chief, brought to her senses, turns to me: "Here, take the whole business and go back to the workroom, hurry up, I'm wanted on the phone, and I certainly can't leave you all alone HERE with all this!"

I obey at once, while she rushes off to the telephone, leaving my junk where it lay and scattering a few stamps as she breezes by. I take the steps two at a time, with the voice of the boss-lady shouting after me: "And shut the door behind you!"

I insert two quivering fingers into the peephole of the door and pull it shut, and here I am back in the workroom in the midst of the ladies, who are gabbing and eating bread and margarine and getting on one another's nerves; they have always been like that, but I am no longer Prisoner No. Such-and-Such, I am a free woman, my sentence has been suspended; in my bosom, between my bra and my slip, held in place by the same hand that is trying to restrain the accelerated beating of my heart, I have my red cardcase, my driver's license, my identity card, my passport to freedom.

When I go to be interrogated, the next day, I cheerfully pretty myself up.

"You're going to court."

Three words that knock my heart off its base and send my head into a spin. The examining magistrate! That was one guy I had completely forgotten about. Maria, stash this away for me in your bag, will you? it's personal papers. Gina, lend me your lipstick . . . no, no lipstick: instead look as if I'm at the end of my rope?

For an instant I wanted to appear in court in that potato sack of the prison, "just to put a bee up their ass," but, on second thought, it was smarter to look decent for the judge and attractive for Zizi. After all, Zizi has already seen me in every possible condition.

Oh, yes, the Bic, to scribble notes on the back of the pack of butts. Nadine slips a few pieces of candy into my pocket: I really like to suck on candy during hearings.

The inevitable 2CV Citroën, the inevitable good-natured cop who tries to feel up my thighs while his partner at the wheel is too preoccupied with the traffic to risk taking his eyes off it and seeing what's up; the inevitable grope at my sweater, followed by a bored and automatic "keep your hands to yourself" from me: I have better things to do and have done to me.

The Runaway

Jesus, the streets are beautiful at that time of year!

Too quickly, the 2CV gets to the place I wish it never would reach: lobby, benches, people waiting and watching you walk by.

Office of Such-and-Such; Public Not Admitted: my eyes search for something that will bring back the delightful summer which I have just had a taste of: at the end of the corridor, I spy the reassuring profile of my lawyer. We shake hands, we immediately make a little makeshift desk out of his briefcase, watched by my groper of a few minutes ago, whose eyes are again cow-like.

A general review: it was almost like the oral exam for the *bachot.*

The door of the hearing room opens, Zizi's lawyer is hurriedly introduced to me; Zizi himself is still having a set-to with the magistrate, I'll have time to decide, with his lawyer, what it's best to say in a few minutes.

The door opens again and discharges Zi and his handcuffs.

He's not in good shape, that's obvious: a pillow would have better color. But he smiles, he waves: hello, baby, yes, I'll take whatever they dish out, and we'll always love each other. His angels haul him off to the stall labeled *Prisoners.* Time to put on my act. All right: back hunched, arms stiff, voice barely audible. Done in, in other words.

The hearing drags on endlessly with its questions, its clacking typewriter, its depositions to be signed in three copies. The minute I am outside the door again, I light a Gitane at once: *no smoking here,* the cop protests. Fuck this sudden stickler for the rules, the sneak! I turn to my lawyer and laugh: "Don't you think I'm entitled to it, counselor, after making a horse's ass of myself for a hour?"

. . . Back at the prison, I go right upstairs to the dormitory, the girls are already in bed. To come back from a hearing at seven o'clock at night is really big stuff.

91

I find my bed made, my mail and my newspapers laid out on the pillow, with the sandwich that Nadine has made for me with special care out of my favorite cheese; exhausted, my head rattling, I have just enough strength to thank her, crawl into the sack and stretch my poor beat bones in every direction at once: days and months of living in low gear drain you of the capacity to think and act at the same time: when you do something half-way worthwhile in stir, it's better to have it all worked out first, or, if not, to forget about it afterward. Because you're far too beat to be able to handle your head and your legs at the same time.

(11)

Soon, soon now, we'll get into action: one evening we'll quietly sneak a few balls of cotton, with which, throughout the night before the battle, we'll weave our silken thread. Serious evening after serious evening, my head and Maria's head are together whispering.

Sometimes the atmosphere of the dormitory is magically changed, the rope goes into the closet, the runaway mare goes back to the stable, and everything is suddenly very cool and crazy. The popular belief that transforms women's prisons into so many reproductions of the island of Lesbos is a childish myth. And a pretty stupid one, when you can get a morals rap just for giving a kiss to someone who's feeling down, or being found with your head on some other dame's knees when she's tweezing your eyebrows; but, on the other hand, to pretend that we are all pure spirits . . .

Mona is generally supposed to be willing, and, when she prances from one bed to another in panties and pajama top, her impudently long heavy hair falling to her waist, you naturally feel a desire to return the hospitality. You feel like an expert in vibration massage.

Mona has a certain amount of lard on her, which she tries

to hide as best she can; Gina doesn't want to ball with anyone (what about Tony?) but it amuses her to con the lesbians: her repeated "hey, doll," and her generosity with cigarettes has persuaded Mona to lay a blanket on the floor between Gina's bed and Nadine's. The two of them are making her show off:

"Crazy, how she moves! Fat doesn't mean a thing."

Mona plays modest, pinches the tires round her waist, and shakes her mane: like a ham actor, like a runaway mare.

"What about you, Anick? You must be dying under that blanket. Come on, be like us, we're all girls here!"

To please them, I fling my fucking clothes off, and there I am, in nothing but panties, on the blanket next to Mona, where Maria was the other night. But now Maria is sleeping. But, though there were four of us talking together that night too, this time other matters entirely are under discussion.

The escapes that occupy all our thoughts with their pro-jected shadows will be something for Mona later, in three or four years, if her petition for parole is refused, or if she gets a kick in the ass on a morals charge . . . for this is transfer time, mass transfers to the Central Prison, and Mona is on notice that she may be moved from one day to the next; it's a matter of duty to put together some comforting little going-away present for her. Cigarette packs grow empty, and so do heads; it isn't too bad on the floor, we may fall asleep there. Before I conk out altogether, I shake Mona: "Got to get back in our sacks, hon. If the matron finds us here tomorrow morning . . ."

"Hell, you'll wake me long before she opens up, won't you?"

"Sure," Gina said, "Anick swallowed an alarm clock. Whenever I wake up I see her reading already with her specs on her nose. Christ, when do you manage to sleep? Matches scratching all night long, papers crackling in the morning; you . . ."

94

I interrupt her: there is no point trying to explain to her that my strength comes from nothing but having none of those common needs like eating and sleeping, because they wouldn't fit with what is going to happen later. For the lines of what was going to happen were laid out as regularly as ruled music paper.

I persuade Mona to jockey a mattress down between the two beds in which Gina and Nadine have gone to sleep with their backs to us; I share an apricot with her, one of the five per week provided by the establishment as a dessert.

After that we don't move, we don't move a muscle, our little carcasses watchful under the ragged blanket and our toes mingling in a fantastic prelude.

Maria hasn't waked up.

I go back to her in the morning, because as far as I'm concerned Mona doesn't amount to much . . . Weave, tie, twist, baby, that's much more important. With my pen and paper on my pillow, I illustrate everything that I say with scribbles, sketches, mechanical and ridiculous geometrical figures.

We have reached—in theory—the possible frustrations that the laundry door might cause: it sometimes happens that the matron calls to the office during the exercise period and locks us all outside, locking all the doors behind her, including that of the laundry. "In that case, it would be impossible to go back upstairs to the dormitory . . ."

Then we'll have to take the rope with us when we go down for our walk; instead of hiding it in the workroom, we'll just plain carry it down in a bucket, underneath some dirty clothes and a box of detergent: "Oh, yes, matron, I thought I'd do my washing today."

If necessary—if the rope still stuck out—a basin could be put on top of the bucket. Even if the door of the laundry should be left open, time would be gained in this way because the trip to the workroom to fetch the rope would be eliminated: Maria would simply go upstairs with the bucket, and . . .

"Yes, but suppose it is locked, the way you said?"

"Well . . ." I say, moving my Bic up and down over the same line. "If it is locked, we'll have to find a way of hooking the cord to the dormitory window right after the exercise period."

"Great! how do we do that?"

I must not disappoint Maria, I have to find a way out. Once my friendship with her has taken root and she is sure of it, then I'll be able to explain to her that this was all a drive-in movie. But the friendship is still too fragile.

"Gee, I like you, Maria . . . Yes, yes, I'm thinking . . ."

"Suppose we throw it up? With a hook? . . ."

Back to that! Sure, ask Gina for the hook yourself, maybe she'll give it to you . . .

"Uh-huh. It's something to think about, you're right . . . But remember, we might have to make several tries, that window's fifteen or twenty feet above the yard, and after all these months of rotting here we aren't in the best of shape . . ."

"Oh, look," Maria says, "when you have to . . ."

She is glowing, the plan has put new life into her, it makes her radiant. I notice that she has really beautiful eyes when she takes off those dammed glasses with their Italian frames: just like her son's eyes.

"I know, doll: when we're broke, we can go out and peddle our will power, we'll have more than enough left over. But we have to think of everything: I have the skill."

"What skill?"

"I mean I can aim all right, but strength is another thing— even with all the will power in the world, there's no guarantee. Besides, that'll all take time and excite attention, you don't stop to think of all the clanking of metal every time we miss! No, all the hook is good for is to get us ninety lousy days in

96

the hole, with an attempted escape on our records: and that's
not much good!"

"You're right," Maria admitted, "it's always some crummy
little detail that louses up everything. You see, I . . ."

"No, baby, you've already told me your life story; not tonight. Tonight we're working on the future. Wait, let me
think . . ."

"I've been waiting for years! But I'm sure you'll find
something."

Now I've really put myself up Shit Creek, and all alone. I
pick up the pen again, I draw the window and its vertical
bars . . . I'm really trying. I keep going back and forth over
the transverse bar, which cuts across the middle of the verticals
and braces them; and, simply by constantly looking at this
damned window, I fasten an idea to it, and the hook follows . . .

"Maria, I think I've got it! You know the wall brush in the
laundry? And the wires where they hang the wash? Well, all
of it together should just about reach. If we have to, we can
add the broom."

"Huh? You've really lost me. Explain."

"I cop all the clotheslines, I put the brush and the broom
together, fasten them end to end—a kind of fishing rod, don't
you see? I'll break the broom because all I want of it is the
handle . . . Get it?"

Maria got it loud and clear.

". . . Then on the end of the fishing rod I fasten another
piece of wire bent into a hook . . ."

"And you really think you're going to climb on that?"

"No, you little jerk, let me finish, at least. I'll have a thin
cord made out of crochet thread, I'll hide it in my pocket when
we go out for exercise. At the end of it I'll make a little thing
like a ping-pong ball; I'll throw the ball up into the upper half
of the bars. The ball will pull up the cord and, when it falls

inside, according to the laws of ballistics . . . but that's something else again. Anyway, when it falls, the ball will hang, and the cord now will be on the horizontal bar; the weight of the ball (which we'll make good and heavy) will keep it from falling down . . . are you still with me? Good. With the rod and the hook that we've put on the end of it, we latch on to the ball, but this time we bring it *under* the horizontal bar. The ball jams in the hook, we pull, the cord follows the movement . . ."

"Oh, yes, we'll have to make the cord out of that yellow nylon, the kind that's such a pain in the ass to work with, it's the strongest. Because when we pull . . . oh, God, what a catastrophe if the cord breaks!"

"I'll make two, there'll be a spare. Let's get back to it: I get the ball back. The broom and the rest of the crap we just dump, in their lousy laundry, for instance: they can enjoy themselves undoing the knots. Quickly, we fasten the rope, which we have ready, to the end of the cord, and we keep on pulling; the little one hauls the big one . . ."

"But," Maria objected, "you said a twenty-foot cord. If we do it this way and I've understood you right, we'll need twice as much!"

I think about this; at that moment, one might say, I have a surveyor's chain coiled in my brain. "You're right; I'll have to make forty feet, then. Hell! and we'd gotten so far. Look, let's have a butt. We've earned it, haven't we?"

I'm loaded with butts. My last deal gave me a bit of a twinge: it's the cardigan that I was wearing on the night of the accident, more or less my shroud, it seems that the cleaner had a hard time getting it clean. But its two sides and its collar were blue again, as blue as the sky in which, perhaps, my fairy godmother has strewn the clouds tonight. This thick topper, worn with slacks, is the big thing this year, and Gina, in her mad desire to be right up to the minute in last year's style, always pays whatever she's asked for the duds the new arrivals sell her.

We take the pause that refreshes with Gitanes: it's funny to be smoking a cardigan. When we had crushed out the butts and got rid of them, we remounted our runaway and it took off again on its pleasant imaginary escape. We work out a few further details: which of our panties we'll put on, one on top of another, that morning, where we'll make the first stop to phone our friends . . .

"A stop, huh? It's not advisable: they'll go over the whole neighborhood of this jail with a fine-toothed comb, you can be sure."

"Suppose we tried to get a letter out?" Maria suggests. "Because I know a guy who has a car . . ."

"There'll be roadblocks right away, everyone'll have to show his papers, there'll be squad cars out on the highway, motorcycle cops stopping every heap in sight, the whole works."

"Yes, that's right. Plus the fact that we can't even set a time, because sometimes we're the first to exercise and sometimes the second."

"Oh, no, the girls in the downstairs workroom always go first. Gina told the Chief that we never get our full hour because the matrons never get the girls out to get a tan in on time."

"And that always gives us a short deal on the visiting hours."

"I'm telling you, Gina bitched about it, it seems now the matrons want to alternate the exercise periods. But, like any other administrative project . . . all right, setting up a timetable is out of the question. No, look, we'll have to make the whole getaway on our own. I'll be thinking about that while

I'm working on the string bags. Might as well earn my salt while we're waiting."

"I'll help you if you want . . ."

"Oh, Maria! Thanks, hon. Now it's bedtime. Every one of my broken bones hurts from riding the runaway mare so hard since they put the lights out."

(12)

Fat, lolloping Fatima Benne has managed to get her case dismissed. She didn't walk, however; she still has to serve out an earlier sentence imposed by a court in the south. But, the temperature being the worst of the sufferings in stir, Fatima would like to go back to that torrid jail that she came from and die of heat rather than of cold. For here summertime is a joke. One day you're sweating, the next day everything is back to normal and it's raining again. And winter is really something to make you shiver.

My complexion is more tractable than my character, the sun darkens me in no time; if I go on like this I'll be taken for Fatima. I'm not particularly keen on that.

Nonetheless you have to admit that you don't come across a prison like this one every day, with even a tattoo artist in residence. Fatima's art work had caught my eye and I was dying to get myself tattooed. The trouble is that Fatima can write only Arabic and can't draw at all. On the other hand, she has a good eye, and she noticed right away that I drew really corny sketches to ornament my colleagues' letters and somewhat less corny decorations for my own letters to my friends.

One jailbird, they say, is the same as another: Fatima, who

101

is both convicted and accused, is as big as a whole harem, and she tagged after me constantly until, with my built-in good nature, I agreed to design something to embellish her legs.

So I made a few little nothings, flowers and butterflies, which she copied in India ink. But the next day she raised hell with me, complaining that I had loused up her instructions, what she wanted was certainly not flowers, "and not lice, either," and now she was stuck with them; she yelled so loud that I began to wonder whether I had not lost my touch. It took no less than three or four commissions from others for roses and lilacs, and as many more for St. Theresas and Gentle Jesuses, before I recovered my confidence in my own talent for drawing. But my experience had really put me off the whole business, and so I jockeyed Fatima into retaining the services of the other artist in the outfit, little Mauricette. Really excited at the idea of a live job, she picked up the torch, and soon a fresh series of tattoos began to climb up Fatima's thighs. I waited patiently for my hour of glory. At the first sign of trouble—in the end, of course, Fatima could not help seeing that Mauricette was not the most talented artist in the world—I threw such a meaningful look in the direction of the quarrel that the Algerian tossed her little friend overboard and went out after me, accusing me of jealousy and so on.

I took the cue. "Me jealous of the kid?" I shouted. "My dear woman, I'd like to know WHO there is here that I could possibly be jealous of!"

And that night, in the dormitory, I really laid myself out damning minds petty and nasty enough to think that I could be jealous of a child, especially a nice kid as straight and bright as Mauricette; so I won back my public and gave up for good on the idea of human flesh as a medium for me.

But this certainly did not stop me, after that, from accepting the spices and garlic that Fatima canteens and doles out with the same generosity: I am extremely fond of salad *à la niçoise,* and Fatima was the first one who ever thought of canteening spices in a northern jail. What is more, I got my own back from the dame, and even more, because the day after the hassle, she apologized by decorating my chest with the exact tattoo that I wanted.

Zizi is right on my heart. Christ, that needle really penetrates: she pushed so hard I felt as if it had dug in at least to a ventricle. The matron must not have searched Fatima, because she has her whole tool kit with her: triple needle, tattooing ink, etc. I am willing to admit that I would have been discouraged too if I had had to go through that whole collection of billowing trousers, skirts, and assorted veils.

Be that as it may, the initials were traced according to all the rules of the art. Oh, certainly, the rules of hygiene had suffered a bit: I had to lie down, stripped to the waist, on the filthy cement floor, across Fatima's thighs—she had squatted comfortably according to the custom of her country and got one of her arms into a lock on my neck to prevent me from wiggling, while her other hand pricked the needle into me, following the pattern that I had given her; she muttered to herself whenever blood welled up, and she swiped roughly at my boob with her old dish towel stained with grease, ink, and wine.

I'm a healthy one: the scabs formed without the slightest hitch, and disappeared in the same fashion. Wonderful Fatima! She has a good heart and she knows her way around: two characteristics that it is generally better to keep secret, if you haven't already lost both before you ever get into trouble. Otherwise the whole prison will suck you dry and then throw you away. After that it's up to you to juice yourself up again, if you don't want to stay in the slop-heap until the last judgment and beyond.

Fatima is good at the juice bit, too: when she's forgotten to canteen lemons, she waits for Friday, when the rest of us bring our lemons out of our cupboards for our fish; then she borrows a few drops of lemon juice from each of us, and, with that and a little sugar, she concocts a magnificent depilatory cream that makes the skin like satin and takes off the moustaches of all those in the workroom who are afflicted with them.

And, the minute they were beardless, those butches forgot their brand-new femininity and kicked out the beautician, yelling all kinds of crap about "those niggers, once you let them talk to you, you can't get rid of them."

Poor Benne! We shiver too, but, through heredity or temperament, we have acquired a higher tolerance of cold, and besides we all stick together. But Fatima's teeth chatter in absolute solitude, and she whimpers: "Why me no hot water like the others? Why I not like the others here? All in jail, all in trouble, no understand."

If I were able to speak her language, I would explain to her that it's not because of the letters and the money that come in to her, or because of her clothes (they were loud but "look at the material, that's really high-class stuff"), nor because of all the things about her that make people envy her and have their doubts about her. As curious and interested as these women are, they're even more sensitive to the color of a person's skin. Whenever the orders arrive from the canteen, Fatima immediately tries to share hers with everyone.

"Fatima darling, that's awful nice of you to offer me spices, really it is, but . . ."

Everyone seems absolutely determined to accept nothing; but let one greedy bitch's reflexes send her hand out to take, and the ostracism dissolves. After all, when you come right down to it, fruits and vegetables don't smell . . . they have less odor than cheese, for instance, or feet in the summertime. And those big pears and purple grapes look really tasty and refreshing, don't they?

The Runaway

The other day Fatima canteened a chicken. She quartered it with her bare hands, snapping up bits of roast skin in the process; all of us had our noses buried in paper, scribbling our Sunday letters, but we were waiting.

For, when an Algerian, an outcast, indulges herself to the extent of ordering "chicken for Sunday dinner," it's an insolence and an outrage. We're all making bets, it's better than a horse race: is Fatima going to wolf down the whole thing by herself, bones and head included? She certainly doesn't leave even a bone when she gobbles up our mackerel on Fridays. Will she throw the remains down the john so that she won't have to suffer our "no, thanks"? Or else—but oh, no!

Yes. In order to face down as many Frenchwomen at one time as she could, Fatima elected to offer everyone a share. And we, who had been all ready to throw mud at her, had the courtesy to accept.

After all, the chicken doesn't stink. Much less than Aliette's feet in summer. But I must admit that Fatima has a cast of mind whose twists and turns elude me. She shares, "out of real generosity," but afterward, in her own outlandish language, she curses herself for having offered and us for having accepted. She brings out a collection of apricot pits, lays them out or arranges them in groups on her scarf, and mutters magic spells over them, her voice mumbling on and on and her eyes glaring darkly at us.

"And just imagine, I wrote out her petition to the office!"

"And I lent her matches for her lousy little stove!"

"Why should you lend her anything? She's got bread, all she has to do is spend some of it. After this, do me a favor and turn her down. Hell, I . . ."

"You're just a nigger-hater."

"And you're a nigger-fucker."

To hell with all their spats. Fuck the whole business, chickens and apricot pits included, I've had a gut full of these silly ruckuses. So has Fatima; but, instead of behaving like

105

everyone else and knocking herself out or planning a break, she's busy preparing for a little skedaddle in the direction of Fresnes.

Solange is pregnant; naturally, she doesn't receive the little extra rations, the special foods, and the books on painless childbirth that are distributed in the model prisons. But at any rate she can be certain of getting out of here when she's in her seventh month. This pleases all of us, because we all love the baby that more or less lives with us, and it hurts us that he's being so neglected; and, in addition, Solange's nauseas, Solange's other ailments, Solange's smell were all beginning to really get on our nerves.

Suddenly Solange's face too begins to swell. Her eyes grow smaller, fluid runs from her ears, there are boils in her nose: Gina, the big brain, imagines all kinds of frightful things: fetuses lying dead in their mothers' wombs, septicemia running riot through a whole prison in a matter of hours; and she describes them in the style of one of those life stories in *True Confessions* that make you puke.

And Solange is sent to Fresnes.

All this time, with big, shining, empty eyes that hide what's going on behind them, Fatima is taking in the whole business. When she has it all down pat, she makes her move. On the first day, she complains of feeling weak, she pretends to be about to keel over, she upsets her plate; the medical department immediately orders her put on calcium injections and those reddish-brown capsules so familiar to people with anemia. General whispering in the workroom:

"She'll throw the capsules down the john, I tell you I've seen the bitch do it."

"You know damn well the jigs have it their own way, and the sawbones is scared shitless of them just like everybody else. You just go try to get a prescription out of him."

The nastiest one is Aliette, who, in spite of being congenitally "bilious and anemic," has never been able to get anything out of the medical department except stuff to move her bowels. Aliette's constipation too is a healthy diversion for me. "By the way, Aliette," I say, "if you want pills, I've got plenty . . ."

"No, no, doll," the fat girl protests with some irritation, "when I want them I'll go ask for them. Right now I'm straight; thanks."

I distribute my supply among the other victims of constipation. In the evening, when Aliette begins to go back and forth to the john, I tell her sadly that I'm fresh out of Mucinum. Aliette finally has to get off her ass and go stand in line with the rest at medical.

Fatima is always the first, she holds up traffic for hours, jawing with the nurse, bawling at her in Arabic, and casting spells on the sons of Aesculapius at a great rate, and whatever she wants she gets; the other patients shift from one foot to the other at the door and the jealous tension mounts.

Since the anemia racket doesn't produce any perceptible results, Fatima decides to pull a real job. A decayed molar serves as her Sarajevo, and the war is on.

Fatima takes to the hills, making camp on her bench from seven in the morning until six in the evening, wrapped in a blanket and moaning constantly. Once an hour a trusty brings her a pan of boiled water, followed by the matron, who carefully measures a few drops of something or other into it; then she gathers up her medicine bottle and her trusty and takes off without listening to whatever Fatima is mumbling; she becomes more and more unintelligible as the hours go by and the malady gains ground.

Night brings no improvement; in fact, if you look closely, you can see a slight distortion of the symmetry of Fatima's oval face. And of course, her damned complexion makes it difficult to appreciate how pale the Algerian has become in a single night.

Then, completely thrown off course by her pain, Fatima

loses all sense of caution: she gets up, plants in front of her a mirror, gets out her triple needle and damned if she doesn't ram it into her cheek, tapping it in with a spoon as if it were a combination hammer and drill, so deeply and so ferociously that the next morning she finally has the face of her dreams: the exact duplicate of Solange's—eyes closed, cheek swollen and burning, lips huge.

That is the state in which we see Fatima leave, as fast as possible, because, whether by choice or force, you always leave jail in a hurry. Fatima has won, she's being moved to Fresnes to get the scarred face that she really hasn't deserved; but it's a sure thing that "the big shots aren't going to be too careful with people like her: they'll open her lousy face for her with two strokes of a scalpel, and that'll teach her to fake. But they let us real Frenchwomen rot in stir and send our kids out to be killed in that shitty country of hers."

I am sorry to lose my tattoo artist, my flower, my poor louse of an Algerian.

(13)

The chief matron must own stock in moving companies. It's impossible to rely on being really settled, once and for all, with the same bed, the same stool, until it's time to leave. One evening she bursts in angry-eyed and sends cartons, bedclothes, and prisoners into a mad waltz.

There must be a stool-pigeon's tip behind it, or a hunt for something, for no apparent reason. Certainly, however, there is a hidden reason in the fact that Maria has been moved to the trusties' dormitory, even though she hasn't been made one, and spends her days with us in our workroom.

What has happened? The hacksaw business, squealed on by former pals or would-be pals? The rope job? But walls don't talk; and, except for the walls and us four, no one knows a thing about it.

Oh, well, it'll all come out without having to wish for it. Otherwise I don't want anything tonight: they've done me out of Maria, what else could I want now? I am not one to cry over spilt milk, and Maria's departure is a disaster, a brutal conclusion to our little nightly dream sessions and our late whisperings. You can't dream things up in the workroom the way you can in the sack: the light is not the same, and the only light that is favorable to friendly talk is the sunshine during our walks or the one bulb left on in the dormitory. There is always a stench in the workroom, it's cold and dirty, it's impossible to imagine anything properly there. At the very best, when your back muscles get too sore, you can stretch an old blanket out on the floor in front of the storage closet, grab some of the bunches of string bags—ten in a set—out of the pile of finished work, heap them on the blanket, and lie down, head on the pillow of nets and ass on the hard floor, to try to last out until the end of the day. To get to their snacks in the cupboard, the nibblers have to walk over you, *oh, I'm sorry,* and, the sorrier they are, the harder they've stepped.

The only time I had for being with Maria was the early evening, and the thought that she wasn't there kept racing through my mind.

Since the trusties' dormitory is unlocked before ours now, Maria takes advantage of being in the workroom to prepare for our arrival; I find her there, sweeping away the crap accumulated on the cement floor—papers, bits of thread, ashes: the sight of Maria looking so housewifely with her broom touches me and comforts me. Recollections of little buttered rolls go running through my skull, and I fall into a chair with a sigh. Yes, I have a chair: I kept my eye on the other women who had them and who had been scheduled for weeks to be transferred at any moment; the minute the first one left, I thumbed my nose at all my aches and pains, which had been equally watchful but just because they were weaker than I was, they were also a bit slower.

One morning my usual casual *Where's Maria?* was followed by a frantic *Where's Maria?:* she's neither under the tables nor in the closet. This is when I get the ingenious idea, or rather the ingenious need, to go take a piss; and, opening the john door, I am hit in the kisser by a powerful odor of something burning and, at the same time, by the outrageous sight of

Maria busy heating MY tin pot of coffee. To pull a trick like that! Furious, I closed the door again. The other dames, once they have their hot water and know where Maria is couldn't care less.

No one says a word when she puts the pot on the table, on top of the sardine-tin trivet; no one notices that Maria's eyes are red, that's to be expected since she's been tending to the burning paper.

But I can see, beneath the redness from the smoke, another redness of sleeplessness and tears: and the girl looks so miserable, with her mouth drawn down with disgust, her eyes open wider than usual, and her cheeks pale, that I would have to be much more blind than I am not to see that something has gone wrong. Oh, yes, Aliette has noticed it too. Those owl eyes of hers can see in the dark. Perhaps that's why I've always liked her. Even though I've deserted her in the dormitory, I've kept Aliette beside me in the workroom: she, Maria, and I form a horseshoe at the end of the table.

It has always amused me to spot her maneuvers. Aliette has an inexhaustible supply of pipe dreams, she expounds them by the mile in interminable sessions, leafing through checkbooks and disposing of millions while she sits there like a fat, professorial Prime Minister. When she stops for breath and the smoke vanishes, there she sits, a middle-aged, neglected woman, Aliette in her prison dress, to whom it never occurs to canteen something to make herself presentable and who lives on Maria and me when it comes to a mirror, a hairbrush, and toothpaste.

This is all we can do for her: so, at chow time, Aliette abandons us and goes wandering among the better-heeled. Maria finds all this annoying, but I have begun with Aliette and so I am obligated to go on showing her certain letters and lending her, without any hope of repayment, the last portions of my package of margarine.

111

"What's wrong with Maria?" she asks maternally.

I reply that I'll go find out right away: I get up and go over to the corner where the sink is, where Maria is piling the breakfast dishes.

"Maria? Baby?"

Maria is not *baby* to me. She makes it clear with angry shrugs. She sulks over her dishes. Finally I get pissed off: "Look, are we still friends? yes or no?"

"Yes, of course," she replies, fiddling with the dishes.

"Oh, shit, talk then. What's wrong with you? You bawl, you don't say anything . . . I like hardheads, I'm one myself, but . . ."

Maria pouts; she looks like her son as she does so. Aliette, the ambassador in residence, approaches us with a conciliatory air; not at all deterred by Maria's *oh, it's you,* Aliette questions her, makes suggestions, shows sympathy, and is so persistent that in the end it all comes out. It burst out of Maria like the juice out of a peach that's been squeezed too tightly.

"Anick! If you only knew . . . Our plan to split . . ."

"What about it? Have you changed your mind?"

"Who do you think I am? When I say *yes,* it's *yes;* I don't chicken out; I don't talk my head off to everybody."

"What do you mean, *you* don't? What are you getting at, dear? I don't, either, and you know it. Who's yacked? And to whom?"

"To everybody; the whole joint knows about it, the downstairs workroom, the trusties, everybody, that's who. With all the details: the rope, the dormitory window, all of it . . . I found this out last night, in a note from my friend Suzy . . ."

"Suzy from downstairs?"

"What have I got, a dozen friends named Suzy? I'm sorry, sweetie, I'm just burned up and sick, plain sick. It really makes me mad."

Aliette has listened to the whole thing, pretending to hang

112

up a dish towel here and stack plates there. "Take it easy, Maria, take it easy," she whispers. "Who do you think would've . . ."

"Who do you think? Who lived downstairs before coming up here? Me, of course; but I never even go to see them, I get the girls to bring my food so I won't have to run into the others. Who's always glued to their peephole? Who's always writing miles and miles of notes?"

"O.K., I get it," I say. "What about my papers? do they know I got them back?" (After all, I've shown them to Gina out of sheer boastfulness.)

Maria has no idea about that; at any rate, there has been no talk of the papers. Good; they're the main thing as far as I'm concerned.

"Papers?" Aliette said.

I hesitate: Aliette seems to adore Gina. She's sucked up to her with little gifts, things sent to Aliette by her mother, who apparently loves running out to shop for her grown-up daughter in stir. Gina may be getting princely assistance from outside ("a friend"), all right, but she can hardly ask the guy to send her elastic for her bra. These are delicate matters that no man understands. As for asking the prison welfare visitor or the social worker—phooey. That's strictly for dopes; those bitches are all tied in with the cops and Gina refuses to have anything to do with them.

So Aliette's mama has sent the whole first-aid kit: buttons, elastic, thread, thimble; she has enclosed some religious pictures in her letters but has never bothered to inquire what has made her daughter suddenly so devoted to St. Anthony of Padua . . . Sometimes in the evening we watch Gina's face go taut in real suffering as she tells us again of the magnificent, doomed career of her Tony, hunted by every police force in the world; and the pictures of Tony's patron saint comfort her and ease the pain of his absence . . . While all this is going on,

Aliette is straightening out Gina's closet. There is a voice in my ear: "Well, no man's ever gone broke sending her this stuff."

This whole circus, then, with the elastic and the pictures of St. Anthony, is a phony: what Aliette does with Gina she'd do with me if my glory weren't so tarnished.

My respect for her rises, I am overcome with amusement and fear at the same time, and in all this confusion one idea alone is absolutely clear: to save my driver's license. If Gina decides to sing, my plans, my real plans, are really screwed up. I grab Aliette: "Look, doll, would you take care of something for me while I grab a shower?"

One of two things would happen: either Gina and I won't be in the shower at the same time, and she'll take advantage of that to go through my things, or . . .

"Give them to me," Aliette says.

Secretly, under the table, I hand her my papers. Now I can go shampoo my hair in peace: the worst that can happen is that Gina, or her creeps, or the matron would find some trivial papers, Damien's identity card, in the possession of a woman named Aliette. So what?

The license is not among Damien's things.

Nothing, of course, happens, Aliette gives the stuff back to me at once, and no one ever even hinted at its existence. The ship with the runaway mare sank without a trace as time went by; but now I knew, we knew what to expect from the mentality of the people who shared our prison.

But, even if Maria had given up the idea of forming a team, she still wanted to go with me.

"Baby doll, we'll have to start all over from scratch after this flop, above all we'll have to wait a while."

To help that time to pass, there's work to be done.

The supplier delivered a consignment of materials for the string bags in August and has not been seen since. The prison, in August, is like a miniature Paris: inmates, lawyers, judges, everyone stopped in their tracks. No one new comes in; what's worse, no one goes out, either. The road of officialdom is officially closed: it seems as if millions of light-years must elapse before the rush of the autumn arrivals—no interrogations, no hearings, just a void.

With what is left of the raw materials, we crochet string bags for a week; after that, we go back to doing exactly nothing: the packing case that holds the finished work is closed and its lid used for the overflow from cartons. To judge by its size and the markings painted on it, this case must have held enough Red Cross supplies to keep the medical department going for twenty years. It's a regular legend. Naturally, it's called *the coffin;* but I am sure that once it was emptied of its drugs it never held any cadavers except those we imagined. Standing there closed it was all right; but, in the rush season, the accumulation of bluish, whitish, reddish nets piling up above the sides of the case and halfway up the wall, and collapsing at each weekly rearrangement of the furniture, had a really funereal aspect, like a shroud in shreds on a body rotting with gangrene.

One evening the men's foreman remembered that creatures called women still existed in the world, and that as a matter of fact they were only a few yards away from his own workroom; since the Superintendent saw to it that the men were always kept occupied—so that they would not find other, less permissible ways of filling their time—the foreman loaded us up. Perhaps in memory of our summer loves, recollecting our frailty and our greed . . . whatever the reason, there is a mountain of work: red and green promotional hats, visored country-fair caps that need tops or need elastic put on them.

Maria and I work together: I make the knots at the end of the elastic and prepare the visors in packages of fifty each, one on top of the other; once they're done I pile the fifties into hundreds, put a band of tape around them, and mark them with our initials—after all, if there are defects, no one wants to have to undo the mistakes of the others—and then I count fifty again, etc. Maria threads the elastic into the slot on each side of the visor. I open these slots with a hand punch (fuck their machinery). Our pile grows so fast that the other girls remark, without any cordiality at all: "I can't believe it, you must have a motor up your ass."

They forget that, if we do really hump like that, it's not for our own greater glory. Of necessity, we don't wear our misery on our sleeves; for that matter, a millionnaire who had to thread elastic into holes in order to pay for his Nes wouldn't have a more efficient routine or a prouder bearing than we do, absolutely not. I "detest suffering," but, when I find myself in the midst of it, I do not limit my consolation to quotations from Rimbaud. To console myself for having been jerk enough to let misery get anywhere near me, I hunt it down, knowing exactly why I'm bitter.

But being with Maria is different: I am no longer the lonely warrior, I have an ally. Thus the battle becomes less futile, almost comic. Isn't it, basically, a magnificent burlesque to do battle against adversity with a visor for a helmet and a ball-point for a sword? It would be funnier still, of course, if it did not tire the body and the shoulders so much, but as for that . . . "Old rattletrap of a body, away!" The curse becomes as mechanical as the gestures to stay alive, as the whole of life. I forget that I'm alive, in this shit-hole of a jail! If anyone speaks to me, my head jerks up in such bewilderment that I must be considered some kind of imbecile or nut. A nut with flashes of genius, granted; but the genius is just random chance, and not worth mentioning.

Speech! Since a certain inability to articulate properly— which, it appears, will linger on for some three years—is one of the innumerable dirty tricks that that old rattletrap has done

116

me, I take advantage of it to stop gabbing altogether. Or only "for the good of the service," and then in a hesitating, barely audible voice; hence people soon give up trying to communicate with me. I wish neither to be communicated with nor to communicate; that too is why I labor like a maniac on the damned caps.

Christ, how difficult it is to accept things from others! However hard I try to repay everything in postage stamps and acts of kindness of every imaginable kind, I never feel really even. Finally, little by little, I stop showing my letters, so as not to have to read other people's; since my session with the medical experts, I have continued my good habit of not gorging; my only enslavement is the trilogy of Nes-cleanliness-Gitanes, and that I make enough money to pay for.

But, sensible people will say, since there is no longer even a hope of any kind of parole, why break my ass? So that I won't have to thank you for keeping me alive, dear sisters; so that . . . well, just because I want to knock myself out. I'll get away however I can, even feet first.

"Hey, baby . . ."

"What do you want?" I bark like a sick pup. No one must know, no one must be able to guess how much I like Maria. In a collective prison, friendships must be hidden even more carefully than hatreds. In the exercise periods I gave Maria new promises, new counsels of caution: don't trust friendships gone astray, don't trust compliments, don't trust smiles, don't trust anything in life. But Maria is much too far from distrusting life. And I am afraid of her soft eyes, of her *Hey, baby* . . . I am paralyzed by her tenderness.

But Maria is determined to whisper nevertheless. Since her *hey, baby* has an urgent tone and the exercise period is still far away, we stop working and sit down on the floor, in front of the closet. Reclining this way, we can see the battalion of feet, crossed feet or walking feet, clean feet, dirty feet; virtually no pedigree, no grand manner could survive that inspection. Even Gina's rock-and-roll shoes lose their glory. As for the pumps that Aliette has had her mother buy for her at the Monoprix, I won't even mention them. Nor will Maria, but I catch her glance, and we laugh like two naughty young jailbirds, we laugh at the feet of our sisters in misery.

"Actually, you had something you wanted to tell me, didn't you?"

"You know Nadine's leaving in a week, don't you?"

"So what?"

"Well, we could get her to mail a letter, to a pal of mine. I'd feel safe."

Safe about Nadine or safe about the friend? Oh, hell, I'll trust whatever I'm asked to trust. Since Maria is waiting, I say, to please her: "O.K., I'll try to make the connection with her tomorrow."

(14)

The patron saint, the real one, must have gladly pardoned all
the Saint Ginas to come when our Gina announced: "Girls,
we're going to do something for my birthday!"

What? A feast, of course, preceded and followed by a general armistice; a day without shouts, without incidents, without quarrels, a let-me-see-you-smile-and-don't-make-me-kick-
your-ass day.

No one is going to turn up her nose even at a plate of boiled
beef; but Gina, who has a few working cells in her brain, is
not about to be satisfied with roping us in by the taste-buds
and has her eye on satisfying free will, the stomach, and the
calendar all together. My damned *noblesse oblige* was working
away as always, and so I forced myself to reconcile my appetite, my resentments, my scruples, and my penury. A yard of
material from Aliette's mother, Maria's thimble and thread,
narcissus and dragon-fly designs out of a fashion magazine: for
hours and hours in the workroom I sat poking holes in my
index finger and ruining my eyes to reproduce these flowers
and insects, which are absolutely hideous but magnified by
my genius.

Then I wash and bleach my handiwork, persuade one of the

119

trusties to press it, and wrap it in gift paper to be laid away until G-Day. I spoke to Gina herself:

"If you don't mind my mentioning it, baby . . . I know you've canteened a load of stuff for the banquet and you'll do everything just right, but, if you need a maid . . ."

"Oh, baby, don't even give it a thought: I'm doing it all myself, the chocolate mousse, the mayonnaise (it has to be stirred with a spoon, so you can imagine) . . . everything that doesn't come all fixed from the kitchen I'll do myself. When it comes to food, I have the right touch."

"Oh, I know that, baby! I won't interfere. No, I was just thinking about the table . . ."

"All taken care of: I'm going to have real napkins, not those shitty mended rags we get every week; oh, no, real big ones, I've squared that already."

"Great, I'll break my diet. But look, to make the table like in a restaurant with class . . ."

"The beer will be in bottles, I'll ask the matron to let us keep them until two o'clock: it'd look lousy if the beer was poured into the mugs, like every day."

"Oh, we'll all get tight! Look, I've managed to canteen some beer too, so we'll have that much more."

"By the way," Gina said, "if you need anything . . ."

We're getting away from the subject: I had started out with the intention of offering my help, but Gina always manages to turn offers of this kind to her own account at the same time that she shows the most complete unselfishness. I take her example and make up my mind to go her one better. Let's see who's going to come out ahead.

"I was going to offer to make menus for you: the social worker brought me some drawing paper. My mother sent her some bread to have masses said for me, as if I were dead already, but since I haven't got my string bag money yet the social worker thought . . ."

120

Gina has stopped listening. "Shit," she says, "that's right, at Christmas we had handmade ones."

I think back to a Christmas in my youth, a prison Christmas but a good one. All the packages had been assembled on the evening of the twenty-fourth, and I was still waiting for mine. Then, when I was just about resigned to being the poor relative, it arrived. What a marvelous package! Zizi had sent me olives stuffed with almonds, aspic, the kind of huge almond-iced cakes I love, and even two little tins of caviar. But how could I make Gina believe that? How could a loser like me claim to have any good luck, in the past, the present, or the future? I shut up.

"Great, thanks, make me the menus. Can I count on you?"

It was a great honor . . . I said: "I came to ask you what kind of design you wanted me to put at the top and to ask you what we're going to have to eat."

"How would I know? Use your own judgment."

"That's what I thought I'd do, but the main thing I need from you is the list of what we're going to have. After all, you're doing the canteening."

I must have had too much of an edge in my voice: Gina is angry, I was being disrespectful, after all, decorating the menus was just a talent, not something to show off about, I was too egghead for her; after this I could keep my talents for myself because as far as she could see I thought she was a shit. The tirade goes on quite a while; I just listen and don't bitch back at her. A good thing we're standing on cement, or I would have sunk through the floor.

Peace returns toward evening: Gina is too anxious to make use of me, she takes the first step. In the meantime I've been doing nothing but scrawling letters and I had damn well decided to skip the whole thing and get myself thrown into solitary afterward, since there's no other way of being alone. The only thing is that Gina has an extra supply of Nescafé, and she doesn't mind sacrificing one or two boxes of it to get what she wants: for her party to be one of a kind in the annals of the place and be talked about in all the centuries to come.

"Get your glasses, girls," she calls, "I'm buying everybody a coffee." Since she can't decently speak directly to me, she adds: "Maria, doll, you want to heat some water for us?"

Maria sees the picture at once and goes to work. She often acts as the mediator between the petty egotistical monsters that Gina and I have become. No one is fooled by it and everyone thinks she has handled things just right. Besides, the Nescafé brings new life: the blood circulates again, conversations are resumed, cordiality becomes general. Those who are broke are grateful to drink "a real java." So that they could also have "a real smoke," I offer up the second sleeve of my cardigan; then, full of piss and vinegar, I go to work on my menus. By bedtime I have finished: there are ten different drawings and ten different styles of lettering, one for each guest, and each chooses the menu she prefers: the candle in the pottery candlestick, the roses languishing in the silver tray, the bottle of Moët et Chandon. I make mental notes so that I can place them properly without making any mistakes.

There was so much laughing and joking, so much braying and eating, that for twenty-four hours I completely forgot about the outside. Or, rather, I conned myself so well into imagining a fake outside that I forgot about the prison. Aside from the mayonnaise, which Gina loused up for the first time in her life; aside from a few silences in the conversation, between the songs, and the tales of past loves and parties—each of us justified her presence as best she could—everything was perfect. The beer flowed from the mugs (for, in spite of everything, the bottles had to be returned, but what difference did the container make?), pleasantly washing down the chicken, the tuna, the sardines, the assorted *hors-d'oeuvres,* the fresh vegetables, the cakes, the *mousse* and the cookies; when the beer could do no more, the fruit salad took over the job; and the fumes of the sublime Nescafé rose with the smoke of Balto cigarettes to the very feet of the Unknown Saint, up there in her cloud, and so totally wrapped us in bliss that, when the matron came at two o'clock to shout *exercise time,* we were all completely limp and collapsed among the remains of the feast. So much so that the matron's invitation fell flat in the unbroken silence and she vanished without a sound.

It is a commonplace that the Bureau of Prisons would rather be told of an orgy than of a riot. As soon as the inmates start having a pleasant family time and utter no prayers for the director's death, no seditious appeals, in fact nothing—I mean: when all they utter is an occasional snore—nobody, even the Superintendent, that Nobody of Nobodies, would dream of spoiling the party.

As for me, I forgot the most important of all my obligations, the break.

Waking next morning with a big head and my paws more useless than ever, I suddenly remembered my promise to Maria: to brace Nadine about the letter. As quickly as possible I made up for my negligence. It was rather tricky: it was a question of persuading Nadine to play mailman and dissuading her from letting Gina know about it: this time there was not even a thought of letting Gina into our deal. From then on in, we had to do everything just right: real but reserved thanks for all the Nescafés of the past, a cautious *status quo* with an eye on Nescafés to come, and the utmost suspicion and silence with respect to everything else. Now, Nadine didn't have too much room left in the brain division: Gina, with her thoughts on the future, had been loading her for months with a mess of telephone numbers, addresses of people to be asked for money, lawyers to whom this money was to be carried; and, finally, the top-secret address of Tony's hide-out. When Gina found a real friend, a reliable friend, one of a kind, the kind of friend

that there can never be more than one of—at the same moment
—she gave her Tony's address; this was normal. What was
remarkable was that Tony was still running loose.

But that's her business; and the friends of my enemies are
my friends, why not? as long as they are obliging and intelligent, just like Nadine, who made me sorry that I had not been
busted six months sooner, so that I could have known her
longer. And in that case I would have been able to go to trial
before the vacations, and get out, and lie in the sun like a
lizard . . . Cut it, girl. I was beginning to rave, my imagination
was eating its own tail. Back on the track:

"Nadine, darling, if I can be sure that this letter goes where
it should and gets Maria . . . if it helps Maria and me to split
out of here, I'll contact you right away and thank you in
whatever way you want me to. This is a favor no one can put
a price on, you're going to tell me; but I know how much you
like real good ice, and I know you know what I'm in for. All
you'll have to do is come and take your pick."

Nadine laughs like an idiot and tells me she doesn't have
the slightest intention of becoming a fence, my junk could not
have interested her less: she has plenty already, stolen hon-
estly, and, if she gets our letter out, it'll be because risks like
this give her pleasure, and a break . . . "I'm going to have to
buy a paper every day! Oh, lord, all the worry you two are
going to make for me."

We are lying on the blanket in front of the closet, on the
dirty floor, as if we were taking a nap; Nadine is stretched out
between Maria and me, a fact that intrigues those present.
Gina seems nervous, she is pacing up and down; it's not that
she has any doubts of Nadine's discretion and loyalty, but her
face shows as clearly as a mirror that she is being devoured
by curiosity and jealousy. What the hell could we be dreaming
up, two second-hand runaways like us, without a cent, mysteries that we were, with her Nadine, her lifetime friend about

to be let out, well heeled, with plenty of connections? What did we have in common?

But Gina won't interfere: it would be bad for Nadine and for herself if she appeared to think we were doing anything but having an ordinary chat, helping Nadine kill one of her last few afternoons: the last days are the longest. Besides, outside Nadine can play belote and yak forever with Gina, because they'll meet again at the gate and be inseparable forever after; but she won't always have a chance to talk to two characters like Maria and me. So . . . Gina chooses to observe our threesome indulgently but attentively, like a mother hen, in a sense, that would never lay eggs. Nadine promises, with reservations: caution is essential, there are eyes in every corner, for every two of these eyes there's a mouth, and all the mouths are hooked up to a central collection office, Gina's ear. Since we don't want Gina to know our business and she doesn't want us to know hers, Nadine sets up partitions in her mind and knocks herself out as good-naturedly for our errands as for Gina's.

"Write it out first and show it to me," she says. "If the letter's all right, I'll slip you some air-mail paper and you can copy it on that . . . "

"That's all right up to this point," I interrupt. "But, if you don't mind my doing my share of this—I hate roast canary—do me a favor and let me address the envelope too."

"Wait a sec. I'll just file the address in my head: I do everything in my mind. As soon as I'm out, I'll do the envelope myself on a typewriter—even better, on a friend's typewriter. You know how many people have been busted by a typewriter."

What am I supposed to say to that? But I try to square it anyway: "When I said *envelope*, I meant whatever you're going to carry the letter in. All right, look: rolling up the letter and hiding it in your long hair is out: you know the matron would make you undo it, if you had long hair: but yours is short, so that settles that. Elsewhere—well, that's already rented."

"Huh?" Nadine said.

"Come on, baby, don't look dumb. I'm on to Gina, and I've delivered a little mail myself . . . But I'm not trying to requisition any part of you for my purposes: don't worry, we'll find another container. You know I'm not too bad when it comes to screwing the office."

Maria is already scrawling the rough draft: we work together like an assembly line. Finally I whisper triumphantly: "I've got it: do you have an old empty Nivea tube?"

"Yes, but I didn't canteen again because I'm walking tomorrow: I have just enough in it for tonight and tomorrow morning. I'm going to try to get hold of a basin of water."

"Are you sure the chief matron'll put you in the exit cell tonight? Ask her to let you stay with us. Tell her you'd like a good-by evening, you'd feel too down in the dumps all by yourself, that crap."

"Why not? I'd like it . . . But that probably won't work, they almost never skip that part. Except when you've done the trusty bit on a couple of raps here, then they sometimes give you a break before they throw you out."

". . . kicked out without a word about your loyal services. In your case I think they'd go along, if Gina backed you up."

"I'll try . . . But if they shove me into that cell just the same, sure as hell they'll search me tonight, don't you think?"

"Oh, sure, you'll have to give them all your junk, your mail, your rags, everything except what's on your back; sometimes they won't even give back your own clothes till the last minute before you go. Then all you have to do is put them on, pick up your dough at the office—your suitcases are out in the hall all packed—and bang! you're out . . ."

"I'll take you all with me, girls."

There was a general sigh, and then the double shock of remaining there within those four dirty walls, and in that atmosphere of stink that gets worse and worse as the day goes on and all ten of us keep breathing it in and out.

"All right, then, you'll hang on to your cosmetics, whether you stay with us or go into the other cell. Anyway, since you don't have to let go of the letter until you hit a mail box . . ."

"How about trying to get it out with all my own letters? With all the mail I've gotten here, she isn't going to waste her time reading every letter and looking inside the lining of every envelope."

"No," I said decisively, "that stinks, it's older than Job."

"Don't shit me . . . I'm sorry, my dear, I've never been in prison, I don't know . . ."

"Is that a crack at me? Look, I'm not trying to con you out of your Nivea: I don't care what I put on my skin, milk, cream, lemon, and margarine . . . Natural chemicals. No, look: give me the tube and I'll give it back to you in fifteen minutes. That's all."

Nadine isn't pigheaded.

With peace of mind and all the time I need for the job, I prepare the secret compartment.

"How does this sound? Read it." Maria shoves her book of popular songs under my nose: she has used a blank page of it to draft the letter; the girls will think we're learning the lyrics of *Come Prima* or *Arrivederci*. Forehead to forehead with Nadine, I show her the draft next: "You sure it won't be too big for you to carry?"

Nadine approves the contents of the same, as well as its weight.

I lock myself in the john, lay out my tool kit on the footrest, open the bottom end of the tube with a hairpin, roll the letter inside some plastic, shove it into the tube, and close it again, biting on the end to make it tight—sure, it's rough on the teeth—so that it'll look like any other family-size tube of Nivea, harmless and innocent. Then I wipe the Nivea off my paws and deliver the tube to the courier.

If it all works out, I'll have to chase all over Paris and vicinity to get hold of Nadine and hand over the promised ice. Whatever piece of ice she wants out of all those that lie waiting, somewhere in France, for someone to put them back into circulation.

(15)

The mouthpieces begin drifting back. They are still wearing light suits, and their healthy complexions betray the sunshine they've enjoyed, the quitters, far from us and our gray lives. Reluctantly they resume their routine of running to the courts and the judges' chambers to petition for privileges, releases, and records. My lawyer is a good talker, that's his job, but, when it comes to writing . . . I had been waiting weeks for a visit from him, or at the very least for a negative reply to my request that he visit me.

The only one who never stands me up is the church visitor. To make her happy, I pretend to be tormented by metaphysical conflicts, and I kiss her as if she were the Host itself. But, just like the Host, she doesn't stick to the ribs.

I have my belly full of holding my back straight and dancing on the tightrope: I'll wind up breaking my neck. You go along with your head among the stars of vanity and your feet balancing on the hard, treacherous rope; and then one morning you stumble over a bucket of water or a tin of Nescafé.

In the middle of our conversation this morning, she offered me her services, if I had anything I wanted done, naturally provided it was permitted by the rules . . .' So I set forth my

129

instructions for the blessed woman, at the same time protesting that I did not like to ask for favors, but it was not the same thing with her, she was like a second mother, etc.

She was to rush into the first telephone booth she saw—I did not dare to suppose that she would run into the first bar—and call the mouthpiece. The message: "Counselor, come at once. Damien is at the end of her rope." I wait, full of certainty: God and man together can not let me down.

The sound of a telephone downstairs: there he is. No, the lawyer wouldn't come by phone.

Back to the wilderness: an hour goes by. Ring-ring again, doors opening to the clink-clink of keys, lumbering footsteps . . . chow, of course. My God, what is the good sister up to? Perhaps she doesn't know how to dial? But then she should have told me. Or else, as slang has it for something else, the lawyer might have gone out to attend to something outside the courtroom? But I had told her to be sure to call at lunch time so that she wouldn't miss him. But perhaps he had stayed outside the courtroom for lunch too.

The door opens. "Damien! lawyer's here."

Ah! I knew he wouldn't do that to me, his loyal little client in good times and bad, his liege, his gold mine; I've never paid a lawyer with promises and I've always paid him what his services were worth, before or after. And God knows he deserves a lot, going on with a case as hopeless as mine! But today I want to reverse our positions: I want to ask the lawyer to be the provider for me.

I carefully close the door of the appointed chamber and take a gander at the matron: good, she's wrapped up in the mail, what a load of it there is, I hope there's something for me; and I launch my attack even before my defender has begun pawing through my record, that famous record of mine which everyone has put a hand to with pens, red pencils, typewriters. I don't want to even look at this file. It makes me sick to my stomach.

"Let me steal a Gitane from you, counselor."

"Please do! Well, keeping your spirits up?"

Out of politeness, I ask for and give news, and then: "Counselor, I've had a brainstorm: you're going to have to help me."

I have often performed the feat of leaving my lawyer speechless: I had put my mouthpiece through surprise, dismay, horror, anything that can momentarily deprive a courtroom tenor of the power of speech, just like anyone else who has only the usual gift for it. I must point out that we had been dealing with each other for several years. This time he can't even open his mouth: he sits there behind his thick eyeglasses waiting to see what in hell I'll trot out for him this time.

"As a matter of fact, since I've transferred funds from my bank account to yours (oh, please don't hesitate to dip into them if you need gasoline money), you're by way of being my creditor."

In fact, as soon as I learned that the judge had not yet got wind of my bank account, I didn't wait around, as you can well imagine, for someone to come and tell me regretfully that he had finally got his mitts on the few lousy bucks that my mother, with a punctuality that suits me fine, deposits each month in the vaults of the bank that I have honored by entrusting my affairs to it. True, the risk is minimal: my mother is not a thief, and, with all due deference to Vespasian, her money has an odor, an aroma of a sergeant's widow's pension, of good middle-class cash—in short, an honest smell. But I larded out my mother's deposits with others of my own, considerably larger, and they most certainly did not have any odor of respectability.

Retirement, pensions, little hoards in desk drawers, jewelry grown musty on three or four or ten generations of plump or dried-out fingers, on swollen bosoms or flat ones—no, thank you, darling not for me: that kind of stuff stinks and there are records of it in antiquarians' trade publications. People like us have no interest in putting anything back into circulation that

131

is come by in that fashion. What we like is to steal bank notes in bulk, or stuff by the truckload, the pleasure of caressing fresh crackling bills; when we're older, perhaps, we may be able to adapt ourselves to the kind of loot that will be appropriate to our age, something fairly old and respectable.

In the meantime, having the appetites of youth, I've gone through quite a bit of healthy young money; but, being frugal by nature, I've picked up the crumbs. My man raised hell every time I made a deposit: "You and your bank account! You'll see what will happen to that. The day *they* find out about it, they'll grab the whole thing, and that will be the end of that. Good God, a bank account!"

I used to laugh. "You're getting old, darling, old and suspicious and a bit of a sheeny; just let me handle our finances whatever way I think best. Why should we knock ourselves out hauling all that dough around everywhere when it's so much better off lying in the bank? To say nothing of the fact that, if we have it on us, it will go sure as hell on helping friends out, buying cars, and paying uncountable tabs in uncountable night clubs. No, baby, you'll be hitting forty soon, it's about time we began to sober up a little."

After the court blocked my prison account, then, I didn't want to be caught twice with the same hook, not to mention the fact that I would have been a bit pissed off, just the same as all the other times when Zizi had done the Cassandra act and been proved right. So I had sent emergency instructions to the bank to send a checkbook, a nice fresh one, to me in care of my lawyer. (Checkbooks are so pretty when they're new; but, what with shifting them from pocketbook to pocketbook, from dressing table to glove compartment, mine become real rags.) Now, every time the lawyer came to see me, he brought the book; I filled out a check payable to him, and he snatched that much more bread out of the government's mitts.

Finally there were only a few thousand lousy francs left in the bank: the account had been milked in stages, a hundred or two hundred bills at a crack; just in case someone in the bank might have decided to play games with police headquarters, it was better not to make the payments big enough to give anyone ideas.

The mouthpiece bitches, but he does what I want: he's fond of me, and I must be a change from the general run of his clients. Always the same hustlers, murderers, and other yardbirds—it must be damned dull for him. I'm an average worker in the vineyard of crime, yes; but that doesn't stop me from receiving him in braids and a little white collar, or designing pretty letterheads for my dispatches to him.

"My mother's still standing behind me—morally, that is—as I've told you, counselor. I suppose in the end I'll get back in her good graces entirely, but it's a long haul. And, that reminds me, I need more phosphorus; the fish here will never build me up, I burn it all up. Write to her? Believe me, counselor, there are times when I have all I can do to find enough strength to write to you. And you come to see me so seldom . . . " Talking to the mouthpiece, I always enjoyed playing the neglected sweetheart. ". . . As far as the court is concerned, any other benefactor aside from my mother is out of the question. Oh, by the way: you did ask permission for me to get money orders from my mother, didn't you?"

"Yes, the last time we were in court."

"Before I wrote to her, though (and I will do it one of these days; promise), just to be on the safe side I wanted to be sure the order had gone through to the people downstairs. Would you believe it? There isn't a damn word about it in the records in that damned office. Just suppose I hadn't bothered to check and my mother had had an attack of generosity, the dough would have been blocked with all the rest and I'd never have known a thing about it."

"But, when they block a money order," the lawyer objects, "they inform you of the fact, don't they?"

"Hell, no, not always."

"Well, why haven't you let me know when something of that sort has occurred? I would have gone back to the judge . . . "

"What's the point? I'm in no danger of getting a cent from outside. Anyway, I've sent another petition to the court, on general principles, and this time it's worked."

"Does the order specify your mother's name?"

"Unfortunately. If only it could have been made a general order. Oh, no, it's very clear: ' . . . permitted to receive money but only when sent by her mother.' Don't think I didn't read it a dozen times before I signed it. So . . . oh, counselor, you will do it, won't you?"

"I'm afraid you'll have to explain. I don't follow you at all . . . Ah, you want me to write to your mother again on your behalf? But you know she never answers my letters! God knows how many times and in how many different ways you've made me write to her!"

"God, no, counselor, who said anything about dragging my mother into the act? Absolutely not; she absolutely mustn't ever know about it. But she lives at the other end of France, and Paris is a big place . . . Go to Paris, please: go into a post office and send me a money order, and pay for it out of the dough of mine that you have. I leave the amount up to you."

"I should prefer to make it a series of inconspicuous transactions . . . Besides, I'm not sure whether I can . . ."

"Yes, counselor, of course you can. The worst you can get for that kind of forgery is three years. Anyway, I'll take full responsibility. All you have to do is write *mother* where it asks for the sender's name."

"Suppose someone decides to check up?" the lawyer breaks in, perplexed.

"What's the matter, isn't my mother allowed to take a trip to Paris? She's gone away somewhere as it is, incidently: I think she's traipsing round Italy. The fuzz wouldn't even find her. Anyway, do you really think any court would set up a whole investigation commission for chicken-shit like this? . . . as I was telling you, there's not even anyone there; and, between now and the time my mother does get home from her vacation, you can be sure I'll have managed to get *real* help out of her."

The lawyer laughs, I know he'll give in. He leaves with a handshake in which his hand makes mine a kind of promise. A few days later, I get a money order.

I can't keep my secret, my joy just burst out of my throat, what a darling guy that lawyer is! Laughing and weeping, I tell the whole hushed workroom that I've worked my way back into my mother's good graces; she's the best mother ever, even if she is a little tough sometimes, it's only for my own good; look, she loves me as much as ever, she can forgive and forget . . . "Maria, darling, get the fire going under the water! I'm buying Nes for the house. No more working on paper hats, no more poverty. Up with your cups, girls! I know you don't drink toasts in coffee, but my mother really deserves one."

(16)

In the midst of a reduced company, which is still quite big enough for me, I cling to my solitude.

You were right, my love: everybody is always alone. But up to this point the bonds of misery and enforced association have made it impossible for me to sever these ties without substance, to give up these conversations without effect or cause. Panic, desperation, indifference: these are star-spangled abysses into which I shall no longer plunge: very soon I will be alone.

All the girls I like are leaving, one by one: Mado, Nadine, Mona . . . One afternoon Mona got her orders, in one fell swoop: pack up, you're leaving. Down from the shelf came her big suitcase—not the little vanity case that is always with you, night and day, but the much larger one that holds sweaters and reserve supplies of all kinds; everyone hurriedly gets out her own stuff in order to give something to Mona: there is already a Central Prison aura round her, and she'll be short of underwear and soap and stockings. They rained down into the suitcase: "Here, baby, take this and remember me. You'll need it there." In all the haste of her exodus, Mona left with shoes of mine on her feet and a good number of my

136

hairpins in her chignon. The thought of Mona departing bare-footed and disheveled into her doom was too poignant: I didn't ask for the things back.

Make it fast, a quick kiss, the closing door; so long, Mona, so long, I'll remember you . . . no, Mona's gone, forget Mona.

Gina will go on trial soon, and so will Maria, if nothing comes up; and God knows how many others are waiting, in all the prisons of France, for the gentlemen of the bench to remember that they exist.

We wait.

Each of the endless days in stir is part of a week that goes like a flash, and the weeks become months in an instant. And all this time waiting vanishes without leaving a single trace, only perhaps a grayish picture or a brief episode in the memory: the luggage of Chronos.

By now it's already necessary to turn on the light in the dormitory if you want to read; and, if the matron forgot to make her rounds on time, it doesn't get turned off. And, since you asked for the damned light, there's no point banging on the door or throwing shoes at the ceiling to get the light out quicker or simply break the bulb. No, when your mind just takes off, it's better to pull the bedclothes up over your eyes and make yourself an imitation darkness underneath. When the click of the switch and the footsteps of the matron indicate that it's safe to surface again to get a breath of air, there's always the same delighted surprise to find how completely dark and cool that air is, a great bowl of night without any spatters of lingering twilight.

Almost imperceptibly we are slipping into winter—yes, already. Coffee, little flower drawings, washing ourselves . . . and the dishes.

"Who's going to do the dishes today? Don't all yell at once, now."

The only element of suspense left is the canteen. The aristo-

crats make a great show out of drawing up their lists as
publicly as possible:

"Let's see, what's the special for Thursday? Oh, yes, cheese;
I don't want any."

"There's butter and eggs too, don't forget; wasn't it you
who wanted butter?"

"No, it melts too fast. Outside, yes; but here margarine's
just as good. Hell, there isn't even one measly butter dish
around here."

"I keep it in a plastic bowl with water."

"But then you have to change the water every day," Gina
objects; "It's too damn much trouble. And . . . wait a minute,
what do you mean, a plastic bowl? Where . . . "

"I had it with me when I came in and they let me keep it.
Naturally, I canteened in the other joint and I have the right
to keep anything that comes from the canteen there, even if
they don't sell it here. The bowl . . . "

Gina is wide awake now; her eyes are gleaming. "I like that
bowl of yours! Want to make me a present of it?"

The bowl is indeed magnificent: bright black plastic on the
outside, dull green inside; the innumerable coffees that the
owner has drunk from it have stained and streaked it so badly
that it looks filthy even when it has just been washed; in a
word, it has class.

"I'll give you whatever you want in a swap—a canteen
order, butts, you name it."

"What, sell my bowl? Not a chance! I'm going to take it
with me as a souvenir when I walk. Unless . . . you got any
Nescafé stashed away?"

"Come off it, girl, what are you saying? All I'd need would
be for my dough to come late, and . . . uh-uh, my emergency
Nes I'm hanging on to. Ask me for anything else in the world,
baby, but not my Nes: no deal."

"That's just why I'm not begging you. I'd really hate to give

up my bowl, I'd only do it to make you happy, I can see you're
really hot for it . . . "

"Never mind, don't try to con me, you bitch. You can
shove your stinking bowl, then maybe you'll see Gina doesn't
go on her knees to anybody. A bowl—shit. If I really want
one, I can get one ordered tomorrow at the latest from the
Department of Extraordinary Expenditures."

The strangest thing was that Gina did put in the order and
did get the new bowl. In her place I would have left the whole
thing in the realm of talk, along with all the other big ideas;
but, if it made her happy to turn her breakfast into a living
advertisement for plastic, and swallow Nes that tasted like
cellophane, to mingle with the masses while drinking from
the same kind of bowl as the first transfer to come along, it
didn't bother me.

What matters is having Nes to drink.

Now that I'm rich, I lavish Nes on the only one who helped
me when I was in the shit: Maria. But even so, by the end of
the month, no matter how many string bags I make for her
or how many stamps I give her, she always has to wait for the
next accounting before she can canteen again. Virtually everyone, for that matter, is equally broke. The canteen tray, which
reappears every morning, is very light today: two packages
of candy. "Catch, Maria!" the trusty calls. "That's it. So long,
la-a-a-adies."

What is this? Maria, you were all out of dough! I'm the
one who watches out for your account, I'm doing everything
I can for you, and you cheat! Maria writes out orders I know
nothing about, probably at night in her lousy dormitory; for
all I know, she's making all kinds of deals so she can stuff
herself under the sheets, after I'd gone halves with her on
everything. What a jerk I've been! Joint food stock, making
string bags in her name, and all the rest. Suddenly a mountain
of little revealing details looms before my eyes, and I pretend

not to look at Maria: those skin blemishes undoubtedly come
from liver trouble, her liver, the candy, it all works out; that
they-can't-break-me attitude that may be nothing but the clue
to prove that her whole morale is loaded with sugar—oh, shit,
it all makes me sick.

All the same, it's impossible that I could have been played
for such a sucker: Maria's my friend, she'll straighten everything out and the whole thing'll wind up in a big laugh.

"Candy, baby?"

Without a word of thanks out of my sour face, I take the
cherry candy that Maria is holding out to me. Christ, the little
bitch remembers, damn it: she knows cherry's my favorite.
She's really laying it on. Worse than kids, these jail bitches,
with the candy bit—really, now, I ask you, at our age!

Laying it on and then some. Because she's showing off
besides. Instead of playing the great lady and passing her
goodies round, she'd be better off to canteen a ball-point pen
for later.

Background noises: paper being crumpled, candy being
sucked, candy being bitten. The only candy that doesn't make
a sound is what's being kept for later. Will this gang of
guzzlers ever stop?

"Hey, what's this?" That's little Mauricette. All red in the
face and panting, she held out her hand; in her palm a paper
folded very small lies among the candy crumbs and a little of
her saliva. "I opened it, I began to suck on it without thinking,
and look what I found."

"God, what a dummy that kid can be!" Gina cries. She's
undertaken to educate Mauricette, and, with her natural impulsiveness, she'd put her out for adoption a dozen times a
day. "No, really, you're a dope. Can't you watch what you're
doing?"

"But it was in the candy," Mauricette whimpers.

"You got rocks in your head," Gina says, but her voice is a

140

bit less harsh. "Sure, it's not your fault if you find a note, but you don't have to tell the whole world. Stop bawling, stupid! Let me see that thing. Shit, it's for you, Maria. That's right, it was your candy. Here, it's your business, I keep out of other people's business."

Maria gives Mauricette another piece of candy and takes the note, which she unfolds and reads silently; then, without a word, she stuffs it into her bra. Her silence has spread to the whole workroom. That's normal enough: the minute any of us does anything at all unusual, the minute she receives a letter and doesn't broadcast the contents to the whole group, as if we all had the same relatives, the same friends, and the same deals going, an embarrassed silence invariably arises. Somebody finally screws up the courage to say:

"Shall we have a hand of *belote,* girls?"

Or:

"This stinkin' place is cold enough to freeze your cunt!"

Which always brightens the darkest faces, or makes even the veterans pull their comfortable denim dresses closer over their chilly shoulders; but the words and actions that follow such silences are as forced as the silences themselves: everyone feels guilty.

When you pull a job outside and keep on breathing the outside air, you can persuade yourself that you haven't done a thing, and it's easy to feel innocent; but in stir, even if you've arrived with nothing on your conscience and your record, the feeling of guilt doesn't take long to blacken you. You breathe guilt into your lungs; you see it dripping down the walls; it gathers in all the corners: like the dirt, guilt has accumulated there for generations: how can you possibly not feel guilty here?

To profess innocence among prisoners is an indecency— everybody knows you've been confined for having given a lead franc to a beggar, that is self-evident. It is equally an

141

indecency to be well educated, well dressed, or hopeful; it is proper to complain of anemia and constipation, to say *"I've really had it"* twice daily (on the average), and to cure yourself on your own hook by repeating that you'll end up croaking in the damned can.

I have enough Nes left for two drinks: "Shall I get it, or will you?" Maria is weakening, but she takes the black pot and the newspapers to be burned under it and goes off, without breaking her stubborn silence. The john door closes on Maria the mysterious, and the workroom speculates; no one says a word about the matter, but I can sense that what passes for minds in my little sisters is elsewhere; but not too far away, no indeed. Just in Maria's bra—with the most honorable intentions.

I let things ride until after the arrival of the official mail, chow, exercise period; but by bed time I can no longer hold out, and I venture timidly: "So you're determined not to let me in on it?"

But the only reply I receive is a vague denial, one of those evasive negatives that put you in your place more definitively than a kick in the ass. I don't insist; it'll all come out tomorrow, or the next day, to hell with it: either we'll make peace, in which case this interval of silence won't matter, or else the silence will go on forever and I can never again rely on anything or anyone, even on Time.

Maria!

" . . . I'm sorry, Anick. But I had to pull myself together before I could talk to you, I had to be sure I wasn't going to start taking it out on you."

"Why, for God's sake? Where's there any connection between that note and me?"

A sudden dizziness: Zizi has escaped, he's been released, he's sent me a letter through someone else going out, he . . . but I'm out of my mind, the note wasn't addressed to me.

All right, then he's been transferred here, he's written to Maria, who's the only girl canteening—no, he doesn't even know Maria. God, what your imagination can dream up!

"It was the answer to our letter," Maria said.

"Huh?"

"The letter Nadine took out, the one where I asked for more saw blades. It was just that, when I first read it, I was knocked flat, I thought Nadine had fucked up, or you—I don't know, I just lost my head. We just don't have any luck, that's all . . . "

"You mean he won't . . . But I don't get you. Where does this note figure? Who sent it?"

"He did. He's been in here, in the men's prison, for a week."

(17)

If I'm driven to crime, too bad.

I find myself muttering like Fatima, and it seems that I've taken to grinding my teeth at night. Come on, Anick, stop bitching: you should follow Fatima's example, yes, but not the Fatima who ranted and raved, but the Fatima who got things done.

I'm going somewhere else, and not to Fresnes: more croakers have already grilled me, more than enough. Result: despite the stitches that crisscross my carcass, despite the fact that I look and say that I'm at the end of my rope, the experts have reached the conclusion that the best nursing home for me is the one I'm in. Imitate Fatima? Not even that. "Pack your bags," she had been told; but I'm going to discard every bit of superfluous cargo and fly away with my head for a closet. Everything is nicely stored there, hung up carefully in mothballs.

But, even before I had really begun to think about an escape, experience was doing its damnedest to convince me that a break, like anything else worth while, is planned and carried out as a solo or not at all. If I want to go ahead, I'll always find the road blocked by loose tongues and watchful eyes.

144

Suppose, Maria, that, as a result of making scale models of the thing for you, I had agreed to really take a chance with you, that curiosity had jogged my ass into action, that I had wanted to forget, to deny that every one of us is alone, absolutely alone, you with your kid, I with my man; by this time I might well be in a punishment cell, doing my ninety days and getting used to your being dead. I mean that: you would have lost your guts up there on top of the wall, you would have hesitated to jump, and I would have pushed you so as to get my chance to make the leap.

I had gone beyond remorse, made a clean break with it— *clean, break,* even the words pushed me as viciously as I would have pushed you.

I quit the game, and yet I'm caught in it; I'll get out, simply because I can no longer do anything else. I don't know the day or the hour, but I know that they're coming nearer, day by day, hour by hour.

The best I can hope for is to spend the next few days in court and be transferred because of the transistor business immediately after the ten-day stay for my appeal: they always need beds here. When I come back from another session with my lawyer and pace back and forth in the room in a frenzy because the meeting had so irritated me, I say to myself that, if that's what that lousy mouthpiece comes here for, he could just as well stay in the corridors outside the courtroom. I had been waiting for him for two weeks, I might just as well go on waiting to be tried, to do my time, to kick off. "No, really, I swear, what a goddamned gang of pricks." I spit it out between clenched teeth, pacing up and down from the sink to the closet, bumping into the backs of girls sitting on benches, kicking out viciously at every obstacle, papers or heaps of dirt —they make it impossible for me to pace properly, it's Friday and no one has swept for three days so that there'll be something worth doing when tomorrow's big house cleaning comes.

Normally, I never moved a muscle except to wield the dishcloth or to go downstairs with the others for chow or exercise; or to go talk to the lawyer . . . oh, no, don't even mention lawyers to me. Tonight I prowl, I boil. "All alike, damn it," I mutter, kicking an empty matchbox under the food shelves, "every damn one of them."

My behavior begins to get to them; they must think I've infected them with my own helplessness, because obviously, since I'm able to go right on cursing the bar and kicking all their shit under the furniture, there's nothing wrong with my throat or my feet. Aliette's the first to risk a question: "What's the matter, Anick? Something go wrong? Did your lawyer have bad news for you?"

I see what you're up to, Aliette, with your passion for fish: you're getting ready to soften me up so that I'll give you my portion. Or you want to make me so blue I won't even eat, you want me to get so mad telling you how society has fucked me that I'll refuse to swallow the slightest bit of the lousy fish provided for me by the aforesaid society. I decided to get one up on her.

"Aliette, you can have my fish tonight, and the potatoes too —everything. I'm absolutely disgusted."

"But what will you eat, then, hon? You mustn't get all worked up; when you get a little phosphorous in your system you'll feel better, wait and see, you'll give off sparks . . ."

"You're not kidding. I'll send that son-of-a-bitch of a lawyer a poison-pen letter. You're right, sister: eat, you never know who's going to eat you. Watch, I'll be the first one in line with my plate."

This sets off a minor riot round the pile of dishes and utensils: "That's my knife . . . Who the hell's seen my plate? It's got A.L. marked right on it. Who the hell took off with it?"

Clutching my coffee mug to my heart, I finally explain: "Can you imagine: he simply forgot to bring along my file! I wonder why the hell he bothers to lug a briefcase around with him: it was absolutely empty this evening, as flat as a flounder."

"But he told you your trial date anyway, didn't he?"

"He received his official notification, he told me: sometime pretty soon. But his brains are in his ass, he left the notice in the file; by this time he must be going through all the crap in his office to find it. I told him to let me know in writing, but this is Friday and I won't hear from him before next week, you know that. My counselor and his weekend!"

All of them had something to say. When everyone talks at the same time, I withdraw inside my ring of silence; I am its center, the tangents brush against me but cannot wound me —evil tangents, mocking tangents, self-regarding tangents. People I like I invited into my circle: Maria is always there, and her sweetness weaves itself into my solitude.

They're all howling now because God-knows-who is missing God-knows-what. Sometimes, in such circumstances, a girl will coil up like a spring and leap from closet to carton, from table to suitcase, turning everything in the dump upside down until someone says to her: "You lose something, baby?" Since that's all she's waiting for, she bursts out: "*They* stole my . . ." This is followed by the description of the article, the threat to cut off the culprit's hands, to search everything and everyone. . . . As a rule the next step is a second, more careful inspection, excited rediscoveries, and universal embarrassment: it's not funny to know that the thief is there, somewhere among us, but it's just as disturbing to learn that it was a phantom thief. And the victim prefers to be out of pocket rather than be sneered at and treated as some kind of suspicious nut.

With completely phony indifference, packages of cigarettes and jars of Nes are left lying unattended on the table, available to everyone; but out of the corner of her eye the real owner never loses sight of the position of her butts, her coffee, her string bags, and everyone takes inventory of her carton every morning under the pretext of having to look through it for some urgent need.

Any packs of butts I got I always paid my pound of flesh

147

for: thieves don't steal in stir. I am Someone Else, I am Damien the willing one, who conceals terrible things behind her nice smile. I work for the group much more cheerfully than for the prison and the string bag dealer: I fashion decks of cards out of Gitane packages, I do the dishes when no one else pays any attention to the bucket of water steaming in the corner—a bucket, for that matter, that I lug up from the laundry often enough: "Bring me up my bucket, darling, there isn't a clean plate in the house for lunch, and I'll go for the water."

And gentle Maria climbs the stairs with a bucket in each hand and her back erect, exactly like the popular figure of Justice, the soapy water balancing the soaped panties. While I'm knocking myself out to be useful to them, the good ladies forget about me and don't worry their little heads about what I am. I'm thinking but I'm also drying dishes.

I don't want to talk any more, I don't want to dream any more; I let the days fall from the calendar like the petals that I embroider on these ladies' little handkerchiefs, and I let their thorns prick me. Soon I'll come to the end of all this: I'll be tried, my man has done everything he could to clear me, the lawyers' final addresses will be based on sentiment: I can imagine their voices as, with much support from the sweep of their broad black sleeves through the air, they sketch the profile of a fictitious Me, a poor misguided little girl living with a crook but no different from any other: yes, granted, he goes out at night but I have no idea where he goes, I'm at home laying out his slippers and making his coffee, because you see, Your Honor and gentlemen of the jury, I lo-o-o-ve him.

I giggle, and the girls wriggle uncomfortably: that poor bitch is losing her mind, look how she's beginning to laugh all by herself now! Acquittal, or at worst a lousy six months . . .

Maria goes on trial in January; perhaps—no, why perhaps? —she will certainly be put on probation; we'll get together again and take wonderful trips together, waiting until it's time to go pick up our men at the gate, because every day that goes by makes that day closer for them too. I'll be driving, and beside me Maria will be rocking her son; the glove compartment will be full of candy for him; Italy, the marvelous little shoes they make so beautifully there, what we would have to do to pay for them . . . Oh, hell, I'm incorrigible.

It's getting closer, it's coming . . . Time doesn't matter: I'm still in my twenties, or barely thirty, I can feel my heart running smoothly on all its cylinders.

I think of the water that has washed over the wreckage of the escape ship, and I relax, closing my eyes in the sun, waiting until it's time to stand up and run barefooted to the beach.

Part Two

Part Two

(1)

"Oh, lord, I'm going into a coma!"

I won't hear that moan from Mado the gypsy any more. Today I joined a new club, and I'm the one who's in the coma.

The matron was pretty decent about it: instead of springing the order to pack on me this morning, five minutes before the car was due to arrive, she began preparing my mind and my luggage the afternoon before.

Now I felt very, very worn out; there was no special prison car, my convoying cops marched me off to the station at double time. Train to Paris, compartment reserved in advance; Paris; the paddy wagon between stations; train again; paddy wagon again . . . ugh!

But I've been brought here directly. "You want to see a magistrate? What for? He must be out to lunch now, and . . . matter of fact, I ought to be thinking about lunch too, my wife must be wondering what I'm up to. Well, Miss . . . or is it Mrs. . . . ?"

I sigh. "Whichever you like; if you recognize common-law marriage . . ."

"Get in, we have to take you to the prison. If you have to see the judge, someone will come back and get you in a while. We don't have any other orders for now."

153

In the best style of a girl in the life, I get into the vehicle casually, drape the fur that had been flattened in the property room as best I can, check my hairdo in the rear-view mirror, and we take off again.

We've arrived.

So here's the new prison, where there is nothing new in the gray shadows: the superintendent is away, the receiving officer scribbles the information on me, pushes my index finger into some thick ink and then rolls it over the registry book; he and my angels, who are relaxing in armchairs, their legs stretched out on the department's carpet, exchange a "Have a good lunch" and a "Thanks, same to you"; they hand each other the envelope containing my dough, count it and make me sign for it; finally everyone takes off, the screw throws me out of the office, and there I stand between my suitcases in the desert silence and the smell of burnt fat in the corridor. The screw goes outside and calls the matron: it is the season for love, and I have no idea whether my man is already here or whether he's still waiting for his transfer. I had hoped so much that we could make this trip together! No luck, though; even if the government could have saved money on the deal, it was willing to pay for two trips and two escorts: the main thing is that we shouldn't see each other.

Here comes the matron's blue smock. Come on, make it fast, I'm dead, and there are still miles of red tape between here and the cell.

"Where did you come from?" Where could I have come from, matron, except another prison? What I said was that it didn't make much difference where I came from and that I was up for trial in this *département*. The cell, the cell! The suitcases are pulling my arms out of their sockets as I am led into . . . Oh, no! This is hardly what I expected: I am being shoved roughly into the medical office. In my numbed state I am aware of a table. "Climb up." Built-in closets with enameled doors, a sink with a bar of soap and a towel; no, it

154

couldn't be true! . . . Certainly I'm not going to be subjected to the speculum, just like that, fresh out of another jail and without even time to wash myself . . . The lady adds to my bewilderment by ordering me to undress, and I just look at her, in shock.

"Get undressed," she repeats; "I'm going to search you. You don't seem to know the score. Weren't you searched in the other place?"

"Yes, just before I left. Why go through it again?"

"That's the rule. All right, get . . ."

She must have swallowed a phonograph record. As innocently as possible, I ask: "All the way, matron?"

"Yes, naked."

The word gives me goose flesh. This pseudo-checkroom is not heated and I'm shivering already in spite of my fur. Strip here! I think of yogis sitting in the snows of Tibet, I take a deep breath and make the plunge. Strip tease, with an expectant pause after each layer. "Stockings too, stop wasting time." Of course, look between the stocking and the foot. That stash was such an old trick I hadn't even thought of it. Finally I stand there with my feet and my clothes on the cement floor, a pitiful figure of Truth trembling and purple with cold.

"Turn around . . . All right, that's enough, hurry up and get dressed, it's not very warm in here."

I glimpse a flicker of humanity in the matron's face: she has big blue eyes; that's a good sign, blue eyes, they're easier to figure out. In this moment of grace I can read frozen things in them, hieroglyphs cut into an iceberg: there's no doubt about it, she's as cold as I am. There is a vague aura of fellow-feeling between two frozen beings, I almost feel like breaking the ice, but then I remember how completely beat I am. All I say is: "Isn't this prison heated?"

"Oh, sure. I'll just go through your things, then I'll take you in by the stove with the others."

So it's not the individual-cell prison that I hoped it would be. "By the stove"—back to 1914, as Aliette will no longer say.

"The others?" I asked. "I thought there were separate cells."

"No; but you'll be alone in spite of that, or almost alone: there's only one other woman. You go to the workroom all day; it's important to get as warm as you can during the day, because the dormitory . . ."

My luck hasn't changed: crowds and cold. But I was too bushed to get myself worked up. First of all let's see this stove: a Nes, a Gitane, and that will be plenty for today. The matron goes through my stuff like a master: the gingerbread is inspected slice by slice, linings and hems are fingered, my bun is taken down; she gives me a sixty-second massage and shampoo, then leaves me with my hair undone and goes back to my luggage. She seems to be irritated that I have so many things: until this morning I thought I had only the minimum number of necessities, not being one of those cons who love their comforts. and load themselves down with two cartons full of yummies, four heavy sweaters, and knit underwear: no, all I have is a few rags that I didn't have time to sell, a few packs of butts, some tins of Nes, and what I need for washing myself and writing. But it's still too much to suit the lady: she tries to prove to me that I don't need my Nivea cream, or a glass bottle . . .

"But that's my shampoo!"

"If you want to wash your hair, let me know in advance: I'll get the bottle for you, and you can give it back to me when you finish."

What a business! There's no point insisting; I numbly sign the property receipt, pile all my stuff together—strange, I still have my mirror, I'm surprised that I'm allowed to keep that and my glasses, because after the shampoo I had already resigned myself to seeing nothing, including myself, until I was turned loose—in my dressing gown, stuffing the pockets;

what's left on the examining table I hastily· gather up under my left arm, and we go out of the room.

The workroom is very light: a window as high as a woman's head and a door topped by a big fanlight look out on a court-yard that measures a good hundred square yards; near the window a sink is quietly dripping, and . . . ah, the stove! Only after I've spotted the stove do I notice the inmate sitting quietly over some sewing: without the faintest interest, I eye the old skirt she's sewing snaps on to, and, not knowing quite how to get started, I pull up a stool, sit down on it, and grope through my stuff for my cigarettes.

"Fine," the matron says, "I'll leave you to get settled. Dufon, show her everything." And she takes off.

The woman fiddles with her work and I with my things; this goes on for a minute, until I find the butts and venture a friendly "Do you smoke?" shaking the pack in her direction.

She comes to life at once, oh, yes, thanks, she gets up to clean out one of the wall closets for me, and, while I get started piling my things into it—one shelf for clothes, one for papers; on the floor, next to the food, my sanitary needs; a whole closet to myself, what a joy!—she gives the stove a few pokes.

I turn toward her, Nes in my hand: "What about a java?"

"Give the water time to heat."

This Nes is divine; the coma begins to recede.

Pinkie extended, let's start sampling and savoring this new slice of life; this half-life, which this time must be made com-fortable and on no account be allowed to get screwed up. Furthermore, I'm like a bird on a tree here: I don't expect to molder here more than three months.

Let my man get here, let the proceedings get going, and before they were over, if possible, I would split. My head is full of Maria and my friendship with her, of Zizi and my love for him; I won't forget anything. Just because I'm in a coma today, just because the lazy purring of the stove makes me feel sleepy, is no reason to let myself conk out. On your feet, Anick, pull yourself together.

I rinse my glass in the sink, I savor the pleasure of the water running over my wrists, and I begin to size up my companion. I ask questions sedately, I answer hers, it's like a drawing-room. Obviously she can't sling con lingo herself, and she's very reserved, very much the model prisoner, and certainly not a two-time loser . . .

I want to be sure of it. I know the essentials already: she enjoys reading, smoking, and filling herself with Nescafé; we made excuses in advance for our future silences, which would not necessarily mean that either of us was sore; we philosophized on the liking for solitude and proclaimed—in the abstract, of course, so that neither of us would seem too smug—that it is the mark of the superior being. I launched my probe:

"Yes, madame, I've just been living in a collective prison. Believe me, it's no fun, a workroom fifteen feet by thirty with a good fifteen women parked in it. You can't imagine, unless . . . I don't mean to pry, but . . . is this your first time?"

"Yes," the lady grudgingly admits.

"I didn't mean to make you angry. I asked you because I'm accustomed to it—to the extent that one can get accustomed to prison, that is." And, in a warmer tone, I go on: "What would you like me to call you? I'm Anick. The way I see it, since we have to live together . . . as a matter of fact, when is yours due?" She looks at me as if I were speaking of childbirth. "I mean your release?"

"Oh, pretty soon . . . You were saying about names?"

"Yes, I was saying that here *madame* seems a bit too formal . . . May I call you by your first name?"

"Oh, of course: it's Jane, not Jehanne; Jane with one 'n'."

"Like Anick, then. Delighted to meet you, Ja-a-ane." I hold out the Gitanes. "Go on, take one: I have more."

Jane says that she appreciates my offer all the more because at the moment she's somewhat embarrassed . . .

"No need to be embarrassed, you know."

"I'm expecting some money. Look, before you got here, I was down to this." She points to a box of cigarette stubs on the table.

Well! Jane saves stubs. When I came in, I had knocked the ashes off my cigarette into that box because I thought it was an ashtray.

"Don't you skin them first? The idea is to roll ten or twenty, real tight, and put them in an empty package, it makes you feel flusher. I know what that's like, you know: I've smoked everything down to broom straws, dead leaves, and garlic peel. But right now it's all more or less O.K., everything'll work out. Don't beat your brains out, Jane, grab one: it's dumb-asses that lose out."

Easy! I've frightened her, it seems: Jane looks down, the white band with which she's set off her hair comes into close-up, and I can no longer see her face or her eyes—they are black—or her rather thin nose, or her somewhat pinched mouth. On the other hand, emerging from her turban and furrowing her hair all the way to the forehead, there is a horseshoe-shaped scar: has the girl had a skull operation?

Sound her out on that at the first chance. I make a mental note: "Talk about our operations," and I let silence fall once again.

I sniff our cage and the invisible city all round it. I don't know the place; from the bright sunshine that splashes over the buildings at noon, I sense that I've come to the Ile-de-France. Accustomed to exile, a wandering minstrel, I feel comfortable, empty and sleepy. Suddenly I am overwhelmed by the loud-speaker above the door.

"What's that, Jane?"

After so many months with no other radio than our own voices, this music seemed vast to me, it crushes me and goes right through me.

"The radio's turned on for an hour every morning and evening," Jane explains. "See, you can turn it off if it bothers you: read the sign." Under the switch for the light, there is a double socket: one side is empty, the other has a plug in it, and a wire runs to the loud-speaker; the card is tacked up below the socket. I read it: "If the inmates prefer not to listen to the broadcasts, they can disconnect the speaker. Do not pull on the wire; be sure to grasp the plug itself."

Disconnect, pull, grasp. The instructions are followed by the penalties for those who pull on the wires. I won't pull the plug out until Sunday afternoon's ear-splitters, unless of course Jane likes them . . .

"Oh, no, I don't like sports either. But the head matron knows that; she has me cut off at the central switch in the office."

No question about it, with a little more heat the hotel would be livable.

The evening vigil begins, with fits and starts of small talk; the music fills in the gaps, finishes off the ends of sentences, and helps start over again. My coma has returned, my dreams are demanding other rights; the radio turns them back toward childhood and brings back the old fairies. Enter, all you "kings and puppets and ventriloquists," come in, you are the ones who are the hosts . . .

The loud-speaker brings us an accordion; then the quick traceries of a harp. My head is spinning like a mad top, then I feel like swimming; I see the possibility of a slow swim through splashing blue water . . . But all the same I want most of all to go to bed. Before chow, I had gotten out my writing kit in order to let the mouthpieces know where I am, but I had not been able to get beyond *Dear Counselor.*

160

The Runaway

Suddenly there is a splash of light on the blank page: the lights in the courtyard have just been turned on and they are reflected in our window. The head matron is getting ready to put us to bed.

Jane runs to the window and waves frenetically, and meanwhile I stash smokes for upstairs. Jane has made it clear to me that this is forbidden, but I can't be expected to know all the laws and customs of the place on my first night: thirty-six jails, thirty-six sets of rules.

I can see the huge red head of the matron, sawed off from her body by the horizontal bar of the window, cut down the middle by the black line of one of the vertical bars: undoubtedly she has seen me stash the butts and I'm going to be searched for the third time that day.

I put the package of Gitanes back into the closet as I hear her fumbling for the right key on the other side of the door; and I go over to the window, which Jane has just left.

The bars are shining in the light; I sense—in a flash, then I am drifting again—that these bars look funny: they seem lighter, smoother to the eye . . . tomorrow I'll have to measure the distance between them. Yes, that was it: they aren't firmly anchored, they wiggle . . .

"Well, you in there? You rooted to the floor?"

(2)

The matron's frustration that night, when she found no cigarettes in my pockets, made up for mine in not being able to smoke in the dark, which is an old habit of mine: twelve hours in the sack is a long time. But in the morning I could have asked for twelve hours more: I was sleeping like a log when they opened up.

Evening comes quickly in the winter; you're back in bed before you've really finished getting up. Since I have had a good rest, I take a chance and smuggle some coffin nails upstairs: Jane will be quite pleased to smoke and chat in the dark, I think.

During the day I picked up the routine of the new place; I learned the week's—and therefore the year's—menus by heart, I had my anthropometric measurements taken, I wrote to everyone I knew . . . As soon as my letters arrived at the office, they came back in the hands of the chief warden.

We got to know each other in a reasonably loud encounter: According to him, I was entitled to send only "two letters on Sunday, plus one on Thursday provided that I requested permission for it in writing and that I had collected no bad-conduct marks." It was no use my arguing that I was up for trial as well as a convicted defendant; he made me take back everything except those letters that dealt with my actual defense: "That'll save you the trouble of writing them over again on Sunday."

Oh, hell, I'll write to the mouthpieces, then, they're my foul-weather friends, and I'm not in this joint for the fun of it. I have none of the things I like, so I'll have to learn to like what I have. I resolve to learn to adore the stove and the flowers in the vase, to remain faithful to Zizi in fog and heatless sun, and to give my imagination plenty to do.

"*Ça ira, ça ira, ça ira, les aristocrates . . .*" I hum as I wait for the incoming mail. Jane has spent the whole day picking away at her sewing, and I saw hardly more of her than her back except when she pivoted on her stool to get into my pack of butts.

This damned woman who's blowing my dough out of her nostrils, this rationing of letter-writing—in contrast to my hopes of being able to slip something for Zizi into the pile of letters I would casually give to the matron—the dryness of my skin without its Nivea, all combine to create a certain confusion in my nut. I have just got in here, I'm in no position to make any definite plans, but one thing is certain, with all due respect to the superintendent, and that is that I don't have the slightest intention of taking root in his flower bed.

"What a break for you, Jane, to be walking soon!"

"Break? Why, I've paid the price, I think. Three months, three full months . . ."

"It's better than three empty months, isn't it? At that, it's no fun."

. . . Zizi is here! Barely a hundred yards away from me! I dance all over the workroom with the lawyer's letter, being careful not to bump into the stools. Jane knows nothing of this: in three weeks she'll be back with her own . . . No, I remember suddenly that she is going through the interminable skirmish of a divorce that is going to call for someone to do a Solomon and cut the children in half . . .

So I keep my joy to myself. I'll wait until Jane has fallen asleep tonight so that I can think in peace: I'm going to frame various requests, try to persuade the new magistrate to authorize us to write to each other; I'll go down on my knees to the mouthpiece to petition for the right to give each other news of our health and to fight for what I'm asking for; I'll . . . In the meantime, what I have to do first is to get Jane to sleep.

"Oh, tell me more, tell me more," she laughs from her pile of bedclothes, "it's like reading a mystery story!"

"I know: the story of my life is a first-class barbiturate. Why do you insist on taking that damned Optalidon of yours as well? Between my voice and my Gitane you shouldn't need anything else."

Why am I knocking myself out so for that dame? I canteen for two—or perhaps I should say for five, for Jane can down grub and guzzle beer enough for four people; I do everything possible for her except peeing and washing, I do all the dirty work and thus become, *pro tem,* the slavey around the place, because all the leisure that I create for Jane she uses to sew for the establishment, to do the laundry for the staff, etc. It keeps her busy, she says.

If I am willing to hump, it's for Jane's sake, not the administration's; I can fill my time beautifully with my own imagination, a tough crossword puzzle, or the mere contemplation of a boiling kettle. Nor am I acting out of thieves' honor: all the business of coping with the lousy tricks of prison managements, sweet talk and mean talk, breaches of prison confidence, long ago made me disgusted with playing Girl Scout in stir. Nor is it out of friendship: the way I see it, friendship, whether it's years-old or born yesterday, means letting your friends handle their own affairs, up to the point where you can see that they're losing their minds and screwing themselves; but I have never carried friendship to the point of asking for work.

164

Jane seems O.K.—I mean that she doesn't have anything bugging her; but she's a dope, just the same. So?

Quite separate from the skin-deep friendship that we share, something else impels me to spoil her a little, to take care of her, as if she were a good-luck token, a vein to mine—in short, someone important. I pretend to confide in her, telling her everything I'm supposedly thinking. Certainly the superintendent won't take the responsibility of letting my guy and me see each other in the visitors' room, not until he has a court order for it. So I do the impatience bit: "They sure aren't in any hurry, Jane. What the hell do they care? they can make love every night if they want to."

Actually, I prefer her to take a long time to reply, or even to say nothing: so as to hear myself say that I'll have to produce a "certificate of concubinage,"—what an expression!—so as to find myself empty-handed as usual, without a single document "attesting to our relation"—since that relation did very well without our ever settling down anywhere; so as to bad-mouth and work myself up a bit more. ". . . But they'll see: I've got something in mind that'll knock them off their asses . . ."

Jane can't seem to get used to my way of speaking. She doesn't ask questions; but, to get her to take her eyes off the knitting she's knocking herself out over—the matron wants the sweater done by Sunday—I have to really get her interested. "That will what?"

Jane's eyes are kind, indulgent, almost amused. She's really giving me the business, she doesn't believe me, she's not with it. I go back to my silence.

No matter what I try to cook up now, I can think of nothing. Absolutely nothing. But I have to figure out something, fast. My imagination goes into top gear. What am I doing here, why am I here, why should I be here? My position as a prisoner awaiting trial gives me the privileges of wearing my own things and writing to my lawyers, who hardly bother to answer. If I make a break . . . I study the bars: that would hardly knock them off their asses, and the risks were the same as always: a bullet in the leg, a dog's tooth in the butt, and, if I don't make it, ninety days in the hole. The risk is minimal and the profit may be immeasurable. When you go out to pull a job and the watchman is asleep, you take pains not to wake him . . .

"Jane, dear?"

"Yes?"

"How far have you gotten with that sleeve? Have you finished the decreases? Good, go pour us a Schnapps and let's drink a toast to all these slobs. Cheers, deary."

We sip our beer. Jane goes back to her knitting at once, and, to distract her from that sorry hunk of wool, I read the front section of *Paris-Match* aloud. "It's not so bad, something to read at night, the radio news at noon. And you . . . oh, you're worse than my mother. After all the work you've done for the matron on that sweater, I'm sure she'll let you have a little flour. Don't forget, I canteened eggs purposely so that you could make us *crêpes*."

I'm between the devil and the deep blue sea: I have to make Jane understand that she's being exploited and that she's not going to get anything in return; but, if it seems that I'm feeling sorry for her for being the slavey, she'll get up on her high horse and come back at me in a way that is already familiar: "she knows her own worth, if she is behaving like this it's because she wants to have a good recommendation when she gets out because that'll help her go straight," or else "the matron's a human being, she's very understanding, she's done everything she can to make it easier for Jane here . . . while Jane was alone; now, with me there, matron has to pretend to be stricter in the beginning, but, when I get to know her better," and so on.

166

The Runaway

I'll be very careful not to tell Jane that she doesn't know the score and keeps hitting false notes, and that miracles are rare among matrons; that in any case this one was certainly no miracle, and, besides, even the best of matrons was too much of a shit for me, and so forth and so on. But let's keep away from trouble, let's join Jane in her devotion to "our really nice matron." I drink the coffee that she brings to Jane, because it's better than the regulation slop and more invigorating than Nes, and because coffee leaves no odor pisswise; in memory of my mother, and because I provided the eggs, I feel no shame in whipping up the *crêpes* with her flour; but, beyond these few concessions, I never let her get chummy with me.

I pull myself together, I shrink into myself; when she comes in before the bell for bedtime rings and sits down to yack, I ignore her, I simply am not there. Jane does all the honors, while I wander from the sink to the closet, brush my hair and braid it for the night, and stash our butts and her pills.

"That one's always up in the clouds!" the matron laughs. I pull my cloud tighter, disintegrate inside it, disappear.

Nevertheless, this woman is my superior, she can give me orders, and so I make it a point to forestall her commands: when the fog begins to close in in the afternoon and she and Jane are bringing in the wash that has been hung up in the courtyard, or in the early morning, when we hang it up again "because it smells better when it dries in the fresh air," I always offer to help: "Can I give you a hand, matron?"

And so we load our arms with sheets and shirts that are still dripping, or else frozen stiff; we jump like goats to reach the wire clothesline strung six feet above the muddy ground; once everything is hung up, we have to stand guard at the window to watch for a change in the weather so that we can sound the alarm at the first drop. "Don't forget, Anick, two rings for matron. Three is a general alert."

"What about one ring?"

167

"One? Oh, I don't know."

It couldn't be true! And when Jane has been discharged, will I perhaps have to lug the wash around alone, with my bad arm? Even if they put male inmates in the laundry, I'll have to hang out the wash and listen to the matron's complaints because the men in the laundry have forgotten to scrub them.

The more I think about it, the more the runaway mare begins to prance again in my noodle. Guards' shots and watchdogs' bites fade out, the hunger for the outside fades in, becomes an obsession. I think of the rain that makes the rounded surfaces of the walls like wax at night, of the beckoning blackness below, the surge of nausea before the hands let go . . . die trying, a princely way to go . . . No, that's a crock of shit: if I do get to the top of that wall, I damn well will have taken along something to help me get down without breaking a few more bones. Then I would sniff the familiar old warm smell of cars hidden out from the cops, and the hesitation-waltz of bars and roads would begin again, the breakdowns in the sun . . .

"It hasn't started raining again, has it, Anick?"

"Don't worry your head about it, Jane, I'm watching—that's all I'm doing."

. . . As long as I can't see Zizi, what difference does it make whether I'm in stir or on the run? I dream of all the things that I'll be able to do for him—packages and money orders, naturally, but above all seeing the mouthpieces, keeping after them, giving them as much money as they want, everything to help Zi get the two sentences made concurrent and get out of there sooner. Then I can relax.

We'll soon know for ourselves whether it makes no difference to a hoodlum whether his woman is inside or outside. Oh, sure, Zizi is going to balk, "Just lie low," he'll say, we're too unimportant . . . unless I don't let him know.

I'm going to leave without permission.

The Runaway

While Jane is down talking to her lawyer, I make a test: my head can go between the bars. Just beyond my ears, but, when your ears can get through, so can the rest of you. So I was as good as at the foot of the outside walls.

All right, what then?

The first wall isn't very high: if I start from the ground floor, I can climb it; if I slide down from the second floor, I'll land on the little barrier that separates the courtyards and forms a right angle with the outside wall and is not too much lower: I can hoist myself from the one to the other.

What shall I do? Climb up or slide down? There was plenty of time to get down from the window of the dormitory: the whole night: after she makes her nine-o'clock rounds the matron doesn't come back again until morning. But this means that I have to be alone after Jane leaves, and that the bars in the dormitory window have to be as far apart as those in the workroom. If only no one new comes in! Every time the bell rings, I die . . .

"Anick! There's the bell! This time it's sure to be that fat Polish woman."

"Oh, Jane, I certainly hope so: poor dear matron would be so pleased!"

The fat Pole is an inmate who is expected to arrive for the heavy work. Even a thin one would do as well, provided she has the strength; and a Pole . . . good God, why a Pole? But dear matron finds that quite a clever idea.

After an examination of my wretched arms, she put it up to her husband to assign some of his men to the washing, and it seems that they battled one another for the privilege of working under her. Without the Polack, they'll start their new jobs next week, so that the matron's pet prisoner can take it easy for her last few days.

The rules provide for extra rations of beer and steak to workers in the laundry. Jane is going to have to give up hers, but the matron intervenes: "You two ought to be able to work something out, for once."

I take out a canteen slip. "How shall I order the steaks. Jane? How do you like yours? raw, medium, well done, rare?"

To avoid trouble—the laundry and the workroom had a communicating door, and we could try to do likewise—the matron will leave us in the dormitory on laundry days. So that we won't die of cold there, she got hold of me to help her lug a stove into the room and we set it up together, while Jane began her rest cure in the workroom. The poor matron pushed it one way and pulled it another, while I, doing my best to thwart whatever she tried to do with the old mass of iron, ran happily over my memories: little, light-weight jewelry safes that you could put under your arms, and monsters that left you moaning and gasping and sweating . . . until I finally suggested: "If I may say so, matron, why not do it this way, zigzag: first one foot, then another . . ." To make her happy, I left her alone to get rust all over her mitts when she put the pipe in place.

So now, instead of washing, we loaf. In the evening we take all our junk upstairs: knives and forks, toothbrushes, newspapers. I didn't take Jane's tape measure: I am watched constantly, and sometimes searched without warning, and I'd have had a fine time trying to prove that I had taken the tape to measure myself before and after meals, for purposes of comparison: the matron would find it difficult to believe that and would simply confiscate it: only Jane is allowed to use it, because she's always sewing things for the staff.

I've measured the distance between the workroom bars with a piece of string, which I took upstairs in my writing kit; all of it right in front of Jane, since I am surely going to have to let her in on it: she never stirs an inch away from me, except when the lawyer comes, and since he isn't coming to-

day . . . A break isn't an easy thing to explain: therefore I
explain nothing, I simply do my little job without hiding anything. Time to climb, Anick: "Lend me your chair, Jane, I
want to climb up and see what there is to see." I get up on to
the back of it and grab the window sill: the sky is straight out
of Verlaine, there is complete calm all around the prison. I
let go with one hand to get at my string, and measure . . .
good, the distance is the same, there's a standard interval between the bars.

"If you'd like a shot of oxygen, Jane," I say, "I'll get down
and you can climb up. I'm not used to it any more, it's beginning to make me dizzy."

"No, thanks, I don't want to take the chance of breaking a
leg . . ."

"That's right, not when you're almost out. By the way, have
you got a minute? There's something I've got to tell you."

Jane has a minute: she puts *Paris-Match* down, I pick it up
and look for the crossword page, I lay down on my belly on
the blanket, the puzzle under my nose and a pencil in my
hand. "If she comes in, we'll be crosswording like mad, O.K.?
Now listen to my serial story."

Scribbling on the margin of the page as I speak in a low
voice, I read aloud to Jane: I read her what is going on
inside my noodle. As I expected, she comes back with an
endless supply of exhortations to be calm, to be brave, several
times she says "oh, come, now," and mentions childishness.
But her logic can't beat mine down: my logic has held its own
against the most inconceivable absurdities, and sometimes I
have won the argument.

"But can't you see it's my duty? Give it a capital *D*, laugh
at it, I couldn't care less. I was dumb enough to let myself get
hooked, even though everything about the jobs pointed to my
being innocent, what my man testified, the most elementary
logic . . . For once elementary logic—mine—and the judge's

coincided: imagine a shrimp like me, weak and crippled, being a burglar! Anyway, Zizi always played it cool where I was involved, he . . ." I make my voice break: "He was just wonderful in court: 'She's my woman; my woman, not my assistant . . .' Look, not just because he's mine, but . . ." By now I was falling into Gina's jargon.

"But if he exonerated you, the way you say," Jane objects, "how come you're here?"

"That's just what's so unforgivable, girl: I'm not charged with breaking and entering, but I do have the goods, in both cases! You can imagine, you can't just leave stuff lying around, especially two lots of it . . . No, believe me, I must have been out of my mind. In a way, everything really is my fault: that stuff led them to Zizi; and it was no use his telling me not to beat myself over the head, that it was bound to happen, that I had nothing to do with it and that he was the one, I can't forgive myself. So now I have to get out . . ."

"Not so loud, Anick! Suppose she comes?"

Ah, Jane had called her beloved matron simply *she*! She's coming round . . .

"We're both in stir. How can you expect me to stay here putting lard on my bones when all that stuff is lying loose outside? Look, I'm not breaking out of here just to have a decent cup of coffee, and not because of any 'animal love of freedom,' like the kids that go over the wall of the Good Shepherd. It's for him, Jane, just for him. My God, the last time we saw each other in court, he frightened me. I could always make some little deals with the other girls, but him, all alone in his cell . . . having your own cell when you don't have any dough is like training to be a jockey, and he sure didn't need that. How can I really know how he is? He always sends me some crap like 'Don't worry, everything's fine,' when he can get a message to me through the lawyers, but that just means he's got a tough skin and a tender heart, and

that all that interests him is *my* health and how blue I get and
how I shouldn't let myself. Zizi takes it all on himself, see,
because he thinks that that way there won't be any rap for me.
Hell, if he were outside, I'd sing my way through my time. But
that's all out of a Grade B movie, and . . . oh, Jane, here I am
getting high on words, and you must be bored to death. I'm
sorry."

"I'm going to grind some coffee," Jane says, getting up.
"Real coffee, I mean, at least that's real, isn't it?"

Stop. Now let's talk about Jane's knitting and Jane's
rheumatism. I've made enough progress for the moment. It's
a pleasant port of call, and the night air that comes through
the window is gentle; and the matron's real coffee tastes good
in my dry throat too.

Too bad that I have to leave all this behind.

(3)

Sitting at the end of the table with a butt in my mouth, I'm brushing my hair; on the newspaper that takes the place of a tablecloth—the matron gave us just enough cloth for Jane's mending—I spread out the hairpins, and balance the mirror on the box of butts: there is no point leaving it lying out in the open as an invitation to Jane to dip into it and roll herself a cigarette; as long as there's a machine-made Gitane, she reaches for the package and helps herself. Therefore I've taken the five-day ration of forty cigarettes and divided it into five daily portions of eight each; and I watch Jane, who gets nicer and nicer as the day wears on and her four cigarettes burn away; when she's finally used all hers and some of mine, she overflows with tenderness, and I, like a good girl, prepare a stock of handmades for the dormitory.

"I'm about to ring for matron, Anick, I fear that it may rain. What do you think?" She speaks like a Latin grammar. "Look at those huge clouds."

"Fine. Do whatever you like. But the good Lord certainly wouldn't pull a lousy trick like that on us, when we've just hung out the sheets. Besides, look (I get up, putting the towel round my shoulders), how pretty those shirttails and all those old lousy rags look flapping in the wind."

"If there's a wind, that's fine, the weather may hold until evening. But if the wind falls?"

"Then the rain will too. Go on, ring, since you're so anxious to. Then we won't have that job on our hands tonight."

"I have never been able to understand why the laundry absolutely has to be brought in at night."

"You mean she's really never told you? I'm surprised. Hell, it's to prevent people escaping."

"But how?"

"Some guy would tie the sheets into a rope; to avoid being caught right away, he'd roll his prison things into a ball, leave them on the pile of laundry, and wear whatever he found outside over his pajamas. Which means, if the staff's laundry just happens to be out that night, good-by to the superintendent's white shirts! You can imagine the excitement: for the guy, it's escape aggravated by robbery, which means a double hunt for him. I don't know which would bug the superintendent more, the loss of one of his prisoners or one of his shirts. Come on, Jane, live a little, it isn't going to rain before chow. Trust your soothsayer. By the way, do you want to read the cards for me?"

The re-cut and redesigned cigarette packages are the only way we have of reading the future. But today the cards don't feel like talking: when the weather's on Jane's mind, she's like me when the dampness gets into my bones. Jane wants to ring, she's worried, and my future laid out on the table doesn't inspire her.

"One, two, three, four, five, a large sum of money," she predicts mechanically.

"Never mind, it makes you nervous. Let's talk about the laundry instead. Or let's console ourselves by making up our minds to bring it in now, it'll prevent trouble and help the prison. For the same reason they make us undress in the work-room at night."

"Oh, no, that's to prevent us from contracting our death of cold up there."

"Contracting our death or kicking the bucket—you can phrase it both ways. In any case, it isn't true. The men leave their clothes at the door too, or didn't the matron tell you that? Now, if they'd have us leave our shoes so that the matrons could shine them while we slept, that'd have class, it would raise the troops' morale. But that little mockery of a search every night; just when we're all nice and toasty we have to show our asses! That really makes you cold, I can't sleep, my ass is so frozen . . . You laugh at it, because your rheumatism entitles you to Optalidon, you even fall asleep sometimes in the middle of a sentence . . ."

"Me? I don't sleep the whole night!" That Jane is divine.

The rain stayed in the sky and Jane didn't dare ring. In the meantime I had stayed at the window, broadcasting weather predictions at regular intervals, until Jane got mad and cried: "Stop it, Anick, for pity's sake! You're ruining my day, you're killing me . . ."

When the matron came to fetch us to lug the stuff up, I leaped to it: my spying had led me to notice some new details, and it was essential that I examine the outside of the dormitory from the lower courtyard. This is an exercise yard similar to ours but converted by the superintendent into a combination chicken house and rabbit hutch. It lies directly beneath the dormitory windows, and, if I miss my jump, I'll land in chicken shit: it would be better to succeed. This court is also used for hanging out the wash; so now is the time to get into it, full of good will. "Onward . . .

". . . and downward," Jane and the Matron finish in a duet. All of us go into the chicken yard.

I mutter that "we'll still be eating chicken when those bastards are eating shit"; I feel mean and frozen stiff. My fingers grow numb as I keep jumping up to reach the clothespins.

"You have to eat more, you poor thing," the matron said, laughing and warm in her heavy cape on the threshold of the chicken house.

"The Polack will help me," I answer, making a mental photograph of the building from behind my damp parapet of sheets. Crazy! there's a rain gutter about a foot from our window.

I would stuff the Polack with beer and starchy food, and while she was snoring away I'd skip the joint without even having to damage the sheets by making them into a rope. All I'll need to take with me is a heavy sweater and my family photographs: the rest I'll have the said family recover. I have three years to make a claim. I won't steal the Superintendent's shirts, I won't break one pane of his windows, but I'll see to it that in return he sends back my few lousy odds and ends.

All that will still be in my way is the main wall. I studied the top of it carefully the other day, from my perch on the chair back: that wall will be a ball! There's not even one piece of broken glass on it; it's flat and broad (that lousy wall is really thick); sired by the dew out of the stone, soft little patches of moss and lichen grow here and there to add a poetic touch to my break.

As the logical prelude to days hanging out laundry, there is usually a steaming pot waiting for us on the workroom table: the matron never forgets to bring us coffee when there are still prison clothes to be hung outdoors. That was not possible yesterday; since the men had not wrung them out, we couldn't hang them that day. The bastards would have to come back to finish the job, the whole place had shaken under the vibrations of their warden's angry voice, and this morning the clothes were dripping their last drops from the trestles in the laundry.

But there is no sign of a pot on the table and the boss-woman seems to be foaming at the mouth. It couldn't have come at a worse time, because there's not a particle of Nes left in the cupboard.

"Come hang out the laundry," the matron says. But, as I move to obey, she shuts the door in my face and there I stand with my hands pressing against it. I hear her whispering to Jane: "The two of us can do it faster." If she thinks she's going to make me mad by forbidding me to freeze . . .

Since we're out of coffee, I go to get some cocoa started. All the same, I'm annoyed; I go to work on yesterday's ashes, trying to get the stove going without making it either smoke or spit; normally, Jane is the vestal, and, because I'm out of practice, I get dirt all over my bathrobe. That does it; I'll throw the whole bucket of slops in their faces and teach them to go feel each other up over coffee in the laundry. No coffee for Jane? like hell!

When they come back inside, glowing and blowing on their fingers, I have my back turned and my ass riveted to the stool; I'm absorbed in my mug, stirring it hard on top to let the mixture get a little air and blend properly.

Jane comes up and stretches out her hands above the stove. "Well, that's that, it's done; everything hung up."

I don't say a word.

"Brr! I'm frozen. Say, that smells good, what have you got there?"

Too bad; I choose Jane. "It's our brunch, dear. I made some chocolate, just for a change. Give me your glass, it's going to boil over." The matron almost boils over too, and leaves. I wink at Jane. "She knows when she's not wanted. Tell me whether there's enough sugar in it."

Good lord, I'm winning Jane back through her belly! Jane's belly? Wait a moment: when I arrived, was the understanding between Jane and the matron founded on anything other than mutual self-interest? A matron and an inmate friends? come off it! All I have to do is watch the disgust with which the matron throws my canteen stuff on the table every morning: it gets her goat that we share food.

She really has no choice but to go on spoiling Jane, who continues doing the same work for her and treating her with the same warm deference as she did before I got here; Jane is equally obliged to turn over her goodies to our kitty, because we've made an agreement to that effect and have my heart and my money on my sleeve; and the matron is pissed off to see that I'm profiting by her benefactions without having to thank her for them or to do anything for her in return, since I get them from Jane.

Jane herself must be well aware that she's making each of us grind our teeth in turn, whether by being nice to me in front of the matron or by kidding around with her while I pretend to be somewhere else. But, far from losing anything by this, she comes out of it on top: for different reasons, both the matron and I have to remain on good terms with her. And, while we compete and, like good competitors, hate each other, Jane goes right on taking from both sides.

This seeming robot has a perfectly sound brain; her rheumatism has done no harm to her trepanned skull; I am more and more certain that Jane is a goddess, or rather a woman, which is what I require.

While all this was going through my head, I drank like a pig, my chin is smeared with chocolate, and the rings in my glass mark the successive stages of my thoughtful lunch. I go and wash both at the sink.

"Jane, if we happened to run into each other outside, would you have a drink with me or would you cross the street?"

"I'd say: 'Waiter, the same thing, please.'"

"Great, we'd get stoned! No, that's right, you don't 'get stoned': you 'have a drink,' a tall one, a Ricard, right? All right, make it two . . ."

"In the meantime, you and I are going to make leek juice.

179

That's why matron took me out alone this morning: we picked them in her garden. She didn't say anything to me, but . . . I've put them in the laundry, I'll go in and clean them right away. They'll wash out our kidneys."

"Fine, I'll drag up an extra chamber pot tonight. Waiter, one leek juice! Can you picture the look on the jerk's face?"

I wanted to probe kidneys and hearts, and here I was invited to a pee-party.

"The leek juice of friendship . . . I'll write to you, you know, when I'm out; you'll give me your address, won't you? I enjoy writing so much! it's what I miss most here. I'll get right to the Waterman and the paper."

In the afternoon, for no visible reason, Jane begins to tell me little anecdotes; by chow time my head is reeling with them: her deals during the war, under the counter and under the noses of some frightening guys; and "my dear Anick, you're too young to remember that, but in those days a deal for a pack of cigarettes with the wrong person could cost your neck," and so on.

If this is Jane's way of taking me into her confidence, she's being heavy-handed about it. A red light flashes somewhere, but I have hardly any choice and I continue to probe anyway.

A bottle cast into the sea: "Jane," I'll say tonight, "please smuggle out a business letter for me. Suppose I said I'd pay what it will cost you for your defense and your divorce, and send you a truck loaded with Ricard. And, if you say no, no hard feelings, love and kisses forever, I'll work things out alone. Just the same, it would be more comfortable to think wheels would be waiting for me on the other side of the wall, friendly wheels; oh, not yours (Jane's wheels had been confiscated), I have no doubts of your skill, with wheels or anything else, but I certainly wouldn't want to get you mixed up in this mess. When the law starts trailing you . . ."

That's the catch: they will certainly see a tie-up between

my escape and Jane's release; and the super-catch is that Jane will see it too. If she refuses for this reason, I would have to accept her no with good grace, after all the crap I had spouted about fuzz and how I hated to see them at my door, or at any-one else's door because of me. I still had one chance:

"Violation of censorship is no crime, what do you expect them to do to you? My letter would be written in code and sealed, no one could make any sense out of it and no one would accuse you of complicity. There's the question of the address, of course . . . Hell, you'll engrave that in your memory and never tell it to anyone, I'm sure of that . . . "

Ugh, the whole thing is farfetched. If only I could locate that red light! The boats I built for Maria had more substance than this plan; the date's getting closer, the rough plans are accumulating, and yet nothing is happening, nothing's really cooking. This runaway mare was born tired, she keeps missing her footing and slipping. Am I perhaps going nuts after all?

What is this new demon that enrages me and numbs me at the same time, that slyly gnaws away my heart, that refuses all contact with my own inner Furies? I grit my teeth, I never relax my defenses, and yet I am constantly tempted to give in and let myself drift in passive trust . . .

This prison is no good for me. I much preferred the other one, where every day was stolen from death. This one is not such a bad deal, it has no more than the normal amount of stupidity and dirty dealing; the contents, animate and other-wise, are the same as those of any other. But I'm afraid.

Afraid of this cleanliness, this silence that masks outcries, the bright stones that sweat a kind of anguish, constant vague threat; the banality of the days batters at me, penetrates me, blocks my pores; neither dangerous nor of any consequence, the routine rocks me and lulls me . . .

The demon remains anonymous and motionless; he's biding his time.

My old cunning, remembering how often I had sent it an SOS, hums to reassure me. No, nanny, I just won't be good! I want to turn and toss with pre-dawn worries even if the flaying about twists me all out of shape. "Let go, let it pass, let it be . . ."

And so the demon and the cunning relieve each other in their vigil over me, until the thousand prickling tingles give up their endless chase along my skin, until I resign myself and fall asleep, my heart torn in two, my carcass submissive.

. . . Jane said she would smuggle out the letter. I am to write it a day or two before she leaves: it might just as well stay in my head, where it is, until the last minute, nothing will happen to it there, no search will turn it up, it will have had the benefit of a hundred redrafts and revisions.

We whisper, we go over the same ground again and again: Jane will ask permission in a couple of days to get her winter coat out of the property room in order to shorten it; before she refastens the lining, she'll sew the letter into the thick shoulder padding. I now think that, after all, if there comes a time for splitting, my friends can really make an effort and scale the wall themselves in order to haul me up; there was something of the sort in the original project that hasty thinking and my sudden transfer had not given me time to develop. They owe me a little help . . .

Oh, now that I have Jane's yes, I can easily enough imagine their no; I know that things are forgotten very quickly: dough given or lent, favors done, secrets kept; everyone has his own little sewer, which sometimes bubbles unexpectedly . . .

But the first thing is to get the letter off.

I'll ask; but, if they don't want to help me, fuck 'em all, I'll find another way.

(4)

The letter is there on the table, right in front of my nose. It is a three-color job: the text is written in blue hieroglyphics, with touches of green and red on the key words: green for *I hope,* green for the date that I have chosen after consulting the calendar for the phases of the moon; green again for the code phrase that, in a harmless letter from a country cousin, will mean O.K.; red for a refusal, if indeed they can find any way of refusing other than simply not answering.

I prayed to God for a heavy fog, or else strong winds, but please, dear God, don't make it rain, even if you think that it will throw those giant dogs off the trail. I don't want to slip, I'm afraid of that pretty moss soaked with water and mud.

Suppose the dogs do get the scent? No poisoned meat: they don't care for that. I'll simply stay out of their reach: no rump steak for them, either. It's simple enough: one guy climbs to the top of the wall, the big one outside: he flicks a flashlight against the dormitory windows, I answer with a match, and I wait for him to throw me a rope. It's the old gimmick: he tosses a light ball attached to a strong and weightless nylon rope, which in turn is attached to a thicker one, which is fastened to another, which . . . I'm already out of breath at the thought of hauling up all that cable of constantly increased caliber . . .

I put my pal's biceps to work: "If you come alone and have no one to help you with the ladder, you can always pull it up onto the wall and let it lie there flat while you pay out the rope to me: there may be patrols around the jail, and there's no point making the guys trip over the stuff. The rope will get me up on the first wall: from there I will be separated from you only by the six-foot-wide guard-path between the two walls . . . It's up to you: take your pick, with all that strength of yours you won't have any trouble: which do you want to do, reach the plank over to me (the ladder would do just as well), or throw me a rope and haul me over and up? I may bash against the wall when I jump but what of it? I won't lose my grip. Either way I'll be out of reach of those dogs." I can hear their jaws snapping on nothing, a couple of inches away from my toes. I'm going to open a jail-break academy, I thought as I bent over the letter again.

There was even a good four-color sketch: the people in the building across the street turn on their lights about six o'clock every morning, and the reflection of them comes in on the left of the dormitory ceiling; I had drawn all that, as well as the outside wall of the dormitory, from the perspective of the end of the street, showing both sides of the street; in order to make the thing look more like a picture postcard than a diagram, I had even drawn leaves and fruits on the trees—which are really nothing but dry old skeletons—brightened the neighbors' gloomy roofs with sunshine, and in general portrayed a day in summer for a break at night in winter. It would be understood and enjoyed.

Jane has left; unfortunately, for her shoulder was a soft one. But my letter is no longer in her lining: it's there on the desk in front of the warden, and the head matron is there too. The superintendent, who talks on and on . . . I gather, without

listening, that my punishment will be light, more or less
nominal: a month in the hole.

"You damned little fool," the superintendent is now saying,
"you could have put my wife on the spot with that nonsense!
Or suppose I had let your pal go out with your letter and then
notified the court. What would you say then?"

I have nothing to say.

"Your friend doubtless knew the address, didn't she?" (Oh,
Jane, why did you let me down?) "And I suppose it isn't worth
the trouble of asking you for it, right? It's like all this scribbling: what is it supposed to mean? Come on, talk, be honest
for a change! You're bright enough to see it isn't going to do
you any good to go on lying . . ."

"I'm not lying, sir: aside from the sunshine on the roofs, it's
all legit."

"What? Speak up so we can hear you. All right, you little
fool, let's hear it."

The drawing swims before my eyes, its four colors run
together . . . it can't be, he wouldn't send the letter and the
drawing to the court! I must do something, I . . . I try to make
my feet respond, yes, I'm off and away, in a flash I'll spring . . .

"So you wanted to grab your letter back, huh? Tear it up,
swallow it, huh? No use."

Obviously he has already prepared against this. Is he
perhaps about to tell me that he's had the letter photo-copied
and decoded?

"I guess it really isn't any use, sir."

"That's right. Wait a minute: take a good look at this trash
of yours. Watch what I'm going to do with it."

Instead I close my eyes; when I open them again, everything of mine has vanished and all that I can see on the desk
is the worn blotting pad, the inevitable blotting pad criss-
crossed with a thousand mirror writings. The superintendent

finishes rolling my trash into a tiny ball and flings it into the waste basket.

"All right, out, and try to behave yourself in the hole. Otherwise I'll leave you there two months instead of one." He turns to his darling wife, who is already hurrying toward the door: "Give her a blanket for the daytime and see to it that she doesn't catch cold: she's the kind that'd do it on purpose. All right, Damien, you can go. Where did all this get you?"

Alone in the workroom with the matron, I wait for her to take me to be fitted for the regulation uniform, tell me exactly how many days I will have to serve "on bread and water," and order me to cart off my mattress and bedclothes to the hole. "You'll have to return them every morning and you'll get them back every night," she'll tell me. "You may have toilet articles once a day; and if you want to write to your lawyer or to the authorities . . ." I know it all by heart.

But what's going on? Matron says nothing of the sort: she pulls up a stool and sits down on it, close to me. I remain standing, looking down at her; her head is lower than mine and I can smell the brilliantine in her hair. She opens her big blue eyes and says: "Poke up your fire a bit, it's almost out. Aren't you going to make your usual drink?"

I stammer something to the effect that, if she'll permit me, I'll have one more before going into hibernation; then, growing bolder, I add: "And, if you'll also let me have one more cigarette . . ."

"Look, Damien: I'm not putting you in the hole. I'll assume the responsibility for that. You did something very serious, I'll admit: if I hadn't found that letter, we would have had to answer a lot of questions about lack of supervision . . ."

"But no one would ever have known!"

"On the contrary: Dufon might have boasted about it, or you might have. The regional director . . ."

"What's the difference, as long as you did find the letter? Even if you didn't find it on your own, you got it."

"But I did find it myself, woman! When I was going over Dufon's coat, I pricked my finger on the pin that held the paper. Your roommate behaved too well while she was here for me to spoil things for her: you saw for yourself this morning that I acted as if nothing had happened . . ."

Pin? Jane had sewed up the padding and the lining right in front of me. I was absolutely certain that there had been no sign of a pin or a basting. So the matron, who didn't know how to make two stitches consecutively, must have taken the trouble to do a little sewing herself during her nocturnal examination so that her little Jane would not go out of the joint with anything on either her lining or her conscience. Pretty nice, huh?

"You'll do your punishment here, in the workroom. I'm not going to put anybody in the hole in weather like this, it would make me heartsick. What do you think I am?"

Oh, shut up, and let the facts answer that. A little flower of a matron? a little flower without poison? I don't believe it.

I knew the routine of frozen feet, of pissing on the hands to ease the chilblains, of broth-bread-coffee-and-that's-all three times a week; I wasn't afraid of it and I wasn't asking for favors. Why should the matron seek to console herself with me the minute Jane has gone? No: her spouse is certainly on to what she's doing, in spite of the little hint of a threat just now: she's not about to spend a whole month listening for the bell in this wing so that she can haul me to the cell lickety-split every time the warden or a big wheel comes and then get me out again afterward. Anyway, her husband has the keys to the women's side.

They take me for a real d-u-m-m-y.

They're afraid that if they send the letter to the court, some judge may manage to decipher it or make me reveal what it says; they do their jobs conscientiously—I had the proof of that—but they're haunted by the fear of not doing them efficiently, and anyway who can ever predict the lengths to

187

which prisoners' nasty minds will go? Suppose I say that this is a nice prison with *crêpes* once a week, washed down with oceans of real coffee? all right: abuses of this kind are over-looked in many jails. But suppose I began making things up? suppose I exaggerated the *crêpe* into deficiencies in their work? Screws would much rather take a chance on our future revenge than on being BLAMED. "It may take ten years, but you'll pay for this!" we howl when they do us dirt. But the screw laughs as he locks the door: right now he's the one that has the keys, and in ten years . . . Why should the prick bother to answer? he knows very well that once we're out, we'll have better things to do than think about him.

Therefore this superintendent is no more afraid of revenge from me than from my would-be correspondents. If he gives me a break, it's just that and nothing more, because it's ice-cold in the hole. And, as he said a few minutes earlier, I might just be mean enough to croak on him in there, and he doesn't want to be burdened with my corpse.

They likewise wanted to absolve the good Dufon: "No, I had no confederates, I was acting entirely alone," good lord, the matron must have mistaken me for the prosecuting at-torney. She knows that, if she laughs and says: "You see what your friend Jane is? she couldn't wait to turn you in," sooner or later my pals would just snap Jane up off the street and turn her over to a gang of big shots to teach her how to die. Even if the matron is so blinded by inordinate professional pride as to convince herself that her intelligence alone has trapped me, she still recognizes that sending the letter to the court would only bring on a complete investigation and open a whole new file, and, if the facts warranted it, my accomplice, Jane, might find herself back here: matron doesn't want any bloodshed on the premises, not to mention the chance that, when Jane is released again, etc.

In short, it's much easier to be nice.

Be nice, show that you're human: but either you're human or you're not, and being human has nothing to do with a job that very often they have not even chosen: being a screw is passed down from father to son, and the wives go along with the husbands' profession. It's hard for me to analyze: guards' faces, hospital nurses' faces, faces in the life, how could any of them be separated into a part that was human, a part that was lousy, a part that was sentimental? I was in stir: the rap was disgusting, the concept is execrable; and there is no one I can either excuse or accuse . . .

Everyone in stir, no matter which side of the bars he's on or what his reasons are for being there, always seems to be making excuses for the fact: the screws by doing us little favors, we by accepting them with thanks. (If I knock you off, it's because of your uniform; so long, screw, you weren't a bad guy.)

I raise my head, my cheeks burning from having poked up the stove; the matron is free to interpret that flush as a sign of shame or excited gratitude; let's get on with it!

"Thank you, matron, and thank your husband for me. I'll try not to misbehave, I give you my word."

A con's word against a screw's honor.

Yes, indeed, my runaway mare is fatally wounded; but she'll recover, tomorrow or next year, she'll come back to life in one way or another because I can't be done out of an idea in my head as I've been done out of a letter. But this is going to delay things somewhat.

"You see we aren't savages," the matron says. "But . . . tell me, Damien, whatever were you getting at in that letter? And why did you draw a picture of the prison?"

"Well . . . I wanted to give my friend some idea what kind of place I was in. He would have liked that . . ."

"Oh, now, come on, you don't expect me to believe that!"

". . . and besides I wanted to get him to take care of me:

189

he's rich, he likes me, it's just that he doesn't know . . . never mind, really it's O.K. this way. You're right, it might have stirred up a fuss."

"But what about . . . your other friend on the other side of the prison? does he know?"

"Maybe he does, maybe he doesn't, I don't know. Anyway, it doesn't matter: it's such an old business."

Apparently it's a little too much for even a prison matron to swallow; but, since I'm always going to give her the same crumb whenever she asks, she might just as well get used to it.

I spend the whole afternoon brooding over this strange mix-up; and I go on worrying in the dormitory with the sheets pulled up to my nose and my eyes wide open in the dark. It's pretty nice to still be in that bed, no matter what: in the hole the sheets scratch and make sores, your face loses all its color and gets scaly, you forget your own face . . . It's really a nice break. Every screw must be tempted, at one time or another, to give us a break; but he has to be neither too tough nor too easy; he has to be a walking book of rules to whom no one has ever said: "Hate (or love) crime" but rather: "Guard that man" and: "Beware of him." Every kind of caution, how-ever, tends to be relaxed in the long run; to live with something is in a way to accept it; even I, when I happen to run across those long lines of gentle puppets moving about in prison denims in the corridor leading to the lawyers . . . hm! The screw who keeps them moving, who is sometimes hard, some-times relaxed, must think somewhere inside himself that these guys are more to be pi. . . what, do we have to feel sorry for them? More to be blamed than to be feared.

"Up your goddamn ass! I'll cut off your fuckin' ear and eat it so they can't sew it back on, you keyhole-spying bastard!" Through ill luck or ill will, a loony has been shoved into his squad.

The nightly report: "Everything all right in the men's quarters?" "Oh, yes, chief, quiet enough, all in all."

The ultimate is the "model prisoner."

The screw has an extremely dangerous job: double doors, spy-holes, passkeys, and, if necessary, straitjackets are visible weapons; while the prisoner is sly. The screw has a public-welfare job, which, if it does not bring him big pay, at least gives him a certain importance, which is also gratifying. A kind of aura travels with him wherever he goes: "That's So-and-So—you know, the Prison Guard."

The heartless watchdog is a myth, a popular print: the severity, the harsh voice, the arrogant strut . . . That is all appearances; actually the screw is not a bad guy. Except that he has been taught that the basic equation of his profession is: being nice = getting into jams.

Oh, those jams! He is just getting ready to take a little break, half-duty, half-rest, in the warmth of the office; and a "jam" comes up and stirs things up; he risks losing the good opinion of his superiors and the food on his children's table if he doesn't immediately restore order. His children . . . who, with breakfast still on their faces, kissed him in the morning, "Daddy"; the captive kid brought here in the last paddy wagon . . . no, there's no comparison, my kids are kids, not thugs.

Daddy has to work with bad men.

The screw wears stripes and gives orders: "So-and-So, straighten the place up fast, get a rag and a broom, an inspector is coming."

He wants to get promoted and therefore he obeys: a sardine lying between two layers of his brain like an unheard-of sandwich. He watches the big shots go by, he opens doors for them deferentially; out of the corner of his eye he inspects the copper pots and pans and scouts for cobwebs, while the inspector wanders through the entire prison, bored and eager to get it over with.

In short, the screw too is all alone.

That is why he associates with us. Even when we're resting, our fingers merely dreaming, he has to look at us. Yes, the toughest part is at night. We toss in our beds, our mummy-like bodies mutter and snore; and the solitary keeper waits for us to return to him.

In the guardroom his colleague has finally corked off, having nothing more to gossip about; the screw on duty looks over the day's accounts, does sums in the account book, everything in proper order right up to the end of the month; and then he puts his head in his hands . . .

"Now you can send the fat Polish woman, God, you can show pity or not, whichever you like . . ."

"Oh God, send me good prisoners."

Not one of those crummy little hoods that have to be cleaned up and calmed down with the shower treatment, no, not that! A good one: not crafty, not a troublemaker, one that can be depended on . . .

. . . whose nice underwear it is a joy to search through in the suitcase marked "Clean Linen" that a girl friend brings him every week; one who canteens a lot and writes little; who will be respectful, willing and compassionate toward us. Who will take us into rich and horrible worlds, or who will simply talk to us.

But it is not just in the nice clothes but "in everything" that the screw has his hands; he yawns as he counts the strokes of the bells.

The blessed knell of retirement drowning in the toasts of a testimonial dinner: an apotheosis.

O God, do not blame him.

(5)

"Having the laundry done this way by the men isn't as practical, any way you look at it," the matron says, plopping down on a stool. "This way I still haven't had time to go make my beds. Well, I'll go now, Damien, I have to get to my cooking."

"All right, matron, I'm going to do some stewing too: three onions will be better than boiled potatoes. Have a good lunch!"

Once more I am alone in my workroom-kingdom. I turn a stool upside down so that I can sit on a level with the stove, which is broad and low. There's a hole in the frying pan, which I've tried to plug with a thumbtack, but it goes on leaking grease just the same. Watch out for spatters; I have no more jumpers, and to do wash today . . . Enough talk of laundry, I've heard nothing else since the day began. The men are scrubbing away, as planned; I can't be responsible for the housekeeping, the mending, the care of my own carcass and my clothes, and the laundry in the bargain. Anyway, I'm in the hole.

Dufon gives no sign of reappearing, the fat Pole has not materialized, and the matron is quite annoyed: "Oh, Damien, I hope we get some good ones soon, not more loafers . . ."

The poor thing! On laundry days she has to stay here to

make sure that the men scrub, that her own prisoner is not writing—this time for them—any love notes or letters to while away the time . . . I could get along without those men in the laundry; but, if more women arrive and they're not "good" . . . the regulations have made no provision for maternity arising out of the two wings and the matron has prepared me for restrictions to come: "There are some, you know, that you just can't be so good-natured with."

The crossbar of the stool cuts pleasurably into my mid-thighs, and my shins are being comfortably grilled. I stir my slices of onion and think about the matron problem, not that this matron is any different from all the others who have kept watch on me but because this class of humanity is worth a certain amount of comment.

She wants more inmates because that's all to the good for her: once she's got past the nuisance of searching them on arrival, ten make no more work for her than one, and ten can do a lot more for her . . . Matron has a good heart: it hurts her to see us sitting idle and downcast, she brightens our lives by "occupying" us. A knitter means pullovers for the whole family; an embroiderer means so many more doilies. Oh, matron, what lovely linen you have.

What is all the more commendable is the fact that, when women play her the dirty trick of being released before they've completed their work, the matron tirelessly passes it on to their successors. The difference between the inmate's wages and the retail price is still enough to compensate her for these unfortunate occurrences.

And, in a way, I am shanghaied too: I don't make pullovers or doilies, I keep my talents carefully concealed, I work . . . for the wages I get, I'm the good conscientious girl, a little slow, "mustn't hurry that Damien." But I do have to talk to her, smile at her . . . How can we converse, and about what? Her mind, which is connected to other circuits than mine, concentrates on actions, on people's behavior, she needs signals: she's observant, but she doesn't look, she spies. Her eyes seem always to be digging in behind things, her ears seem to hear something under every word. It's a deadly bore to me to talk to her, but, if she thinks that I'm cutting her short, I'll have to put up with angry looks and barking words: might just as well smile, let my imagination work in peace and pretend to breathe in every word of hers. I don't need sweet talk or a calendar to help me do my time; but, since the seizure of my letter, I've accepted the fact that a few weeks will have to be lost in a step-by-step reconquest of the staff's confidence: I've lost these weeks as a sort of payment, because it seems that I owe something. Basically, the matron is much more bored than I, and it's an act of charity to let her amuse herself yakking with me.

We gab when she gets me up in the morning, again at lunch at eleven o'clock, again after the so-called walk at two o'clock, again at supper at six, again at bedtime . . . The worst times are the eleven and six o'clock ones: when she pulls out a stool from under the table and sits down, I know my meal is loused up. I have never been able to get much down in front of someone who doesn't eat a thing, and even less when I am being devoured by a pair of eyes. Matron's big blue eyes drill into my forehead, bowed over my plate. "Eat, eat," she used to say to me at the beginning. And then I would make such obvious efforts to chew and to move my spoon that in the end she understood: now she goes off to check up on her locks, or count the linen in the infirmary again, and thus leaves me ten good minutes in which to shovel it in in peace. On days when there is something special, she has the good taste to leave the wing altogether: "My husband asked me to come by the office, I'll do it while you're eating."

Hurrah! I get into my bathrobe, now I can eat like a pig. Outside, caution, if not good manners, compels a certain restraint: you cannot eat like an animal in any restaurant you please: the owner may be a stoolie and you're on the lam, you don't want to be spotted, etc. But why bother in stir? Those who don't like it can leave . . . I sink my teeth into the local version of beef stew, or I use the heel of the bread to construct tremendous sandwiches soaked in gravy or fish sauce, with mustard and plenty of fat running down my wrists.

"I'd like to keep you company while you eat," the matron says sometimes, by way of a change, "but the way you crunch that toast sets my teeth on edge . . ." She is always inventing dozens of ways to get herself sent away while seeming to leave of her own free will.

She also embarrasses me with little gifts. "Here," she'll say, unwrapping a piece of cake, "eat this quick, it's still hot, I just took it out of the pan." Or she'll bring me a pot of coffee: "This is really good, it's the best brand."

Or else she'll excavate a piece of candy from her pocket, the superintendent gave it to her, she took it to give to me, because when it comes to a sweet tooth . . . They're still in the candy stage: I find these two really touching. I know the whole story: the wedding, the childbirths, the disappointments of approaching middle age, their lives, the lives of their former charges, the price of groceries, the little cherubs' achievements in school . . . And I listen to her in rapture, I tell her that she has every right to be proud, that she was beautiful when she came back from *the* hairdresser, that she looks terribly chic when a new collar peeks out of her blue smock . . .

Naturally, she continues to search me every evening when it's time to go up to the dormitory, she never forgets to make sure that the canteen knife and the spoon are in plain sight on the table, and I often have to straighten up my closet, turned upside down by a nocturnal raid—talk about the joys of the morning. But the book of rules is part of matron, she puts it on with her blouse and doesn't take it off again until night; and, even more than her big eyes, it's her smock that exasperates me. Aside from my guy, I have no passion for anything, but . . . if some mad wind should blow through my noodle and I should make up my mind (and manage) to escape by means of a spoon, or commit suicide with a knife . . . Matron searches, searches as she has been taught to do, always accompanying the operation with all her own special sense of humor:

"Well! here I am, harping on the same subject," she announces each evening, her fingers reaching out for my clothes. They slide down my flanks until they get to the pockets of my dressing gown, into which they plunge for a nice little dip for a few seconds; and I, like a docile automaton, holding in my upraised hands my handkerchief and an apple to gnaw on under the blanket, smile thinly: "Make a good search, matron: don't miss the saw blades and the extra batteries for the flashlight."

In spite of herself she can't help frowning, but I am sure of my code and I could have recited the whole of the wasted letter to her without her seeing in it anything but an attempt at a joke. I've buttered her up so well that she even allows me to take cigarettes upstairs for the night, on condition that in the morning I sweep away all trace of the orgy "in case there should be an inspection."

Dear God, let no one come! Let the inspectors and the cops apply for unemployment insurance and let me remain solitary in my little realm of silence. Silence is an easier habit to acquire than is the prison of which it is born: I like the night, when the ear is no longer alert for bells or keys, and the cold makes the birds in the rain gutter nestle together. There's the radio, but now that Dufon is no longer here to ask for it in her nice way, they often forget to connect it for me, and only the echo of the loud-speaker in the men's quarters comes through the wall, a faint background of noise.

"But you must tell me when you want it, Damien," matron cries.

Tell her? But . . . I thought I was in the hole. Even so, don't count on me. I'll never make a request. I'll never stool-pigeon. If your good women do come, I won't be your intelligence staff. The most that I might bring to your attention, in an extreme case, would be the presence of a rat in the laundry, because in any event you'll put out your lousy traps and the poisoned flour that I sweep up after you've gone, because I am fond of rats.

The other day there was the tiniest baby rat caught in the trap, and it looked so piteous with its crushed neck and its bloody fur that it bugged me the whole day. I had had the grim task of removing the little corpse and burning it in the stove. Thoughtfully and remorsefully, I poke at the little bones among the ashes . . . But that reminds me that a monster of a rat had run between my shoes as I was coming out of the shower this morning, and I am going to have to turn informer again.

In short, I'm going nuts, absolutely. A kind of tepid dopiness is taking hold of my mind, I'm barely simmering and I feel myself getting soft, like some dull dish cooking on the stove that refuses to get done; that matron is doing me no good at all . . . She's offered me the same bait as the rest, coffee, candy, and smiles; and perhaps, in return for these things, which I value more or less, I've behaved like the rest, I've sold my soul, I've listened, I've opened up . . . I wonder whether the matron appreciates it. She likes talking to me, simply because she likes to talk, because gab and gossip are the only pleasures of a job that bores her; she hangs out with me not because she likes me but out of a kind of possessiveness: I've been put into her care, I belong to her, body and property. Since she doesn't want any trouble, she won't force me, she tries to con me by being friendly: and I, slob that I am, instead of giving her the air, let her get away with it.

She's told me often enough that when you came right down to it she was in the same boat with me, that she was always in prison, she couldn't even go out at night, that she knew better things before she married a prison guard . . . A guard whom she adores and who's given her the loveliest children, who . . . well, what does she want, then?

Gab and gossip.

I'm willing enough to offer her distraction, but at the same time there has to be some fun in it for me. To get it, I give her the philosophical bit, I talk to her about chance and the diversity of things, I quote various authors with the invariable prelude, "Of course, ma-a-a-tron, you probably know . . ."; when she arrives right in the middle of a broadcast of classical music—the screw downstairs has forgotten to change the station, the male inmates are bawling: "What is it, mass today?" and I'm saying nothing—I play deaf, I don't hear her key, I don't see her come in. She says: "Good evening, Damien," twice, and I open eyes heavy with mists of inspiration: "Oh, excuse me, matron! Good evening. I was just listening: it's beautiful, isn't it?"

For the sake of appearances, matron rolls eyes charged with sorrow—great music is always sad—oh, take off that funereal face, ma'am, I'll turn it down, here's the volume control. Then I can go on listening while I endure your cackling. Th-th-there, now. Comforted, she draws up a stool: it's she, not the music, that I prefer. "You're right," she says, "a little music is nice, but then it begins to get you down." I don't reply.

An administrative reflex: she doesn't attempt to poke around at this level. Besides, I've come down again, which shows that when I take off and soar, it's only because I have nothing better to do. It's impossible that I can enjoy the heights as much as I say I do, that's only an act I put on.

The upper level is the dormitory where she would lock me in. Ignorance is like a nice pair of well-worn slippers.

"But how can you expect not to catch cold, Damien?" the dame says, observing my mules, old sky-blue ones clumping across the floor. "You don't have anything to speak of on your feet!"

Oh, yes, matron is quite capable in her own sphere, which is that of the elementary. Having grown weary of her round eyes, hungry for peace, I try not to upset her too much, I play it dumb, keeping spontaneity and being argumentative in reserve for some future time; upstairs at night I pull myself together again . . .

In the darkness of the dormitory, after the Hand of the Law has shut me away for twelve hours, I wake up, I turn over, pull the sheet up round my neck; and, with my nose pressed to the cool gray paint of the wall, I chuckle and chortle. A madcap urge climbs into bed with me and explodes in brighter and brighter sparks.

Shhh. Wait a little while, restrain the impulses of the fingers when a shadow passes. Suppress.

I am forgetting nothing, neither the runaways that had got out of hand and been brought down nor the long period when everything was fucked up, nothing; but I don't want to be hurt again by things that cling and betray. There will still be time, unfortunately, to take up the battle again after the trial: the outcome will be yet another kick in the teeth, but I'll bounce back . . . For the moment I'm hibernating in a cocoon of kindness and good faith.

Hot sharp irons have been thrust into my softest flesh; but that happened so long ago that all the surrounding tissue has forgotten the pain and formed calluses; I can stand up all right to these grafts because I know that they don't have a hope of taking.

The pincers of the absurd leave dark, lasting marks on me; the big paws that search me and feel me make me tremble with revulsion: "Always harping on the same subject!" . . . Behind my submissive smile my teeth are clenched over surges of hot words.

But I shut up.

In the old days, I screamed, I broke things; I broke everything except the prison that watched me passively and confidently. Now I don't scream any more: it is I who watch the prison, I study the old contraption; I'm learning to detach the shouting part of myself, to peel it away without breaking the skin. And, when I have my belly full of thinking about the joint, I simply put a heavy foot down on the analysis in progress, get up, and go to the window to watch the sparrows in the courtyard.

I dream, and my flights into fantasy became more frequent; I'm coming to enjoy them, and I almost don't mind being where I am . . . I set up ingenious detours, strict barriers for the times I'm sick at heart.

Even more than the utter lack of any interest in my daily life, constant association with no one but the matron contributes to my taste for imaginary escapes. I'm not undertaking anything, I'm not getting hold of anything: I want only to remain entirely within myself and to keep this Me far away from here, somewhere where nothing and no one can make it other than what I want it to be.

In a walled, barred cell, where the grub would be shoved in to me through a slanting hole—and not an anti-germ partition like the one in the office here—in a cell where I would not have to yak or fake, it seems to me I would be able to tell exactly where I am more quickly; but here there's always that matron . . .

(6)

There is a transparent curtain of rain on the other side of the bars.

In spite of three Nescafés, I'm yawning; what's the point of getting up, getting into your clothes, and making yourself beautiful when you're going to have to reverse the whole procedure at six o'clock, go up to bed without having seen anyone, and get in between those damp sheets where it wouldn't be so bad, just the same, to do the rest of your time . . .

It's no use glueing my stool to the stove, holding my legs as close to the heat as I can stand to, the skin turns scarlet and marbled but inside they stay frozen, my arteries run with snow and my head is like a tasteless ice. Under the reign of Dufon we used to go up to make our beds before chow, and matron has allowed me to continue this. "When we have new girls, of course . . ."

From now on it'll be the usual thing. So I flood myself with coffee until the bedtime bell rings, and, when the matron comes to fetch me, I dive into the corridor, climb the stairs full steam ahead and ensconce myself in the bedclothes with a minimum loss of calories.

202

The Runaway

There the lady is: I can see her head bundled up in a scarf outside the window. She's moving fast, it must not be very warm out there. I'm already at the corridor door, tapping my foot, my crossed arms in the sleeves of the heavy sweater I've put on over my nightgown.

"Ah, matron, there you are, finally! Quick, let me get into the sack."

"No, Damien, the bell hasn't rung yet, and anyway you have to go to court. Get your clothes back on fast, the officers are waiting."

I panic: I have just washed my slip and my stockings as I do every night; I have wiped off my lead-pencil eye shadow with margarine, I . . . quick, my comb, oh, God, I've already braided my hair. I can't care less if I go to court bare-assed; but without eye shadow!

Well, there's no choice, matron shoves me into the infirmary dressing room in my nightgown, my skirt in my hand; she performs intricate gymnastics to reach up to the top of the wardrobe where the suitcases are: since we have no hangers, my fur jacket has been stashed up there since I came. To speed me up, she holds it out to me by the shoulders, the sleeves ready for my arms; but I want to let the engine warm up a little. "Aren't you going to search me, matron?"

She hesitates a moment. "Well, you had no time to prepare for this . . . and besides I watched you getting dressed. All right, raise your sweater, that'll do."

I lift my arms so that her big red paws could scrabble over me; the nightgown re-emerges, all stuffed into the waistband of the skirt. On my way out, I make sure it's not showing, and then I say innocently: "Oh, didn't I tell you? I thought I had. No, that's right, you gave me my lawyer's letter and went right out, and afterward I forgot about it."

"But I didn't give you any mail today."

"No, but you did yesterday morning. But then I thought the

203

lawyer had made a mistake, because they always tell you on the morning of the day you have to go to court."

In fact the mouthpiece had told me that I would be called "in the near future," which, in mouthpiece language, means "I don't know when." The lawyer earns the fees that you pay him by punctuating your waits with comforting little scribbles. But I was certainly not going to let the matron know that I was getting nothing for my money and that what my lawyer and I talked about was anything and everything except my case: she would have been much too disillusioned.

What about my shoes? There's no time to go back to the workroom: I'm going to have to appear before my interrogator in a fur jacket and mules, my ankles stained by the puddles in the courtyard and my braids done up in rubber bands. If only I had had a chance to make up my eyes a little! But I'm lusterless; or, rather, I'm all aglow with margarine, and I look like a little kid who's pinched her mother's jacket.

To top it all, Zizi is among those present: I see him standing in front of the paddy wagon. I duck behind the cops so that he can't see me in this disgraceful shape. He must have had advance warning: he's freshly shaved, a very close shave, with that brand-new appearance that I've always loved. I sit as far from him as possible in the wagon, too bad, I'd rather seem angry.

But I can't keep that up for very long, I raise my margarined face, smile and tenderly call: "Zizi!"

"Hello, baby," he says, with an automatic wave, and then he looks away.

What's going on? Always, the minute he sees me, Zizi breaks into a smile and gets as close to me as he can, and now he doesn't smile, he doesn't stir; he looks irritated, like a man who's been hounded and wants out of the game, and his eyes never leave the window. I can see all the lights of the city reflected in his eyes, but we're at the justice building and he hasn't made the slightest move. My angels shove me into the waiting room and my man goes directly through the next door, into the judge's chambers. I plunk down in a chair and sit there, absolutely drained, imagining things, and smoking cigarettes that give me a headache.

What is wrong with Zizi? I'm eating dry straw, I'm chewing thorns, I just can't understand.

"Well, beautiful, getting your lies straight?"

"Oh, it's you, cop. Sure, the prisoner has the duty to lie to save his skin, everyone knows that. But since I don't know what this is all about . . ."

"You been inside a long time?"

"Centuries! I've had it up to here . . ."

"Aah, you're not so bad off in that joint. Seems like a good place, and everybody we bring to court says the screws are nice."

"Oh, yes, you can eat the grub, you have a bed, with clean sheets . . ."

"What's more, you're both in the same place: one thing you don't have to worry about, anyway, he can't cheat on you."

I give it up. Watching the gloomy street through the rain-streaked window, I want to go out on the balcony and just howl, to pour my tears into the gutters with the rain, I want to just dissolve and flow away.

There have been so few clouds, such brief storms in the time our love has lasted! Today, when I'm in no position to ask questions or answer them, why not spare me this fog, dearest? Don't you want to talk? Not to the judge; to me. Just a couple of words, even if those words kill me; anyway words, even the most reticent ones, should be divisible, refinable, split into infinitesimal bits . . .

The door of the hearing room opens again; "our turn now," my angel says, getting to his feet. And the interrogation begins once more, slow and tortuous.

I'm not too aware of the answers that I give, but it doesn't matter, I think it's just as well this way: for too long I've been feinting, evading, inventing; the questions that are put to me, in their involuted, jaw-breaking legal language, make me fashion my answers automatically. After a while the defendant acquires the reflexes of a chauffeur: there is no need to think about the road, one part of my attention functions as an automatic pilot and the other takes flight with me.

Then, little by little, what with the bad light, the clacking of the typewriter as it repeats what I've said and the magistrate has translated into normal language, the motionless silence of the lawyer sitting next to me, the angel on guard behind my chair, I begin to feel anesthetized, I slide down in my chair and stretch out my legs as far as I can; somewhere in the clouds there's an airplane, its engines like a lullaby. I'll take a little nap, and the magistrate will wake me when the session has ended.

BANG!

Shattering, like a shot at night, that bang jerks me upright, my heart pounding, my ears split: the magistrate has just leaped out of his chair and slammed his hand down in fury on his desk; he begins to shout, and suddenly I realize that I'm the one to whom this tirade is being addressed: "Since you refuse to talk, I am adjourning the hearing. All right, on your feet, get her out!"

I look round me: the stenographer stops right in the middle of what he's recording, fingers in mid-air; the lawyer is latching his briefcase and beginning to rise; and the cop already has his hand on the doorknob. For a second or two all these people seem rigid, frozen in action, like people in a film that is abruptly stopped; even the magistrate, shocked by his own outburst, is still on his feet, his lips still forming that word *out,* his mouth taut, his hand pointing at me.

I haven't budged.

I must put the plug into the socket, I must make them run

off those frames where he flips his lid again, backward, I must—ugh! I have to say something.

"Please don't get upset, Your Honor . . . If that's the way things are, I'll answer your questions. Could I ask you to repeat the last one?"

Everyone sits down again and the interrogation is resumed.

To save my arm, I give a finger; I rephrase my earlier statements in new versions; apparently embarrassed, I admit things that will certainly come out on the slightest investigation. And the typewriter echoes me, while I search my mind for what I can say next, anything at all just so long as this interrogation goes on and on, until I collapse with exhaustion and boredom and I am hauled back to stir without regaining consciousness, without seeing Zizi again. If a shadow has come between us, then let me croak fast!

. . . That's all for today; continued in the next issue. I go out of the room shrunk down to size, dragging my feet. The lawyer joins me, shakes my hand, and says: "I'll see you soon." I go back into the waiting room marked *Prisoners*. Zi is sitting at the other end of the room, near the window, on the same chair that I was sitting on a little while ago. He's smoking, and raising both palms with every puff because they've put the handcuffs back on him.

When I come in, he turns his head toward me, and his eyes meet mine, uncertain and a bit glassy . . .

Before the cop could move, I ran, I was with my man again and now I stood there against him as he sat there, I cradle his head in my arms and his legs in my legs; I weep into his hair and sob his name . . .

Finally Zizi's eyes recognize me, he moves me a little way away from him and I feel the minuscule sparks of his flashing eyes run all over me from under the heart-catching sweep of his eyelashes.

"Anick . . . look, explain, tell me . . . Why did you do that? Don't you realize I'm going out of my mind?"

The angels speak: "O.K., get going, the wagon's waiting. You can yak some other time."

As we go down the corridors, our four hands interlaced, our bodies swaying like those of lovers in the streets, thrown off balance by the handcuffs, I find out, piece by piece, what has been torturing Zizi.

Matron had told her husband my damn-fool story about the letter addressed to my lover; the Superintendent had sent for Zizi and lost no time warning him: ". . . he told me that you'd shot off your mouth about it to his wife, with a dame like you I'd always have dough, etc. . . ."

"Oh, darling! Certainly you didn't believe that! Imagine you believing what I tell screws."

"Uh . . . I admit at first it got to me. Then I said to myself that if it was really true the screw would've got a kick out of reading the letter to me . . . or anyway quoting something from it: even when you wrote to somebody else I'd know your style . . . no, it didn't make sense. But still I couldn't figure it out. I knew from the kitchen that a girl had walked, and I figured you'd jump at the chance to write. But this 'lover' that the bastard harped on: where . . ."

"Darling, you know as well as I do that tail can be the best cover possible."

"All right, but did they really grab the letter? Did they read it?"

"They grabbed it, but they couldn't read it, it was all in code: it was a plan for a break."

Zizi jumps. "A what? You're absolutely loony! Anick, Anick, you're going off your rocker . . . Please, don't be a horse's ass, stick it out a little longer, at least until the trial. You'll get off, you'll see. But you have to hold out, the same as I'm doing, toughen up . . . I'll do my time, don't worry, I'm thick-skinned. What the hell's the difference, three years, five years . . ."

"You won't do five years! I won't let you!"

". . . more, even, if we're together afterward, and free, you and I? I love you, Anick, and you know it. And you'll be outside, I'll share your life, I'll feel free along with you . . ."

"No, Zi. Because I'm not going to walk. I know what you tell the judge in there, he reads me parts of it. But you're wasting your time trying to get me out of it . . . He's not an idiot, you know. I'll get mine too, a little less than you, perhaps, but nothing like a walk! anyhow, I still have to finish the earlier time, so I might as well split now, before the trial. If I don't make it now, I will later, but, no matter what, I'm going to break."

"Your neck is what you'll break. When I think that that letter could have gotten out!"

"At least I'd be out and I could be helping you. The way it is now, with both of us inside like a couple of poor slobs and not even allowed to write to each other, what the hell? . . . I admit I was a jerk to trust that Dufon, I was a bigger dope than she is. Imagine, I thought I'd greased her enough to get her to do it: 'We superior beings' . . . Ha. What a shit, though."

"I'm sure you went overboard on her. Why do you think I keep telling you not to mess with slobs . . ."

"I didn't have much choice. But don't get mad, the next time I'll handle it all myself."

"No: you're just going to lay low. And I want you to take your punishment without bitching, because you've got it coming to you: not because of the letter (to tell the truth, I'd have tried too) but because you went off on your own without letting me know. If you were absolutely hot to break, I couldn't have stopped you, damn it; but I could have kept you from lousing it up . . ."

Zizi would bet on my mare, Zizi had come back to me, everything was all right . . . Then the panic came back. Let the smallest wisp of cloud darken our sunshine for a second and all my happiness flees, the whole world goes black and full of shameful spider webs: "Zizi's stopped loving me, Anick has another guy" . . . The spider is groping about, sorry it ever left its home.

"Me write to a John! Yes, if it's you. Anyway, the magistrate still isn't on to it . . . And that superintendent, why do I worry about him? Or that other hypocrite, his wife, who felt so sorry for us being separated! Just wait till we get back, I'll smash her face."

"And get yourself another month in the hole."

"But I'm not in the hole, Zizi! Not at all. Look, it's much too cold there, and they got scared . . . And she plays big-hearted! She brings me coffee!"

"Easy, easy, baby, not so loud . . . The hole on the women's side doesn't have a double door or a window—it isn't regulation. That alone could have got you off half the time. But, as long as you aren't in it at all, I think you ought to be careful not to make them change their minds . . . Tie your hands together, damn it, keep them off anything I'm not in on. These interrogations are going to stop, the judge is tired of seeing us, they'll send the file along pretty soon. Look, wait out these few weeks, baby. After that . . ."

"After that we won't see each other at all. We'll be sent to Central and then . . ."

Yes, we'll forget even the color of each other's eyes. Look how upset and frantic you got over a lousy intercepted letter, darling. At even the smallest slip or misunderstanding the acid of prison comes into the picture. Our glass shivers and gives way, like those cups that collapse when your fingers press on them. So I might crack our love out of rage, out of indifference. Forgive me, Zizi, and be my master. Let me learn and grow up with the years, or else let this damned paddy wagon turn over . . .

"Zi, I'd like you to beat the hell out of me . . ."

"I know. Even better than that: later, when we're together, we'll beat the hell out of each other, the way we ought to . . . But for now we have to just go on living, the best way we can, even the life we have in stir . . . As far as the letter goes, forget it. Besides, you're going to have to forgive me, too . . ."

"Forgive you?"

"Yes, because I did something too without letting you in on it. I just talked to the judge. I asked him . . ."

". . . I know, to let me walk."

The paddy wagon had stopped for a red light; our two heads, close together, touched lightly several times with the vibrations of the engine, and my cheek scrapes against the shoulder of Zizi's jacket, where I used to nestle at night. O God, take this heap out of here at a hundred and twenty miles an hour in this dazzling rain and let us take off for somewhere else . . .

". . . To let me walk! What we're taking off for is years in stir, that's what. . . . Well, what did he say?"

"Nothing, because it doesn't just depend on him. But I'm going to write wherever I have to, to the prefect of police, to the regional director . . . Oh, yes, I forgot to tell you: I asked him for permission to marry you."

(7)

Monday: not a hope of getting any mail today, my people write over the weekend. Unless my little local lawyer is feeling friendly toward me again? That's like expecting midnight at eleven o'clock. Monday's menu: round sausage or flat sausage. And a chunk of bread that I eat the inside of. I barely have time to gobble the sausages, which is a shame, I would have made fried potatoes to go with them but before I can cook I have to deliver the mended linen: I promised it to the matron today. Afterward I'll have plenty of time to myself until the next laundry day.

Ring! It's not the sausage, it's the courtyard bell: through the window I can see the matron's head as she runs, ring! again, someone's in a hurry. What was making somebody so impatient all of a sudden? A special-delivery letter? A cop coming to eat me alive right here? I read the cards yesterday, and they were full of spades, brr . . . The matron's taking a long time to come back, and I can breathe again: bad breaks move faster than that. It must have been the superintendent longing for his little wife, or the kids longing for their little mother. Bing bang, she comes back, this time by the corridor door, bang, she opens the door of the infirmary. It's not croaker day, and the voice accompanying the matron's is not that of the nurse. I have to accept the evidence: it's a new arrival.

She's here. Young, old, intelligent, stupid, broke, boastful, whatever she may be, I'll have to put up with her just the same. Always give in, always appease. All right, I'll clean out one of the closets: the girl may have some luggage, and I don't want to have to make my retreat after she's been installed in my principality . . . good-by, princess!

The dusty, greasy shelf paper I fling into the fire. This closet is used for non-personal things or things intended to become part of the community property: sewing materials, newspapers that have been read, empty boxes. I keep the other two closets, marked *Personal* and *Food;* this time both will remain my private property. I've had enough of feeding double-crossers. I separate those of the old newspapers that I want to re-read, and arrange the rest on the table as neatly as in a dentist's waiting room. I sweep and then I get out my writing kit: too bad about the promised linens, I had better have a discreetly superior attitude and not let my good room-mate get used to the idea of being patiently listened to by an empty head. Let's start writing.

"If someone does come," I told the matron, "I'm just going to stay in my corner: a favor, a bit of information, all right, but she'd better not start beating my brains in if she doesn't want me to knock her out. Oh, matron, you will keep her busy, won't you?"

"But you talk as if she were here already, Damien."

"Because I really want someone to come . . . because of the laundry, I can't do it alone, and she'd do yours as well . . . You don't want me to help you with it: I can understand that, because I don't like just anyone poking into my things, either."

Carried away by her good will, the matron had replied that I was not "just anyone," and then she had gone off on the

tangent of my infirmities and "you have to take care of yourself, you're not going to be outside tomorrow."

She has a real gift for the comforting word; half-honestly,
half-mockingly I justify my bootlicking to myself by ingesting
the best brand of coffee and reassuring myself that I will never
be a turncoat, at least on the inside, since my peace and happiness require that I give the appearance of being converted.

That bygone conversation is running through my head while
my fingers are setting down what's happening right now: tomorrow friend lawyer will know what's up with me, and perhaps it will jog him into speeding up the petitions for our
wedding and our trial. As I lick the envelope I raise my eyes;
the door has just opened. Oh, matron is alone. Hell, if I
dreamed up that other voice, I'm going to have to chuck my
letter into the stove.

"Damien," she announces, "somebody's come."

Strange how she has suddenly gone back to her old reserved tone, the voice she had at the beginning, the voice of
a head matron determined to demonstrate her authority.
Equally suddenly I go back to my submissive voice to answer:
"Very well, matron. I've already made room, look . . ."

"Oh, good."

It always amazes her that I can recognize a step, that I
can identify events by their sounds, without any need to be
told or to spy; inevitably, having guarded so many keyhole-
peepers, she had turned into a keyhole-peeper herself. I had
elaborated my theory of auditory intuition during one of those
evenings when I felt like making her shove off, and I had explained that my own talent had been sharpened by many nights
as a lookout, in a special profession that is not eligible for
unemployment insurance.

"Would you also prepare . . . oh, no, I'm not thinking, I
have them all in the coat room. There aren't too many of
them here already?"

"What's that, matron?"

"Plates."

"No, I have my two and my mug, and my knife, that's mine, I canteened it. Look, I could fix up Dufon's old knife for her with the help of the stove poker and some heavy cord for a handle . . ." But matron doesn't smile. I go on: "Excuse me, matron, but, if you don't need me any more right now, I'll go on with my mail, I have an important letter to finish between now and chow."

She scrams, and, as I'm writing the lawyer's address, my imagination is already at it again: since the girl hasn't been dropped off at the workroom, they must have had to clean her up first in the shower. The rule book bathes every new arrival, but matron allows the clean ones to come in with their outside smell. So this one must be a pig.

Sub-sections: pigs by accident, those who have spent a night in a police station without a chance to clean up, and pigs by incrustation, which covers a wide range: from the man-killer who never wipes off her make-up to the poor bitch for whom a bath is a vacation luxury.

I hear water spurting in the shower and in the big zinc tub: the tub means that the new girl's clothes are not acceptable. With a sigh I go back to my calligraphy.

A new invasion by the matron: "I swear, in this job you have to put your hands into everything! If you could see that one! I'm going to give her denims. She comes in here without even a change of clothes, just a purse and nothing in it, not a handkerchief, not a cent, what a pitiful thing to see, and especially anybody so young . . ."

Becoming my sympathetic self, I shrug. "You're right, it's terrible. You know what I promised, I'll get along with her, but I sure won't let her make a shit-house out of it."

"Good," the matron says gratefully, and goes out again. I catch the sound of cloth rubbing on wood, she's tobogganing the denims down the stair rail. This is a universal habit: every item of penal equipment is thrown down the stairwell, to save labor. Since there is no well here, they use the rail and slide the stuff. It's one way of shining the rail. When matron is wearing her Sunday smile, I go downstairs the same way, astride the rail. But, as long as the new girl has not won the matron's affection, I'll see no smiles, on Sundays or weekdays. I fish in my mind for some words of greeting, for the cleaning process seems to be over and the stranger is approaching. She enters, followed by matron, who makes signals I don't understand over the girl's shoulder.

"Sit down," she growls. "This is Damien, she'll teach you the ropes."

So here is the end of my solitude and I am face to face with this woman who stands there looking at me, motionless and dazed. My frigidity melts and I say cordially: "Are you cold, madame? Come close to the stove and get warm. You can get settled later."

But the girl goes right on shivering all over. I observe her purple hands, her soaked tennis shoes; the shower has also drenched her hair, without bringing back its color; locks of it are dripping down her neck, and spots of moisture already appearing on the penal gown. She is still clutching her wet towel in her hand as she sits there awkwardly on the very edge of her stool, her knees together and shaking.

What in God's name am I to do? I slide over to get my pan. I say MY pan, but in fact it belongs to the house. So many inmates have used it to heat their coffee, so many fires have browned its bottom and burned its handle that it looks like a blackened pentagon. When the cold weather lets up and I get up enough nerve to stick my nose out into the frozen oxygen of the courtyard, I'll take the pan along and scrub its ass with earth, squatting down with my sleeves rolled up. I had said: "Matron, you can be sure that when the archeologists uncover this prison a few centuries from now, this pan will be worth its weight in gold to antique dealers and collectors. Someone will stick it in a museum with a card on it: 'Pan, twentieth century, discovered by X at Y, and used for coffee and coffee-substitutes.' "

"If you like it, you can keep it," the matron had said; she too had appropriated it.

"Oh, ma-a-a-tron, I'll put it in my collection of prison souvenirs, between the locket made from a beef bone and the file of money-order receipts."

And now with this dame I'm being robbed of the glory of the pan, "you're all alike"; I now will possess only half of it. I start it boiling and the talk going: "Listen, it's not so bad here: you can heat water whenever you want, there's a pitcher, a bucket, a stove for frying . . ."

The woman is still trembling. It's gone on so long I'm beginning to be scared. "Are you really that cold? Wait a second, if you'll move your stool just a little, I'll poke up the fire . . . It is pretty cold, isn't it? Even here on top of the fire and wearing this big sweater, I'm frozen. I'm going to make a coffee. Hand me your glass and I'll give you some. It isn't like what you get outside, but it warms the body."

"Yes," the girl brought out in a hoarse voice, "it does do that. Thank you very much, madame."

"Oh, don't call me madame, the name's Anick, what's yours?"

"Simone, no madame, I'm not married. Do you know Fernand?"

"Fernand? He has nothing to do with me, who is he?"

"Well, he's my friend, he was in here, he was in the laundry, he was still here just last week: yes, in prison he works, but when he's with me . . . All he's good for is to take my money, come home drunk, and knock me around. Here, take a look (she turns back her sleeve), that's yesterday's fun and games."

Simone bends her head, sweeps the hair off the back of her neck, and I can see Fernand's fingers: four bruises; she opens the prison dress: Fernand has scratched her skin . . . a curious skin, half brown, half milk-white.

"You must work outdoors, right?" I say. "I can see signs of sunburn."

"Yes, on a farm, dear, and it's a hard job. Beets, peas in season . . ."

She is trying to close her dress again, but there are no metal hooks, just little loops of thread that her numb fingers can't manage. "Why do I have this dress, anyway?" Simone complains. "The guard told me to wash my things and then I could put them on again."

As a matter of fact, matron doesn't like to see her charges in denims and she lets all of them keep their clothes, whatever they're in for. If she's had Simone's taken away, they must have really been . . .

"They came to get me this morning," Simone explains. "I was still in bed, they didn't give me time to take anything, not even to wash my face, so here I am. Oh, I know, I should have been expecting it, it's two months since my trial . . ."

"Oh, you've already been sentenced? How much, if you don't mind my asking?"

"Four months."

In this part of France, it is quite common to let convicted defendants go free after their trials and then pick them up a few weeks later and haul them off to jail. That is, of course, when the crime is not too serious and the person is reliable— that is, unable or unwilling to remove himself from the court's jurisdiction. To judge by the confused explanations given by Simone, which I listen to with half an ear as I scribble on an

envelope, she has got herself her four months in some obscure
business with stolen poultry and leeks, which she had received
from the thief and eaten; in addition, she has a suspended
sentence of a month because of a fine that she had not paid; I
explain to her that she can count on doing five months, because this second offense would cause the sentence for the
first to be reinvoked. Some of my words seem to baffle her, but
she gets her back up at the words "second offense":

"Oh, look, I'm no beginner, I've done plenty of time, during the war my bitch of an aunt turned me in for collaborating.
Families are really nice. I never collaborated, I swear it: but
a man's a man and my aunt turned me in out of jealousy, because I was doing the best I could with the boches so I could
feed my kids."

The kids? They were grown now, and, in spite of everything
that she had done for them, they had never turned a hand for
their mother and, if the welfare people had finally taken them
away from her, it was just to make it easier for her . . .

All this drunken-woman crap is beginning to make me
drunk too. I detest lies made up so clumsily. And the vague
feeling that might rise in me at the sight of so miserably
wasted an existence turns into irritation precisely because
Simone is trying to reach my emotions. I too have fallen into
shit; I got out of it all by myself and without whining to anyone for so much as a butt. And, if I never had just potatoes to
live on outside, that too was my doing alone. Receiving stolen
leeks is the same as receiving stolen jewelry: the crummiest
jeweler has insurance, he gets money for his junk, but the
owner of leeks . . . No, anyone who would steal leeks is a
disgrace to the profession. And then on top of that the crap
about collaboration . . . Have no truck with Simone: as of
this moment, I declare her ears hostile and her mouth dangerous.

She is leafing through the newspapers. I notice that she's

219

picked up a magazine and is holding it upside down. "It's good to read a little, isn't it?" I said.

"Oh, it won't take me long to get through it; I never learned to read or write. I just like to look at the pictures. See this whole pile of papers?" She laughs and I see that she has no upper teeth: courtesy of Fernand, perhaps? "I could 'read' them all in an hour. I wish I had my watch. I have a nice one, gold plated, but they took it away from me when I came in. Why do they take your watch? They took my earrings, too, and my ring."

Good God, how she runs off at the mouth! "You're lucky, you'll get them back. I don't have anything left: no more jewelry, no more family, no more man, no children, no more name . . . I've even lost interest in laughing and talking."

"Oh, yes," Simone says, looking important, "the guard told me about you in the shower. She told me what you were like more or less—oh, nothing bad! Don't get upset, we'll get along fine together. I like hard work."

Go on, you ninny! "All right," I said, "it's all yours. Here's the mending, if you want to start . . ."

"No, I like HEAVY work: they've been waiting for me to take Fernand's place ever since he got out. The superintendent was real pleased to have me: you should have seen what a welcome I got! He stood there with open arms, the cops couldn't believe it . . . I'm going to take care of the matron's chicken-house too, and her garden, she promised. As far as the laundry goes, dear," Simone continues, making a funny face, "that's just play for me. Fernand told me all about it. You see, he worked there . . ."

"Yes, I know, you've already mentioned that he did."

"Oh, I did? If I'm bothering you, then say so."

"Me? Nothing bothers me, that's why I can take anything. When I'm plugged into my own circuit, you can talk forever and I won't even hear you. So if it makes you feel better . . ."

"Hey, would you write a letter for me? I have to tell Fernand to send me my things."

"He's going to have to take care of you now."

"Huh, that's what you think. I don't need him. When he was in here, I left him for good; hell, I turned him in so I could get a little peace. Now he's paid me back, I'm sure he's the one who went and tipped off the cops this morning. So he can keep his money: we don't owe each other anything."

I am utterly nauseated. "Are you going to canteen? You have to give your order in at supper time. You said you came in with money, didn't you? Tell me what you want and I'll write out the order for you. Matter of fact, today's miscellaneous day: writing paper, soap, toothpaste? Wait, I'll go get the list."

I take the canteen placard off the wall, it's covered with dust: unfortunately it has been a long time since I have had any reason to consult it. Dufon reeled it off to me often enough. But Simone stops me.

"I don't need much stuff, you know: the matron gave me some soap, and she promised me good pay if I did her work right. Seems like a good boss, that one. As far as toothpaste goes (Simone opens her giant cavern in my face), I can't use it, all my teeth are either gone or going. And I don't have anything to wash myself with, they didn't give me a shower mitt or even a decent towel, just this old rag . . . That's not very nice of them. Well, I guess they're not generous. And what am I supposed to do my dishes with?"

Wearily, I explain that that's the way it is here, I show her the jug full of soap powder that the princess provides at her expense to clean tables and plates.

Matron takes us by surprise. I had not heard her coming back. Then I remembered that one day she told me that she kept an eye on the new ones through the peephole for their first few days to see how they behaved when she wasn't

around . . . Knowing my nasty nature, she must have been
there at least a quarter of an hour, listening to our conversation and watching to see whether I pulled too much rank. So
she's quite surprised when I say: "Simone has no shower mitt,
matron. Would you give me some material so I can make her
a couple right away?"

"But Fernand will send some to me," Simone protested.
(Always having to wash!)

"Oh, no, it'll only take me five minutes, and matron likes us
to wash ourselves every day. Isn't that right, matron?"

The matron recites the code of penal cleanliness, including
the ban on running about less than fully dressed, and winds
up: "Take Damien as your model."

I sigh: this is the end of my pleasant half-dressed mornings,
of my Sundays without bed-making (there is no inspection on
Sundays); I have to set an example! And I have an idea that
with Simone I'll have to bathe myself from head to foot three
times a day if by example alone I hope to persuade her, on
days when she's feeling particularly energetic, to clean so
much as the tip of her nose: in spite of the shower, her wrists
and ankles still have thick bracelets of dirt, and her hair . . .

"Did you take a look at her head, Damien?" matron asks.

Did I take a look at it! I reply that I would not have done
so without a specific order, Simone might have taken offense.

"But that's the rule, you know that!"

"I'm clean, though," Simone objects, "I don't have any
lice. The policemen wouldn't let me get washed, I asked them
to but . . . and last night I didn't have time, you can imagine,
with all the work I'd had all day. But that doesn't make me
lousy. When you're working you don't have time to make
yourself pretty . . ."

That's a dig at me: I don't have one hair out of place and
there's not a single spot on my cardigan.

"All right," matron cuts her short, "that's enough. Come

into the laundry and finish washing your clothes. Don't forget your soap."

Simone goes out, shuffling her tennis shoes behind the clacking little heels of the matron; I hear them jabbering a moment in the corridor, then there is the sound of the wash-tub, and the door slams, but not very hard. The matron comes in: I'm standing on the table, taking dishtowels down from the wire clothesline overhead.

"Damien, you'll absolutely have to keep her clean, I'm counting on you. You should see her underwear! Especially her panties!"

Clinging to the very edge of the table with my toes, which are on a level with the matron's navel, I am mistress of the whole situation, the soiled panties and the abandoned news-papers. "Of course, matron, of course. She's a hick, what do you expect? I don't mean that to be nasty, mind you. But I hope you'll put her to work somewhere away from me, because if I have to have that forced down my throat from morning to night, there'll be a bloody crime on page one."

"She'll do the laundry, the inmates' to start, and mine if she knows how. What a pleasure, Damien, to have a laundress again!"

Simone kills the rest of the afternoon looking through the papers, yawning and talking to herself. She's made a few trips to the sink and drunk vast quantities of water: hangover from yesterday probably. Finally she confessed that all the money she had was four hundred francs that she had grabbed up in a hurry when she was picked up, "just lying there on the table, imagine . . . anyway, it's that much that Fernand can't drink up." I had sworn to myself that I most certainly would not offer her another drink: with a parasite like this I'd be flat in a month. There's one piece of luck: she doesn't smoke: that, in fact, was the only question that I put to her . . . Her monotonous uninterrupted soliloquy is like an anesthetic: I

can hardly stay awake. I wash myself while Simone swallows
her soup, pretty noisily, never taking her distrustful eye off the
plate of rice that I've added my portion to. I get a potholder
in order to turn the bread that I'm frying on the stove: when
Simone has finished guzzling, I'll take her place and she'll take
mine.

"You can start now, I've finished," I say. "Personal hygiene
is optional, but the cup and plate have to be washed so they
can be sent back to the kitchen in the morning."

And thus matron finds us: Simone vigorously scrubbing her
muscles with the bath mitt that I have made for her, me enjoying my bread fried in margarine. "Well?" matron says with
fake enthusiasm, and my "Everything's all right, matron," is
purely automatic. Both of us stare at the intruder's back because we don't dare look at each other: the matron senses my
annoyance and I sense her confusion; she's wondering how it's
possible that Simone and I haven't murdered each other.

The matron has no way of knowing how much I prefer a
simple-minded vegetable to poisoned honey, and she smiles
because she doesn't know what to say. In the radiance of that
smile, obedience can be a pleasure, an act of thanks. But I
refuse to play the game.

That night I am back in my real situation, a certified
prisoner "just the same sort" as my little sister the vegetable,
who is orating again as she sits in MY place, wrapped in
borrowed garments that matron has unearthed for her in the
stock kept for indigent inmates: a cast-off nightgown and a
bathrobe that's losing its nap.

Simone has stopped shivering; she barely belches, as un-
obtrusively as she can, giving off a vague vapor of soup and
rice blending with the aroma of prison soap. I have finished
my snack: I light my Gitane-for-the-digestion and pull up my
stool. When the bell rings for bed, I know that my mornings
have been salvaged: entranced by every bit of work in the

lower courtyard, Simone will be taking care of Madame's chickens and rabbits.

Tonight I'll refuse to chat, I'll say: "With my old fractured skull, I need plenty of sleep." And the minute I'm in bed I'll go into a coma.

My nose under the covers, I'll be working out the best way of handling the vegetable and giving the lie to our beloved matron's "just the same sort."

(**8**)

A month has dragged by. The official permission for our marriage has not yet arrived.

I make a kind of thermometer of the calendar, the lines marking off the degrees accumulate, the column of mercury rises; and when my temper starts rising too, I turn to the mercury of the local thermometer, brought in by the matron and adorned with gaudy landscapes; a month in Alsace, a month in Ardèche.

Matron brings in a double portion of coffee, and, to prevent mayhem, she fills our glasses herself: I'm still sipping the first mouthful and already Simone has finished her glass, washed it, dried it, and put it on the shelf. Her greedy absorption of the coffee is an index to her nature: she digs into everything, destroys all my obsessive-compulsive arrangements, smashes all the little piles of coal I carefully build up on top of dying embers in the stove. "What a lousy fire!" she bawls, thrusting with the poker. "I'm going to make a real one. A roaring one!"

She manages to extinguish what fire there is, she waltzes around frantically, making drafts round my composure. In the end I start yelling too: "Fuck the . . ." Simone's eye being trained on me like a rifle and the poker being in her hand, I finish in a quiet voice: " . . . time we're doing in stir."

By now Simone is more herself, her cheeks are full, there is a little lard everywhere on her, to say nothing of her self-assurance that borders on insolence. She has robbed me of half my kingdom, and, to keep the peace, I've been self-effacing enough for her to take over the whole of my share of prison. But, no matter how much I say: "Yes, Simone," or "Fine, Simone," she remains behind her own frontiers, which her lack of education and her lack of money keep her from crossing except in thunderous outbursts and apostrophes such as "that whole gang of assholes!"

I spend the evenings charming Simone as I charmed Dufon: I simply make my cars a little more American, my cops a little tougher and a little stupider, and my hauls a little bigger. The movie of my adventures, with a deliberately monotonous sound track, lulls her gently to sleep; when I observe that the intervals between her "Really?"s and her "Great"s are longer and her breathing more regular, I heave a sigh and finally begin my own day: general review of the situation, confusion of what I've just reviewed, and re-reviewed: in the process, I munch pounds of winter apples that compensate for my fasts in the workroom: I have a good appetite, but Simone's is revolting. Note that her gluttony of the early days has finally subsided: she very soon grew bored with dusty beans and potatoes with bouillon cubes, but she has gorged herself so much on bread and margarine, has drunk so much bad coffee, that she is stuffed to the gills, and therefore more demanding. With her peasant logic and her vegetable stupidity, like all women winos, she arrived with the famous slogan: "They put me in here, it's up to them to keep me alive." But I'm the only one who canteens. Since matron gives her little extra tidbits in return for her work in the garden (lettuce, fresh eggs, rabbits' heads, killed chickens), the sly bitch proposed to share

227

them with me. I could see what she was leading up to: in return I am supposed to turn over half my canteen stuff, put my closet at her disposal, and guarantee the survival of that big body.

We call each other *baby* now and generally address each other like old friends, it is more sisterly that way:

"No, baby," I answered, "keep what the matron gives you, it's just that much less that you'll have to canteen when Fernand starts sending you bread. I'm O.K., I canteen. Oh, the damn dough, how I envy you not having any, not always having to make it last . . . Share the coffee, the real stuff, too, if you want, because I could drink coffee out of a lousy beggar's bowl; and keep the extras you get from the matron. A sip of beer, for a toast, that's all I want. Besides, you work like a horse, you never stop, naturally you have to eat a little more than I do, sitting closed in here all day without doing a fucking thing."

Let us not attempt to introduce even the most primitive notions of esthetics and delicacy into this charming head: keeping clean, taking care of one's hair, writing, drawing, whatever Simone is incapable of doing is therefore not doing a fucking thing. As for knowing how to behave . . .

"Oh," Simone belches, wiping her greasy mouth with the back of her wrist, "I know how to act outside, all right. I hung out with guys from Paris too before I met up with Fernand. But he's a real hick, so what can you expect? Would you believe it if I told you it meant a real fight to get him to wash himself every Saturday? He stinks, he don't know how to talk, he sounds like a rube. What did I ever do to make the Good Lord send me a guy like that? Here at least I have clean sheets but with him there's never a cent to get the laundry done." And on and on.

I tirelessly clean up the shit that Simone drops from morning to night but never makes the slightest move to get rid of. "The workroom's your job," she says.

So I scrub away the evidence of lunch—her mug filled to the brim with regulation coffee with bits of bread; I sweep up the crumbs and the other dirt that accumulate under her stool: and I sew the rips in the seams of her indigent-inmate wardrobe, which she splits open again with one of those vigorous flexings of her masculine biceps; and matron is pleased to see how well her girls get along together.

"Here, have some, baby."

A tidbit for the dog. Simone is hardly the one who will compel me to change my ideas; it seems to me that whatever worth she has—all of it in her muscles—is more than canceled out by everything in her that is negative: she has had children and a husband, she has had a thousand chances to learn, but she was born and will die a simple-minded vegetable, I don't like simple-minded vegetables and all I feel for Simone is an indifference vaguely tinged with pity on my good days and an impulse to slug her the rest of the time. Yes, my constant desire to smash Simone and put a few stitches in that big stinking mouth of hers reassures me that I still have the qualities of a good pal: Simone doesn't disgust me at all. When that desire gets too strong, I suggest writing to Fernand so that the ballpoint can drain off the insults in another direction: "Well, girl, shall we do that letter?"

Immediately Simone becomes a serf, a serf who has to go to the public scribe. All of a sudden, the smoke of my cigarettes no longer drives her into fits of coughing, my feet can find all the room they want between hers on the rungs of her stool; the crumbs and the dirty mug vanish to make room for the writing pad. Simone listens thoughtfully to the phrases that I suggest, and her eyes, which never lose their lively suspiciousness, are hidden behind lowered lids.

Fernand darling, we'll still have lots of wonderful times, we'll make love again in the haystacks; but in the meantime think of your poor woman who has such toothaches and can't pay the dentist, and who works so terribly hard for just enough to pay for the stamps on the letters that she writes to you . . .

"Don't put that," Simone says, "he won't understand it."

When the envelope has been addressed, when Simone has made certain that I've placed it with my own to be sent that evening, the vegetable in her comes back to the surface: the writing pad flees before the mug, and the rest follows.

"If the poor guy only knew! Imagine, the dentist! But just you wait and see, that letter of MINE'll make him send me some dough!"

But once she gets outside, to hell with Fernand. The social worker will find her a job, far away from here, and Simone will take no chances on letting Fernand know where she is, he can stop counting on it, she's had her belly full.

"Yes, Simone," I say. A week after she gets out, she will have sold every last rag that she has acquired here, bought a couple of bottles, and gone back to Fernand, drink, and love in the haystacks. If it could be called love to be laid once in a while, when Fernand is tired of his mother and the neighbor ladies, by a man who has not shaved or washed for a week and who stinks of onions and wine.

Oh, Zizi darling, thank you . . .

In this fashion, by dint of little favors asked and given—you must occasionally ask for things in order to win the affection of a vegetable—and with inexhaustible patience, I recapture my kingdom.

True, Simone would never learn to close her closet in any manner other than slamming the door; and, if she wears reasonably quiet slippers in the morning, it is only by way of imitation: the things had been mine—a pair that she barely saved from cremation one day when I was house cleaning in earnest—and I move so noiselessly that, even on Simone's feet, my footwear kept the habit.

But she humors me, and I do as much for her. The shouting-matches usually wind up in the evening with bedtime reconciliations; like the first night, when Simone began to divert her public with various eruptions at both ends, and I pointed out to her that here she was neither at home nor, what amounted to the same thing, in a pigsty, but with me, and that these nocturnal noises, etc. Thereafter, every time she farts, Simone excuses herself. In return, I stop smoking in bed. I came to this resolve after a number of harsh awakenings by Simone at six o'clock in the morning: "Shit, it stinks in here, I'm being poisoned by the filth, the bucket, the dust . . ." Of course the real poisoner was my Gitane. I am beginning to believe that yokel hygiene differs in every respect from urban hygiene. My dream of retiring to the country one day, when Zizi and I reach the end of our careers, my dream of life among my hens and rabbits takes a precipitous plunge.

As a matter of fact, this has made me cut down by one pack every five days.

In addition to the ration, I also have access to butts from the lady prison visitor. This lady has nothing of the condescending, patronizing woman of virtue: she is pleasant, her hair is always freshly done, she is a bit heavy, and she always arrives loaded with packages, and not only butts. Simone's eyes begin to gleam, she is all politeness as she waltzes back and forth; arousing a certain amount of amazement in the lady, she unpacks everything at once and pulls out skirts, blouses, underwear; she puts on everything at once and begins showing off like a drunken old gypsy woman:

"Nice, huh? Madame? . . . That's real nice of you to bring all this. I'm going to look like a duchess: oh, yes, indeed, madame, we're not rich in here, we work real hard, but we have our pride, we like to look pretty too, you know . . ." She holds out a purple skirt with garish flowers. "Hey, that's really something. Maybe I can get somebody to let down the hem."

Somebody, in this instance, was me. I ask the lady about news of fashion and literary gossip, I open her pack of cigarettes, I offer her a light; that good fairy's fur transforms the workroom and I breathe in its smell as deeply as I can, stealing a few perfumed seconds from the ugliness and the wretchedness. Seconds of grace like that do not come sixty to the minute, but they do exist.

So, when one day the matron tells me that I am wanted in the office, I am neither surprised nor upset, for I have sinned against neither hope nor the rules. It must be the decision on the wedding, it can't be anything else. Thank God the lawyers have told us what line to take. I would never have believed that so many yeses were required in order to be able to give our own. But in stir you have to beg for everything.

As we walk to the office, matron at my heels, I ask myself whether it is more important to me to have a *yes* or a *no;* hell, I'll react later, when I know: what matters is that there has finally been an answer. What it is is still a matter of indifference to me.

It's yes.

At once matron grants me rights that until now have been forcefully contested: she goes at once and gets a batch of letters out of my suitcase . . . In the first one, Zizi apologizes for the indigestion he is about to give me, but he will write every Thursday and every Sunday, since he is confident that sooner or later I'll get the whole batch at once. On each envelope the prison censors have written "To be withheld" in large letters, with two underlines, of which the first is always the heavier: knowing what is under negotiation, the censors didn't dare send the letters back.

And that woman had never said a word to me! I am astonished, she's such a bigmouth.

"Matron, what about the actual wedding? Do you know anything about that?"

"That I can't answer, Damien." This was to be translated as "I don't want to tell you."

The Runaway

I hold those letters like a slice of tart, very awkwardly and with a certain absent-mindedness. I must be undergoing some kind of paramnesia: I have already read these letters a thousand times in a room just like this one. The vegetable is not at all pleased: this has all been my day—the office, the letters, who knows what next?

"A husband."

"Did you ever tell me about him?"

"Yes, I told you I was going to be married."

Oh, if only I had a little drop of schnapps to help me make the transit from anticipation to reality, to really feel elated! I know now that all that mattered to me a few minutes ago, on my way to the office, was to get a yes. Because that was the only thing possible, I had always been sure of it. My will is limited by refusals of others; there is an area of recoil there and it can be traversed only by enthusiasm.

Zizi and I had been utterly without resources: all we could do was to ask and then wait patiently in a corner for their decision. "The strength of the spirit is also important," Zizi has written. "Just have confidence, and we'll have our wedding."

Before I learned how to drive, when I could sense how tired my man was at the wheel, I used to watch the road and clench my fingers as if that would correct our course . . . I don't remember the night of the accident clearly, but I am certain that I fell asleep and that was why it happened.

In order to win this yes, I had put everything in myself that was not related to it to sleep. I kept my whole body relaxed and my mind concentrated on a tight nucleus, one tender dominant thought. Wrestle with the judge, get married, fantasize—oh, just for the fun of it—some kind of runaway, was a lot to do; I opened the window and chased all the stubborn blind flies out of my brain, one fly at a time.

Oh, Zi . . . let me still remember this morning when I am

very old, or very weary. Let me tarnish nothing of it, distort none of it.

Simone is as sentimental as an old madam now that she knows: certainly, when she went out to look after the rabbits, she had asked matron about it and matron had finally talked about it. You see, I can shut up like a trap, when I'm not supposed to tell a soul, I don't tell her. But how she makes up for it!

Simone is right, it is my day alone; so, to be in on things, the vegetable shares my happiness. What an afternoon I went through with their voices rasping in my ears, their presence, their attentions, their barracks humor! Matron left us only when she had to satisfy her natural needs, a piss, a little cup of coffee, a little kiss for her little husband, and every time she came right back and immediately started talking again about the same thing. I have never longed for evening as I did today.

At last we were alone. Then Simone too leaves me: she is snoring, and I can picture her toothless mouth gaping into the dark, her stinking mouth that has been talking all day about my love.

I would like to get up and smash that mouth.

Well, well: I'm turning jealous! It's other people's doing! As if I could feel the reactions that they ascribe to me, as if I needed their complicity, as if I didn't know how to make love, as if I were getting married for that!

But I am like you, my dear Simone, I'm an unmarried mother who hasn't had any kids. My marriage is a whim, something off-beat; I had been careful to have something to drink first, I would be able to make it as far as the river without stepping into the puddles . . . The ride, the city hall, festive clothes—incidentally, I'll have to have something decent sent in, I've smoked up all my good things—matron will let me have my make-up, she's promised, we'll be able to kiss

234

each other . . . Cut it! this is just distilling the essence of being down in the dumps.

What has been and will be, what is between Zizi and me: these are the constants, the essential signs.

My marriage is not going to be a brief abortive flight into the promised land; I'm not going to be overwhelmed—certainly—by a desire to hide under the desk in the city hall like an overjoyed kid among all the noise of footsteps and voices; a transaction of this kind between my man and me can be no more than a formality: wife, the functions of the wife, madame, monogamous . . . Crap! all of that I already had. If I want to, I can have my bridal night right away, and a good late morning on top of it. A late morning! Even more than the night or the wedding, I want a day in bed, just one, without having to jump up and rush into the water that takes your breath away and the workroom that freezes you . . . The day I get out I'll find a pad and hit the sack. And tomorrow . . . tomorrow I'll wake up two hours ahead of the morning bell, fill my nostrils with an imagined aroma of coffee with cream, loll back on familiar pillows . . .

I had already tried, but I had fallen asleep again. It was better than a marriage in a prison, it was a metamorphosis: Zizi was a bird, he came for me and turned me into a bird too. A beak prodded at us, and silly little black claws; without the slightest surprise, we drank in the pre-sunrise light above the tilled furrows; our claws gripped the loose moist gold, the lightly granulated gold of the earth, heavy like something good to eat; and our beaks were washed in air so fresh, so pure, that it was certainly the beginning of the world . . .

My bird dream grew, grew to the limits of my body, I was singing of a life of joy, a moment without a memory . . .

Matron unlocked our skulls with the end of her key.

All right, then, girl, sleep, stop dreaming your old dreams;

235

you're going to be married, and that is not a dream, that is a concession granted by the prefect of police.

Does the prefect ever dream of being a bird?

And now don't mention this marriage to me any more, don't ask me to talk about it; tomorrow I will be deaf and dumb, I will not go in search of a friendly voice or ear, I will listen to the violins inside me, I will be married to the sound of violins, I . . .

"Simone! Don't snore so loud or you'll knock the joint to pieces!"

(9)

It was laundry day, and hence my day for being kind: relaxed by my morning of solitude, I was quite ready to spend the noon rest period with Simone in the same euphoria. The sun was almost shining, it was almost hot; we had eaten well; the water for the Nes (which I treated Simone to on wash day with an eye to a sip of her cocktail-hour beer) was beginning to bubble in the pot. We wandered up and down together in front of the closets, chattering casually: in another moment we might have had our arms round each other's waists, like a couple of vegetables under the young elms.

This was when catastrophe came down upon our heads.

Absorbed in our nattering—Simone was telling me how one night she had got hold of a young sow that had wandered out of the sty—we had heard nothing, neither bells nor keys. Matron arrived like a cyclone, howling: "Here comes a new one!" and latched on to Simone "to give her a hand." I expect her to come back with all the gossip, but she must have had to go directly to the laundry room, I can hear the wash-paddle again. I knock on the common door and go to watch from the window. Soon the washwoman's blowsy head appears between the bars; I give her a big questioning smile and make words: "Well, baby, what's this mouse like?"

Simone lets a few of her dull locks fall between the bars, and her toothless mouth shapes itself into a hen's ass to utter an imperious "Ssh!" All right, she is still being searched, the watch will have to go on. Hell, it's going to take much too long, and I sit down again.

Re-banging at the window, re-Simone: "She's an old bag," she said, grimacing, "a grandmother."

I have known grandmothers who worked the streets, grandmothers who were second-story workers, grandmothers who . . . oh dear! Out of the noise of the wash-paddle I can distinguish the pounding stream of the tub, this is going to be a dirty grandmother.

Simone's locks reappear at the window; this time her eyes are rolling and there is a bit of lip-biting to accompany the whites of the eyes.

If Simone can be moved to these schoolgirl imitations, the sight must be really revolting; because after the men's linens, the sheets caked with sperm and the towels full of hairs, any other dirt seems clean. And now the woman appears, between Simone, who leads the procession with an angry expression on her face, and matron, whose blue eyes give the lie to the harshness in her voice: "Go on. Go dry yourself at the fire."

It seems to me that I have only just finished being a spectator at a similar display. But this time I will not be under orders to take part: this grandmother is by way of being a savior, Simone will forget me to a certain extent. In fact she is already gabbing, running back and forth, cleaning out a closet, tossing her property and mine helter-skelter onto the floor. "Here, grandma, put your things there, make yourself at home . . ."

In a word, she is doing exactly what I had done for her when she arrived, and her protective manner makes it obvious that she has completely forgotten the state in which she herself was; now she is making up for her wretchedness on her arrival with the grandmother's misery; a trembling, cold-blue grandmother in a wet prison dress with hair dripping water down her neck.

"Wait till the matron goes," Simone whispers to me with a sly look, brushing against me as if by accident and crushing my toes with a discreet nudge of her heel; "I'll tell you all about it."

I need no explanations, but how can anyone muzzle Simone?

"Did you check her head?" matron asks, as always.

"Oh, yes," Simone says obsequiously, "nothing there, she's clean." As soon as the door closes, she turns to me. "That really gave me a bad time! I hope you never have to do anything like that, doll, when I'm no longer here to handle it."

"Shut up for now; tell me later, upstairs, when things are quiet . . ."

"She doesn't hear us; look at her."

Grandmother is sitting hunched over on her stool, her chin in her bosom, her back stooped, her legs apart; bent over this way, she's making little snoring noises. I murmur: "Poor woman," and this sets Simone off again:

"Oh, come on, she's not worth feeling sorry for, anybody as crummy as her . . . Look, you don't have to believe me if you don't want to, but there was . . . there was shit all over her thighs and her back, her man must love that! Oh, yes, she's got one, he's on the other side, it seems he's younger than her, matron says they're funny ones. And then you know there's a thing in the shower, an iron basin, like, a . . ."

"A tub."

"Yes, that's it, a tub. The old bag got into it, tried it out, and it rocked a little, she began to fall out, and I had to go in the shower to help her: look, I'm still wet—and I had to scrape the shit off her myself. She must be on her last legs, she can't even stand up. And to think we have to put up with THAT!"

I join the maledictions enthusiastically, but mine are directed at "the bastards who still keep bothering people when they're that old."

"But we have to live with her! I hope they'll make her sleep in the other dormitory, because if we have to breathe that poison of hers all night . . . These old jerks are unhealthy, you know, they stink of real rot, you could catch anything from them . . . Anyway, dearie, we won't pay any attention to her, we'll still be friends, won't we?"

"Well, you know how I am, on good terms with everyone and always on my own . . ."

"Sure, you don't give a fuck for anybody, you sit there warming your ass while I have all the filth with her . . . oh, shit." Simone gets up and bangs her stool. "I'm sick of it, I'm going to talk to the matron, I'm always the one who has to do everything around here . . ."

I say nothing. Simone can try forever to get to me, she'll never make it. The noise of the stool had awakened grandmother with a start: she looks round the room empty eyes. I can see the beautiful irises, a glowing purple like hazel nuts, and pity knifes into me again. I ask her what her name is; for answer I get a kind of groan, some complicated handle, undoubtedly. I point out that all I need is her first name, and mine is . . .

"Oh, hell," Simone growls from the corner where she has taken refuge—she couldn't keep her tongue idle more than five minutes—"I don't go in for fancy manners. As far as I'm concerned you're Granny, and that's that."

Then let it be Granny. "Get your bowl ready, Granny, I hear chow coming."

But it's the matron coming back for Simone; they go up to the dormitory, they walk about above our heads, I can hear

240

a bed being moved . . . so the three of us will sleep together tonight. It's strange how this rearranging seems to have soothed Simone's nerves: when she comes downstairs she's glowing, and almost friendly. Possibly just because she adores being assistant matron and these signs of importance (washing away shit, moving beds, etc.) make her feel superior to me, the scribe hunched over my writing.

Granny merely took a sample of sleep just now, she has the whole night ahead of her. From the way she punches the mattress, it's obvious that she's no first-timer; when it comes to unfolding the covers she's as quick as she was at twenty. She must have had an enormous amount of sleep to catch up on, to judge by how she goes for the sack. She gets under the covers fully dressed, falls into a comfortable sleeping position and closes her nut-like eyes. But matron is peeping through the spy-hole: she suddenly jerks the door open and begins to bark: "People get undressed here! You're not in a hayloft, you! All right, do as you're told."

The old woman gets up clumsily and tries to open her dress; her frozen fingers stuck in the loops, she begins to tremble again, and her lower lip pouts like that of a child about to weep. It's too much. I get out of bed: "Come on, Granny, I'll help you. Get up."

Finally, what with matron pulling, me pushing, and Granny interfering with both of us, we get her out of her dress, her chemise, and her cotton undershirt. There is a stained gray rag that must once have been a nylon slip still on her bowed, bony back. The matron gives her back her undershirt, throws the dress on the foot of the bed, and goes out, saying that she's turning the light out: time to sleep.

Granny has gotten back under her covers, being careful not to make too much noise as she breathes.

"Oh, shit, isn't that ever going to stop? I couldn't even close my eyes! Do you hear her, Anick?"

It's nowhere near dawn; Simone is thundering in the dark. With considerable irritation I open one eye and half my mouth: "Yes, baby. It's really unbearable." And I go back into my coma. But it is written that this morning I am not to have the kind of peaceful awakening that I prefer, a "How do you feel, baby?" or even a "Can't those goddamn cooks let us sleep instead of rattling their pots that way?"

This morning my darling roommate is really at it; she keeps turning toward the wall, then toward me, back and forth, so often and so restlessly that in the end I resign myself to listening and trying to find out what has put her into such a state.

There is indeed an unusual amount of noise. It's not the cooks, either; tomorrow's the day for grated carrots; and it won't be tomorrow that the Bureau of Prisons will supply an electric grater: the Bureau is poor, the carrots are tender. The stubborn frantic rasping that is audible is much nearer and louder than the almost imperceptible scraping that usually goes on.

It's coming from Granny's bed. By now the filmy dawn makes it possible for me to see her bedclothes moving, and there can be no question: she's scratching herself. Last night, when I was undressing her, I saw red streaks on her shoulders, but I supposed they were the signs of some recent beating, or of a night spent sleeping on straw; and besides I had been reassured by Simone's "There's nothing there, matron."

"This can't go on, I'm going to tell matron, that's not turning anybody in, it's a duty." What a big word so early in the morning!

To be honest, I am far more moved by Granny's fierce scratching than by Simone's wretched smirking. And what makes her talk that way is not any concern for hygiene, but the nasty pleasure of finding someone filthier than herself; what frightens her so much is not the lice—which she must be acquainted with herself—but the thought of being given

242

hell; because after all she should have mentioned these bugs yesterday.

At the morning bell Simone springs into her slippers and shouts like a sergeant: "Everybody up! On your feet, you there!" Granny too tries to leap into her high shoes, painfully zips them shut, and bustles about, folding the bedclothes. Simone kicks the neat pile away and sits down cross-armed on her own bed, looking like a model prisoner. When the door is unlocked, she rushes downstairs, ignoring the chamber pot (although it is her turn to empty it), to make her report. "It's the truth, isn't it?" she shouts at me.

Like a singer walking down steps onstage, I go down the stairs, the nightgowns over my arm, my braids tangled, my eyes stuck together, still in a fog. Simone comes back up to me and grabs me: "Tell her, tell her. See, matron, I wasn't lying, she heard it too!"

The two of them go on whispering back and forth, while I escape to the workroom to start emptying the stove; for I have now been forbidden to poke up this poison while Simone is stuffing herself on dunked bread. It's harmful, it seems. Good, the big mouths are taking their time, I'll have time to build a decent fire and get it going.

Simone comes in with her coffee and the usual bread ration. "No bread for her?" I ask.

"I left it on the table; is she supposed to be waited on? Let her clean up her own shit, the old sow."

The old sow then arrives, propelled by matron, who says: "Look here, I think there's something wrong here . . . Damien, you inspect her: her head, her underwear, everything."

It's an order. Simone withdraws into the shadow, her eyes are pieces, I can feel them firing into my back. Nevertheless I do my little inspection job without turning a hair. In the first handful of hair I see that there's no need to go further. I pat the hair back down on Granny's skull, I place my hands on her shoulders, and, as solemnly as a croaker giving the family a dire diagnosis, I announce: "She's full of them, matron. There are egg cases. A whole lot, almost one per hair."

Matron and Simone bite their lips, their schoolgirl lips. A state of emergency is proclaimed: the plague must be isolated before it can infect first us, then the men by way of their laundry, then the matron's family, the . . . I join the clucking of the two others over Granny's head, and she sits forgotten on her stool, her spine bent in shame and her ears burning, a poor bag of bones and lice whose soul we completely ignore.

"What about her body, Damien?"

Matron has sought refuge close to the door and is allowing me to conduct the operations. I make the old woman sit close to the stove, which is growing warmer, and rattle away at her, whatever comes into my mind: this is our job, the same thing has been done to me, she mustn't be ashamed, it is all for her own good, etc. Now she is naked, her back on public view, her knees pulled in. Well! This is prison aggravated by corporal punishment; this back has been whipped.

Three hours later, all heads had been scrubbed and combed; I had encased Granny's in a towel held in place with pins, a shock treatment for her, a whole bottle of louse medicine had been poured over her. It was paid for with her man's money: he had some bread on him when he came in, and it seemed that he had approved the expenditure without argument, with eagerness even: "Whatever she needs, whatever will make my woman comfortable," he told the guard. And the existence of a population on his head, coupled with the striking difference in age, has made for talk: it is generally believed that they have been busted for incest, that Granny has been sleeping with her son. Fine, when I get married we two couples will visit each other and I can really find out what it's all about. What matters much more to me right now than Granny's matrimonial state is that of her feet. At first, you might think that her inability to keep her balance came from her hitting the bottle hard, but now?

She totters like a baby taking its first steps, and I spend all my time watching her so that I can jump up at the first sign that she's falling. Especially when she falls asleep on her stool after lunch, all fed and toasty warm. But she doesn't tumble off, a way she has of balancing her upper body keeps her in her place. Simone, delighted to find a woman who can eat as much as she does, takes advantage of the fact to discard the good manners that she felt constrained to practice in front of her housemaid: again the table is strewn with crumbs, fish bones, grease spots, and coffee stains. All the same, this three-sided life is more to my liking than being paired with Simone: she couldn't care less whether her remarks are understood and answered; what counts for her is to yak; she sounds off to Granny, who sleeps. I find the same pleasure in Granny as in an old doll.

Matron chooses to pay no attention to the instructions on the medicine bottle: to her way of thinking, the more you scrub, the better you de-louse. So I have to administer the treatment five or six times every day.

"Look, Granny, if it stings too much, just lift your hand. All right? If it's not, I'll dilute it with water."

Granny shakes her head for me not to, as happy as a dog being relieved of its fleas, and mutters: "You're all nice girls here, and matron's nice too, I'll always think of you, that's right, ladies, I'll always think of you."

Matron oversees everything, angry at Simone's myopia— "just think, Damien, if you hadn't been here to double-check" —and she explains that she has given herself a de-lousing and made her husband and the children do the same. "One thing, it does make the hair prettier. Too bad it smells so."

"Oh, matron, your perfume takes care of that. It's Lanvin, isn't it?"

She mentions a very cheap brand. "No, but this one's good too."

Simone comes back from the chicken yard, dirty pots in her hands. "Pfui," she bawls, "it stinks of rot in the damned place! Here, baby, you like to wash dishes, here's a job for you. What were you telling me, matron?"

"Nothing, I was talking to Damien."

Vexed, Simone settles herself with a mug of coffee with milk. "Fuck it, I'm going to eat something, I think I deserve it with all the work I did this morning."

Matron looks thoughtfully at her pail. "Why don't you warm that a little?"

"Hell, I'm no princess! I had worse than this in the war."

A little matter of deportation on the horizon. I laugh, the cup of coffee with milk threatens me, Granny in her turban looks like a dervish in a nest of serpents, let's get out of here: matron allows me to take over this poor body's hygiene as well.

In the laundry room I fill the big tub with warm water. "Try it with your foot . . . All right, sit down in it if you like. Pay no attention to me, I'm a bath attendant outside, and I have kids as big as you are. My God, you're tiny!"

"But I'll get you all wet."

"What of it? I'll change my smock. Let me have a foot and I'll soap it for you."

No wonder she hobbles along, with feet like these: between each toe is the dirt and filth of years, and they are all cramped together and bruised by shoes that are too tight; I have to work very carefully, sliding the bath mitt gently between the toes; Granny whimpers and clutches at my neck: "Oh, my corns, please, please . . ."

I get some ointment and some old slippers, and I settle my Granny near the stove, her feet on the floor while her shoes sit drying behind the stove. I clean and cut her toenails, I treat her corns; Simone watches it all without saying a word. She is thinking that with her dainty feet she can probably get into these shoes easily, and for working in the fields this winter . . .

(10)

The water from the faucets is less cold: soon it will be possible to bathe in the washroom. When the men's things no longer hang there dripping, when all the launderers and laundresses have been set free. But that is nowhere in sight—on the contrary: the good ladies are now coming back in pairs.

When they enter, I had resolutely turned my back in enmity and gone to lean on my elbows at the window: I am bitchy as hell and it's no time to step on my toes. Simone connects at once with the two new arrivals, mentioning names of people, or dumps where those ladies too might have worked; she inquires into their names, their ages, their family status, she assumes her magisterial manner in order to bring them up to date on a code of rules of which she knows nothing of the *why* and still less of the *how*.

"Right, doll?" . . . "Isn't that so, doll?" I knew that in Simone's gab *doll* is the form of address reserved for days of ardent friendship; the rest of the time it's *slob* or *bitch*. But that's the way it goes.

"Oh, baby, do me a favor and fuck off for a while."

"All right, all right! Anybody can see you're making out with the priest."

The Runaway

The priest! . . . I can see him again in my mind, the way he looked in the visitors' room just now, with his transparent eyes and his miserable big red nose, and I wonder which of us, he or I, is unhappier . . . And in the mirror hung beside the window I see Simone pointing to me and indicating: "She's nuts," her finger making circles at her temple. Good, I hope she'll make out better with those two than she has with me.

One of them is called Solange, I think: she has great brown cow eyes, wide-awake in a round face, with beautiful coloring; and it seems to me that, once she has dried the big tears with which she had arrived and has blown her minuscule pug nose mightily, she'll be easy enough to live with. The other hasn't told us her name; she remains standing, her hands thrust into the pockets of her blue jeans . . . I wonder why she's been allowed to keep her pants. I was put into regulation clothes the minute I arrived and had to wear them until my own dresses came . . . Then I swallow my bitterness and smile at the big girl via the mirror, because I don't like people to go around bawling and because her eyes are not red but blue.

"Don't pay any attention to her," Simone says. "She's going to get married and that's all she thinks about."

Exactly: all I needed to make me angry. I had requested a baptismal certificate to be used for the religious ceremony, and had sent a letter, since my parish was too far away to ask the lawyer to go there for it; assuming that the chaplain would not raise any problems, I hadn't even bothered to ask him what he thought. And he refused!

"My dear," he told me, "what you are asking of me is a very delicate matter."

And I was so annoyed that instead of conning him I said curtly: "All right, then, let's forget it."

I had already risen and gone to the door of the visiting room, ready to knock for matron to come and let me out to go

back to the workroom; then the chaplain rose too, came over
to me, and took my hands: "If you really insist on it, my dear,
I cannot refuse you this marriage, of course; but you must
understand . . ."

"It's all right as it is, Father, I told you that," I interrupt
him. With one ear toward the door and one hand offered to
him, to make it plain that I thought the whole thing had lasted
too long, I said: "Good-by, Father."

My desire for his blessing was completely pagan, I know:
blessing, or fingers interlocked, or cut wrist on cut wrist and
the blood mingling . . . I would have agreed to any ritual, I
would have agreed to all of them. But simply because, as long
as we were doing it at all, we wanted to have it sealed completely, perfectly . . . We had had to hide our love under a
bushel so long, Zizi and I!

Granted, we had still treated ourselves to the luxury of putting on a great show, we made quite a display of ourselves as
a couple . . . at least our wedding rings were the real thing;
and we made it a practice whenever we moved our hands to
make them catch the light, we played with them as we spoke,
as if we were doing so unintentionally . . . Sometimes we
played mother and daddy, "borrowing" children from this or
that friend: for a few hours these kids were "the fruit of our
love," and in this capacity they were handed back to their
parents loaded down with candies and money—how was it
possible for anyone to run out on his kids? We delighted in
ingenuous showing off, in kisses exchanged in public, not so
much for the kisses—which we didn't enjoy all that much—as
for the show we gave others and their reactions of resentment
or sympathy; we joined the nameless, winged race of those who
love, and we crossed all frontiers. And yet any dressed-up
puppet would have had a greater claim on love than we.
Living always on the run, trailing wanted notices, skipping
from one hide-out to another, we found an escape in lovers'

prattle, we found a shelter there. Love could be made into many things by us . . . but not into marriage: the court's rejections of our petitions for the right to see each other had been enough to make us recognize that marriage is an act, and that the fact of being together and the act of love are not enough . . . Now we had elected to bow to the law, we wanted it to be known and ourselves to be approved and helped by everybody, even by God.

Chaplain, chaplain, you were not very decent, your *no* is the only one: even those who parted us are willing to escort us into marriage, setting up a thieves' nursery under the auspices of John Law, and you . . . You're a pessimist, you know from experience that prison loves don't "keep," you've performed other such marriages; in a word, you generalize us. And if I insist? What business is it of mine what dilemmas you find yourself in? I will have nothing: no incense, no echoing arches, no bridal train, no grandly dressed church officer, not even a uniformed policeman. And, on the threshold of the nuptial cell, farewell to the bridal night! . . .

Yes indeed: to make your kind of marriage, there would have to be a consummation: one cup for two, without straws. Hell! Out of the cup from which we cannot drink, our letters will draw everything, like little straws. We're marrying in order to be able to write to each other, that's true; but, whatever you may think, we'll always write. Whoever walks first will write a little more often, that's all . . . Because there is such a thing as faithfulness! Oh, you forgot nothing: "Are you sure that, if he is released before you . . ."

Let him go free, Father, let him whore around! As for you, sleep in peace . . .

I say nothing, I try to keep my eyes stubbornly lowered, I count the demons passing by behind my eyelids. If I fight for my rights, it's only because I'm angry. You can keep your charity. When I found love I was hunted, broken, homeless;

and suddenly I became a refuge and found my own: we were
there, mingled and bound by that thread of love, without a
way out, without props, and we needed none.

To shore up is to doubt: but it's others who doubt, it's for
others that we shore ourselves up.

Summer and silence and perilous joys . . . There were no
vows, only words, invented whispers, the ghost of a whisper,
free ones . . . And now this *yes!* I'm getting married, I'm getting married! Ah, let us forget these sacristy problems: flow,
my joy! I throw myself into you, I negate myself in you, I
make myself a vessel, a conduit . . .

My nose pressed to the windowpane, I laugh and laugh.
Simone must be afraid I've lost my mind. Better reassure her:
"You know how it is, all right," I said, turning back toward
the workroom, "you're getting married too. When's it going
to be?"

"Wait till I get out, I have to go see whether Jojo's written
to me." Jojo is one of Simone's fiancés, a seasonal lover who
comes back for the harvest every summer. I must say a few
words about him; it's worth the trouble.

One Sunday, after I had finished my customary letters, I
had got off a few out-of-the-ordinary messages: I had written
a letter of welcome to our President, who, according to *Paris-
Match,* had given us reason to hope that he might pay a visit
to our part of the country one of these years, I had written
to the mouthpiece to ask the croaker for the X-rays of my
back and bring them on his next visit so that I could compare
that old straight back with the one that I was sure I now had,
crippled by my prison stool and threatened with scoliosis;
then, running out of ideas, I had asked my little sisters
whether they "wanted me to do anything for them . . ." It was
so unusual to see me idle that Simone beat her brains out to
think up something she could prevail on me to do, or, rather,
get done for her: "Read me the letter to Fernand again."

This letter provided her with a fine entering wedge, a logical transition that Simone must have taken days to carve out: to be exact, ever since the dentist had begun work on my bridge. When I came back from the first visits to him, Simone would make me show her my teeth that had been drilled deeper, and deeper, suffer with me, warm my coffee . . . All this solicitude was cleverly calculated. In return I was supposed to ask the dentist: "How much would it cost for a denture, just the uppers? No, no gold or silver: just little white pearls like they make nowadays." I repeated this inquiry word for word to my dentist, and both of us had laughed so much over it that our hilarity had taken hold of the cops escorting me and the five of us had spouted like so many whales until the captain of my guard had looked at his watch and recovered his composure, then his cap, and finally his prisoner.

In all this I had forgotten to find out the price of the apparatus, and I could not guess at it, inasmuch as I was neither covered by medical insurance nor toothless myself; I got myself off the hook by saying: "Baby, the guy couldn't tell me anything, he'd have to examine you himself first: I don't have the exact map of your jaws in my head, but the next time, if you want, I can take him the impressions: all you have to do is bite into a big ball of bread . . ."

It was after this conversation that Simone had abandoned —provisionally—her plans to have her front redone and that she had talked to me about Jojo: "He wants to marry me and take me back to Spain with him: I'll have everything there— a house, a car, a trousseau . . . The trouble is, he spoils me; he's no Fernand: he caresses me, he treats me right—mm, it's good with him. But what bothers him is my teeth; he wants to pay for a dentist, for whatever I need afterward, everything so that I'll be beautiful. But what about me? If I have to go without teeth for weeks and weeks, waiting for the gums to heal! . . ."

"But you don't have to look nice for anyone here. Why not make the most of it and let them take out your three lousy teeth that you can't even eat with? When you get out, you'll have the choppers in a week and you can buzz right off to Spain."

"That's right . . . But tell me, how much does it cost to have three teeth yanked?"

"Hell, you're so brave, it can all be done at one time . . . I'll ask the dentist. It would be a good idea if we went together."

So on this Sunday I had composed a letter to Jojo: "we" gave him poor-mouth sweet-talk, rich only in promises, promises of the summer soon to come when Simone will be with him, her skin clear and her breath warm, her sweet gums offered up to the plaster and to all the coarse vices of the peasant.

But Jojo hasn't sent the money for the dentist yet. Simone explains to me that he must not have gotten the letter yet, but that he'll soon be going back to the job to which we had addressed the letter, and, as soon as he's read it . . .

Jojo is in the land of castles.

(11)

"Would you do me the honor of being my witness, counselor?"

It was essential that the profession be represented at our wedding. But, since one mouthpiece would be quite enough for that, we would have friends as the other witnesses.

Friends know—sometimes from experience—what someone in prison lacks: love, and not necessarily fresh water. Ours, in addition, know our favorite brands; so they arrived with their pockets full of small bottles and two big ones of champagne in a basket.

But I hadn't yet had a drink when I almost bumped into a tall character in a gabardine suit at the door of the prison. Instead of excusing himself and making room for me to pass, the brute grabbed me and tried to kiss me.

My bridegroom was already ensconced in the radio car, on the back seat; I was about to shout to him to help me when I recognized my attacker . . . and I threw my arms round him.

"Good old Maurice! Oh, how nice of you to come! . . . I'm sorry, I thought you were a cop, I didn't put on my specs."

Maurice tripped over his own tongue as he poured out phrases and filled my arms with flowers and boxes of pastries. I asked him to keep all those things for me until later, when

I could take care of them; right then it was impossible, I had too much to do with this wedding. I climbed into the car, sat close to Zizi and threw myself into his arms—the handcuffs had been dispensed with. I would never move an inch again. Never again.

We set off for the mayor's office, not having quite burst with joy, and not one passer-by looked at us any differently from any other people in a police car; we were calm, pensive, a little out of this world. Our witnesses had all piled into the same heap, except the lawyer, who was to go straight to the mayor's office. The witnesses chatted politely with our angels and passed bottles to us right under their noses, those gentlemen having refused to drink on duty but granted permission for others to slake their thirsts: not every day is a wedding day, and angels can be as nice as anything when what they have to do is nice too.

We drank out of those bottles, one after the other, like people saved from the desert, to an accompaniment of "take it easy! take it easy!" from our friends as they tried to get us away from the bottles. When the little bottles had been drained, we called for the big ones; but how could the corks be pulled without drenching everyone in that mass of arms and legs? I abandoned my betrothed for a second and turned toward Maurice, speaking slowly and sleepily and with great effort: "Don't worry, we'll all go drink the champagne at my lawyer's. I've asked him to lend us his apartment for five minutes."

Another prisoner had been able to get an emergency permit, having unfortunately to accompany a dear one to the cemetery on the same day that our business was a wedding; consequently our ceremony was run off somewhat in the manner of Gretna Green—nine minutes, according to Maurice's watch. And we were carried back to jail at top speed: the cops were already fixing their facial muscles in the set for the next ceremony, and there was not a hope of distracting them, even with the smell of the Moët.

It was a shame; I would gladly have listened to the mayor all morning. He was fatherly and garrulous, the schnapps taken on the way made bubbles round all his words, and I would have liked to go on drinking by way of tribute to them.

"As for you, little lady," he said, threatening me with his index finger, "you must not desert the marital residence, understand?" I replied that at the moment my only concern was to get back to it.

The mayor seemed rather taken aback; at this point, my counselor-witness intervened and discreetly whispered something to him. Though the mayor had been told that he would be marrying a couple of convicts, he had not recognized them in this well-washed, well-dressed bridal couple. "Oh," he cried, "excuse me. I seem to have made a blunder. In that case, madame, I wish you both every happiness and . . . and an early homecoming."

In view of the damned funeral ahead, the cops would have nothing to do with the idea of keeping us out a little longer. Counselor, as usual, was "distressed" . . . but I didn't give up. "There's plenty of time for dying," I told one of the cops with a smile. "So why not make it easier for yourselves with a little Moët? Oh, come on, you can find some excuse, it isn't as late as all that . . ."

To demonstrate the powerlessness of his good will, he shoved his wrist under my nose so that I could see Time's needle jogging along. "If we aren't back at the jail in ten minutes, we'll be late for the cemetery. But wait a second: I'll tell the driver to stop before he gets to the gate, and you can have a drink in the car. But just don't say anything about it inside, huh?"

Maurice got out in order to pull the cork. I felt gay and blissful. They passed the bottle to me, the bright lava solemnly

257

pouring from its mouth; I licked the neck, then thrust it into my mouth and drank, drank interminably, until the bubbles were coming out through my eyes. I drank to our night, to the dawn that would follow it, I drank to *us*.

I have no idea how I got to the workroom, where all the girls jostled one another to kiss me while I was trying to get hold of the rusty old scissors so that I could open the flowers and the pastries; I kept repeating: "Where are the scissors?" And then: "Matron, can I give everyone a flower and share all these things?"

Like everyone else that day, the matron said *yes, yes* in a mixture of indulgence and prudence: I was at the same time a young bride (to be handled with kindness) and a drunken prisoner who had to be talked into going to bed. Since her delicacy coincided with my own languor, I did not have to be coaxed into following her to the dormitory. And so the Bureau of Prisons included among my wedding presents the little long sleep that I had been dreaming of for so many mornings.

Even without my husband it was a fine gift. I had never seen the matron allow anyone to go to bed in the middle of the day, just like that, without medical orders, without my even having to justify myself by claiming a beastly migraine or a menstrual hemorrhage; in prisons, it is either off-to-the-hospital or die-where-you-sit-on-your-stool.

But I was just knocked out: for this place it was a case lacking all official precedent. Matron would have given me hell if my bed had not been made officially and rectangularly; she turned it down for me, helped me to pull up the covers and disappeared without a sound, turning the key with a light, airy *clink-clink*.

I placed my feet on the footrest of the other bedclothes; my toes were still pinched in my beautiful shoes of the morning; I got out of them, put my glasses into one of them and my butts into the other, and got ready to sleep until the visiting hour.

The Runaway

My first conjugal visit, especially lengthened to a full hour. But how could I sleep when it was the time for feasting and there was neither feast nor time? In slow motion I reviewed the film of the past days, all the battling and pleading that I had had to endure in order to obtain all this, this nothing, these nine minutes . . . Zizi: "Yes"; me: "Yes," two seconds. The same amount of time as an X-ray exposure.

For the pre-marital examination I had refused to change my clothes; I had gone in my smock, dragging last summer's slippers through the dirt. The dispensary was gloomy and filled with women in nondescript swollen coats, who waited with documents in their hands and who were questioned by a cranky, sexless secretary with an exasperated voice, constantly saying "what?" and making them spell their names. For the X-ray I had had to go bare-breasted into a little cabin; a male prisoner taken out at the same time as I, a tubercular skeleton, was meanwhile getting dressed in the damp corridor and coughing: "Poor France, poor France . . ."

An angel at my shoulder and I about to be a bride . . .

Stale smells and heartbreaks, wiped out by those two seconds.

Oh, my darling husband, we are not to be like those children who go hand-in-hand-into-the-sunrise, we are not to pose for garish beribboned photographs of our wedding. Just photographs of our lungs.

We are far from paradise, we have to make a path for ourselves on earth, kicking and punching; we are sleeping on piles of damp sheets, you alone and I alone.

"Ah, the bridal night is still far off!"

Don't make me scream, girls, when I come back later from my first visit: there's no *madame* here, get that? The only call of the flesh has to be the litany of food-soap-laundry. I make my bridal *toilette* every day: you harass me enough. I wash myself meticulously, yes; fiercely, so that, when washing time is over, there is no point talking about it any more. So just leave me in peace. And, if you don't mind, please don't call Zizi *Zizi* when you talk about him.

Coming down the steps from the mayor's office, my husband said to me: "Well, that's the last of that. I'm not going to get married again."

But you will; you'll see, we'll be married again. Don't worry, Zizi, my body is obedient; it is my guitar against boredom, I play on my body, I deprive it, I indulge it, I offer it to silence, I create in it your image and the radiant touch of your hand.

I walk toward you and I walk beside you, the sun is on my back.

Let us walk in its reflection, let us be neither shadow nor flame. Or, rather, let the flames die down and become a great attending brilliance.

Suddenly I thought: the cops took our new family register to the office. I turn toward the wall again, the champagne gurgles inside me, and I smile into my pillow, remembering that booklet full of blank pages.

(12)

The last bites are the best; Simone hurries to fill her belly and admits through her busy jaws: "Maybe I won't have as much to eat outside."

She gets up to put her mug into her cupboard, quickly inventories the other contents, and announces to the world: "The first one I catch in there, I'll cut her hand off!"

Since no one appears to have been impressed, she slams the door of the cupboard and clumps back to her place—to her place "No different from anyone else's": she is no longer the deputy matron, no longer the sergeant-major, just a miserable corporal whose stripes are obviously fading.

"Would you have a match, baby?" she asks me. I have learned the routine: I carve it to a point with my knife, stick it into my thumbnail and present it to her with a smile: "Here, clean out your pantry." Whereupon she digs and digs into her gums and her few teeth with the match, clicking her tongue and breathing hard: a combination of actions that causes you either to blow out your own breath or to turn away in order not to be overcome.

I grant that each of us in her own way is disgusting enough and irritating enough, and, when the wind changes, the smell

261

of shit gets on your nerves; there are days when a girl who merely scuffs her slippers along the corridor makes you want to leap on her and force her to sit down; even I, in spite of the fact that since my wedding I feel like a new, serene person, relapse at times into behaving like the rest of them, deliberately becoming angry at abstract objects—the static on the radio, the over-salted soup, that Loving God of Prisoners who has forgotten our existence, etc. But fundamentally it's all the same to me. These months of group living have taught me how to make negative efforts: for instance, how to laugh like a maniac at ancient, stupid jokes, not to raise an eyebrow when some girl decides to take a piss in the bucket less than a yard from the table where we're all eating, and to keep eyes, ears, and nostrils hermetically sealed against all unusual sights, sounds, and smells. But Nicole is still in the stage of positive effort. Nicole is the tall girl in the blue jeans. That is, she used to be: on her second day, the matron confiscated the pants and put her into a dress.

It is evident that she has never been in prison before: she has the first-timer's reflexes, some clumsy, some subtle; she seems brazen, enthusiastic, a bit cynical, a bit sentimental; clever with her hands and reluctant to do a damned thing, clever with her head and expert at playing dumb. Before she arrived, I got tired of making puns and singing in foreign languages: to vegetables, puns are idiocy and foreign languages are nonsense. Now I'm able to fence respectfully with the matron or listen to the chaplain's sermons (we are enemies, but, since he's a magnificent speaker, why not listen to him?), I know that Nicole too listens to me and enjoys it. On the first morning, she asked me whether it was possible to strip naked to wash, whether the noise of her tooth-brushing bothered us . . . if only she knew that the majority of prisons have not yet been equipped with soundproof bathrooms, and that, when it comes to annoying little private matters, there is plenty that is worse than wiping your ass in public . . . Simone at once pointed out that the girls on work duty had priority in the bathroom and that "it would be a good idea" to finish fast in there because she had to wash herself and do a million other important things afterward.

I said: "But why do you wait to go in there? You're always the first one up."

"I don't have the time. I have to bring *your* coffee, I have to empty the slop, I . . ."

"Come off it, matron never told you you had to take care of the slop or the other stuff: in fact, she's always telling you to take your time and drink your java. You're the one that always raises hell and kicks the door if things aren't done fast enough."

But what's the use of nagging at her? Simone always finds and always will find excuses to get out of cleaning herself. I haven't seen her breasts yet, except now and then when she hooks her bra; as for her thighs, they are more often to be observed marbled from the heat and ringed with dirt than soaped by the bath mitt. As a matter of fact, you would never see them at all if Simone didn't every now and then feel a need to reassure herself and to ask us, as she warms her bottom with her clothes lifted above the stove: "Tell the truth, girls, don't I still have nice legs for my age?"

When there are waltzes on the radio, she starts whirling and showing off her brown mesh stockings, a bonus for some private laundry job done for the matron; it's Sunday, we're all gay. "Come on, baby, I'll show you how . . . Listen to that: God, could I dance to that when I was young!" It is at such moments that I become aware that the only grace Simone possesses is just this perpetual motion that makes my hair stand on end: when she stops, she's once more the ripe vegetable with gray hair and thick muscles. Aside from her gams, Simone has nothing. Certain phrases that come out when she's in a temper make me want to cut her tongue out, to snap the rusty scissors through every word, and then devotedly cut her throat, thoroughly, until her soul trickles out through every puncture . . .

"Calm down, girl!" I shout. "Oh, baby, who the hell ever gave me such lousy scissors? Sharpen them on your glass for me, be a good girl . . ."

I rewrap my thumb in the bit of rag that protects it against the scissors: they cut so badly that you have to press and press until your own meat begins to bleed . . .

"The asshole of all scissors!" Simone yells, lubricating the glass with lard.

Neighbors, friends, lovers, big shots, and nothings, they're all assholes to her. Simone's heart is a negative heart with room for nothing but the opposites of love.

The evening Nicole arrived, she tried to get me to go along with her in a bitter travesty of the girl, "that one's a loud mouth, she's another one that knows everything, she's such a show-off . . ." I replied that I left it to experts to make judgments on people they didn't know and that I liked Nicole very much precisely because of her manner.

Now no one mentions Nicole in the evenings. During the day, I'm the one who speaks to her. Nicole has no money, no clothes, not the smallest personal possession; she seems to be on excellent terms with loneliness and to have a solid foundation of pride; I can lead Nicole along the same roads on which I accompanied Maria, I'm not in any danger of forgetting the way . . . The problem of shit can always be solved, inside or outside. But Nicole doesn't give a fuck for the shit of being in stir: all she wants is to see her John, who was busted at the same time she was and is now in the men's wing.

She wrote a request to the superintendent, who sent it back with one word written on it in red: "Refused." The same as happened to me earlier. I suggested: "Write to the court: you'll be turned down, of course, but you have to follow the routine. Hope is a killer, we know that, but . . . in stir it's always good to have some request or other in the works. Here, take my pen: write to the court, I'm telling you."

Two days later both of us were called down to the office: for me there is a notice of trial. Having signed for it, I moved aside to make room for Nicole: meanwhile, to pass the time, I read the alphabetical list of inmates posted on the wall and, backward, the envelopes piled up around the mail guard, who was sighing as he did his censor's job . . .

Back in the workroom but out of range of the vegetable tribe, we began to talk somewhat more seriously. By way of preamble, I said: "I'll be going to trial soon . . . We'll have to have a coffee to celebrate that: it's freezing down there in the office. Your eyes are all red and your nose is blue . . ."

Nicole blew her nose, told me that the court had refused her request, and showed me the picture of her young lover. "You know, it's no lie to say that this photo is the only thing I own in the whole world right now . . . I wonder whether they send him my letters: I mark them *to be paid for on delivery,* but . . . is that allowed?"

Here it is impossible to buy stamps through the canteen, and so I can't give Nicole the one thing that I would like to give her. I suppose the protective manner and the paternalism from which I had suffered so keenly during the time I was broke must be equally repugnant to her; so, instead of giving outright, I swap: I buy her Wednesday egg or her Friday fish and pay her in cigarettes, I sell her writing paper "on condition that she help me with my math lessons because I intend to start a correspondence course," etc. I also have her read my letters before I mail them, on the pretext of having her correct my mistakes, for it's not easy to discuss mail with a girl who never gets a letter and is sick of writing them.

Yes, if I, the savage, the silent, the suspicious one, who hides her letters and numbers her cigarette packages, can make this terribly difficult movement of the hand, this "Here, read this," with which the letter is offered, I must once more have been caught in the velvet trap of friendship. Friendship is like those playful little kittens that it is better to drown at birth: they grow too fast.

At exercise time (it is beginning to be really pleasant in the sun), we half bare our chests, and push our skirts halfway up our thighs, and sit on the ground, not too far from the vegetable tribe though, so as to be able to enjoy the spectacle without taking part in it.

Simone and Solange have their heads full of school-day memories: they've drawn a hopscotch diagram on the ground and jump about on it like little girls, shouting: "Heaven!" "Earth!"

There they are in paradise; watching the clouds, I think that God the Father will receive them into his Eternity in the hope of giving them pleasure and that they'll play hopscotch with the angels to make the time go by; a thousand ideas, sweet ones or odd ones, go through my mind, I tell them to Nicole before they can get away, and we laugh . . .

Simone stands there suspiciously, one leg in the air: to her, laughter can't have three meanings: either you're sharing her fun or you're laughing at her. Then, when the laws of equilibrium remind her of her precariousness, she shrugs, makes her "off-your-rocker" gesture and goes back to heaven, pushing her pebble with the toe of her shoe. Although they were good shoes when matron gave them to her, Simone has worn them when she does the laundry as well as for her Sunday dancing: no, Simone will never have decent shoes, she will never have any other paradise than this.

"Hey, your turn, fatty, it'll make you thin . . ."

"Well, anyway, we aren't freezing our asses, we know how to have fun."

Their hair is falling in their eyes, their shoes are dusty, their

cheeks are red. The only harm I wish for you, my hopscotch-
ing Simone, is that you should have no soul and not have to
go and be bored in paradise; that you should live long enough
to drink the bottle dry and then break it on Fernand's head,
or Jojo's, and that you won't make the mistake of investing in
a set of teeth, because, you see, I'm not at all sure you'll be
able to barter them later.

The wind carries the scent of flowers and the sound of voices
above our heads, and you can't be sure whether these were
other flowers and other voices than those of last year. But
the wind moves along better than time does: reality weighs
tons; perhaps we'll be here forever. To make the film move,
one must resort to dates, to other Mays. "You know, Nicole,
there's something funny about May in the plural."

Once, on the first of May, a social worker brought me a
bunch of plastic lilies of the valley "because they won't wilt":
and, in spite of my low opinion of imitations, I thought of this
durable bouquet as possessing the mobility of a jewel of the
woods; there was my first first of May with Zi, when our love
was still as frail and soft as these two inches of lilies of the
valley . . . I dig into the grass and find things starting to grow
there.

"I swear to you, Nicole, people really do get stir crazy . . ."

"Pull down your skirts, you there!" the queen-mother cries.
"Everything's showing."

All I know how to do, matron, is show my ass, but that is
just childishness and not impertinence, believe me.

"And stop muttering behind your hand to the new girl, that
isn't going to get you anywhere. And what's more, after this,
the first thigh I see, I'm going to put an end to the exercise
periods. Instead of enjoying yourselves quietly with the
others . . ."

Very well, August One, I obey.

Let's go back to May, my heart: there was love then, although so different, so good! You put your hand over my heart, my love . . . I wanted to die so that nothing could take away that moment; I had so much need of hope in those days! And it had been necessary to despair and almost to die in order to arrive at certainties.

In six months it will be winter; now I find full-grown leaves in the grass, there is the wind, and summer is not far away.

But hell! As long as you love me, Zi, in May or June or January! . . .

(13)

"Hello, Callipygian Venus, did you sleep well?" Every morning I watch Nicole as she comes majestically down the stairs in her prison underwear, her knees bare, the chamber pot held away from her. The trap closes its jaws and opens ours. But I want to forge other bonds besides the shared chow:

"My friend—no, I mean my husband now—is on the other side too. What a lot we had to go through to be able to write to each other . . . officially. Your turn will come too, you'll see."

"If it doesn't come, I'll make it come!"

"The trouble is that in this joint it's almost impossible to get in touch with somebody."

"*Impossible* is not a French word," Nicole says.

This makes me impatient. "Look, old girl, I'm not a baby. Otherwise my man would have let me grow up quietly at home instead of taking me out to work with him . . . But that's something else again. I was telling you: we've been in plenty of jails together already and we've always found some pipeline to get through to each other: cooks, office personnel, even prison visitors . . . So you can imagine that we tried here too. Especially Zizi, because I . . . well, I was working on a more

269

radical solution, I'll tell you about that later. Anyway, it's impossible: the screws were smarter than we were, they had the canteen inspected, they probed pots and pans, etc. And aside from the laundry workers (who are well guarded and aren't there much anyway), I've never seen a man put a foot in the women's wing: the superintendent himself comes up to fix locks and lights, so there isn't even a chance of latching on to a workman either. We thought of everything, you understand . . . And then there we were in front of the mayor. Now we can write: but if you only knew the unbelievable censorship they do on our letters! Look, here's one of the latest: Zizi and I have been together five years. So he wrote, to mark the fifth anniversary of our meeting: 'We are about to begin another lustrum.' Well, they must have thought he meant a break, or a mutiny, because 'lustrum' was crossed out a dozen times. I had all I could do to make it out at all . . .

"Sure, I'll try an acrobatic escape act. Why not?"

Easy, Anick! "For the moment," I reply, "I want to wait and see what happens in court. Then it will depend on how tough the sentence is . . . But we *must* wait: Zizi and I, Roland and you: all four wait until everything is definite. Here, have a piece of chocolate: not too good, is it? What I like is those big sweet rocks, all full of nuts and cordials, the disgusting stuff that knocks hell out of your liver and your complexion . . ."

"Oh, yes, Anick, to go through a box of chocolates in bed on a Sunday, when it's raining for example, with a good book and plenty of butts . . ."

Automatically I add: "And a bottle of cognac and a good John . . ."

When the imagination takes off like that and memory carries you outside, the taboo is rescinded, and the conversation soon goes off on imaginary tangents, you gratuitously abandon the path of wisdom and in a flash you've turned down the lane of fantasy . . .

270

Certainly we're not spending all these years in stir for nothing; certainly we've managed our affairs properly and, the day we get out, we'll be off in a big car parading our decent clothes: we'll be peaceful and tolerant, we'll have lovely children to whom we'll be the most devoted and wisest of parents. The healthy joys of family life, work, chickens and rabbits, ten times as much water as alcohol in the aperitif, *et cetera.* But on the other hand money is unreliable; it melts in the heat of our hands; gasoline prices are always going up, and we're not fond of walking; perhaps life will last a long time for us, longer than our savings.

Yes, but in any case you need a passport . . .

Then go to the Prefecture.

I know, but I'm on the lam . . .

Oh, Nicole, this sun is making me lightheaded, I want it to be winter already. Summer in the can is murder for me.

"Let's face it," Nicole says. "Undoubtedly I'm going to be here all summer, it'll soon be vacation time . . ."

"Oh, please, let me have my trial first. There's still a good month and a half. But that's no guarantee against pissing away the whole summer in this rat-hole, you're right . . . You just wait and see, Nicole, those long June and July evenings, the night that never gets here, the days of sunshine in the dormitory . . . Oh, well, the birds at dawn will console you. I'll be gone by then, but, if it's any comfort to you, you can remember that I'll be locked in somewhere else and that I'll be just as lonely as you. Because, once the trial's over, it's everyone off to his own place. Men's Central Prison for him, Women's Central or some other joint for me. Unless . . . unless we can appeal."

"Would you still stay here, in that case?"

"No, but we'd be transferred together to the house of detention in whatever big city the Court of Appeal sits in. Mind you, the prospect of a weekly visit together is hardly a consolation: if we appeal, it means that we'll really have gotten it in the neck . . . Logically, we should be able to have the sentences made concurrent: that's 'juridically possible,' as the mouthpiece puts it so beautifully. Although he always adds right away: 'But the court has the faculty . . .' "

"The faculty of Law and Sciences and Jurisprudence."

"Exactly. But anyway, Nicole, I'll be leaving you in a few weeks, and I'd like to keep in touch with you."

"Well, then, write to me."

"No, that's 'strictly' forbidden. If I'm outside, I'll sign *your affectionate sister-in-law,* but from one jail to another . . . I'm not going to give you that crap reserved for those creeps that insist on knowing where you nest: 'If by chance we should happen to run into each other, dearie.' None of that; but all the same I hope we will have a chance to see each other. I'm not trying to pal around with you, or make any claims on you, but outside there's always something to do with people you like: something you find out or a job to put you on easy street or a way to spend money or just a chat or a drink in some late bar."

"Where shall we see each other again, then?"

"I'm telling you . . . but then who knows whether we'll want to see each other again, once we're both outside? who can tell how good either of us is at forgetting?"

"No, Anick, because this is my first time, and it'll leave a mark on me for good. I'll never forget all this shit, this suffocation, this pettiness, this loneliness. And by association I'll always think of my morning cigarette and . . ."

"Oh, please! You pay me back with that wonderful smile of yours, even in the mornings, when you come down the stairs and we say good morning to each other . . . What's your secret for smoking and still having that whiteness of yours?"

"Whiteness?"

"Yes, your teeth."

Nicole tells me the name of her toothpaste, some American

stuff; I write it down on the cover of my *Crossword-Puzzle Magazine: Fun for Everyone,* which is my weekly ration of this diversion.

"While you're at it," Nicole said, "write down my address too: Mr . . ."

"Easy, girl, easy! That's something else and it gets written somewhere else: in your brain. Spell it out for me very slowly, and look as if you're all involved in my crosswords; then you can whisper it to me now and then, the way people hum Sunday hymns during the week, and it'll just etch itself into my mind, never fear. My address—well, no fixed place of residence, like everyone else in more or less of a jam. But hang on to my lawyer's name, he'll always know where to reach me. I won't bother you with his phone number, they have directories outside; or, if you want to send him a note for me, he'll forward it. That's all. But wait a minute . . . Oh, yes, if you want me to ask Zizi to do any errands for your friend when we go to court, just tell me. I can see how you might think I don't mean any of this, but it's as much for myself as for you, I love rolling loaded dice."

"I don't think anything of the kind, Anick, and . . . I think I'm going to accept: this silence is so horrible . . . There are times when I'd like to blow up this prison, and even everything here around me—the girls, the stools, the dishes . . ."

"Oh, that! that just wears you down. Much better to fight the enemy with his own weapons: silence against dirty tricks, cunning against double dealing . . ."

I explain to Nicole the various techniques of prison notes, the variables and the constants. "Don't do it until just before I'm due for a hearing: since everyone is always writing like mad, no one will pay any attention. Write two lines together, on ordinary notebook paper, and condense as much as you can: one page should be enough. Give it to me, let's say during exercise, and forget about it. I'll stow it upstairs that night, and in the morning I'll simply come downstairs with it in my shoe . . ."

"Why in your shoe?"

"Suppose she gives me a surprise going-over when she opens up? I put the notes in their final hiding place only after my bath . . ."

"But she'll search you even more carefully than usual! She made you strip even for the dentist, I remember the day when she made you get undressed here . . ."

"Oh, yes, there's no heat in the infirmary dressing room and she was so afraid that I might catch co-o-o-old! Well, did anything extrude from my glorious nakedness?"

"But you don't exchange notes with the dentist, after all!"

"Why not? . . . Anyway, it will be the exact same thing: look, Nicole, the only foolproof stash, if you will excuse me, is *in the vagina,* as the English say . . . and you can be sure that in a triple plastic envelope it won't stain. That's the one place where no prison employee puts a hand. At the very worst, they ask you to put one foot on a stool and cough, or to urinate into the pot, but, if there's no croaker present, hands off. So . . . it's too bad there's no way of tipping off your friend, otherwise you'd have an answer, as long as I'm making one delivery I might as well deliver a letter going the other way . . ."

"I'm sure he's doing his damnedest to get us permission to write, but Justice is so negative. Why would the court say *yes* to him when it said *no* to me?"

"Who can ever tell, Nicole? the court might very well grant in the end what it refused in the beginning. It all depends on the way the investigation goes, and also on your own persistence: the pain-in-the-ass tactic. Everything comes in the end, Nicole, particularly what you've given up hoping for."

I was right. That morning Nicole could not believe that the envelope that the matron tossed down in front of her was

really hers; at mail time she no longer even looked up from
her book: there was no palliative for the pain of waiting, other
people's woes don't console you for your own, and their joys
are a matter of indifference . . . their joys and their faces and
their questions. I am still waiting for the right moment to
give my letters to Nicole.

"Well, are you going to read your letter or don't you give
a damn?"

"What?"

Her eyes still full of her novel, Nicole stares at me without
understanding.

"Yes, your letter: aren't you Nicole M.? I took the liberty
of looking at the address . . ."

In an instant the blue irises and the reaching fingers, though
still controlled, are voracious. "It's for me; oh, it can't be true!
I swear, Anick, these people will give me a heart attack. Oh,
Anick, it's from him! He got permission . . . they . . ."

"Don't get so excited. Read your minor miracle in peace and
then, if you want, you can tell me about it."

In the midst of her reading, Nicole stops to announce
coldly: "The superintendent is a swine." At once all the good
ladies look at her. Automatically my eyes swing round in
search of Simone, but all is well: she's cleaning the dormitories.
All the same I motion to Nicole to be quiet. But she shouts:
"Let somebody tell him I said so, I don't care. I still say he's
a swine." She gets up and begins to pace up and down with
long strides. "No, really, imagine that jerk sticking his nose
into my business! All right, he has to do his job. But there
are limits!"

"Look," I said, "the walls talk here. Sit down and just wait
until you cool off. Otherwise, matron will turn up and want
to know what all the noise is about, and we'll all be in the shit.
If your business is no business of the office, don't shout it out
the window for everyone else to know. Matron is not more

than ten yards away, reading her little love stories in the infirmary."

Nicole sits down and rolls a wispy cigarette with a shaking hand. I give her the sardine tin turned ashtray. "Take all the butts, they're all mine. All right, I have good ears. Just don't shout, and don't make it look as if we're hatching a plot, either. Here, here's my trigonometry book, there really is a problem I can't work out, pretend you're explaining it to me. Here's the protractor too: you hold it. Now, tell me why that bastard of a superintendent is such a swine?"

"You remember, in the beginning I tried to connect with some of my friends so I could have some clothes and some books: I showed you the letters, you could see there was nothing dirty in them, right? Well, the superintendent called my John down to the office, he tells me about it here in the letter . . ."

"I'm surprised that they didn't cut that out of it."

". . . and he told him . . . now listen to this . . . he told him I was writing love letters to a whole bunch of lovers . . ."

I recognize at once that this is the fault of my Christmas letter, the lovers bit is rapidly on its way to becoming a classic here. "At least the superintendent could have found a new gimmick," I murmur.

"Pardon?"

"Nothing . . . You have to understand that what the superintendent did arose out of a natural goodness: he disapproves of common-law marriages and does his best to get them made legal: careful, Nicole, or you'll wind up like us with a ring on your finger . . . The superintendent is no home-wrecker; quite the contrary. It's just that he isn't used to wives like us."

"All I know is that he's stinking bigmouthed. I'm going to ask for a chance to talk to him, what do you think?"

"I think that's the best way to put an end forever to the right to write to each other. Furthermore, if you don't make matron your ambassador, if you give her a sealed letter for her John, you're going to have doors slammed in your face as long as you stay here. If you ask me, the best thing is to forget it altogether." The same old advice, wearying and irritating, I know; but what else is there to say? "You have your love and your youth, and they're a lot stronger than all the stupid silly arguments. You two are like us two. You say you want to write? Fine, then write—but not to the superintendent. To him."

Nicole takes the notebook that I canteened for her. "Can I put two sheets in? one seems too short, and since they don't have a microscope any more than they do a dictionary, maybe if I write two lines together . . ."

"Well, why don't you ask me for a piece of decent writing paper?" Roughly, I set my pad and a package of envelopes on top of the photograph of Nicole's friend. I'll never learn how to give. "Look, keep it all, because . . . You're going to do me the favor of writing to him every day, aren't you? You can, you're only being held for trial. But be careful what you write, just talk about love, the little birds and the flowers, so that you don't get them against you right from the start."

(14)

"Matron's coming just the same, I'm telling you: she promised me she would. She'll let me have a coffee with you, girls, you'll see me all made up, hair done and all . . . street clothes make a difference. Don't tell her this, huh? Well, she put in my bag—you know, the pretty plastic one she gave me . . ."

"Oh, yes, that tired old thing from the five-and-ten . . ."

"Or three-and-four," Simone said, for once picking up on a pun. "Well, you know what she put in it? two of her own tubes of rouge, brand-new ones, and a box with some orange thing, something hard, it has a puff with it, what do you call that stuff?"

"Foundation powder? A compact?" Paulinette suggests.

"Yes, a compact, that's it. Imagine, with the good color I've put on here . . . Fernand will be waiting with a taxi (well!). I'll tell him to blow the horn. If you hear anything, doll, you'll know what it is."

"Are you going to walk to the station? Won't you go have a drink in the bar across the street?"

"Certainly not. Don't you remember what I told you about the job?"

I remember, even though I've slept since and want to sleep

again tonight. But after all Simone is leaving in the morning, one could make some last little effort. "Oh, yes, matron's friends are taking you on, aren't they?"

I speak very carefully so that Paulinette can laugh as much as she likes under her covers. Paulinette came in just as Granny went out, and has taken over her bed. (The rest of the harem is housed in the adjoining dormitory, which is larger.) She's always sleeping or reading fashion magazines, and it's up to me to keep up the nocturnal conversations. But Paulinette relieves me in the workroom; you have to make these arrangements if everyone is to remain friendly. This evening Paulinette can't sleep, she's too tired, she's "having her bloody time," as she puts it. This blood comes on late enough to save us from a lecture; if the sheets and the mattress are stained in the morning, the new laundress, Solange, will take care of them more readily.

The blood has not yet begun to flow: half asleep, a heavy blanket folded between her legs above the other covers and a good thick sanitary napkin under her bottom, Paulinette doesn't stir; but now and then one eye opens and sparkles between its lids. I play the idiot in order to try to take her mind off her cramps.

"It's a good thing you didn't wait for that damned social worker. (And a good thing that that really nice woman couldn't hear me.) So you're going to be a lady's companion?"

"Yes, she's old, and loaded with dough, and she has a bachelor son . . . Being as how the matron recommended me, I'll be in solid in no time . . ."

"In other words, it's just your dish?"

"And, if Fernand isn't there, I'll just ring the bell at the prison gate and ask for matron, and she'll phone her friend . . ."

I wonder where Simone, who can't even read, has dug up this romantic tale. No doubt matron has given her a synopsis of one of those little novels that please her so much, and thick-headed Simone has taken it as applying to herself. Well, we'll find out tomorrow.

"You all right, Paulinette?" I whisper. "Not too miserable?"

"I'm all right, darling, but I don't know if I can sleep, it hurts, I think I'm going to hemorrhage again . . ."

"Well, we'll let you sleep. Good night, girls."

Dawn is just breaking, but already the bundle of bad linens has been thrown on the floor near the door, the mattress has been stood up against the wall, and the tapping of Simone's feet is beating out a German march on the floor where our beds are resting; as for us, we've all given up being able to rest.

Paulinette has her nose in an old annual reader, and I am doing a crossword intended for calm mornings: Simone must have thought there was a shortage of tears and gnashing of teeth. But I no longer have the strength to put on an act for her: her ghostly silhouette in her ragged underwear, her sagging jaw, her beat-up shoes, the whole of Simone suddenly revolts me and fills me with admiration for the amount of inertia and pretense I could call upon until this morning: safe in port at last, one is amazed that one has been able to survive the ordeal, and then one is caught up in weariness . . . But this dawn is gentle, and it seems less sorrowful than most: I feel that soon we'll be joking together. It is matron's day off, but since she has promised in spite of that to come herself to release Simone . . . Ring-ring-ring: up. I give a hand to Paulinette, who is having great difficulty in all the welter of her covers and her preoccupation with keeping her knees together in order not to lose her sanitary napkins, which make a strange lump under her nightgown. The poor kid had spent five years in the House of the Good Shepherd before marrying on honest mulatto who has given her five children, and at the age of thirty she still has a childish convent-girl turn of mind; I find Paulinette at once irritating and touching.

Simone is beginning to simmer. "Well, what the fuck is the old bitch up to? Hell, they must have forgotten all about me!"

"Is it possible," I suggest, "that in spite of everything the deputy matron will be the one to let you out?"

"Of course not! But by the time she goes and has her coffee at matron's, and piddles around in the office, and then goes to get her keys . . . All that's so much more important than my getting out, I suppose! You work like a nigger, and then all you're good for is to get tossed away like an old shoe."

Finally, a quarter of an hour later, the deputy matron opens the door. All alone, of course. She takes Simone and locks the rest of us back in: "I'll be right back."

When we are all in the workroom, the morning is well along and Simone has not got out yet. "I'm going to take her downstairs as soon as the coffee's here," the matron explains; "she insists on having some, and on taking her morning bread serving with her when she goes. She has the right to it, hasn't she? I've locked her into the infirmary: now that she's been searched, I can't put her back in here with the rest of you."

In the heavy silence that follows all this news, there is the sound of spoons and jaws, and above and beyond it the noise of Simone's Hitlerian heels pacing up and down the infirmary. She must have finished her final mug of prison coffee . . . We all go to the window to watch the cow go by: there is not a sound in the workroom now, it is a solemn moment.

Finally we see Simone emerge outdoors. "Shit, you'd think she was coming back in!"

She does seem to be in a hurry. In each hand she has a beach bag; the five-and-ten job is nested in one armpit. One of the bags, which is broken, reveals part of a striped dress, the dress that she wanted to wear today and that only a chorus of "It's out of season, you certainly have enough other things to choose from" had persuaded her to thrust it back into the bag destined for bartering; her lips are carefully parted, perhaps so that she won't make herself any more of a mess: she has given herself a frightening job of make-up, with three layers of ochre foundation powder and an equal number of coats of purplish rouge, which is in perfect harmony with the rest of her outlandish costume: the matron's checked dress, the faded blue jacket in which she had arrived ("it stinks of gas and oil because I always wore it when I worked on the tractor"), the yellow scarf, the ...

"A real gypsy ..."

"Tap on the window to make her turn round, I want to see whether she managed to tease her hair into a World War I bouffant hair-do ..."

I drum on the glass with my wedding ring: Simone gives us her characteristic smile, waves *so long, girls,* and that's that. Simone has gone and we're still here, looking at one another rather stupidly, not knowing what to say or where to go.

"It can't be true!"

"You know, we're going to miss her."

"Shut up, I feel as if ten girls had been let out ... "

I cross my arms on the table, bury my head in them, and, my shoulders shaking, I pretend to be sobbing; all the girls rush to comfort me and it ends in a wild orgy of laughter, one of those mad laughing debauches that are as good as a prison beefsteak because they shut your epigastrium and twist your guts until they ache.

But it was a shoddy Eden that we had imagined: as it happened, the loss of Simone brought on a moment of silence among us like the pause that is observed in periods of national mourning. A minute extended into an endless Thursday, during which we drank our coffee and ate our spuds without being one bit hungry: it was all too clear, too calm, we were too relaxed, and this alone was enough to make us uneasy. No more fear of what might be said, no more hasty rushing about at coffee time; no more belches, no more farts, no more picking of teeth: in short, one of our prime irritants was missing.

Shit is one of the essential elements: in prison or at large, it is as much needed as air or fire.

The supply of it was replenished the next day . . . Oh, what a marvelous night it had been, without a single bang of lid on bucket, not one "shit-ass cooks," no cavernous snores: Solange limits herself to the burblings of a good-natured mother. She was absolutely astonished this morning when she opened her eyes to the walls of our dump: she all but bashed her jaw into one on the way to her morning piss.

"I thought I was still with you, girls," she says, ladling out the coffee. "All right, come on, who wants some of this slop? A step more and I'd have landed next to Paulinette. Which reminds me, Paulinette, how do you feel today, hon?"

Paulinette doesn't answer: her head remains stubbornly hidden in the hollow of her elbow while her coffee grows cold in the glass, deserted beside the packages of biscuits and other goodies (Paulinette can canteen as much as she wants, her Algerian is a generous husband). As gently as I know how, I say: "Darling, you must put away your canteen things . . . I know how you feel, it's awful. Come on, baby! Wait, I'll warm your coffee again, you have nothing hot in your tummy."

I put the coffee on my grill. The stove had gone when the warm weather arrived; and here there was not a hope of buying an alcohol burner or a charcoal stove through the canteen. "As a rule the women get their water from the laundry," the matron told me. I had tried it, but what I had drunk then, after the water had crossed the hall and been treated and stirred, tasted like the house brew, only worse, and gave one an idea of the taste of donkey piss. Tired of drinking piss and irritating my esophagus, I constructed my grill, which I lend only in special emergencies.

This apparatus is composed of an empty coffee tin whose upper part has been perforated and whose lower part is filled with oil; a piece of cork wrapped in tinfoil with a plaited rag through it serves as a wick. A second box is placed, slightly off center in order to admit air, on top of the first: this is my pan. A fatty, stalactite-like deposit accumulates on its underside— according to what Nicole tells me, these are oleaginous macro- molecules, but, macromolecules or not, they're certainly filthy. At any rate, this keeps the good ladies from using it when I have my back turned. In order to enjoy a steaming coffee, it is necessary either to be half dead, like Paulinette this morning, or to canteen enough oil to keep it going.

"Stop crying, you dope," Solange said. "We're all women here. Give me your clothes and your sheets and I'll scrub them right away, with the Johns' things, so that you can have them back dry tonight."

Paulinette's internal anguish is complicated by the embar- rassment of a little Good Shepherd girl; she goes on weeping. "No, no, I'll do them all myself, thanks. Leave them alone, I've been through this before . . . "

Then the java begins to work, and Paulinette comes back to life: with shining eyes and grieving hands, the hands of an Oriental dancer, she acts out one of her confinements: "This is nothing today: when I had my second little one . . . Say, Anick, do you think matron would give her permission if I asked her to send for my outside doctor?"

My "Why not?" is evasive: how can I explain to the girl that she is entitled to nothing but the medical care provided by the Bureau of Prisons, except in emergency or when a specialist is required, but that this mischance (an unpleasant one, admittedly) is only a mischance; that, if it were necessary to send every prisoner who hurt somewhere to the hospital or to her home to be examined by her private physician, there would be considerable more traffic in the joint, that . . . I couldn't do it: Paulinette is clean, cooperative, fashionably dressed and all, but she is not much disposed to listen to argu- ments based on practical considerations. She'll have to make the best of it; each of us is all alone, baby . . .

She was stained to the loins, and the blood had made serpentine streaks all the way down to her slippers; but, in direct
proportion to the disappearance of the red linens under energetic scrubbings and to the manipulations of the bath mitt
(we had all forgotten about our regular turns at washing),
Paulinette recovered her normal pertness and gaiety; taking
hold of one handle of the bucket, she says: "Then you'll boil
this stuff for me, Solange? Thanks, you're really sweet. Excuse
me again; I scrubbed it as well as I could, and I put a handful
of coarse salt in the water."

But staining bed linens is prohibited: matron was quite
angry.

While Paulinette repaired her mattress in the sun, the rest of
us told funny stories during the whole exercise period in order
to cheer her up a little. And to such good effect that, when the
supper bell rang, she was still gabbing with us. "Oh, damn, I
forgot all about the time," she said.

"It's all that Simone's fault," Solange said. "If we hadn't
talked about her so much" . . .

"And I could tell you plenty more," matron says. "But in
our job you don't have the right to tell everything. All the
same, when I think she had the nerve to say I was going to get
her a job with a friend of mine! . . ."

"That did surprise us a little," I say, making a flank attack
on my fried herring (for I was not about to let go of my
portion of fish for all the gossip in the world), "but we know
you're so kind that . . ."

"You know very well, Damien, that I never listen to
prisoners' gossip, and a good thing for you: if I had believed
everything she told me about you, you never would have got
out of the hole."

"No shit? Oh, excuse me. But I'd certainly like to know
what makes the imagination of a veg . . . of a Simone tick.
What did she say about me, then?"

"Oh, I can't even remember, there was so much of it! Oh, yes, one thing, when I had you take the stove out of the workroom: was it really you who helped her?"

I look sadly at my skinned herring . . . But, as long as matron has taken off on Gossip and Scandal, might just as well get rid of the vegetable once and for all. "Well, I did clean the stove and wash the workroom afterward . . ."

"She got me off in a corner and said: 'Look, matron, I have to tell you something: Damien hid the poker inside.' I said: 'Good, she's neat and tidy, if she put the poker inside the stove it'll be found again in October, when the heating starts again. You have another one for the laundry.' But she kept on about it, she even took hold of my blouse: 'No, matron, you don't understand. Inside, I said—I mean *inside herself!*' "

This time I forget all about the herring, I can't stop laughing, I'm crying and choking, I'm going to suffocate . . .

"Oh, lord! A poker as long as my forearm! It's not so much peritonitis, there's always a chance of escaping that . . . But since the other end would have had to come out my mouth, how could I ever have denied it?"

286

(15)

The supper bell had rung and Nicole had not yet come back from her hearing. To liven the atmosphere a little, I take bets: "Do you think she'll have a chance to kiss her guy? . . . Will she come back with bail? . . ."

I bet along with the rest of them, but my heart isn't in it. I'm too lazy to wash my plate and I give it to Solange ("take the soap powder that's in my cupboard"), I keep uttering stupid platitudes, and all the time my ears are on the alert, hoping to hear the bell of the gate before the bedtime bell. But we go upstairs without Nicole. On the way, in the corridor, my bathrobe brushes against the bowl of rice that, like us, is waiting for Nicole, and getting terribly cold: what a fine supper after a day with the law!

Solange's voice is intoxicating and Paulinette's is lulling: I soothe myself with their two voices, paying no attention to what they are saying, my nose pressed into the tarred wall. When my own trial is so close, I have no desire to stuff myself with these girls' tales; I have more than enough already tonight worrying about Nicole.

Nonetheless I must have fallen asleep: what made me open my eyes was the loud noise of the lock. What is it? A new arrival? A fire? The windowpane is still black . . . Ah, yes, it's Nicole. Good, then she had not gotten out on bail. I'm ashamed of my delight.

Sol and Paulinette had waked up too. The kid was rather frightened, and good coarse jokes are called into play to calm her down: "Baby, I sure wouldn't want you to split tonight. The matron didn't lock the door: all those big guys from next door are on their way over to give you a ball . . ."

"Oh, shut up, please!" Paulinette implores, half laughing, half trembling. "Solange, get up and see whether the door's closed . . ."

"What do you mean?" Solange teases from the warmth of her covers. "Aren't you a big girl? Go see for yourself. Oh, look! there's light under the door . . ."

"Where? where?"

Paulinette is sitting on her bed, examining the shadows and reflections made by the watchman's light as he goes his rounds. I think again of my runaway mare that has died this winter: "Hey, listen, there's someone on the wall, he's throwing pebbles at the windows . . . and there are more outside the door, listening to us talk, they're going to get a hard-on and bang-bang-bang they're going to batter down the door . . ." All the miseries of prison can be wiped out for a moment in a joke.

"It must be midnight, at least," Solange says.

"That's what you think! If it's nine-thirty, I'll be surprised."

"When you come down to it," Paulinette says, "sleeping like that cuts your time in half . . ."

When Nicole comes down from the dormitory, she's hollow-eyed. She must have spent the night weeping instead of sleeping. The girls grab hold of her and all of them start questioning her at the same time. "Well, was your guy looking good? You gave him a big kiss, I bet. That must have been great, I'll bet you'd go to court every day for that . . ." And on and on.

Their excitement makes me sick: these stolen kisses while a cop tugs at your arm—not for me. I'd rather get a letter.

"Come over to the window," Nicole says, "I have some decent cigarette butts, I grabbed all I could find, but there aren't too many. I didn't dare get into the magistrate's ashtray."

"I was just thinking: what about the note? you still want me to deliver it? Now that you've talked to him face to face, I wonder . . ."

"God, yes, Anick, more than ever. The hearing gave me a better idea of what's going on, I can go into more detail, that's all. Oh, yes: I found out what was behind my so-called love letters: the superintendent was shocked because I called some of my friends *darling,* but Roland knows damn well that that doesn't mean anything, he just laughs it off."

(*But he didn't ask her to marry him. Hurrah for us.*)

"Does your friend know my husband? I don't know whether guys waiting for trial have any contact with the infirmary." (Yes, Zizi is there: his old back fractures are acting up again.)

"Yes, he does. Just imagine, Roland's managed to wrap the superintendent round his little finger and he can go anywhere, emptying garbage, peeling spuds in the kitchen—a real servant, but it gets him around . . . and he knows your husband. I tipped him off, he's going to try to get into the infirmary the day after you go to court so he can pick up my deathless prose . . ."

"You should have told him to write to you too."

"I don't know whether he'd have the nerve . . . I don't mean to write, but to ask your husband to deliver it. Even I . . . but let's not talk about it, I know you hate thank-yous. Incidentally, I wanted to ask you: suppose she makes you urinate? She forgot about that yesterday with me, there was no time, and anyway I'm not as big a case as you."

"So what? Does Tampax fall out when you urinate? The

principle is the same. Besides, the note is super-absorbent. What always fascinates me is how my man can ever manage it. Almost always, he produces it like a miracle, right out of his hand, and when I ask him how he does it he just laughs like a madman . . . imagine, when we were in X he managed to bring out every note I'd sent him the whole time we were there: I think it was three months for breaking parole. So it's no use trying to figure it all out . . ."

"The same system as yours? Why not, if it's waterproof?"

"But hell, Nicole, in X there was a whole package of them! Everyone always keeps these notes with his personal things and takes them out to read now and then when they're feeling sentimental. You can't imagine how loving you can be in a note! But this time we're not dealing with love letters: I'm going to write to Zizi too, I want to spend the summer outside with him."

"Oh, I certainly hope with all my heart you make it, but . . ."

"There isn't any *but,* Nicole, I've got my mind made up to split, and it's all your fault, you woke that runaway mare of mine again. No, I'm serious, don't tell anyone a thing about it. I was kidding."

On the following Sunday the mass is crowded: now that the weather is warmer, God draws a full house. We can at least carry on our little deals all week long, but the men don't have as many opportunities of saying hello to their friends and doing business, exchanging letters and cigarettes, and blows and all that.

Matron herds our little troop into a triangular recess closed off by a wooden partition, and then waits until we've all sat down, neat and clean and silent, before she motions to the guard. At once he barks in the most charming tone: "All right, send them in!" and there's a noisy stampede: shuffling of shoes, murmurs and whispers, and our Johns make their appearance. Nicole has plunked down at the apex of the triangle, at the very end of the row, and I spread out as much as I can in order to hide her maneuver from matron, who keeps twisting in every possible direction to keep a constant eye on her flock; I know that Nicole is trying to find some aperture through which she can see Roland. I even had to stop her from stealing my scissors and sneaking them into the chapel so that she could use them to drill a hole in the partition: "Cut it out, Nicole! Don't you think I'd like to smash that partition too, jump over it, and just howl? You're not the only one, you know. I need those scissors for my mending. You don't drill holes in church, you cough."

"Oh, of course, you mean at the elevation?"

Exactly: at the elevation of the host, I slowly count to ten and then go *hum-hum-hum,* and ten seconds later Zizi answers.

"Roland had the same idea," Nicole continued, "and he picked the elevation too, but I told him no, it was already reserved. So then he had nothing to say . . ." They had finally fallen back on the Sanctus. In addition, after the Ite, there are about thirty seconds of general confusion during which Roland hopes to be able to pass a note to his beloved, and so this morning she's rather nervous. I smile reassuringly toward her end of the triangle. But from now until the Ite one has to devote oneself to singing.

The nursing sister had handed me some sheets, hymns from the First World War that no one knows and that she had detailed me to teach to my chorus of virgins. Talk about a job! Between Father Dupanloup and the love songs, there wasn't much in our repertory. During one of our rehearsals, Nicole had called attention to a couplet in a hymn dedicated to the Virgin, which had been inserted in the program "so that everyone could sing that one": the couplet was an invocation for which all of us should have had a special enthusiasm, for it began: "O our advocate."

I was in a fine mood; Zizi had well and truly rasped out

his cherished little *vocalises* ten seconds after I had rasped mine; Roland and Nicole too had exchanged greetings; just before Communion, the little sister, at the organ, had played a little number that no one knew except herself—and Paulinette and me, a little, in the chorus; I always like it when no one knows the music, it reminds me of those winter masses when I made it a point to stand on my freezing feet so that the sound of my voice could reach my man's ears. Our men are always on the alert for the slightest personal sign, a throat clearing, a rustling, the response to the Ordinary: "*Ad Deum qui laetificat,*" darling, how you too brought joy to my youth.

We had sworn together that, when we came to "our advocate," we would all be as solemn as prisoners in the dock; we were sure that we had run completely through all the jokes on the subject. It was Solange who was my ruin. First of all, the copy that the sister had given me was typed on watermarked paper dated 1899; on the pretext of helping me to follow the words, Solange shoves it under my nose; all right, I am still able to keep a straight face in spite of that; but, when we reach the fateful phrase, I automatically glance at the ancient paper and there is Solange's black fingernail underlining the word for me as she bawls ADVOCATE into my left ear and Paulinette batters my right side with meaningful jabs of her elbow . . .

It is impossible to die laughing while trying at the same time not to swallow your handkerchief and proceed with your part in a chorale, and all the more when it's a chorale as anemic as ours was: this couplet opens a sudden cavern of silence, in which only the wretched raucous voice of the sister persists in discordant flourishes; the chaplain, who is changing his clothes, sticks a surprised head out the door of the sacristy; seeing that there is going to be trouble, I both resume the couplet and regain my composure just before the final words.

And, as I accepted the plaudits of the good sister after the service, while protesting modestly that "in any event it must have been pleasant to God's ears," I feel my heart beating regularly and joyously: Nicole has smiled at me, both relieved and somewhat disappointed, so Roland must not have made a move and it would still be up to me to play mailman . . . I'll take this opportunity to ask Zizi what he thinks of Roland. Cynical thoughts go through my noodle: perhaps desire coupled with inaccessibility had endowed an empty little jerk with a glittering aura, Roland was a talker who did nothing, but Zi did not behave like that. Then it occurred to me that I was poking my nose into other people's business. Then again, I may be taken in by appearances, Nicole may be up to something that I can't fathom . . . And there's always the question whether she herself knows what she's doing.

But Roland's not what is bothering me . . . It's my friendship, which every so often comes alive and tenses, for instance when one or another member of the crew issues a hearty invitation: "Here, big girl, have a butt," or: "Be my guest and have a piece of bread and butter, and no arguments!"; or when Nicole laughs at their jokes, or when she supplants me as the scribe squatting down for this one or that one.

At night it's "Good night, Anick," and "Good night, Nicole," and I scowl into my pillow when Nicole's laugh reaches me through the wall; I scowl because, instead of spending thirteen hours locked like a sardine in a tin with Solange and Paulinette—second-rate sardines without much savor—I would prefer to be lying in the bed next to Nicole's and talking with her late into the night. Then I say to Solange: "Hey, old bag, take your shoe and give the wall a couple of knocks. Use the old beat-up ones, Sol, and be careful you don't break down the wall, that's all there is to protect us. Just listen to those old biddies in there!"

We are indeed even more like sardines than in Granny's

time: in order to be able to jabber more comfortably with Solange, Paulinette has moved her bed between Solange's and mine. Every night we have to perform like acrobats when we arrange the covers, if we're not to be constantly bumping behinds. If I sigh, there's no air, we breathe in each other's noses. But, since their intentions are kind ("mustn't talk too loud, poor Anick's asleep"), I have to keep my mouth shut. The first of these sardine nights, I suddenly came wide awake about two or three in the morning; I sat up and tried to figure the source of the *woo-woo-woo* that was ringing in my ears, wondering which of the two was breathing so loudly . . . *Woo-woo-woo,* the poor bitch was having a bad time, I had better wake them both . . . Then I realized that it was simply a bit of blood pressure in my eardrums. Well! I'm really beginning to fall apart, just the approach of the sword to my poor little ears makes them ring, darling!

What about it, Anick, getting scared?

Yes, I was afraid that, in spite of our pedigree, of our lack of haste to return to the "straight and narrow," etc., the court would give us the works; or else afraid that it would but that the sentences would be made concurrent; in a case like that, there would be no sense in appealing: nor could we plead not guilty and then appeal to be spared all punishment . . . especially since we have already taken so much of it. And besides, if they think they're being played for fools . . . If I appealed, so would the prosecutor: so then an increased sentence . . . No, none of this would fit in with my plans. For I cannot and will not try to carry them out without my man's approval and help. Let's take off together, dearest, for the same jail or the same freedom, I don't give a damn; but let's stay nice and close to each other.

I've been in this dump six months, as it comes: so it goes. To celebrate this anniversary, or rather semi-anniversary, a package comes. A fat package, friendly and honest, wearing glasses and speaking shrilly. My mind, long since allergic to soft soap, is immediately suspicious of her declarations of sisterly good will: "I'll canteen my cigarette ration and turn it over to you girls, and then all of you will have a little more, after all we're all here to help one another," and more of the same.

But, as time goes on and carries me closer to the courtroom, all sounds grow remote and merge somewhere behind me into an even monotone. This morning I washed myself all over, did up my hair, made up my eyes with a writing pencil; I look important, I'm waiting for my lawyer. Matron probes my hair, makes me take down my underpants, then leads me to the visiting room. It is a typical prison morning, guards and inmates wandering about comfortably in the halls, amid a lingering smell of coffee and nice stale bread.

The mouthpiece touches paws with me and we invite each other to the best place beside the cold stove and the moth-eaten table cover; we spend a good quarter-hour chatting about the possible amnesties in July, which we may be able to latch onto, because of course you won't appeal or only appeal part of the sentence, right? Oh, no, counselor, anyway I hope it will be nice on trial day, inside as well as outside the courtroom; and I take pleasure in observing the excellent cut of counselor's suit, his brown leather gloves . . .

I would like it to have already begun, to be there thigh to thigh with my darling husband; even if all those ridiculous mistakes had to be paid for, even if we are no less stupid than our punishment . . . After all, we did not have the right, we never would have the right, to commit such terrible errors.

What amuses me is matron's sudden solicitude when I return from the visit: "Well, Damien, is everything going to be all right, finally? What does your lawyer think?"

"Life at hard labor without deduction of time served awaiting trial and sentence," I say, to make her feel better.

The big package, who is with us to defend herself against a judgment by default, asks me about my lawyer's qualifications, for she needs a local man; she's from Paris, where she's been in La Roquette, which doesn't keep her from yakking on and on like a woman of the world, with her big mouthpieces and big mouth, and as far as I'm concerned she can shove 'em all. "Nico-o-o-le, my lawyer told me something awful; I'll tell you about it as soon as I finish this book." And I dive into my reading, deaf to every effort by the package to get through to me: she goes into raptures over my hair style, she weeps at my youth; in a word, she's a ball-breaker.

Excessive delicacy is as out of place here as the cultivation of sweet potatoes. "You can't imagine," the lady says, "but when I was in La Roquette some of those other gir-r-r-rls were *so* vulgar! One day one of them called the church visitor a . . . but I couldn't possibly repeat it. So I . . ."

Turning a page of my book with as detached a look as I can manage, I begin to hum. "Oh, take that little broom, Oh, take that little broom, And shove it up your a-a-a-ss." Then I whistle it a couple of times, and observe that a shocked silence has set in; I look up and turn toward Paulinette, who has no idea what it's all about: "Tell me, my darling little dyke, does it bother you when I sing 'up your ass'?" Seeing that Paulinette is getting ready to weep, I get up, go over to her, and slip a square of chocolate between her lips. "Will you massage me tonight, darling? I'll get some liniment sent up, my bones are aching." And, to finish off the package's revulsion, I kiss poor bewildered Paulinette almost on the mouth. Then I go back to my own kind. I have things to discuss with Nicole.

"Well, my lawyer's willing to act as a mail drop for me when I'm out, so you can write to me in care of him. But, as far as sending money to your lawyer goes . . . he doesn't want to do it. That's really going too far, since it's my dough. But what can you do? he's consumed with jealousy, he's afraid I

296

want to cheat on him. So we'll do it another way. Money's being sent to me now, there's no further danger of its being blocked—and I have plenty of time to pay off the costs of my trial and the civil damages and interest . . . they can all go fly a kite. So in the end there's going to be too much dough in my account here. You want to help me cut it down? I don't want to canteen for both of us because it makes talk, because there will be jealousies, because I have certain principles, because all the rest of it. But I do want *you* to be able to canteen. If I send bread to your lawyer, that's going to upset the Bureau: everyone knows who is whose lawyer in these small towns, it's all in the family. But, if I thought he'd pass the dough on to you, I wouldn't care about the Bureau."

"But don't you see? if you send him money 'for Nicole M.' he'll interpret that to mean his fee, there's no question."

"True: if I send my lawyer money for the appeal (oh, yes, I'm going to appeal, you'll see), with ten bills for you, he'll hide behind 'his professional integrity,' which forbids him to have any part in our deals, and simply latch on to the whole lot . . ."

By lunch time our imaginations have worked hard enough to have found a solution: I'll send the dough to last year's lawyer, the one whom my mother retained for me; I'll tell the superintendent that this is the balance I owe on old fees, he can hardly refuse to let me pay off a mouthpiece who might be *ex* but who's still been *my* defender. And this guy's hands will be tied: he'll have to do what I want; otherwise I'll spill the whole thing—my mother, the money that he sent to me on the side, all of it: a detailed letter written right away (Nicole, the paper, please) will tell him exactly what I want.

I'm becoming quite disgusted with the staff's bad behavior, which is making Nicole feel absolutely worthless, because she refuses to wash and sew for the whole joint, because she's taking it easy since she's only being held for trial, just wait until afterward and she'll learn, she'll have to give in and stop writing her "bullshit" every day; matron is having a wonderful time because Nicole can't talk back. And those bitches making a show of their charity! "We'll whip something together for you so you can look decent when you go to court."

Nicole is wearing a skirt contributed by the social worker, which I altered to fit her; her ballet slippers, which she has worn since her arrival, are getting more and more holes in them . . . I know her outfit's not "decent for going to court." But then why be "decent"? One might wish to seem pathetic, or upright, or as seductive as Phryne, but being "decent" is the least of our worries. "You know, it's true: you're always being watched in this dump. It's sickening. But, if I'm lucky enough to be outside this summer, I'll help you, and much more than I can here, I give you my word . . ."

Suddenly I remember that just a year ago I said exactly the same thing to Maria; what can she be thinking now? True, I sent her a package for her kid, and another at Christmas, I wrote to her mouthpiece . . . But that's not what Maria wanted most: I also promised her I'd split . . . The unexpected court action and transfer put it off, but . . . a year has gone by, and the horse is still whinnying in the desert between the two sets of walls. The time is endless and the sun is shining. Nicole's heels are full of chilblains, it's still cold, your feet are always cold in prison; we read old newspapers, we talk a great deal about our men, and we guzzle heaps of bread and margarine; I tell Nicole how lousy people are and how they have to be made use of in spite of that; I explain to her how frustrating and useless explanations are. "We have to turn ourselves into foxes, Nicole, and then at the proper moment we have to spring and bite like wolves . . . It's a matter of learning to wait for the moment to lunge, years sometimes, but sooner or later you have to lunge, lunge ferociously . . ."

I think of the importance of nice things, useless things,

imagination, a touch of lunacy; and here we are still, in this workroom where the linens drip mournfully onto the place where the stove was, where the sun hardly penetrates the windowpanes veiled with soot and dust.

Nicole seems lost in reverie as she stands at the window, her back to the room; but I know that she's plucking her eyebrows, I have lent her my tweezers, which I manufactured out of the cover of a metal box and usually keep hidden in my toothpaste. One hair, then another . . . a useful tool, that. Nicole comes back and secretly slips the tweezers to me; there are times when I can sense in her movements a solid ground for less innocent operations, for the dangerous life; and the absurdity of this life, so routine and gray and shitty, rises to my lips in words as I laboriously get up to take my turn at eyebrow care: "One thing sure, there are still a few people I'm going to make pay for all this before I'm through."

Careful, Anick, if you go on like that you won't have any eyebrows left.

(16)

I stirred a little cream into my coffee to finish off my snack, and then I changed my mesh stockings for nylons; it's one-thirty and I'm waiting for the police, my third coffee in my fist.

By now the package calls me Anick and I call her Margo. Margo is going to court at the same time as I am, almost immediately. She drones on at me: "You know this court a little, do you think I can get my time cut down? If not . . ." And so on.

You know this court . . . You know prison . . . Forget me for a while, the whole damn lot of you! I mumble "yes, yes, of course," I put more sugar into the java, and I let my mind go wandering. Footsteps and movement, Margo is consulting the cards, perhaps they'll give her better advice than I can. At the sound of the bell, we both put on our jackets and give ourselves a final brushing.

"No, not you," the matron says as we both rush for the door. "Just Damien."

It's only the lawyer, who has come *in extremis* to check once more that all the instruments are in tune; he doesn't even sit down: "I haven't had lunch yet." Poor fellow! and

300

me stuffed full of fried potatoes! "But I came anyway, I had
to try a case this morning in X, I've just come from the station.
All right, here's how it is with us: the chief judge has it in for
you, I spent a good half-hour yesterday with the prosecutor,
who promised me that he was going to stick to the letter of the
law, which is at least something. But the atmosphere is as
unfavorable as it could possibly be . . ."

(That figures.)

After he had put the bite on me for an extra fee, counselor
split; in spite of the said extra money all he'll eat today will
be a shopgirl's sandwich.

Waiting for the real ring-ring, I light Gitane after Gitane
and drink coffee after coffee: it's forbidden to take butts into
court, let alone a thermos. From now until tonight it'll be
impossible to smoke or drink.

Simone in the car: no, not Simone any more, it's Margo and
I whom the other girls are watching from behind the window
this time:

"Step in shit, it'll bring you luck!"

"We've all got our fingers crossed for you!"

How much clover there is in the courtyard! I thought that
our trial would be enough to fill the afternoon . . . Now I see
in my mind's eye: the funny judges, the summary questioning
. . . I try to get closer to the Johns, but I am separated from
them by a bunch of cops and attendants and all that I can see
is blue cloth. On an off chance, as I climb up the high tailgate
of the paddy wagon I hike my clothes to mid-thigh: if Zizi can
get an eyeful . . . But it's not until the Palace of Justice, just
before we go into the room marked CRIMINAL COURT OF
GENERAL SESSIONS, that we manage to brush lips.

Damn, there are no stalls here. On either side of the central
aisle there are ordinary benches with plain backs, and in these
the cops seated us, sorting us out, naturally: Zizi on one side
of the aisle, me on the other. Margo is pressed against my

301

right side, some man has my left arm pinned, and I am right in the first row, with my feet sticking out on the floor of the courtroom. I sense that, after it's all over, the same process will be repeated in reverse, and perhaps even more hurriedly . . . and I somehow have to get the smuggled notes out of their hiding place—they have been there since I got dressed, I was beginning to be aware of them—pass them to Zizi, grab the ones that he has certainly prepared for me, and stash them away . . . How is all this to be done? I begin to feel slightly nauseated.

A bell rings: Introit. The presiding judge, the assistant judges, and the prosecutor enter and take their places. At a little side table the hack from the local scandal sheet is already scribbling.

The first defendant comes up for questioning. While he is answering questions, I twist in every possible direction, pretending to straighten the seams of my stockings, modestly pull down my skirt, scratch a sudden itch in the ass . . . at last I have the quarry in my hand: the notes for Zizi and Roland are in a piece of plastic tied together with thread, inside of which there is a second plastic, and the whole is contained in a shampoo capsule sealed shut with a match.

My eyes follow the proceedings attentively; my hand, at the bottom of my pocket, is busy undoing the packets. I crumple the containers, useless now, into a ball, which I intend to drop into the gutter on the way out.

Margo is the next one called; now that my mind is partly relieved, I really listen carefully: I shall be an eyewitness so that the girl won't try to bullshit us again tomorrow with her courtroom virginity . . . My lawyer, whose services she had wanted, hasn't budged, and I forgot to say anything to him about her just now: he seemed so tired and so hungry! Oh, hell, let her take care of herself: he was there, in the lawyers' section, all she had to do was to ask to speak to him.

Oh, yes, our darling mouthpieces have all turned up: I eye their faces to see what they're cooking up. Counselor has pulled back the sleeves of his robe, so that his shirt sleeves show; his cuff, lying casually on the rail alongside his seat, makes me think of my husband's cuff in the breeze that sometimes comes in through the open window of the car. "Hands at ten after ten, baby!"

My love . . . I lean forward and go *hum-hum-hum* in his direction. Zizi doesn't see me; but my lawyer does, and he moves his fingers in a little greeting, which makes his cuff link sparkle, and I answer with a wink. He has taken off his glasses and he seems dreadfully bored; thus deprived of its solemn frame, his face seems secret and seraphic. It occurs to me that this must be how counselor's face looks when he wakes up in the mornings; I think of his bed, and, for about two seconds, my love is transferred to him . . . *hum, hum*. This time my husband, who is shifting his feet like a schoolboy in disgrace and gazing stubbornly at the tips of his moccasins, hears me and smiles. I wink again. Fortunately, Margo's back —she is still bullshitting at the bar—prevents the judges from seeing what we're doing. True, the prosecutor can see me out of the corner of his eye; but, inasmuch as he's concentrating on applying the law . . .

And in any case the result is already a foregone conclusion: in these provincial courts, the defendants appear, the lawyers plead, other defendants appear, other lawy . . . and in the evening, when everyone has finished, the discussions begin: the court retires to deliberate, then comes back with all the files in a bundle, as if they were prizes to be distributed; each winner's name is called, and he steps up to the bar again to hear his sentence. Whence my views on the worth of the verdict and the futility of putting up any system of defense whatever against it: you need only reflect that, with six or seven defendants coming up between the pleading by your lawyer and the court's decision—if indeed it does decide then —it is hardly likely that that decision will be influenced by the vocal exercises or the crocodile tears produced three hours earlier. It's a lottery, it's luck, it's a circus.

Under these conditions, why bother to assume an upright and repentant pose? I devour my love with my eyes, and neither grills nor bars exist.

Margo has finished, I push against the clown on my left so that she can have room to sit down again. She seems worn out. "They're going to give me the business," she whispers, "I can see that. To be finished off like that, without a lawyer, without any formal proofs! It's outrageous! Tell me, Anick . . ."

"Later, Margo, there'll be time to talk about it then: I think we're next."

Now I fall back on the principle that forbids me to touch the bar, I lean on my elbows, my ass to the room. I look weary and fearful; at my left, Zizi stands straight, not moving, but his hand rests lightly on the wood. I look at this hand, I see again the veins under the blond down, the familiar little scars . . . Interest and life are halted a yard ahead, where Justice is watching me. Keeping my eyes on Zizi's hand, I answer the questions, I take the hurdles, without emotion, without terror: I feel drunk and dreamy, all that's worrying me is those notes in my pocket—oh, not too much, but still . . . I want so much to put them into my husband's hand, and put my hand over his . . . poor baby . . . oh, lord, compassion is on the prowl, I'm going to smash the whole circus, I . . . and my anger crumbles into bits of laughter, because the presiding judge has a nervous twitch and now he's the one I feel sorry for: after each verse of his interrogation he throws in a drawling, nasal "Eh?": "And where did those treasury bonds come from, eh?"

Besides, he must be a little on the deaf side, so that my

quarrelsome tone of voice becomes a necessity . . . My deference, my weary, terrorized attitude, all that deserts me. It's
been a long time since I've stood before the bar with schoolgirl braids and collars, since my woman lawyer combed my
bangs with her own comb before I went into court, like a
mother teaching her big girl the art of being pretty: pretty for
the court, in other words without any frivolous hair style. Oh,
yes, in those days everyone was full of illusions and hope.

I take a deep breath; those were the days. I turn around for
a second to see whether counselor is paying attention to what's
going on: all O.K., he's awake and leafing busily through the
file. We go back to our seats as he begins his flight of rhetoric:
"Your Honors . . ." It is a fine specimen of eloquence, always
worth hearing, even though I find it quite difficult to recognize
myself underneath the verbal make-up with which he is
beautifying and improving me.

The judges take turns napping. The assistant judges have
comical faces too. One has hair that looks pasted down in
sections, the other looks like a leonine cattle slaughterer.

Counselor is caressing my ears, I feel fine and light, we'll
have our sentences made concurrent . . . Stop! I don't want
that. What the mouthpiece is saying is true, just the same: that
we've never been given a chance, that ever since adolescence
all we've known is one kick after another, and none of the
scars have had the time to heal . . .

My weariness returns, as well as a vague euphoria and
a whirlwind of possibilities . . . no, no, no matter how you
look at it, it's too long a haul, there's too much cold and too
much hunger before the end, I don't want that. What I want
is the sun shining through the high windows of the courtroom,
I want Zi's hand on me. What is being discussed, of course, is
not sunshine and the hands of loved ones: the theme is "the
need to compel understanding, through an isolated action, a
bold rebellion, of the injustices under which all of us labor; to

do, in the name of all the prisoners in the world, what all prisoners dream of doing." The present seems to have shifted somehow, to be lagging far behind, and my hard head has already gone leaping ahead.

"My play is finished, all I have to do now is write the poetry." The poetry? I thought of some that sounded wonderful, but the verses didn't rhyme; Zizi will have to make them hang together, and then, instead of being spectators at our own drama, as we are today, we'll stage and act it ourselves. Ah! just now counselor said something about the "ill-fated couple," this *us* from which we can never again escape; bravo. Never fear; there is more joy in our sorrow than in your joy, gentlemen. So suppose we do prefer to live, to live high, to get drunk, laughing the while, and then suffer and wait until we can laugh and enjoy again? You walking corpses, get out!

"Clear the court," the presiding judge orders.

It can't be true, I must be dreaming! No, the cop is already giving me a push in the ass, "Let's go," and suddenly I am in the corridor again, in Zizi's arms, his lips are biting into mine: "O my darling, my dearest . . ." I am dreaming: I'll find myself back on the bench, squeezed between the unwashed prisoner and Margo's gray coat. Never mind, the dream is worth it. Zizi is crushing me in his arms . . .

My head is spinning, and I have to free myself. "What's happened?"

"Don't worry, just some cunt case being heard in closed session, it gives us a break for a minute . . . Anick, Anick!"

This time my husband's body is quite real against mine. I lose myself in a kiss that embodies the whole sum of our exile and our hunger. Laughing cops and prisoners watch every second of it.

Then I remember. "Business first, Zizi: can I have a minute?" I go to ask one of the cops to take me to the wee-wee room.

"Gotta wait," he grumbles, "somebody's in it." In fact, a whole line of males is standing patiently at the foot of the stairway. I go round all of them, my angel at my ass, and take the stairway that I know so well, for the road to the john is the same as the road to the chamber—the magistrate's chamber, I mean.

When I go back downstairs, I nestle against my husband again; but this time I had the forethought to get my back to a window: what with emotion, high heels, loving nervousness, I might stumble any second. Margo started maneuvering to turn us into a trio, but, after introductions in which there was absolutely no warmth, followed by strictly private exchanges of glances and whispers, she finally got the message: isolated now beside a radiator, where she pretends to be absorbed in the various documents that she has brought in a bulging brief-case (and that she had tried to offer in evidence just now), she makes me feel ashamed, and I want to call her back . . . My lawyer bursts out of the courtroom like a gust of wind: I have an idea, I'll introduce him to Margo, since she's so keen on it, and let the two of them take care of themselves.

Before he leaves, counselor says to me: "I won't wait for the decision; write to me tonight about it, would you? and . . . try not to laugh when you look at the judges: my dear lady, that makes a most unfortunate impression . . ."

I gave Zizi the notes, but I can't help quoting parts of them to him, of course. I remember to ask him where he'll hide them: "In my mouth, naturally, since I don't make chit-chat with the screws . . . I have a feeling that we're going to get a real kick in the ass. But then, if they run the two things together . . ."

We're getting away from the subject. I bring us back fast, sitting astride my runaway mare: "You and your concurrent sentences! The lawyer did a beautiful job, I'll grant that. But how can you hope to get anything good from those people? If they give us concurrent sentences, then at the same time they'll add something to one of them: if you get a year added to the two you already have, or three years to be served concurrently, it comes to the same thing . . ."

In the end we're really battling each other, each head butting the other with its own logic, our irritated kisses become bites . . . Zizi really wants to have nothing to do with any runaway! In his hands, mine have become cold; I want to bawl like a baby deprived of its hobbyhorse, I want to smash my love's head because inside that head there are things that I reject, that I don't know, that I hate . . . "What are you looking for, acceptance into society again?"

"Oh, Anick, try to understand . . . I need you, I need your love for a long time, forever. What I want to do is get this rap over with and then be with you until I die, without this dread of prison, of being without you, of . . . You know damn well that we could be picked up in twenty-four hours— remember Christmas—and get six months extra for the damages, with ninety days in the hole . . ."

I can feel myself getting nasty. "So that's what you're afraid of, the ninety days!"

"Oh, baby, what I'm thinking of is . . . everything."

"No, Zi, not that. Give me any other reason you want— good sense, being practical, weariness, anything you like—but please, please don't let fear influence you. What we deliberately chose to be, and what keeps us in this circus of the can and the courtroom right now, can't live with fear. If you don't want to split, all right . . ."

"You fool! I want to split as much as I want you, and you know it. But later, on the up and up, with a decent set-up . . ."

"And a dozen bastards in the house . . ."

"Don't be cruel, darling. I've had plenty of time to make you plenty of bastards today. Say, how would you like to go make love on the judge's carpet?"

The Runaway

"Ah, that's more like you! But let's be serious. Do you remember the last time we got back together on the up and up, to use your phrase—full of good resolutions and all the rest of it? what happened? . . . After a couple of weeks of taking it easy, we got right back on the job: and that was where we made our big mistake: trying to go on putting up a good front. The law had its eye on us, and we were just suckers . . . We thought we could go on forever leading a double life right under its nose, working legit in the daytime, stealing at night, and on top of that having fun and keeping things up and taking care of our friends . . . What was the result? six months later we were back inside. And how did they manage to bust us, eh? By finding us quietly at home because we were so sure that we had thrown them off. More bullshit: one address that was really ours, and another for front, which made twice as much work and twice as much expense . . . Whereas, if we just plain vanished into the landscape . . ."

I am well aware that Zizi is counting on leniency from the court to get both of us off that runaway horse that I'm dragging him off on against his will: if we don't appeal, we won't be able to plan anything together because then we'll be sent to separate prisons.

Zizi, you love life more than I do . . . I know, I know well enough that I'm just making it tougher for you, I'm making you put up with all my dirty little female tricks, inventing all kinds of fake pretexts . . . And you're trying to bring me back to my senses, to time that marches on, you're putting all your hope in the future . . . But the future is so far off! All right, if you refuse to go along, I'll repeat that Christmas, even if I break my neck trying . . .

I start again: "When I get something into my head, you know . . ."

"But at least wait for the court's decision! You never can tell, they . . ."

"Oh, that! Look, I hope you do get concurrent sentences, for yourself. So then you can do your time and scratch your back raw in prison denims . . . But if we could just have this summer together, Zi, the way we are now? don't you think that's worth the chance? And, if we have the summer, why not the fall, and the winter, and years and years more? Just a minimum of caution, fake papers . . . Why wait all that time?"

"No one ever serves a full sentence, you know that as well as I do."

"Oh, sure! Paroles, petitions for clemency! The Bastille Day amnesty that you hope for every year and that never comes! Oh, sure, it helps to make the time go by, and sooner or later there does come the day when the gate opens . . . But that's all old stuff to us. And we've tried everything outside too: you in stir, me in stir, or both of us on the lam together, or taking it easy somewhere—everything except one thing: breaking out of the same prison together."

Zizi's eyes are beginning to fill with a strange light, almost excited; his hands are hurting me. "You know I always listen to you in the end, Anick . . . Is there anything I wouldn't do for you?"

"Is there? . . . Do you think you can move fast enough, then? The appeal could be made before vacation time, that doesn't take long . . ."

Zizi smiles: that's a good sign: because when he does the sphinx bit there's always a place for me in the puzzle.

We get back to the jail long after bedtime. Matron searches us in the empty workroom; my bathrobe, neatly folded, is already on my stool: a little gesture by Nicole, no doubt.

The matron is nice enough, in her own way, which amounts to little outbursts like: "Oh, well, then, that's not really so terrible," when she hears the verdict, and to suggestions that she go into the kitchen to see whether she could find us some hot soup . . . broth for women who had just spent the day being torn apart! I'm tottering on my pins, the cigarette is shaking between my fingers; Margo has sat down and is telling the story of the whole afternoon.

"Are you planning to spend the night here, then?" I ask her.

"Oh, I'm not all that tired, but my throat is parched, absolutely parched . . . If only I had some fruit, but I forgot to canteen any . . ."

That's enough: I understand. I unearth an orange from my supply and toss it to her: "Here, suck on this in bed . . . Time to go up, matron?"

I drape myself in my bathrobe, bullfighter style, so the office will know tonight that Damien is taking it well and is ready to resume the battle. But just the same, even though it doesn't bother me too much, I have to admit that, as always at the end of a trial, I'm surprised by the harshness of the sentence. I didn't want concurrent sentences and I didn't get them, and neither did Zizi.

Solange and Paulinette watch me as I come into the dormitory: what I say will tell them whether they should smile or frown. But I say nothing, nothing about my case at least. "Oh, say, Solange, our pride and joy, is wearing a nightgown: it must be going to rain tomorrow. What a disappointment not to see your knockers. Who gave you that present?"

It must be a gift from the matron, who is no doubt about to start the same thing she did with Simone . . . I ask how the afternoon has gone, whether everyone behaved well and ate nicely, whether they had managed to get by without Damien, the pain in the ass, etc. "Oh, you made my bed for me—thanks. I'm ab-so-lute-ly beat, ab-so-lu-te-ly. What bothered me even more than the sentence was having to make my bed when I got back. You're good kids, and I'll do the same for you when it's your turn."

Since both of them have already been sentenced, this doesn't get me very far. I slip quickly between the clean sheets —they had even been changed—and bite into my evening apple. "God, it feels good to stretch out the pins! Believe me, girls, it wears you out to fuck standing up in a courtroom corridor!" Then I tell them what has happened; I announce the sentence without putting special emphasis on it; I avoid the prying questions:

"What about the old gal? how did she make out?"

"You'll rub her nose in her own shit, won't you, if she starts snowing us about it downstairs?"

I pretend to have understood absolutely nothing of Margo's case; as far as I knew, it had merely been adjourned for a week. Having thus finished my job as court reporter, I turn my back and press my nose to the tarred wall.

It is impossible to shut Margo up the next day; in no time she gets our goat, and we mockingly conclude every sentence she speaks with an "Eh?" just like the judge's; at ten o'clock I begin singing all my jail songs, beginning with "Comrade, where are you now?" and going on to today's "Marie, Marie"; by two o'clock we are muttering against all the bastards and singing the *International*. Little by little, then, as the afternoon goes on, "Eh?" is heard less often, our miseries recede into a secondary plane of reality, and the smooth old routine once more alternates with little rows and little vexations.

I for my part am waiting for the mail. In the corridor, Zizi gave me a big light green envelope with a piece of paper the same color inside. "Just as a change from the prison stationery. Keep this for something important." I had entrusted this envelope to Margo to keep for me in her huge portfolio of supporting evidence, and then just now I had used some of the new paper for my bi-weekly marital letter. "May this butterfly bring you all my love," I began.

On the day after the slaughter you always feel sentimental

and a little groggy, like the day after a good night of love-making; the pain does not really hurt yet. In my letter I was careful not to make the wound bleed: I wrote about nothing but love. I asked forgiveness for the wretched fact of being me, with my thick head, unable and unwilling ever to backtrack on a road I had chosen to take. The letter also contained a code phrase by which, in his next official letter, Zi can let me know whether he agrees to split.

Evening, night, dawn, day.

I wait for that letter as for the Second Coming. To keep myself from screaming, I pace up and down the workroom, I sweep it, I clean the little burner.

Will Zizi choose to follow me along my desert paths or to pursue some other wilderness road of his own? Perhaps because I'm younger, the future is less important to me. I have plenty of time left for suffering. Of course we'll have to do our time. But we'll prepare it, we'll decide when it will start, we'll stop being the thoughtless clumsy idiots that we've been before. "Oh, Zi," I whispered that night as I bit my sheets, "I'll do and be everything you want, I'll make you forgive me for having forced your hand, you'll never blame me for this runaway even in your mind."

I dreamed then, and a film seemed to be shown on the virgin screen formed on the dormitory wall by the windows lighted by the watchmen's flashlights.

I don't dare superimpose the pictures of the past on the days of the future, I feel superstitious; awake, I uncross knives, I raise hell when some girl says *bad luck,* or throws spitballs . . . the stupefying surroundings have an osmotic effect today.

"Has the mail come, matron?" I can say that without exciting curiosity, everyone knows that all that I live for is my letters, and that this morning I have more reasons for waiting than ever. Zizi's letter will bring me back to life or kill me.

Had I been loving enough, humble enough? Had the pressure of my body against Zizi's in the corridor reminded him of all his promises?

All but dead inside, I wait, quietly smoking my Gitane; the most terrible thing is the knowledge that nothing will kill me, I was exaggerating . . . life and hope are more thick-skinned than I, than a rejection or a defeat. "It's hard to be hard," I say to Nicole, who is all absorbed in some love story, turning the pages two by two.

I assured her that her note had been properly delivered to Roland, I read to her—while pretending to sort out all my various documents—extracts from my husband's note: it is an unsure note, as unsure as he himself was in the corridor: "If they throw the book at us, I'll choose my destiny . . ." I burned it, and threw the ashes into the bucket.

I know the mean Zizi and the nice Zizi: all I hope is that our shared anger will be stronger than our diverse intentions, that the sentence will have smashed only his dreams of yesterday, not those of tomorrow. Tomorrow is summer and happiness. I smile, remembering that when I arrived here the dream had been just as close, just as warm: but the date for the break was also the date for Father Christmas. And it had had to fail, furthermore, because I had chosen the short-cut of solitude instead of staying on the road of *us*.

I tell Nicole about my spoiled Christmas. ". . . and I got it from a good source that the superintendent had not been all that kind, that he had sent my letter to the court officials. And I, like a jerk, had given my word to take it easy, I was full of thankfulness and good will! He had thrown my letter into the trash basket in front of me, but he had taken care not to tear it up . . . anyway, my promise did one good thing, it calmed Zizi down and forced me to behave myself until we get out of here. But otherwise I didn't promise anything . . ."

Yes: the lone wolf, the desperado until we met, Zizi always reckons with the possibility that I may wake up one morning with a big *no* to love, just as I said *no* to prison and to everything else that no longer means anything to me; he loves me without big talk and without holding back; and I have always gambled on the absoluteness of that love, I took it lightly, I'm a little disgusted with myself, but there was no choice . . . I repeat in my mind the promises made at the Palace of Justice: I'll never again be sulky, never again be nasty: if Zizi gives me this break, it will become a source of marvelous memories; far above and beyond the pleasant dream I construct infinities of tenderness and joy . . .

"Damien! the mail's here."

I run through two letters, from my lawyer and from the church worker; then, taking advantage of the minor confusion arising out of the arrival of lunch, I go to the window to savor the third, oblivious of the girls who are guzzling and at the same time reading their own letters aloud.

My heart melts, I think I'm going to scream . . . My hand covers the letter, my eyes wander toward a vague heaven, I manage to get hold of myself, the ticker calms down in my chest, good. Now I can read the letter again: yes, the code word is still there, it has not fled into a storm cloud, Zizi really wants to, Zizi has chosen *us*, he . . .

"If you've finished eating, Nicole, come here a minute . . . Look: he's in, he agrees, he . . . here, read it yourself. The code word's there, it's *yes*."

Nicole hands back the letter with no comment except a big smile. "Men are really a wonderful invention, just like those birds on the wall . . . look at that one there, near the garbage can: isn't he pretty?"

Yes, Nicole, I feel light, just as light as that bird on the wall. But it is time to talk of heavy responsibilities: "The superintendent will certainly order us transferred as soon as the appeal has been heard: this pair of burglars who walk through walls creates too many heavy responsibilities for his wife and himself. As far as they're concerned, the promise I made at Christmas is just shit. He judges and prejudges everything on the basis of the damned past, the precedents that frighten both of them. I split, I tried to split again: so, logically, I'm bound to re-try to re-split. Before I got into the life, I was a Girl Scout, but I have to admit that, if a really sure thing had come up, my scout's honor might have wavered . . . especially because this kindness of theirs . . . if they didn't shove me into the hole, it was only because it's not warm there in December and the discovery of my poor frozen corpse some morning . . . but then they have my word, let them hang on to it, and may it do them a lot of good: I don't belong to this world any longer, in ten days I'll be out of it . . ."

Nicole wants very much to be tried before my transfer, because she has had an idea, and a very simple magical one: "I'll appeal too and I'll join you . . ."

"I'd love it, Nicole, but . . . Don't forget that if you appeal that automatically acts as an appeal for everyone that's in the thing with you: what would your friend think of it? If I'm lucky enough to still be here when you go to court, and see you get all dressed up, pick up your possessions and walk on parole, I'd love that just as much . . . But look, talking about parole is just talking in a vacuum, like talking about splitting or anything else: we always talk in a vacuum here, and every time we talk too much."

"Anick, I can't offer you anything or promise you anything: I have nothing and I don't know much. But I'll never forget you."

Nicole's eyes are very blue, they're like a true caress.

The superintendent now appears in person, bringing an extra love letter for me. "I gave permission for a supplementary letter, in view of your husband's decision."

Zizi is now playing the lord and master who settles the fate of the family: "I have considered carefully: I will file an

316

appeal. Since it is the logical thing for us to present the petition jointly, I should like you to take the necessary steps on your side."

A vast endless sigh. I have made the longest leg of the journey, I've won. With Zizi I'll certainly win again: now the road into the shadows will be no more dangerous than the sunlit one, there can never be any accidents so terrible as those that had brought us so close to death.

Don't touch the wheel, Anick, let yourself be driven now.

Therefore I file my appeal on the form provided by the superintendent; I write to the mouthpiece to go and jog the prosecutor, because, "if he would be kind enough to have us appear before the court goes on vacation . . ."

This was the *if,* the shaky part of the program: provided too that we were not transferred before the end of the vacations. Hell, three months more or three months less . . . I discipline myself against impatience, against restlessness, I make myself hold out, eating, writing, being nice and being sly with the good ladies; and I take advantage of these nights before the battle to sleep a great deal.

Part Three

Part Three

(1)

"Is it possible that the bell didn't ring? Did you hear it, Anick?"

"No, but maybe mama matron is just loafing this morning. Come on, let's get up."

Paulinette is still in the arms of her Mustapha. We shake her awake. "Quick, darling, the keys . . ."

"Oh, let me sleep, you girls," Paulinette says, but nevertheless she hurries out of bed and begins to fold her covers so that she'll be the first to be ready: just as in the Good Shepherd. She's a kid among her own kids, the good person among the bad ("I know how to behave"), and how to behave is just about all she knows. When we play belote—the only vice that anyone has managed to teach her—she's my partner; ten times in every game, and always with the same pleasure, I say to her with an unctuous solemnity that the Mother Superior would have respected: "It's your turn, Paulinette, my child."

Paulinette hurries and hurries . . . Too late, the matron's footsteps are at the landing, the key turns, and the first one ready is Solange. She gives an enthusiastic "Morning, matron!" and disappears, the chamber pot in her hand.

"No, no, you can stay in bed, it's not time yet," the matron says. "Except you, Damien."

I recover immediately. "O.K., so long, girls, I'm on my way. Say good-by to the others for me."

My fur jacket is hanging on the stair rail; matron knocks it off, "oh, I'm sorry!" (she addresses the animal), I pick up the opossum, which is ingloriously wiping the dirty floor, and, throwing it over my old bathrobe, I ask: "Am I leaving, matron?"

In the workroom my suitcases are enthroned on the table among the regularly placed knives and spoons, the lids-turned-ashtrays full of matches and butts: obviously, if I forget to empty them . . . Suddenly I picture the empty space today at my place, I imagine the women quarreling over my part of the cupboard, my soap, my ragged slippers . . . I'll leave them nothing else, I have nothing. But Nothing occupies a prominent place this morning. It must be pointed out that matron is much more skilled at messing up a suitcase than at packing it: she has made a hodge-podge of all the odds and ends that I had her arrange every time a new arrival was searched, losing a little more ground each time . . . And to think that when I arrived I had thought I was in heaven! True, I was just coming out of hell, and the roomy closets, the steaming shower, the quiet nights spent smoking and chatting with Jane had all seemed good to me. And then . . . the loused-up escape, the euphoria of good resolutions, the wedding, the comfort, but also the vegetable, the lice, the crowded workroom, the resurgence of bad resolutions . . . Yes, it's about time for me to take a powder, my nerves are getting ragged again.

Matron has become a kind of Marie-Antoinette all bursting with hypocritical compliments; I refused to lie in the grass with the rest of the vassals to lick the queen's feet, and little by little she has caused the light of her respect and her interest to shine upon me.

As for me—instead of rubbing my nose in the grass that the queen's chickens and ducks had fouled, I had chosen to pay my homage to friendship, I had shared the warm stone of the steps with Nicole. Stones barely made clean by the scrubbings, however violent, of the cleaning women, dirtied by a thousand feet, a thousand feet in shitty shoes. We repaired the soles of these with pages out of old magazines; and the matron, who doesn't approve of people tearing up newspapers, was annoyed that we gave her no ground for criticism because we were careful to use only paper from publications that I canteened. The stock of back numbers of *Confidences* and *Intimité* was treated with ostentatious deference.

Yes, we had lost the favor of the queen because the queen doesn't like subjects who escape her domination. Ever since my lawyer has become Nicole's, she has virtually ceased leaving herself open . . . The clothing problem has likewise been resolved: once more it's the social worker who got us off the hook, with a lovely summer dress, almost new, which she had intended to give to the homely ones, the ones who really know how to wheedle; but, given the length and the width of the thing, no one could wear it. So Nicole had suggested very sweetly: "Well, perhaps a big horse like me . . ."

The vote to give her the dress had been unanimous, or almost; the only opposition vote had come from the matron: "It's bound to be too tight for you, with those big hips of yours . . ."

With money and clothes once again, Nicole no longer has anything in common with Marie-Antoinette's lambs, and the queen, whatever she may try to make us believe, prefers to have everyone bleat in unison.

This morning she is smiling, distantly; and, as I repair the mess she made in my luggage, I catch the thread of her silent thoughts, I sense the meaning of the triumphant little corners of her mouth. For some days I have already been giving Nicole my final counsels:

"Don't run through your dough too fast: that's all they're waiting for to clamp down on you again. You'll manage to get more sent in once I'm gone, I'm sure of that; but the superintendent is opposed to letting Roland share part of his account with you, as you remember; and, once you've been sentenced, you'll have no more chance to apply to the judge or the lawyer, you'll be even more at his mercy. What's more, your dear friends may very well persist in sending you nothing to help you along except the assurance of their eternal loyalty. Keep all that in mind, Nicole, and roll more cigarettes out of butts instead of giving them away or passing round the package."

Matron's thread of triumph is winding itself in with my thread of anxiety, and I say: "As far as what's left of my canteen goes, and my worn-out shoes and the other junk, let Nicole have all that. As for my old clothes, the girls can make themselves ribbons out of them."

"Sure, sure, but hurry a little, for heaven's sake. The police'll be here. I came to get you an hour ahead of time, but you're dawdling so . . ."

"I'm not dawdling, matron, I'm washing myself. Matter of fact, could I have a little coffee, please? You see, I'm dawdling so much that I won't even have time to make myself a lousy java. Usually there's a day's notice. Anyway . . ."

"You've finished with your suitcases, haven't you? All right, I'll take them down and go get you your breakfast. You can put in your toilet articles afterward, outside . . ."

"Oh, no, matron, I've finished, there's just my toothbrush, and I'll put that in my hand bag. I'll lock the suitcase now, might just as well get that out of the way." Then I add: "For heaven's sake, to use your expression, what a way to wake up! I'm sure my husband is furious."

"Oh, him," the matron says as she grabs the suitcase; "he's already sorry that he ever appealed. He wrote to the judge to withdraw the appeal, but you can see it's a little late now . . ."

What's all this she's telling me?

The workroom begins to spin, I barely recover by picking

up my toothbrush. But I quickly recover my poise: with a stupid look and just a touch of angry stupefaction, I say: "He's had ten days to think about that, though. Too bad he didn't use them better. So, if he's sorry now, too bad for him! For my part I don't regret anything."

I promise myself that I'll get all this out into the open as soon as we're on the train, even before I kiss him, this repentant husband of mine! He couldn't really have done that, I think as I try to fasten my bra without having first reversed it, as I generally do. But I can't manage it: nothing can take the place of my old habits: let's start again. Three minutes lost, and the police on the way . . . But that too is the matron's fault: all she would have had to do was let me pack the suitcase the night before. But not a chance, she's always so scared that I may be up to some shady trick, or sneaking out letters or addresses . . . But what the hell, I'm doing just that anyway, directory and a note, an oral note which I'll try to remember word for word . . .

Coffeebreak: "I brought you your bread," the lady says, "because you probably won't get any there." Very well, queen, we'll eat cake.

I am about to snap back that every new prisoner, regardless of whether he arrives from inside or outside, has the indisputable right to demand chow even if he's not listed on the roster for that day, that there is no point loading myself up any further, that . . . but, at the sight of that crisp half loaf (I forgot that this was fresh-bread day), my heart melts and I break off a piece of crust that I pretend to eat with zest. A healthy swallow of burning coffee to wash it down, and I go back to doing my hair.

This task having been completed and the police not yet having rung the bell, I put a couple of touches of shadow on my lids and touch up the corners with a pencil. Now then: will I do, darling?

"Are you sure you haven't forgot anything?"

"No, the mirror and the eye shadow are Nicole's, I'll put them back in her closet . . . Just a moment, let me check everything once more . . ."

Ah, yes, there's still one thing I want to take with me: the knife. The damned canteen knife, whose constantly dismounted and sharpened blade always seemed to me to have been specifically planned to provide a harmless method of helping the prisoner kill time and nervous irritation. I slip the knife into my purse and go out of the workroom without another look at the mug of slop getting pitifully cold on the table or at the setting in which I had spent the past seven months. I open a suitcase once more to stash the bread in it: it'll be crushed when I take it out, and its crumbs will mildew for years among my clothes, for now it will be mandatory to wear prison dress: in the big houses there was no fooling around with the sartorial preferences of the population.

While I'm sorting out my cigarettes, sitting on one of the suitcases, matron goes to work on me; in the contest that is shaping up, her standing position gives her the advantage of at least a couple of feet. I begin to hone my defensive weapons.

"Well, anyway, Damien, I hope they won't be as stupid as us in the new place . . ."

"Oh, I've been there before, it's nothing new to me: that one's no holiday resort either, but, since they have individual cells, at least I'll be left in peace."

"Of course, Damien, of course. In the beginning everything was marvelous here, you were always singing our praises, and then you tried to put one over on us, you began looking down on everybody . . ."

"In the beginning it really was marvelous. Everything's relative. But now I've had seven months of it, and that mob of women always in my hair . . . I don't like prison and I don't like company . . ."

No ass-kissing at the last minute, Anick. And no hell-raising either. All this bullshit is getting me down, I've had enough of the sight of the queen's pins in their heavy stockings, I've had enough of this courtyard where I'll never again sit in the sun: soon Nicole will be alone, and then another Anick will turn up and life will go on, like jail, like eternal friendship. I look up at the wall: on the roof over the john there is a litany of little patterings, my morning sparrows, and, beyond in the distance, the gently stirring green of the chestnut trees.

Everything is ridiculously new and spring-like on the other side of this wall; inside the prison the birds and the dew display their saucy youthfulness. I can feel the coffee coming back up my throat: if the cops don't ring soon, I'll go throw myself down on the grass and pour my tears over the little wet green blades . . .

But I can hear the solemn tread of my convoy, the sound of gates being opened, of handcuffs being closed; the guard in the hall bellows: "Send her out!" and the door of the work-room opens.

I crush out my cigarette and grab the handles of my suit-cases. I can never carry all that! The guard shuffles in, without making a move to help me; finally one of the cops comes up and takes the suitcases. I follow him, my purse hooked on my arm and my hands swinging.

I wave hello to Zizi. Behind me I hear a snicker: the queen has interpreted that as an *au revoir* but it was a good-by, a last farewell.

The wagon starts off toward the station.

Zizi is braceleted on one side to a fellow who is also being transferred and on the other side to a cop, who's holding his handcuff in his hand. Since only one of my wrists is in custody, I light cigarettes that I put between the lips of Zizi and his pal. Prisoners, by definition, are always short of tobacco: I put the package away without offering any smokes to our angels.

"In a little while, in the train," Zizi whispers between two puffs, "I'll slip you some things."

We whisper back and forth, his mouth to my ear and then my mouth to his ear: the cops take it for granted that what we'll talk about is love-making, and listen with depraved attentiveness.

"Look," Zizi says: "I'm going to kiss you: there's a note inside my chewing gum. In case they separate us in the train. The rest isn't so important."

"I'll go to the john at the station," I say. "With all this being knocked around, I didn't even have a chance to piss."

Zizi raises an eyebrow. "Did someone knock you around? Who was it?"

All at once I remember the letter asking for the withdrawal of the appeal: I shouldn't have kissed him, even for the chewing gum. I grit my teeth on this mailbox.

"Who, you say? Did you get yourself shaved by the screw? I had to do everything in five minutes, and the matron always at my ass."

"But why didn't you get your things together yesterday?"

"Because the management didn't deign to give me notice, that's why! By the way . . ."

No, in a few minutes we would be at the station. The guy chained to Zizi extends his free hand and relieves me of my briefcase, which is heavy with all my accumulated mail; the cops take the biggest suitcases and boxes and jump out of the car as soon as it stops, come on, let's go. The people in the station turn and look as we march past: I stare hard at a point just above their eyes until they look down or away. Bunch of assholes! And to think how much you knock yourself out to get back into that stupid crowd, instead of just taking it easy in your prison as long as possible . . . The love of freedom is indeed the worst of vices.

The basement hall is long; my purse, with its three apples

328

and a handkerchief, weighs two hundred pounds. But Zi is walking behind me and I can feel his look whipping my legs and straightening my back; in my cheek the note has a cool, menthol, plastic savor.

"Gentlemen, do you think you could let me go pee before the train comes? I can't hold it any more . . ."

"Sure," the cop says. He turns to his colleague. "Coming, pal? You can give the joint a once-over."

The three of us head for the doors marked *Men–Women:* it's a pleasant little provincial station, bright with sunshine and formal flower beds, and full of loafers who have to be stared at above the eyes. Methodically one of the cops inspects the toilet, then says: "O.K., she can go in."

They leave me alone, the bracelet still on my wrist and the chain dragging on the ground. I spit the chewing gum into my hand, stash it in a safer place, and then, relieved, I diligently pull the chain and come out again, adjusting my skirt: "Well, I sure feel a lot lighter, I must have been carrying more than a quart of it." Then I remember my dignity: "You are very kind, gentlemen; thank you . . . What a beautiful sky, isn't it? I'm sure it'll be a magnificent day."

"Yep," the law belches, "a day like this is great for all kinds of fun and games." He sighs and puts the handcuff back on his wrist.

We cross the rails, and I step high so that my heels won't catch in the ties. My skirt is too tight, and each step makes it climb higher up my hips; by the time I catch up with the rest, it's halfway up my thighs. What with all the bread and margarine and the endless nights, I really put on plenty of lard. I'll eat less in the new place; I'll ignore the lunch bell for an orgy of reading and thinking. *There* is full of hopes and plans, and the new prison—where once I had dragged through weeks of living death—now seems like a new paradise, it's always like this, even though I know that no paradise-prison exists, that soon enough *there* would be an old story, just like the joint we left this morning and all the other jails we'd been in.

But it doesn't matter: we still have an hour's train ride before we get there, I want to stretch out this hour and keep the memory of it forever. Zizi's arm has fallen into its familiar arc round my waist—he now is manacled on only one side—I rub my cheek against his chin and my belly against his leg; the moment is sweet, all thought and all desire are far away, all I want is to stay and stay like this, my eyes closed, my limbs slumbering. But the train is coming into the station and we have to move.

Ahead of me a woman has trouble climbing the steps. She has a short skirt on and she has pretty legs: I pretend to push her in the ass, with hollowed palm and widespread fingers, and the whole convoy bursts out laughing. Good, now they're in a good humor, they'll let us sit close to each other. I head for a window seat, on the right, so that I can face my husband; but the cop attached to my right wrist, whom I had forgotten, objects: "Let me go first, damn it: where do you expect me to sit?"

Zizi shoves over toward his companion, and we manage in spite of this to be face to face. I let my angel have his window. Now I have to be careful to look inscrutable and angry until Zizi asks his little darling what's wrong, what's bothering her.

"I'll tell you right now," I say. "There isn't that much time, so we might as well get it all straightened out right away, don't you think?" And I tell him about the letter to the prosecutor.

"Oh, so that's what's eating you. Look: one of the cooks got a concurrent sentence without filing an appeal: all he did was write a letter to the pros' and take a little trip to court, and he got three months taken off—two raps put together. But then he was a first-timer, that's for sure; and, besides, the superintendent himself had written to the pros' to try to help him. You know how it is out here in the sticks: the pros', the

330

judges, the warden, and the chief of police are all pals and stick together . . . That's why the superintendent sometimes knows more about our business than we do, I know this routine by heart. Anyway, to get back to this guy, he was a poor slob with I don't know how many kids to feed, his mouse came bawling every day to visit him . . . so to make a long story short, the superintendent was touched by all this."

"You just try to get yourself out of any other state prison that way! What a circus! . . . But what about you, darling?"

"Well, I played dumb, as always: I noised it around that I was going to try to do the same thing, that there was no justification for what had happened to us, the whole bit."

"But you know very well that an appeal can't be withdrawn! The prosecutor is automatically made a party to it, and . . ."

". . . and so it's almost impossible to get it withdrawn, either before it's heard or in court. But look, stupid, I wrote just because I knew I'd be turned down! The main thing is not to let it seem that I'm appealing just so we can stay together but to make it look as if I'm acting on my own to get my time cut down and nothing else. I got my answer two days later: the pros' simply sent back my letter with something scrawled on the margin. So the superintendent gives me a short course in Roman law, treats me like a smart pal, and all the rest of it."

"It really was bright. You're a great guy, Zi, and all mine. Let me chastely kiss your majestic forehead."

I brush my lips on Zi's eyebrow but he grabs my ear and pulls me to him so that I have to kiss him for real this time. Inside my brain his letter to the pros' tears itself into a thousand minuscule scraps and all of them fly out the window of the train while Zi takes possession of me again, tenderly, with little endearments, with light caresses of his fingers.

"Oh, darling," I say, "we have to make a lot of train trips, on morning trains, like this one; or else sleepers where we can cuddle all night long . . ."

"And what about the back seat of the car? Do you remember that, Anick?"

Do I remember! Oh, those cars, never the same ones, but always big and fast, how we traveled and slept and worked in them! How I waited in them some nights for my man to sneak back!

"That's not all, baby: and . . . What about our plans? I know you haven't changed your mind, but what are the prospects now?"

At once Zi seems thoughtful. "It'll be tough, very tough . . . Especially if you can't get out of your cell and I have to go into the women's side to get you. Because of course we both have to split the same night. What I'm afraid of, you see, is not having enough time: it's summer, and the nights are short. And as far as I'm concerned, there's always the chance of my being switched from one cell to another without warning, so I can't start digging two weeks ahead of time; I'm going to have to be fast as hell . . ."

"What do you mean, *digging?*"

"It's all explained in the note, I don't think I've left anything out. For God's sake, don't lose the thing."

"Don't worry," I laugh, "I'm not having my period. You know me: by tonight there won't be a sign of it: into the fire and then into the bucket."

I take a quick look around the compartment: our angels are behaving themselves, they've got out their sandwiches and their newspapers and two of them have fallen asleep; another is doing crossword puzzles . . .

"We can talk," Zizi said, "they're not paying any attention. Hell, as soon as they're sure we aren't going to try to lam . . ."

I laugh. "Did you notice? One of them does crosswords. The ones in that paper I can do in five minutes, by the clock. I'd like to talk to him about it."

"For God's sake, don't stir him up! Oh, by the way . . ."

Zizi pats his pockets, moving slowly because of the awkward-
ness of the handcuffs: little by little he pulls out a heap of little
packages, which he sets one by one on my lap.

"Oh, darling, chewing gum! I'm going to chew it right away,
because the matron will confiscate it. What else is there? . . .
This is wonderful, dearest—a Camel and a Yacet!"

"All presents from social workers, I've been keeping them
for you since Christmas . . . That stinking screw didn't even
want to let me give them to you, at court or when we had our
visits. So I fixed his ass: I asked the superintendent to keep
these things for me in his desk. You know the screws, always
nosing around at night, they're always short of tobacco or
grub . . . See, baby, there's candy too, six pieces, and two pictures that a guy drew for you: he got a look at you one day
when you were on your way to the lawyer, and I think he
really fell."

My funny little hoodlum, with his big male hands that are
good at making little packets of candy for his woman. I feel a
bit unhappy that I wasn't able to fix anything for him. "Oh,
sure, I guess I could have written to you in advance and
smuggled the thing out, but it looked like just taking a needless
chance. Besides, from now on I expect you to give all the
orders, I don't want to do anything without your approval . . .
not anything ever again. It was my carelessness and stubborn-
ness that got us into jams too many times. From here on in
my place is in the kitchen, I promise you. Now let me put my
treasures in my pocket . . . "

"Look, here's your last letter, I didn't have a chance to put
it away with the others." Zizi unfolds it and underlines a sentence with his fingernail. "That gave me a laugh! Damn right,
'our fancies will always be better than our maddest dreams'!
But does that refer to bed or to the deal we're cooking up?"

"*Deal* has a bad ring for anyone who might hear, or for the
mail censors: when you want to talk to me about splitting, call
it *our ideal state.*"

"Very well, boss. Well, then, is it to be ideal-talk or bed-talk?"

"Both: I'll scribble the most obscure things I can so you can have a wide choice of meanings."

"For a second I thought you'd guessed how I was going to go about it. What am I going to do, in your opinion?"

"Uh . . . I suppose you're going to get hold of some hack-saws and . . . "

"No, you didn't catch on at all, so I must be even brighter than I thought. Sure, I've already gotten in touch with people to get the saws from outside: through someone walking, some-one whose brains I can rely on, you know that there's a mini-mum of people I trust for stuff like that. Except . . . The only guy who could bring it off right—you know, B.—is away until the middle of August, and I didn't know how to reach him directly. So I sent a letter to his usual address. His mouse may have forwarded it, but as a rule I know that she gives him his mail personally, when she's the one who receives it. So, by the time he gets back and gets the package ready, the thing will drag on for two months. On the other hand, if I do everything strictly on my own, without using any of the old tricks—saw-ing through bars is really square!—we might be able to try next month."

"A month is a long time," I sigh. "At least, with you, wait-ing has no uncertainty in it."

"Almost none, baby: because—I always come back to this —you have to remember that it can always get loused up: and then it means extra punishment, immediate transfer to Central Prison, strict surveillance . . . "

"Transfer? But they can't do that before our appeal's been heard!"

"I thought of that too. But . . . this is the end of June: so you have to figure that that can happen before the vacations, during July; or even during vacation, there are some hearings then. If that happens, get yourself sent to Central, or the hospital, or anywhere you can: I promise you absolutely that I'll get myself out of wherever I am and come and get you."

"That isn't going to solve anything . . . Why not ask the mouthpiece to get the thing dragged out? Anyway, Zi, the only reason why we're appealing is so we can be in the same joint, and now you want to snatch me out of the hospital."

"Sure, that's the reason for the appeal. You think I get laughs out of taking the chance of a longer sentence? Either by losing or after a lam . . . So we *must* make it. And then stay outside as long as possible."

I'm getting edgy. "Where's the connection between how we behave in stir and our sentences? If they want to give you more time, they'll do it without waiting for you to try to run. That's like becoming a trusty or taking correspondence courses in the hope that they'll take that into consideration in court: it doesn't stop them from kicking you in the balls, anything but. As far as they're concerned, intelligence is an aggravating circumstance. We aren't going to be able to con them into thinking that we do all that shit because we've genuinely made up our minds to reform in the future. But I'm getting off the subject: the decision's been made, I tell you."

"Well, but . . . suppose in spite of everything they did make the raps run together?"

Oh, Zi, I think wearily, has that got hold of you again? That formless hope, that thought that so seldom had any basis: that the courts would show some understanding for our misfortunes because they were so moved by our sincerity and our zeal? the same zeal that we employ in the commission of acts that they're paid to punish? Oh, Zi, you're out of your mind.

" . . . We won't get anything—anything, do you hear me? Not one hour less, not a bit of clemency. Both of us are undesirable citizens, black as coal, said to be dangerous: granted, we wouldn't kill a sparrow, but go tell the judge you love sparrows! We're burglars, so there it is: the seed that grows into murder and social upheaval; as far as courts go, there will never be anything for us but that fucking record that is brought out every time and copied into the file of the next case, which can't get us anywhere either. Look, there's still one good job we can pull on them, and that's to appeal, to win the appeal, and then to skip in the interval between the decision and the transfer. Then the judge would certainly hang himself. Unfortunately there's still the warrant for the car accident, in any case, and you'll be sent up for that the minute there's a decision: a warrant is even more urgent than a transfer order to some Central."

"Yes, damn it . . . and the joint I'll be sent to for that business has no individual cells, it seems to me. Oh, shit and double shit, it's a mess . . . "

"On the contrary, it's perfectly simple. There are only two choices. Either we split before the appeal, prepared to lose by default and get extra time, because you're so hot for that—that is, we have a summer in the sun followed by a few years abroad to recover our health and pull a few little jobs before we grow too old and helpless. Or else we split afterward, the day after the decision, for example, to skip out on the transfer, and . . . "

"That would be better, because that would give us the perfect excuse: 'I just lost my head, it was my last chance, after that kick in the teeth my wife and I were desperate . . . ' "

"Just try not to do too much damage," I laugh. "Running is no crime, but damage to prison property is . . . A lousy bar can be worth about three months. On the other hand, they can pay for it out of our prison accounts, since we'll have to leave that dough behind . . . I'll write to the superintendent and tell him to have no hesitation about dipping into it to pay for the repairs to his prison, and that way he may forget to wear mourning."

The morning is passing; the sun floods the gay little sta-

tions where the train stops; people come into the compartment, delighted to see so many empty seats, and then, when
they see the cops and the handcuffs, they mutter *oh, sorry,*
and flee. They would much rather stand jammed in the corridor than sit next to people in such impressive company. The
prestige of the uniform and the aura of the criminal.

"I'm going to smoke that Yacet you gave me," I said. I
didn't expect the matron to inspect my cigarettes one by one,
and I would slide the Camel in among the Gitanes; but the
Yacet was longer, unless I cut it . . . No, I have no intention
either of cutting it or of lighting it twice. "Take a drag, my
love, and then we'll have an apple."

"No, keep them, I have oranges and lemons in my sack."

"I insist, an apple, like outside."

"Like outside" means that I'll peel it with my teeth and give
it to Zizi naked and tooth-marked, a dirty habit, as is the rule
among Lovers.

The other prisoner has sat without a word in his corner ever
since we got into the train. I suggested that he eat and smoke
with us if he liked; even though Zizi has told me he's a pain
in the ass, a half-wit and all the rest; what difference does it
make? I'll probably never see the jerk again, and Zizi will see
him only from a distance, during exercise or at mass . . .

We must be halfway there by now. My angel has slacked
off on the chain and I'm now sitting beside my man, which
makes it easier to whisper and to read each other's faces. He
gives me a rough outline of his plan: all that he'll need to get
himself out of his cell is a large screwdriver: "With my good
looks and my nice disposition," he says, "it won't take me any
time at all to get on the good side of the carpenter or the shop
foreman . . ."

At night, Zizi will cut a hole in the wall and cover it inside
and outside with imitation brick panels painted on paper; using the bars in the window as a pulley, he'll let himself down

into the courtyard on a rope, which he will then draw down after him; after that, all that he has to do is to find me. If I can find some way of getting out of my hole, we'll meet in a courtyard; otherwise Zi will simply go into the women's wing and quietly let me out, since the matron never comes back at night after she's made her nine-o'clock round.

"The worst part of the job, obviously, is going to be the second wall, the one that stands at the street." This is unbelievably high, and the top of it is covered with broken glass; but Zizi has already arrived at certain ideas, and, though he has not yet settled the details, they are a foregone conclusion. Without a pang, I leave the station and walk out into the square in front of it, where I recognize every bar and every shop: this city had long been a favorite resort of ours, until a court order forbade us to go there; I remember that the prison is a little way outside the town, without anything opposite or any nearby buildings in the way; all night long, heavy trucks pass along the main highway outside, making the window panes vibrate.

Now we are at the door, which is really huge, and only a panel in it is opened for us; I enter: but this is not the way by which I'll leave the next time. Far above, on the terrible brick wall, the shards of glass sparkle their threats. During the train trip, I sketched a concise plan of the women's wing on the back of my cigarette package for Zizi, and whispered to him: "Look: this roof on the right, with the two little windows in it, is over the exercise yard."

In the corridor outside the receiving room, the men are sent to one side and the women to the other; there is a pleasant smell of soup amid the surges of music from the loud-speakers. I am quite fond of this prison: it is indeed the "real thing," and the silence in the cells makes a pleasant contrast to the constant passage of lawyers, visitors, and keepers. The canteen has a diversified stock, the staff is not annoying, the superintendent is bright and has a sense of humor. And in addition we'll be sort of the babies of the house. I hope that, in spite of our past breaks and our prison files, which are as voluminous as the others, we won't have to undergo any special watch.

When the customary formalities have been completed, I leave the office and greet the waiting matron like an old pal. I kiss Zizi—on the cheek, out of respect for that lady—I whisper: "See you soon," and I am swallowed up by the door of the women's quarters.

The journey has ended and a new period of waiting has begun.

(2)

The Rule, the sound, purgative rule of the search still has some
tricks to play on me: in this place it is forbidden to have a
garter belt, or ink, or matches in commercial quantities, for
they will be doled out to me in accordance with my needs; but
never has a rule been so decently interpreted: the matron,
whom I don't know really well (during my first rap here, she
was a probationary employee), doesn't wear the regulation
smock, and this friendly civilian look about her is matched by
a gentle, courteous voice, she smiles a great deal, and she
doesn't ask questions. She would have liked to let me keep my
things, but . . .

"You've been sentenced, haven't you?"

"Yes, matron, but I've appealed, so it's the same as if I were
on pre-trial detention . . . "

"Yes, I saw the admission card in the office: 'sentenced
to . . . ' Is that the sentence you're appealing? You understand . . . "

Even if the sentences are made concurrent, there will still be
time for my back to chafe under prison denim. I can't explain
to the lady that I need my clothes for my escape . . . So I am
getting ready to bid farewell to my nice skirts, when the lady

climbs down from the stepladder that she has mounted in order to inspect the upper reaches of the wardrobe room, and says to me as she comes down:

"Look, there are no more prison uniforms here in your size; if I give you one of these, it'll come down to your ankles. I'm going to go talk to the deputy warden; in the meantime, hang on to your things."

The sorting out of my property, scattered all over the floor by now, continues: the food is all mixed up with packs of butts, panties, new soap. I get hold of my bottle of oil, which the lady has mistaken for toilet water and therefore tried to confiscate, and am preparing to cart off the whole inventory by myself. "Wait, I'll get a trusty to help you with all this," she says.

As a matter of principle it is always a good idea to get in good with a trusty: she can always arrange everything for you as long as you're in stir, and, if by chance she walks first, she can always put in a word with the right people so that you can take over from her. It's not that I'm in any great hurry to go back into the mending business, but the workroom is on the ground floor; the trusty sleeps there, the transom is wider than the others, and . . .

"Lerouge!" the lady calls into the hall.

Lerouge is on the pale side and rather slender, and she has no other distinguishing marks except the heavy uniform and the big butcher's apron. She barely looks at me, answers my cordial greeting without a smile but also without nastiness, and holds out her arms for me to start loading her with my things. I take the four corners of the bath towel into which I've bundled all the rest of my stuff, and we start off single file toward the cell: the lady, Lerouge, and I.

"I'll put you on the second tier, there's no more room on the first."

"Fine, matron," I say, pretending to be thoroughly pleased; "then I'll have the advantage of light and air.

341

"The only trouble (I turn to Lerouge) is that that's going to mean more leg work for you when you bring chow up."

"It doesn't matter, because one cell up there is taken already, so one more can't make any difference."

Well! the sanitary equipment has certainly been improved in the past five years! A white enamel bidet, a blue enamel bucket as a highly superior replacement for the battered old rusty ass-breaker; since I have the cell at the end of the corridor, I'll enjoy a double ration of heating pipes: the elbow turn of the circuit is just below my table and will keep my dogs warm this winter. Provided, of course, that by then I have not gotten back to our little hide-out, where Zizi makes a dozen trips a day into the cellar to shake up the furnace and provide a tropical climate as soon as October is half gone.

Before each cell used to have a sliding panel opening onto the corridor, through which the chamber pot could be passed; the corridor door leading outside is now secured by an iron bolt. Even supposing that I can force the bolt, can I make myself skinny enough to get through the space between the two heavy bars that is just big enough for the ass-breaker? The architects who designed the prison must have expected something like this. As for the transom . . . with the means at my disposal it would take a year to even begin to make a perceptible nick in its bars. And, like Zizi, I am at the mercy of a possible stool pigeon, so I can't begin work several nights in advance.

All right, Anick, leave it up to your man: for him it'll be child's play to pick my lock, and, if he's caught, at least I can be certain that I won't get any punishment and hence I'll be able to act for both of us.

I have to put clean paper on the shelves of the gray metal cupboard. "Can I have an old newspaper, madame?"

While Lerouge goes to find it, the lady kills time for me by making small talk. "You can have your writing paper and your mail as soon as the deputy warden gives me permission to give them to you. In the meantime, you're right: a bit of reading . . . "

"But I don't want it for reading, I want to line the shelves."

It is always essential, especially in the beginning, to act like a good housewife who is not too bright. That, in fact, is why I left the math course and the other intellectualities in the suitcase, with the idea of asking the warden for them after I've taken a gander at him: I'm sure he'll send for me soon, to get an idea how I look this year; he's quite fond of me because I take things calmly and because I once spent days and days mending his shorts.

Lerouge tosses a pile of old numbers of *Paris-Match* on my mattress; they promise me that the bedclothes will be right up, and the big door swings shut, leaving me to myself.

Greetings, solitude. I savor my first moment of peace in a year, sitting on my wooden chair and smoking a cigarette. Then I douse the butt in the sink and begin a methodical filling of the cupboard. There is one good thing about an individual cell: each person has her own place with the same cubic footage and the same equipment as her neighbor, and you can see how each of the others uses her oxygen and her bidet.

The lady won't come back before exercise time, unless . . . but as a matter of fact lunch hasn't been served yet. Full of candy, my stomach has forgotten all about listening for the buzzer. Here, if my memory is correct, they ring a real bell. If the bill of fare has been included in the general trend toward improvements, I'm going to have a hard time starting my voluntary diet. Just yesterday I said to Nicole: "By yourself, you throw the slop into the bucket and forget about food until the next meal. I'm taking along a perforated box and some oil, and I'll fuel myself with coffee, tea, and lemon juice."

After the delivery of lunch (broth and split peas, at once

devoured by the john), I wait to hear the bang of the door in this wing, and then, at my ease, I take out Zizi's note and sort out the pieces of onion-skin paper covered with transparent scribbles: one side is written at right angles to the other, to make it easier to read. A still tinier note falls out of the first sheet: this is a new alphabet code, which I copy off onto my package of soap powder. Then I begin chewing it up, while going ahead with the reading of the rest, which I stash page by page in my bra: I'll have to read it all again, etch it indelibly into my mind and get rid of all the evidence before exercise time.

Good: it's a repetition of what I learned in the train, plus various code phrases for use in our official letters: to say whether I could fit myself through the panel in my cell door, to tell what floor the cell is on . . . The cell number has to appear along with the identification number on the envelope, so here the prison regulations work to my advantage. Once Zizi has cased the joint, and found out when rounds are made, etc., another code phrase will tell me the date and the time for our break.

I feel rather woozy, and I would enjoy a quick nap. But the prohibition on daytime sleeping and the lack of a mattress combine to dissuade me. I'm bored, and I wish I had the rest of my things. What is there to do until the lady comes back? I can't start tearing down the prison yet. I look through the old magazines, I'm just like the vegetable, with one difference: I'm searching for the crossword puzzles. But alas! In each square of each puzzle my Bic has been preceded by another, and a smart one. As soon as exercise time comes, I'm going to look for this crossword addict: as a rule these girls turn out to be people I really like.

"Would you like to come and get a little air?" That doesn't tempt me much: occupants of individual cells get individual exercise periods. You spend an hour walking back and forth

The Runaway

round a rectangle of grass and dandelions. But I have to go out if I want to get a line on the exterior of the place, the arrangement of the bars along the corridors, etc.

All the women are waiting on the downstairs landing. I count a dozen of them. But there are only six exercise yards; in the old days, the women used to be taken out six at a time. "Do we exercise together now?" I ask the lady. "The last time I was here . . . "

" . . . you were alone? The rule hasn't been changed. But during the superintendent's vacation I took it on myself to let you out together. You can't do anything wrong just talking among yourselves, and it's less noisy than yelling over the walls . . ."

I've drawn an angel of a matron. It's too bad, because, when I have my mind made up to pull a fast one, I prefer to do it under the nose of some bitch. But then the break will be at night, so it won't make any trouble for her. All the same, she smiles too much.

Out in the sun, my back against the warm bricks, I begin my investigations. Cigarettes all round, first, to break the ice; a few observations of a general character on "how sad it is to be in jail in such nice weather" and "hell, we'll all be out some day anyhow"; then the exchanges of information: prison records, number of kids, opinions on the split peas at lunch. Having warmed them up, I attack.

"How nice that matron who admitted me is! What's her name?"

They tell me; they add that she's "real human" but that "you mustn't let her down, or else . . . "

That's all right: even if she's stern at times, we'll get along very well. The main thing is for her to keep her mouth shut and not go telling Lerouge that I'm an old hand at breaking windows, at breaking things in general, at ninety days in the

345

hole, and a bad actor. By the way, what about the night inspection?

"Everything's really the way it should be in the cells now. And you can sleep decently, not like in Central with that light in your eyes every time they go around. The matron never used to make a night inspection here, but under the new rules . . . "

"It's still the same: by nine o'clock it's all quiet. Except that if you aren't quiet . . . "

Can't she change adjectives once in a while? The girl who keeps repeating the word has round shoulders and glowering eyes; she keeps eying me without any warmth at all, I seem to know too much about prison routine. Pull back, then: she must be a long-termer who's jealous of her domain.

"What about coffee?" I ask. "Still the same pot of boiling water shoved into the cell after exercise?"

"If you have an account," Lerouge tells me, "you can canteen one of those little burners. There's real ground coffee, too . . . "

"Marvelous!" I say in English. "I wish I were three days older right now! Still two days in advance for canteen orders?"

"Yes, but . . . Hey, Paule! (Lerouge is now speaking to the 'quiet' dame.) You have a burner, lend it to this lady, as long as you don't have any fuel tablets for it. And I'll lend her a few francs so she doesn't have to drink slop for the next three days."

Paule agrees, since she has little choice. "All she cares about is her quart of red wine," Lerouge whispers to me.

"Thanks a lot," I say. "In the can, java's fine when you can't get anything better. But in this hot weather I'd rather have a Ricard. What about you, Paule?"

"Oh, I don't drink all that rich people's crap . . . "

So I've annoyed her. What a pain in the ass this woman is!

The walk goes on and on. The lady, it seems, allows us to stay outside much longer than the regulation hour, sometimes until supper time. By the time I am alone again, the day is almost over. I plan to resume my beloved old habits, reading in bed, eating in bed, writing in bed . . .

The other prison is already at the bottom of my memory, without the benefit of that pity that the passage of time usually brings to things: still quite sharp, bitter peaks stand out, a thousand actions, words, and sights that disgusted me there. Oh, no one had put me through the usual blackmail after my wedding: if you don't behave yourself, we'll get your little hubby's ass; every care was taken not to rob us of one minute of our visits, to deliver our mail with irreproachable punctuality. But their seeming kindness was only a system of defense, of invulnerability: no deficiencies in the service, no neglect, no injustice. Negative equity: the "to each the same" and the "everybody" had been succeeded by "no one." Little by little, all the privileges and extras granted to Dufon and extended to Damien had disappeared. But, every time she eliminated a favor, the matron had been careful also to eliminate a chore: she had made Solange take care of the laundry and the mending, without depriving me of the hundred francs a month allotted to me at the beginning, when I was doing the job; she . . . but it's no use looking for something, there's nothing I can throw back at those two, she and her husband were a smart little pair, my hat's off to them, and I'm still the one who had to take down her pants, after that Christmas flop!

Hell! this runaway will make up for all the others, the ones that we tried, the ones that we goofed, the ones that we only dreamed about.

Dawn awakens me; it's four o'clock. This first night, I got caught up on cigarettes and smoked I don't know how many in the dark; the silence and the emptiness of the cell made it impossible for me to fall asleep. Then I got hungry, and made a number of journeys to the cupboard; this morning my stomach is weighted down with chocolate and apples.

When coffee comes, I refuse the big piece of bread that Paule offers me, all I want is "just a bit of the crust"; at lunch time I make a disgusted face at the dish of noodles and stop her ladle in midair as she aims it at my plate.

Paule begins griping, she's sick of dragging heavy pots around to women who think they're too good for the stuff, Lerouge can do the serving after this, etc. I point out to her that, since she's also on latrine duty, filling my plate will only oblige her to carry off my share in my bucket tomorrow morning. I manage to get her quiet by promising to pay her for her burner (which she got as a gift from someone going out and which therefore cost her nothing) with butts or whatever else she wants.

Fortunately she is soon released. Now all that matters is to connive so that I'm not nominated as her replacement for work. Since Paule's cell was one flight up, there would be no profit for my runaway in getting her job. The bars in the door panel are too close together, I can't squeeze through between them, and besides the door itself has been reinforced with iron bars: throughout the past five years there had been nothing but jolly improvements such as this in the whole joint. So there's nothing for me but the door or the workroom window. But Lerouge sleeps in the workroom, and will go on doing so for a long time to come. I'm going to have to play up my injuries, it's too well known that I do fine patching and darning, am good at ironing shirts and all that housemaid stuff.

My wrist will clumsily break a few plates, which I'll pay for out of my account, and I'll make a big show of "this lousy arm that can't do a fucking thing any more" . . . Even if I'm given something to sew in my cell, I'll quietly go about being very clumsy: "There it is, matron, I did my best, but . . . "

The lady comes to get me during exercise period. I clamber over the two girls stretched out on the steps (oh, don't bother moving) and in the corridor I ask whether my lawyer has come. I was not expecting any other visits: I had gone to the croaker in the morning, and I had not found any good pretext for getting in to see him, since anthropometric measurements are taken only once a week . . .

"Somebody wants to see you in the office," the lady said, "and I don't know any more about it than you do."

The office is partitioned into windowed bays: leaning on the radiator in the corridor, I study the functionaries sitting behind their desks over their registers and their various documents while I wait for someone to tell me to go in. Finally one of the screws takes his nose out of his work: "Damien?"

Putting a smile on my kisser, I go in. "Here I am, sir. What's this all about?"

He hands me a gooseshit-yellow document. "Sign this here and write in the date: your appeal will be heard on the eleventh of next month."

I reject his ball-point, leaving it held in the air and the guy nonplussed; I find mine in my pocket, read the paper, and sign. "Well, at least they aren't wasting any time."

"Right," the screw says, "if they ordered you transferred, THEY probably knew . . . "

As I hand back the notification, I see a second paper just like it, on which my husband's name appears in large letters. Let's prepare for the worst, since the worst has come. I put on my little act for the girls: "Imagine the luck! To come up at the very end of the court year, three days before Bastille Day and the amnesties . . . "

"I hope you'll wind up the year with a bang," Lerouge says. "Then you'll leave us in the lurch for the summer."

"Wait a while, I haven't left yet. If you ask me, they make up the lists of transfers to Central months in advance, so I probably won't leave here before the October transfer."

All very well, but what about Zizi? Suppose they had no single cells and had to put him in a three-man cell? "I'll ask for an isolation cell right off," he had told me; "if necessary, I'll enroll in a correspondence course and tell the warden I have to be alone in order to study, etc. But, if they have no single cells left . . . Oh, well, if the two other guys are the right kind and not stupid, I'll manage just the same."

"Bring them along," I had suggested. I have an appetite for big headlines. "I'll send the local paper my sketch of the lay-out . . . "

But Zizi had just shrugged in amusement and I had stowed these childish jokes. I'm impatient for our first visit, now three days off.

Solitude leads me into fantasy, it's true, but it also protects me against boredom. I like this idleness, this deliberate slowness that disintegrates and protracts every action. The day becomes divided into little rituals: washing and dressing, making coffee on the burner, listening from my bed to the hour of broadcast music; lunch, bed again until exercise time. Be still, my head, be still, my heart, make room for trivial clap-trap, for the gurgling of the fountain in the warden's garden that we can hear from the exercise yard, make room for the grass. The courtyard is choked with dandelions. I take my knife down there on the pretext of sharpening it. After I have scraped the blade over the stones a few times, I straighten up.

"Good lord, I'm stiff as a board. Tell me, Lerouge, is it allowed to cut the lawn?"

"Is it allowed! It's compulsory, you mean. One of these days I'll be back in good enough shape to do it again."

"Never mind, I'll do it for you. Try this razor: sharp, isn't it?" In no time I have harvested dandelions from a quarter of the yard. "Want some, Lerouge? With a few new potatoes and a good mustard sauce they can be delicious, you know."

You become a glutton in stir. And besides, making a salad can take as much as a half-hour, if it is done slowly. In the back of my mind, while my hands are busy with it and my eyes

350

take in the jokes in a magazine, certain problems go on nagging: will I be put to work? what will Zizi say? what will he do? what will he be able to do? Each tomorrow brings only the stumbling hope of another tomorrow, my disappointed hunger is no longer satisfied with these little crumbs; I must swallow in one breathless gulp a tremendous draught of the future, weeks and months.

"Hurry up with your dinner," the lady says to me on the evening of the dandelions. "I'll leave your door open, and, when I call you, you can go down and talk to your lawyer."

"But I can eat later, this is only a salad and it doesn't matter if it gets cold."

"Right now your lawyer's busy with a man, so you have lots of time."

Imagine going to see counselor with green teeth! I had better things to do than guzzle dandelions. Hastily I straighten my bun, which has become a little untidy during the harvest; with one hand I Colgate the pearly whites while the other goes through the cupboard for a virgin handkerchief . . .

Counselor would get a good laugh out of watching me. But I can't help being fond of the little guy. I put an ear to my half-open door; not yet hearing a sound from downstairs, I give my shoes a fresh shine with an end of the blanket; I smoke a butt; I straighten my bed; finally, ring-ring, and there is my beloved; I fly down the stairs to meet him . . .

After we shake hands in the central lobby, outside the door of the windowed conference room, counselor lets his hand drop onto my shoulder, and gently maneuvers me toward the table inside, where, with all the warmth of a bodily presence, his briefcase awaits us, that symbol of order, of secrecy and of importance. He offers me a chair and shuts the door.

"Well, madame, how's your morale?"

"Magnificent, counselor!" I answer heartily.

"You didn't take my advice, you appealed anyway. I must

tell you frankly that I am quite uneasy over the outcome . . .
I had written you as much, but . . . "

I want to scream at him that I don't give a shit for the outcome of the appeal: what interests me is coming out of prison.
There is a shout implicit in my silence: "If I keep my mouth
shut now, it's because I'm your client, because I want to spare
you a kind of moral complicity that you would try to wriggle
out of with your usual counsels: 'Be patient, madame, be
brave, my dear.' And yet that comradely indulgence in your
eyes makes me want to delegate everything to the Voice . . .
But my silence embarrasses me, I wish I could hide, because
I've pledged myself to a quick violent outbreak . . . But I'm
still on guard, just like those screws at their posts out there in
the lobby . . . "

I offer my pack of Gitanes, but counselor refuses with a
gesture of his hand. He looks as if he no longer has strength
enough to speak or even to stand. I am touched by him: I
know that he has to be careful of his throat and that on Saturdays he's rather worn out; but tonight I can't take him
seriously. Mechanically, at the same time that I say politely:
"I know, you're especially busy right now . . . " my eyes are
turning toward the lobby, where the silhouettes of automata
are passing back and forth, inmates in blue shirts and guards
in uniforms with stars, and, far beyond them, a black shadow
leaning against the door of the women's ward, the lady, waiting to "take me home."

"Yes, I'm really overloaded . . . I think I'm going to ask the
prosecutor to agree to a week's adjournment of your case."

"Oh, counselor! What a break, another week like this!"

An amused despair flickers in the lawyer's eyes; he must
think I'll never stop being a child. Have a little affection for my
childish ways, counselor . . . And my silence says: "What
does it matter? Take off your lawyer's robe, let me get out of
my prison denim, and let's kick up our heels together . . . "

"When will you be seeing your husband?" counselor asks.

"We're supposed to have a visit tomorrow. I won't forget to convey to him . . . "

"And how is *he* holding up?"

Stop a minute! Isn't there an unpleasant undertone in that *he*? I would swear there was. I'm going to scream. He, he? What do you want from Him? I love Him. I don't want that pitying *he* of yours; soon enough all of you, Mouthpieces, Judges & Co., will get a big surprise from Him.

The canteen cider must have gone to my head, everything is swimming before my eyes, I want to smash this well dressed insolent stranger who no longer has anything in common with my friend, the lawyer, and who takes the liberty of referring to Zizi as *he*. Easy, Anick, get hold of yourself.

"Do you . . . do you think they might increase our sentences, counselor?"

His eyelids and the corners of his mouth droop, he looks like a miracle worker who's afraid his miracle isn't going to come off. "Well . . . it could happen, madame."

Then his eye catches mine and for an instant, far away from the prison and anything having to do with prisons, we are frisking about. I see him again as he was the last time in court, lounging in the lawyers' stall in his shirt-sleeves, without his glasses, with that sleepy look that makes me picture the lawyer waking up after making love, while the prosecutor drones on about the Enforcement of the Law and my Zizi circumspectly studies the toes of his shoes.

"Well, madame, I'll be back on Monday, we'll have more time; I'm glad I was able to get permission to see you: but it's five-thirty now, we have to finish."

Well, well! Observe the gentleman complaining about the regulations of the remote prisons where his work for me compelled him to come to see me! And growing indignant when

353

the screw pokes his head into the room saying: "Counselor, it's supper time, you have to leave."

"In these places (which meant here), I confer with my clients until midnight if that is required . . . "

See here, counselor: like me, like Him, you too are governed by the Rules!

I feel a sudden need to give evidence of my friendship. "So they're getting tough here too?"

Shaking my cool hand without any visible reaction, but with a sparkle in his eye, the lawyer replies in a voice from the tomb: "Like visiting your woman in a whorehouse."

(3)

A lazy Sunday.

In order to have a lazy morning, I had to get out of bed at the first sound of the birds. I can rely on their perception of dawn, they're not double-crossers like that other matron's rooster. It's not necessary to open my eyes to make sure that daylight has come: I jump into my slippers first and open my eyes afterward.

I brush my teeth while the water is heating for the coffee, fold the first two blankets, and take my braids down. Then I go back to bed, just loafing until I hear the sound of the keys and allowing the coffee and the freshness of the remade bed to do a slow job of getting my mind back on its track. When the lady opens the door, I have the broom in my hand and I'm busy with all the little balls of fluff. This brings on a "Well, doing your housekeeping?" that makes me drop the broom to run out, my prison mug in my hand and the regulation smile on my lips.

"Well, Paule," I say, pulling at the half-cut loaf of bread while she tugs at her end, "I guess this is the last time I'll receive my daily bread from your lily-white hands."

"Who knows, between now and tomorrow I may find some way of getting back."

Hell, when it's certain that she would register in this same hotel the first time she ties one on and kicks up a fuss, she might just as well stay where she is. All she has to do is get nasty with the screw who gives her her exit papers. And I won't have to worry about being assigned to her job.

During all these random thoughts, I'm hurrying with the rest of my dressing so that I'll be ready when the bell rings for mass. I'll be taken downstairs for Zizi's visit right after the *Ite, missa est,* and here the visiting room is equipped with neither a mesh grill nor a merciful half-light: let's make ourselves immediately and lastingly beautiful then.

The table in the visiting room is divided in the middle by a frosted glass panel as high as two ping-pong nets, over which, from our respective positions, we volley the verbal balls without ever touching each other even with a fingernail. A guard and a matron stand beside us, the referee and umpire; sometimes they play a game of their own.

Hurry, Father, hurry! Let your sermon come to an end and the flock be locked again in its pen so that I, the lost sheep, can go to my beloved wolf.

The minute we're settled, I drive a well-aimed ball into the volley of kisses that Zizi is sending me with both hands: "Darling, do you know the score on the mail rules? I was worried about your letter, so I asked how the local post office works. Well, this is how: one letter a week, plus two on Sunday, which can be written whatever day you like. They don't need stamps, so the mailman doesn't have to bother figuring out how much they weigh. Now we'll be able to answer each other instead of having our letters cross, isn't that great?"

Zizi makes a face. "I'd rather be able to write to you twice during the week and take the chance of the letters crossing . . . "

So the visit has got off to a pleasant start; what with the bare pipes, the smell of wax coming from the table, and the

echoes of the just-finished liturgy still in my ears, I feel as if
I'm in a convent. Ah, screw, you were looking at your watch?
And Zizi puts it into words at once: "I trust you noted down
the time when we started, sir?" He turns to me: "I caught Mr.
Warden himself with his pants down; he robbed us of nine
minutes!"

This way there's no danger of their pulling the good-faith
trick on us, putting a watch on the table after it's been set a
few minutes fast on the sneak. Since Zizi is much more skilled
than I in the domain of double-meaning phrases, I let him
talk.

"So he wants a postponement?" Zizi says. "Well, let him
get it or not get it, what the hell . . . " His whole arm follows
his hand in a sweeping fatalistic motion of tossing everything
over his shoulder. *Alea jacta,* but careful: it is better not to talk
too much, the lady is neither deaf nor stupid. As for me, my
detachment is much too studied, and instead of sliding subtle
meanings in, I skid.

"I wrote to the prosecutor yesterday for permission to get
my books back from the property clerk. While I'm waiting to
hear from him, I'm going through a whole backlog of the
Revue des deux mondes and *Historia.* I was 'way behind, I'm
having a regular debauch of reading, I'm taking advantage of
being alone . . . "

At this my indifference flounders again: "I thought the men
were put three to a cell."

"Not me." There is a slight wink from Zizi. Good, our
problems are being simplified.

When the half-hour is over, I rise submissively, and the way
Zizi looks at my legs makes me stagger a little. "See you next
Sunday, baby . . . "

Back in my cell, I immediately sequester the visit, my slight
anxiety, and everything I've imagined in a mental vault for
contemplation during the evenings of the coming week; there

will be plenty of time to take them out again after lights out. Coffee, potatoes, crosswords, naps. Zi and I are each alone: the gods are on guard.

"You again?" I am amazed the next morning when Paule, as usual, is there to hand out coffee.

"Yes," the lady smiles, "she insisted on serving breakfast on her last day: busy-busy right to the end, you know!"

If that idiot had left early in the morning, like everyone else, I would have known by now whether I'll have to take her place. The lady went out, but she's not one to spare her legs, and she's quite capable of coming back ten minutes later to tell me to pack up and move. Unable to stop my heart from pounding, I pace up and down my cell in my slippers, listening to the sound of doors. There it is, she's coming back, I've had it. The key, the . . .

"Would you like to canteen, Damien? It's fruit today, and incidentals."

Oh, matron! I pull up my chair, I forestall the gesture of offering a pen by producing my own, I want to throw my arms round her. Damn right I want fruit. Put me down for twenty pounds of each kind.

"Am I right in thinking your husband ordered strawberries last week? He said so yesterday . . ."

What a retentive ear the lady has! "All right, then, strawberries . . . We'll make a wish together. And some lettuce, it'll make a change from the dandelions." Then I branch off. "Is our darling Paule unhappy? That must make a lot of work for you, too: packing her off, packing someone else into her place . . ."

"Do you think so? She hasn't got a thing to her name, and the one that's taking her place is just the same. She's already mending mattresses in her new cell."

"Oh. As for incidentals, I'd better order shampoo and some envelopes. Thank you very much, matron."

Now my heart is back to its normal rate. I don't know who was put into Paule's place, but it isn't and won't be me: the gods are still smiling.

All that Lerouge has to live on here is her wages as a trusty: when she arrives two days later with my canteen order, the bill for which amounts to at least four months' pay for her, the strawberries are stripped of all their gourmet charm by the sudden memory of that immanent injustice of the old days, when I was so broke and had to pay for kindnesses with smiles and the work of my hands: I don't want the fruit any more, I won't want it until Lerouge has accepted half of it. I still owe Lerouge plenty more than a pound of strawberries.

I know the joint: crippled, half dead, pig-eyed, or persuasive, if I had been destined to be a trusty, I would have had no choice. Every night, until the day that Paule left, I had spent in imagining: the necessity of revealing my secret self, my pig-headed self, of demanding hearings, of haggling, with much display of X-rays of arms and threats of calling expert witnesses, all winding up with finding myself in the hole for refusing to work, then coming out a week or two later, wan and docile; docile because in the hole I would have worked out another scheme and found a way to transform the job into a better arrangement for myself . . . Now that the major terrors are out of the way, I can approach Lerouge, in an offhand, detached way; she is perceptive, she can always spot the finger that's trying to get up her nose; but, since I had been careful to coat the finger with plenty of coffee, cigarettes, and other goodies and since I was operating with as much subtlety as she was, Lerouge did not sneeze. Gently my finger went farther, groped, and reached the brain.

"People have asked me what I think, as you can imagine," she says. "Since everyone knows you're a good worker . . ."

."Ha! Aside from my reprehensible activities outside, I've never done a lick of work except what I've done in stir. But

I've done plenty of that: laundry, sewing, all kinds of jobs, even taking care of the warden's kids and making layettes for the ones on the way . . . They haven't left out anything where I'm concerned. But now I can't do so much. Give you a hand, yes; if you're behind with your sewing, just tell me." I feel a rush of remorse and good will.

"Thanks . . . for the present I'm all right, but perhaps later . . . Yes, to get back to what we were talking about: the deputy warden came into the workroom the other night, you may have heard him . . ."

"Oh, you know how hard it is up here on the second tier to hear what's going on on the ground floor, and anyway I don't glue my ear to the hole in the door . . ."

"I know that, it's nice to meet a woman who minds her own business the way you do. Not like that other one . . ."

That other one is Josy, Josy the candy-guzzler, the asker of fool questions who never lets go of anyone, who takes all our guff and, when she can't take any more, talks to whoever will listen, and, when there's no one left, she goes and talks to the dandelions. At the moment she's explaining to two old women, who can't get away, how she expects to be able to get her children back when she's released from here; she punctuates her oration by displaying numerous photographs all crumpled from being permanently stored in her bra.

"Hey, Josy," Lerouge calls, "stop your wagon, the wheels are falling off! The other day you were telling us you'd go out dancing for four nights in a row. Well, what do you want, your kids or the gay life?"

"The kids first, naturally," Josy says. "But that doesn't mean I can't go dancing, does it? The day I get out of here, I'm going right to the social welfare . . ."

"But you're getting out on a Sunday, so you'll bump your nose on the door; you'll promise yourself to go back on Monday but in the meantime you'll find yourself a John and go . . ."

The Runaway

"Dancing," I interrupt. "Cut it, Lerouge, let's talk about something else, all this makes my tits ache. Stir's a dull subject, I'll grant, but I'd still rather talk about that: kids are a sacred topic for me. When I think that she's got four of them!"

"Yes, all out in foster homes . . ."

"And the fifth on the way, or almost . . ."

"Well, thank God we're not judges or matrons . . ."

"Speaking of matrons, ours is really a marvel. It's a lot tougher with the men, believe me. The deputy-shit hasn't been too tough on you, has he?"

"Oh," Lerouge replies, "with me he's always kept his head screwed on right. The other night he even gave me compliments. Imagine, I'd just got through with (she counted on her fingers) six starched shirts, cleaning and pressing his uniforms, his . . . anyway, with that and the prison laundry I was absolutely pooped. So he asked me if he should assign you to help me. I told him I'd need four like you, as busted up as you are . . . Excuse me, Anick, but since you didn't seem too hot for the job . . ."

My darling Lerouge! As long as I'm in stir with you, you'll never go short of fruits in season. We'll do all kinds of little things for each other, I'll draw you floral designs for your letters, and you'll put aside a special prison denim for me and, once I've begun to wear it, I'll even begin to feel a certain affection for it little by little. But careful: prison is in that dress, you must not love it. Thus far, simply through the power of my own possessions, I had managed to erect and maintain an impenetrable barrier between myself and resignation, between myself and the clan of the brown dresses. And soon enough, along with the outfit of the finally sentenced prisoner, I'll take on that character. The absurdity, the banality of words! Finally sentenced—I have been that for years; then I was a released prisoner, and that too, I had thought, was final. But by now I have learned not to believe in words any more, to accept them only on a provisional basis, and that

361

applies as well to such words as *final*. Our state here is a word, just as our entire outfit is a denim dress; in the mind as on the carcass, you are entitled to own only what's underneath, "provided that the general appearance of prison dress is not modified thereby." But this time the dress will no longer exert any power over me: beneath the denim I am patient but prepared to spring, because, before I put it on, I felt the fingers of my love upon me, his impatient, his confederate fingers.

Zizi will never know that there are times when I am tempted by resignation, that same resignation into which he had locked himself and from which I had had to rout him with an angry gentleness. No, Zi will never know of the unending vigil against regret and weariness. Oh, these days! They pile up one on top of another, days without incident that I discard one by one in a scorn without memory. The brain must not be overloaded: to remember one of these days is enough to make all of them come alive again. If I were a first-timer, I would certainly find a kind of pleasure in learning the oddities of the routine and the regulations; but, thank God, I'm an old hand and weary of the joys of prison. For with this laughter I may very well, one fine morning, find myself at the bottom of the walls with my ass full of lead. But then, once I'm free, I can already sense the furies that hide beneath the kindly lulls, and I continue to be watchful.

There are times, too, when I realize what we're going to do and am filled with an awed horror: these poor walls, and these nice reinforced devices that we shall have to destroy; these other people, my betters, whose indifference will be suddenly transformed into madness . . .

"Mad, they'll go mad," I repeat into my mirror; and, supported by old newspapers that had somehow escaped the prison censor with their stories of other recent jailbreaks, American and French, looking at the pictures of the wretched officials painfully wriggling into the formidable tunnels of the

362

fugitives, I picture with a heady sense of shame what will occur here when Zi and I, harnessed to a star, have disappeared into the pale fog of dawn.

Sometimes I get up at night to take a pee or make coffee, and, before I get back under the covers, I go through various exercises and contortions on the bed in order to make the idea a familiar one to my carcass and train it to obey my mind. And the carcass fights back, makes itself heavy and rigid: "Maybe they'll all go mad, but in the meantime you're the one that's acting like it, girl," I think, forcing myself to touch my head with the tip of my toe as I lie stretched out on the bed with my eyes fixed on the transom and its many black bars.

How precise, how frighteningly geometrical everything becomes at night, how worthless the mind feels in the midst of all that motionless real matter!

Once, after the nine-o'clock bed check, I waited a moment and then climbed up to the transom: I suspect the birds of having built a nest there and in the moonlight I may have a chance to see the glow of its strands. My chair, undoubtedly as the result of some earlier neglect, lacks the chain that should have kept it fastened under the table, as is the case in most of the other cells. So I stood the chair against the central-heating pipes, being careful not to bang it against them: these pipes make an endless serpentine throughout the whole wing, which is practical for Morse transmissions, but, as it happens, my own preference ran to the semaphore. I hoisted myself up on the back of the chair, taking special pains to distribute my weight evenly on both feet in order not to make my perch rock: I had jammed my fist between the uprights of the transom, and I had no desire to be hanged by the arm. I brought my nose up to the level of my wrist and took a deep breath of the night. If I had been able to get eight inches higher, I would have been able to see the nest, but the chair too must have been designed with a thought to our possible exercises: from this extremely acute angle of observation, all I could see of the nest was its outer trim of feathers and twigs, and a part of its base, which consisted of old, extremely old chunks of bread, probably tossed up there for the sparrows of the preceding inmate: my own sparrows were invisible.

The windows of the office wing were still lighted; those of the buildings on the other side of the highway were lost in a vague darkness. And, to add to the fearsomeness of the broken glass glinting in the moonlight on top of the main wall, the tiles and the dormer windows reflected the glow on the steep pitch of the roofs. My arm was beginning to feel the bones of the uprights, my head was spinning with fresh air and silence, and I climbed down again. The fuel tablet lighted before I climbed up had long since burned out; I started another and listened to the water as it started boiling again with a tremendous hissing. I had the feeling that it could be heard all the way to the office, that that damned seething was going to destroy me, that someone would come and take me by surprise in my underwear stained with the dirt of the wall and with a deep red bruise on my forearm. But everything stayed asleep: the office and I were the only ones awake, probably, in that part of the establishment. The men's wing is at the other end of the prison, and the only windows from which you can see the men's windows in daylight are those of the wardrobe and storage rooms, ex-cells in which no prisoners have lived for years. Instead, these house dried vegetables and new mattresses: "There were some guys that did things they shouldn't, so you can guess . . ." Naturally, in a world of women like ours, there would always be some poor hysterical thing, or simply one who didn't have enough to do, to call to the Johns and show them, if she could, her ass and her knockers.

As a consequence it had become extremely difficult to communicate with the men's wing on serious business. There is always some point at which the system has a weakness, and Zizi can be relied on to find it; but I would prefer that he restrict himself to our letters and visits, reserving notes for hand-to-hand or mouth-to-mouth delivery during excursions to court: a jailbreak should never be made in writing.

"Whistle while you work," I hum as I get off my couch to go look in the cupboard for a handful of strawberries: strawberries are not the ideal fruit and if they are not eaten they go bad. I can hear Lerouge cleaning the stairs; I hastily roll a little packet of instant coffee and, tapping my wedding ring on the window, I call: "Lerouge!" She doesn't hear me, so I knock harder.

"What is it? Oh, my!"

Poor Lerouge—all the other women exploit the fact that she comes and goes all day long in the wing to get her to run all sorts of errands, or to make her listen to crap they find intensely interesting. And Lerouge, like a good girl, shoves cigarettes and newspapers under doors, carries messages, and, whenever anyone raps at the window for her, runs to answer with her *Oh, my.* "Say, Lerouge, you wouldn't have a match, would you? . . . Come here, Lerouge, and I'll read you the letter I got from my John . . . What time is it, Lerouge? This morning's a real bore!"

"Just you come and do my scrubbing, and you'll see what a real bore is!" Lerouge retorts, because they've finally gotten to her.

Classifications are rather strict in this joint: Lerouge may fall in her tracks, but she's the one who has to do the work, and not anyone else.

It is disgusting but also reassuring. In any case, no one ever dies of the work; you just lose a few superfluous pounds; and, on the other hand, it brings certain little privileges. In a collective prison, those not yet tried and those who have

365

been tried and sentenced are all thrown together and everyone gets into the act; in order to avoid being treated as a parasite by the others and as a loafer by the matrons, you make a show of what you can do, there is always competition for the washing, the cleaning, the ironing. For the sake of "looking good."

When you ask for a work assignment in an individual-cell prison, you should know what you're exposing yourself to; and, if you don't know, you learn very quickly. In the beginning, the calves of your legs ache every night and your arms are dead; then, after a few months, the seesaw moves, and the hope of ever getting out of it wanes, while people's esteem for you rises, along with the hope of finally getting some crumb of privilege from the warden.

It is to be noted, however, that these crumbs are far more concrete than the wild stories that run through all prisons from the first of every January to the fourteenth of every July and actually come true perhaps one time in ten—I mean amnesty. "All I'd need now is that amnesty!" I mutter. "With my luck, the amnesty will hit me right in the back and crush both my mount and me. Good-by, runaway!"

Now an amnesty that would tumble us all out together, political prisoners and criminals in the same crowd, would suit me fine. But you might as well ask God to hurry up the Last Judgment! If an amnesty is granted, it will affect, as usual, only the little nobodies doing two or three months or fined a hundred or a thousand francs . . . as for us, we'll be stuck in the same old cage: layers of stale, immobile disillusionments for our last sacrament.

All right, let's bury all this shit, these remissions of sentence bought with the pound of flesh of prison employment, these paroles that get refused every six months until the whole sentence has been served, etc. All of them call for too much conniving, too many petitions, too much sterile persistence, too much torturing hope. To think of freedom in terms of an

imminent delight that can be brought about in an instant by
a single super-effort is much more stimulating.

A fixed date for discharge is an obsession; but a split is
not. A split is for tonight, or another night, or next month,
or next year; it takes root, even if not in detail, as a background figure that leaves the rest of the mind detached and
alert; it is discreet, like a friend who sits with you without
talking; you continue whatever you're doing without bothering about her, yet you remember all the same to give her a
smile now and then.

I wonder what my friend the runaway mare will be able
to tell me when I make up my mind to ask questions. In every
friendship, especially at the outset, there is a secret anxiety,
a fear of being betrayed or disappointed by the friend, a fear
of your own potential to betray or disappoint. So I keep
myself as busy and aloof as I can, lest my friend the runaway
should suddenly decide to talk.

This triangle household of the runaway and ourselves
makes itself quite at home on my bed, the runaway caressing
my mind and Zizi caressing my heart. We wait attentively,
long after darkness has fallen.

Until the matron makes her night round, the auditory
environment consists of the noise of plates—like me, the
girls have probably allowed themselves the luxury of dining
in bed—of lids being banged down on johns, of coughs,
sometimes of conversations through closed doors; but, from
seven o'clock on, all these sounds begin to be muted, and the
only thing that still makes the walls shake is the sound of the
pedals of Lerouge's sewing machine: the prison is going to
sleep, humming quietly.

The lady comes to make her check: if the night is slow
enough in arriving to allow her to make out our outlines
under the bedclothes, she doesn't turn on the light; and,
even when she does switch it on, her hand is astonishingly

light on the button. The way in which a light switch or a peephole is handled is indicative, much more so than words, which are colored by circumstances and by the natures of our dear guards.

The night is soft and silent. Sometimes, naturally, someone drums on her door: there is a mouse on the premises, a ghost has been seen, a sudden illness has begun. Lerouge is in charge of the alarm bell in the workroom, but, before she turns the place upside down, she goes first to call through a door and ask what's the matter, and as a rule our ladies manage to get through their ailments and their night terrors without the help of the staff or of anyone else.

Besides, I think the bell isn't working.

Mice and ghosts: and they pretend to be grown-up women! I'd be glad to take over some of their fright: perhaps that might save me from disastrous stupidities and an ass full of lead. I remember our farewells on the first night of prison, and the devastating clarity that suddenly made me whimper under the final kisses of my love: "It's my fault, Zi, everything's my fault . . ." Again I feel the overwhelming grief of those days, my silent supplication, forgive me, Zizi, forgive me and keep on believing in us through all the years of exile and misery. This runaway, I swear, will be my last caprice: I won't be careless and fool around any more, no more jeering, no more selfish and teasing games.

When Zizi wants something, he offers it as a proposal, a suggestion; he allows me to do things he disapproves of, without issuing prohibitions, without jawing at me; but I can see the color of his eyes grow darker, I can feel ice flowing into the tips of his fingers: at such signals, I persisted maliciously and clumsily in my whims, waiting for him to hit me one . . . but the first belt is a sign you're settling things by force, and Zizi never has hit me.

I owe a mountain of love, a mountain of friendship.

The Runaway

In order to maintain the tie with friendship, I sought and sought: with Maria, with Nicole, and our tiny brains evolved a thousand projects for the wind to scatter one by one, laughing at us with the sun.

I'm already drafting letters for the future, for of course I'll write letter after letter to everyone . . .

Oh, Zi, I am alone, join yourself to me and me to you. We won't let anyone down, we won't do anything wrong.

And we will be sure that we have done ourselves so much good.

(4)

It is raining, it has been raining whole days and nights, and the mixture of rain and time wipe out the summer. Even to-day, when our appeal is to be heard, the sun refuses to appear. Too bad, I might have made it my ally. Oh, Zizi, what a waste of beautiful weather! But there will be only a chilly caress or two, and it will not be too awful to have to return to the cell . . .

Last night, after the six-o'clock lock-up, I wrote my note. All day the storm darkened my transom: it was impossible to write, and at that time of year it was out of the question to bang on the door and ask for the lights to be turned on: not before October. Sitting in the dusk, listening to the floods pour down the rain gutter, I waited for the lights to be turned on. At seven o'clock I was able to begin.

I had kept a bit of treated paper that had been the wrapping of a canteen sausage. But the grease of this sausage, although it was advertised as "dry," made the ball-point skip; so I had to take a sheet out of my notebook. I used cigarette paper only for the diagrams: the floor plan of the basement and the big sketch of the whole wing. I had sewed all this into some plastic and put it away in my shampoo capsule, as usual.

The Runaway

In order to be able to get at it more easily, I fastened a bit of string to the note: it is better to minimize the gymnastics in case there is no stall there either and asking to go to the toilet would be asking too much.

At the eleven-o'clock lunch the lady gave me my shoes and my skirt. "Be ready to go at one o'clock, or one-thirty," she says, "but wait for me before you get dressed, so that we can save time by relieving me of having to search you again."

"But," I laughed, "suppose I spend the time sewing love letters into the hem of my skirt?"

"I trust you; and anyway I have no choice where you're concerned: I know very well that, if you have something to smuggle out, you'll have a sure place to put it!"

This matron is really a good sort.

This doesn't prevent me from making sure that the string on the note isn't hanging out; I take down my panties, coughing and waving my arms: good, it stays in. The lady is kind, but God knows what kind of shrew a kind jailer can turn into when she discovers that you've tried to make a fool of her. I would simply have to defiantly gulp down that shampoo capsule that tasted like fern; before and after every trip to court I would have to submit to a gynecological examination (after all, this may not be the last time; a second appeal is always possible), and this would run up my bill: to search a woman in that area, the presence of a certified physician is mandatory, and the croaker doesn't make the trip for nothing: everything is always hidden "there," but, if you have been observed or even only suspected, it's "Up on the table," and remember the fees.

I hear the sound of a bell in a belfry.

If only I have time for a final coffee. I start the water boiling. But the lady knows every courtesy, including that of kings, and her keys clink barely five minutes after the bells in the town have rung. I can hear her slamming doors on the ground floor; as she opens my door, I am blowing on the burner to get it started.

"But you have time enough to finish your coffee," she says.

"I've finished, thank you, matron . . . This was just a bonus. It'll taste all the better when I get back." (I shall never be able to eat or drink in the presence of matrons.)

I get into my rags; meanwhile the lady inspects the pictures that I had attached to the wall above my table with rice paste. Helpfully, when she sees that I'm having problems with my zipper, she closes it for me, observing that "you need a shoehorn to get into that skirt."

Then we leave. I start for the open door of the wing, but the lady points me toward an empty cell: the escort hasn't arrived yet, I am searched, I'm like a limb made ready for the surgeon: it is necessary to keep me in a sterile environment.

The minute I'm alone, I bring out my note. Out with the fern; I sling the shampoo capsule over the transom, no use carrying an overload. I hide the plastic goody in my handkerchief, the decorous handkerchief of the woman who has no pockets, that I roll into a ball in my fist.

The lady is not long in returning; in the corridor outside the office there is a huge crowd of yapping policemen, certainly we can't be the only ones going out . . . Inside the men's wing, an attendant opens the gate: ah, here are all the Johns. Suddenly an angel detaches himself from the jabbering mass and pounces on me: "All right, you, stand against the wall and don't move."

No, angel, I won't move, not yet. All orders will be carried out in silence, in order not to stir up the wild beast and to be allowed to sit next to my husband in the wagon on the way back. As a matter of fact, where is this husband?

The men bolt through the gate, and the cops chain them in series, two by two, at the wrist; ah, there's Zizi, the last, as usual; once more I feel the pleasant shock of rediscovering him, that feeling of the unknown and of dazzled possession . . .

Zizi is about to pass the whole line in order to join me, but I put a finger to my lips at the same time that a cop shuts him off with a sharp click of the handcuffs.

The squadron parades before me as I wait there, my buttocks glued to the wall. Finally I too am invited to detach myself.

The wagon has been driven into the main courtyard: in whose honor had the great gate been opened? Certainly not for two harmless little runaways like us . . . We had not made a single move in daylight, taken a single step, knocked out a single guard.

No, there must be much bigger game in the bag. But it does no good to look all the men over, I don't recognize any of them, or, rather, I know them all: my little brothers, the jailbirds, shabby, well-dressed, or tricked out in their Sunday best, but all brothers in their glances, their gestures, their beaten or triumphant or nondescript manner.

Waiting for my turn to climb into the vehicle, I inspect the landscape: the height of the walls, the flower beds, and the rows of vegetables in the warden's garden, and the cartons of Nescafé and margarine in great piles that two characters in blue aprons are beginning to carry into the storeroom. My traveling companions favor me with labored pantomimes and charming glances; to give them pleasure, I give them a fraction of a smile, which I finish by making it broader for my husband, who has also been waiting his turn and smiling.

All of us sit there looking like angels.

In the wagon, the men continue putting it on: they exchange male remarks, smoke, and spit like free men, and pull on their handcuffs as others might on their shirt cuffs. One of them seems as bad at identifying every passing heap as I would be reading the mass, but who persists all the same in naming every license plate that passes us. "Look, a car from Holland," he says at the sight of a Mercedes with a Z on its license.

The cop sitting beside me reacts at once. "They're not Dutch," he insists, "they're from Switzerland."

I look at him like a new friend: "No one can put anything over on you! Anyone can see right off that you know all there is to know when it comes to cars. Like me—I *adore* them." I pull back the sleeve of my sweater to show my wrist. "That was my last accident."

With the eyes of a lovesick toad, the cop confides that he too is all scarred from accidents and he'd be delighted to show me his wounds, but . . . I hush him: "My husband's here."

"Your husband? which one is he?"

I point to Zizi, at the end of the row. "Oh, so that's your husband." The cop is silent for a bit, and then he says: "Say, it can't be much fun to meet like this, not even able . . ."

"Well," I say coyly, "if you wanted to fix it up, we could . . ."

He explains that it's not his fault, that if it were up to him personally, that he has to carry out his orders . . .

"Sure . . . but, if we behave ourselves, do you think we could sit together on the way back?"

"Now, now," the cop says with irritation, "I told you I have my orders."

I drop it. Zizi and I make signals to each other above his head; luckily, both of us know how to read lips. I tell him that I have mail to give him; he replies that he has some for me, and he makes a gesture indicating a toothache: good, he has it in his mouth. We find names of birds to fit some of our companions, we are getting closer to the Palace of Justice, soon, darling, we won't see each other ever again, I hope, as accused prisoners. Don't let them get you down, no-certainly-not, shit-to-the-thirteenth-power-for-luck, kisses being blown and loving glances.

As we enter the main hall, the police divide us into two groups, those going up for sentence on one side and those appealing on the other, and then we start off again. Stairway, corridor, doors with titles on them. The angels must have lost their way, they can't find the right room. Suddenly the leader of the band frowns and says: "Stop, stop. Weren't there six for appeals?"

"Yes," one of his men says, "why?"

I am beginning to be sorry that we had not got on our horse right here at the Palace of Justice: what with all the time involved in realizing that the number of prisoners didn't add up right, in counting us over again, calling off the names —which had to be done twice, in order to be absolutely certain—I could have been all the way out of town. As it happened, no one was missing; there was one too many of us.

". . . five, six, seven," the cop counts again. "There's no way out of it, we've got somebody here who shouldn't be here." Suddenly it dawns on him. "We must have taken one of the guys to be sentenced. Well, which one is it?"

Don't all answer at once. He goes from one to another, waving his list. "What's your name? . . . O.K., you're on the list. How about you? . . O.K. Next man, what's your name?"

The next man says "Grregneugneu," and the cop bawls: "Huh?"

"Gru-gnon."

No luck, Grregneugneu is on the list too. The cop spots us; he separates me from Zizi, who had pulled me to him with his arm, and shoves us apart: "These two we know all about . . ."

I would like to know just what they do know, but it's not a good time for asking questions: the cop is red-faced and angry, all this mish-mash is going to make "us" late. Finally

375

the culprit is discovered: a poor dazed bastard who looks like a chronic masturbator and whose clothes are falling apart; under the flood of abuse poured on him from the mouths of the law, the only thing he knows to do is keep his own obstinately closed, rocking back and forth in his dirty boots.

"All right," the leader tells the nearest policeman, "take him back where he belongs."

But the man to whom the culprit is chained objects: "But I'm not up for sentencing."

"Who asked you to butt in?"

"But look." The man raises his arm to show the handcuff binding him to the masturbator.

"You're right, you have to be separated. Now where are the keys? WHERE are the keys to the handcuffs, damn it?"

Let no one make a move! The arrangements for our custody have been perfected down to the slightest detail: the cops assigned to the other group have our keys, and vice versa. Someone trots off to make the exchange, while the rest of us shift from foot to foot, the cops take off their caps to wipe their foreheads with their handkerchiefs, and Zizi and I take the opportunity to whisper together. But Zizi is being watched, and I wonder how we are going to manage the exchange of goodies. Hell, we'll see when we get into the courtroom.

At last order is restored, the poor devil who has caused all the trouble is hauled off by the ears, and we make a fresh start toward the proper room, which the cop who went for the keys tracked down on his way back; we simply backtracked over the whole course that we had taken and set off into the maze opposite the one that we had wandered into first.

We are even five minutes ahead of time: the clock opposite the judge's bench, above everyone's head, shows five minutes before two o'clock. This tick-tock saves the presiding judge the necessity of making motions toward his watch when the lawyers won't stop talking.

Zizi is at the other end of the bench, separated from me by six feet of cop-criminal-cop-criminal; finally he can't contain himself any longer; he leans toward the angel sitting at his right and whispers into his ear. The angel mutters "hmmm," shifts his feet, looks at me, and then says: "O.K. But two minutes and no more, right? Make it quick, before the judges come in, and just keep quiet afterward."

Zizi promises, thanks him, and gets up, making a half-turn in order not to twist his enforced partner's wrist; I also get up and walk over to him; and there we stand enlaced in the traditional kiss of souls united, during which a tiny parcel starts toward my throat; I stop it on the way, I push it into a corner of my cheek with my tongue, and at the same time I slip my own note into my husband's hand. A vast sigh, delivery accomplished, and all that remains is to go on kissing, in an eternal kiss . . . until our respective escorts yank each of us back toward his respective end of the bench, muttering "that'll do, turtledoves," and the two of us, still breathless, can only repeat and re-repeat our thanks, which at once touches and irritates our angels: "All right, that's enough, now just take it easy, will you?"

Take it easy, take it easy! That's the only thing that they too know how to say. Take it easy yourselves: we'll obey, we'll listen to the decision, we'll make our break, and we'll live and love each other, taking it easy all the while.

The license-plate expert is sitting at my left, and there is no cop between us: being so close to him, I can observe some of the more nauseating details about him: the spots on his trousers, the ear standing rudely out from a field of badly washed skin, in which a number of pores had burst into sores; and he keeps shaking himself and muttering . . . Every time a lawyer pushes open the door upholstered in moleskin, he stands up, then drops back onto the bench; he calls me to witness: "See? they aren't worth the big fees we pay 'em. Can't even see my lawyer before the thing begins. You just wait, he won't even show. I'm such a dumb prick . . ."

"Oh, take it easy," I say (great, it was getting into my blood too). "Your mouthpiece'll show, all right. And, if he doesn't, you just tell the presiding judge you're not accepting any decision without your lawyer, and you'll get an adjournment for a week, that's all."

The guy shrugs and turns his back on me: what a jerk of a girl. Who does he think I am, without a lawyer, without any papers to support my case, without anything? He's loaded down with a bundle of greasy documents that he keeps endlessly consulting and chewing over, looking anxious; he folds them all together, daydreams for a moment, then opens them all again and starts rereading them. Probably he is getting ready to act as his own lawyer.

Ten minutes after two. The moleskin doors spit out a little bit of a lawyer, extremely young, probably a trainee, who fidgets in his robe and waggles his brief case. I sighed with relief: this is a musical-comedy lawyer, in a minute he'll start singing . . . With a coquettish finger he smoothes the hairs of his dainty goatee; then he puts on his glasses and comes up to our bench. "André Maugin?" he asks hesitantly.

My neighbor raises a finger, like a schoolboy called on by the teacher; then, being watched, he changes this gesture into that of the customer in a bar: "Hey, bartender." "That's me, counselor," he says.

He tries to rise so that he can move away from us and talk in privacy, but the handcuff stops him and I have no choice but to hear what the goatee tells him: "Allow me to introduce myself: my name is X, the bar association assigned me to represent you. But I wasn't told about it until this morning:

that's why I was unable to visit you in detention. I have familiarized myself with the file in your case . . ."

Obviously, the jerk doesn't have a sou and has had to accept a lawyer appointed through the court. I take my ass in my two hands: "We must be privileged characters in the women's wing: there's a roster of your Holy Order and, if we insist long enough, we're allowed to look at it."

The goatee smiles, I feel like gabbing, but the moleskin door opens again and I drop everything, because it's my very own lawyer who's coming in, my father, my savior! I turn to him at once, and, when we've shaken hands, I cling to his to pull him toward my husband, who is still manacled; "May I?" I fling at the angels, adding to myself: "And, if I may not, it won't make any difference." The three of us whisper together until the judges enter.

The lawyer still wants to have our case adjourned: first of all, he is not in such good voice today; second . . .

"The third party is here," he says. As a matter of fact, I can see our victims at the very back of the courtroom. "And, now that the vacation period is almost here, we have a good chance of wearing them down: what with the repeated loss of time and money in coming here . . . in short, I'm going to try to persuade them to send their lawyer to the next hearing."

Court is now in session. I'm no longer listening to the lawyer: I'm studying the judges' faces, trying to decide what kind of behavior will have the best effect on them when the time comes. Zizi is better at this than I: when our turn comes, I admire the way in which he walks to the bar with deference and humility, and I too try to make my head bend and my shoulders droop.

We take turns answering the chief judge; for the moment I stand quite erect, my hands far from the bar. But it is useless for me to swear to myself at each session that I will not touch that lousy bar . . . by the time the questioning is over, it's always the same, I am clinging to it.

Counselor explains to the prosecutor that, if it were possible to put off our matter to a later date, this would give him the time to devote further study to certain points in the record. I know that the pros' and counselor have been pals since school days and so at first the formality with which counselor makes his request seems exaggerated to me; then I remember that it would be indecent behavior in court for the evildoer's defender to address the representative of society as "old pal."

The prosecutor conveys counselor's wishes to the presiding judge, who says that he has no objection . . . provided that we too have none. We'll stick to that: since in principle counselor is *we,* let him answer in our place. Very courteously, the judge says again: "Do you agree to a postponement of the hearing?"

In stir you lose the habit of giving your opinion: look here, you, nobody's asking you to butt in. Uncertainly, I look at Zizi, and I can see that he too doesn't seem to have his mind made up. But a decision is imperative: if the judges begin to kick up a fuss . . .

It is one of our victims who saves the situation. "Your Honor," he begins, "I am leaving on a two-month vacation the day after tomorrow: if . . . if the hearing is postponed, it will be very difficult for me to be present . . ."

Counselor leaps on him. "But that is no problem, sir! The court will take note of your wishes: at the next hearing, we will request that a lawyer present them in person . . ."

The chief judge is impatient. "Well, monsieur, are you willing to be represented?"

The complainant can hardly choose otherwise. And furthermore, before the stern faces of the judges, the complainant seems considerably more guilty than we. He was the one bringing charges, he expected compassion, sympathy, equity; and here it is we who are getting the preference and he who is being asked the same questions as those miserable crooks . . .

As a result, all the other complainants were emboldened enough to back out too: all of them seem relieved at avoiding having to attend another session in this joyless hall. Justice will be done here, that has been promised to them: why should they have to be here too?

They declare that they will stand on their requests and withdraw, with little bows in the direction of the court.

"Very well," the chief judge says, "the judgment stands with respect to the civil complainants. The next case please."

If they had dared, our accusers would have galloped out. We, being less pressed, make our little obeisances to the court, inclining our backs a bit; and we go back to our little brothers, our angels, and our bench of infamy.

Since we have "taken it easy," we are allowed to sit side by side in the wagon on the way back. And there we continue our kiss.

In my cell, I unfold the notes, which I had smuggled in in my mouth without any trouble: when a prisoner comes back from court, he can hardly be expected to talk much. Tomorrow I'll explain that the appeal has not been decided yet; but tonight it is to my interest not to open my mouth. The lady respected my silence.

It is just as I thought: Zizi is on my wave length, he advises me not to start anything before I get the word from him. He reiterates that he'll come and get me out, "above all, keep your hands off the locks," and that there will be plenty of time to pack my bags on the last night.

But, with all the stuff he needs and can't get hold of, God knows when we'd get the green light. Counselor's adjournment has gained us a week or two, and I'm hoping that this delay will get Zi the right contacts. But Zi writes: "Darling, the summer is slipping away rapidly . . . When I think of the possibility of letting you down, because I may not be able to find a way out, it drives me up the wall and I want to sit and howl like a baby . . . Try to understand, baby, that all I have at the moment is my teeth, and I can't gnaw my way through walls."

When I read that, I too feel as if I'm about to bawl.

Treacherously the thought of giving in returns, hovering above my resolution . . . It would keep Zizi from being upset, it would mean that for him and for us there would be just the time to be served, these years whose every season is winter and that compel us to re-invent sunshine by dreaming of it . . . Oh, no, I can never keep hope alive that long!

I'll be released first, that is almost certain; but I know too well that I'll come back here every day to share . . . What idiocy, to share! It is always impossible to share in the sense of making burdens lighter: a rap cannot be borne as a cart is pulled: if two of us are serving time, the time is doubled. And all the rap we've already served, and that's a long time, can't compensate for anything, can't help in any way, as long as it continues, for us or for others, as long as it has not been eliminated. If we succeed in escaping from it, other guys and other girls will still be caught in it at the same instant; our rap rolls us and erodes us in an endless tide, and those years —like a thick substance that has to be gulped down—will turn into a liquid and evaporate little by little: even memory will have no trace of them.

We always forget stir very soon—why?

Because—at least as far as I'm concerned—I never "realized" my prisons; I never saw them as anything but intervals, as pretexts for doing things that had no relation to them and to the purpose that had been assigned them; in these penitential precincts I've made jokes, if I have suffered it has never been in my conscience, I've observed what was around me, I've also learned to love better . . . Nor have I ever thought that all these days were bringing me closer to freedom: I have always left jail with the feeling of unfinished business; perhaps because release has already put me on the road toward re-imprisonment; but above all because, since for me the concept of expiation has no validity, it seems to me that I must go on paying until I have accepted it . . . in other words, for a very long time to come.

I confected too much adventure out of my prisons: I could not believe that for the others, the men in the Palace of Justice and the Bureau of Prisons, there is nothing of adventure, there is only a chronology and red tape; and that all this red tape will shape the conclusion of the adventure, regardless of what I may have in mind at the moment.

This is why I always concentrate on making a break.

If I gave in, I would give in too much, and I would need a kick in the ass on the final day; already I feel almost frustrated at the thought of throwing away this jumble of fabricated protheses with which I make myself prop up the absurd and plunge further into it . . .

I toss on my mattress in the dark: "Zizi, you absolutely have to find the tools, prison is beginning to get me down, you have to move fast . . ."

Because in no time we'll be separated . . . And it does no good for Zizi to write: "I'll come and get you no matter where I am," I say to myself that it is precisely here that action must be taken, that there is no other reason for our transfer.

Let the force of things not be greater than our own strength! Let the summer last a little longer! If I accept autumn, then what reason will I have to refuse winter? Warming my feet on the radiators in December, I will be collecting material so as to be patient in spring, and so on . . .

But I know that I'm just spinning daydreams in a vacuum: at the thought of staying here, a pang of eternity twists my guts, exactly like when I was a child contemplating the eternity of the catechism, the horrible eternity of the Good Lord.

(5)

"There certainly seems to be a lot of running around up there! Are there burglars on the roof?"

"The men are cleaning out the rain pipes," the lady explains to me.

Those jerks woke me up: they are whistling louder than blackbirds, and their voices drown out the cheeping of my sparrows. Poor sparrows! with all this disturbance, they're afraid to go on keeping house in my transom: but at eleven o'clock, when the guys go off to lunch, the birds come back.

Up, girl, on your feet. Going back to sleep is out of the question, the big birds are making too much racket. I could talk to them, it would be less painful than having to listen to them: the back of my chair, set under the window, would hoist me up high enough; but I don't want to.

Perhaps the roofers are ambulant stool pigeons. Go get the screw, the broads are breaking our balls.

Being alone, Zizi must look for a delivery boy for his notes: he can size up the various men before he gets in contact with one. I just wait: mentally, I strip whatever comes into my cell, canteen orders or prison visitors; I am forever imagining all the possible mistakes, anticipating the kick in the teeth

. . . If they're the messengers I've been hoping for, the birds will, of course, be able to find me.

During the exercise period, I glance casually at the roof, just long enough to observe the prisoner with one buttock hanging over the edge of the tiles who is trying to peer at our thighs: we are trying to get brown in spite of the clouds, and every dress is pulled up from the bottom and unhooked at the top. When I spot the peeper, I button up and move to another part of the yard; I decide to sit right up against the wall: if the bird wants another look at me, he'll have to move farther out and cling to the gutter . . . and then I may have the pleasure of seeing him spill his guts right there in the middle of the rectangle of dandelions.

But what does one thigh more or less matter? there are still those of the other women, and these women are thinking only of their suntans, it's obvious that they haven't noticed anything.

To punish me, the bird on the roof is chucking things at me: slop out of the gutter, pebbles, bits of zinc, little mud pies. But when a large hunk of tile lands a couple of inches from my shoe, I begin to worry about my safety, and I call the matron, who is prowling about just inside the door. "Could you put me into another exercise yard, matron? With all that work going on, it's getting dangerous here."

The other girls should have paid more attention too. They have started cutting the grass in the new yard, talking and laughing very loudly in order to let the bird hear them, at least. It's not at all a matter of liking to put on the frightened act; but, if they keep up all this bullshit, something or other will happen that will bring on a complete ban on men in our wing, and I'll be up the creek.

Besides, I'm Zizi's woman, am I not? I keep that woman's blemishes and, to a lesser degree, her charms under wraps; I want to be recognized, so that Zizi can be told that I have been

seen, that I seem like a nice little dame; I want to prevent any
funny stuff, any false interpretation of whatever I do or say;
if I flex my body, it is quite a natural thing to do; if I sing my
head off, it is a different song from the one the boys on the
roof are whistling.

They take up what I'm singing, stop to see whether I'm
following. I start another tune, and so the mornings go by, in-
consequential and insipid.

Soon, from the roof or from somewhere else, a letter will
come, just as later freedom and the end of exile will come:
knowing how to be patient . . .

I had barely gotten upstairs again from the exercise yard
when the lady came into my cell with a pitcher of milk in her
hand.

"What, matron, are you on the job detail today?"

"Lerouge is busy mending, this will help her out."

"Let me give you a hand . . ."

"Oh, no, thank you, I just wanted to bring you your milk.
I'll serve chow when I come back: I have to take you to see
your lawyer."

While she is closing my door behind us, I rush down the
two flights of stairs, sliding on the over-waxed steps: for once
I may be able to get a ten-second start so that I can look
round a bit in peace. There is never a chance when we go
back indoors from our exercise: someone asks me to lend her
a book, someone else wants to "borrow one or two matches
. . . and some butts, if you have any," or else I myself have
to go and get some thread from Lerouge; in a word, every
trip to and from the courtyard is frittered away in these un-
avoidable trivialities; and what chance is there, apart from
these walks or visits, to get out of the cell?

I wait, leaning against the main door of the wing, trying to
look as if I were not trying to look like anything, my arms
properly crossed; there are fire hoses on each floor: well,

they'll make fine ropes; as for getting through the bars of the window, hm . . . I don't think I can make it, and still less Zizi, he'll have to get in through the basement transom, and . . . hush, smile, "excuse me, matron," "good afternoon, counselor."

I am reasonably satisfied with my quick survey of the premises: the fire hoses will be more solid and will take less time to get in place than a rope made of bedclothes. Now it is time to concentrate on the mouthpiece; my work has made progress, even though only inch by inch, but what's a prison wall except one inch added to another?

I get in a good handshake: counselor has thick fingers, which usually slip out of mine; but this time I got a good grip on them, a handshake is a comforting thing. An empty visiting room proffers its chairs to us, the other nooks being full of life; good, the joint is stirring: as in a silent film, the lawyers and their clients gesticulate, the prisoners on work assignments—cooks, cleaners, clerks—go about their jobs briskly, the lights are on already, the loudspeakers are blaring the evening hour of music.

Since I'm always waiting for a miracle—though God alone knows what it will be—I spend two hours every morning on my eyes and my hair, experimenting with doe eyes and all kinds of chignons; I soften the harshness of the prison denim with little dickies; I kick off my slippers in order to slip into my high heels whenever I hear anyone coming up to my floor . . . so tonight, as on all the other nights, I am completely ready for God knows what; as for my lawyer, he looks rested, his eyeglasses glisten; each of us is well pleased with the other.

To open the meeting, the question of fees has to be broached. Counselor talks all round the subject; good lord, he's embarrassed.

"Getting a postponement of your appeal," he says, "was very much a matter of professional conscience for me, believe me. We could just as easily have gone ahead with it right away

. . . But I wanted to go through the file again from the beginning; besides, after the vacations there will be a new presiding
judge, whom I don't know; there may also be a different prosecutor. So there we have the unknown, chance . . . Whereas
here I'm on solid ground. The trouble is that . . ."

"That what, counselor?"

"Well . . . I wasn't able to get you on the calendar for next
week, you have to wait two weeks."

"So much the better."

"Except that I'm going on vacation in ten days. You understand, if you absolutely insist that I handle the matter myself,
I can always interrupt my holiday; but perhaps one of my colleagues . . ."

Once again I am amazed by the lawyer's faculty for sweet-
talking, his way of appearing, as the circumstances required,
either very strong or very weak: the court was as well composed as it was disposed; he has arranged for us to be heard
by this court, under conditions that please all of us; now he is
drawing back, waiting for us to beg him to return to us, but
. . . to listen to him tell it, while it is true that the presence of a
lawyer is required in order to have the argument get under
way, it is equally true that all that matters is that some lawyer
be there, either counselor or someone else . . . What modesty!

"Oh, please come back!" I say, to make him happy. But in
the last analysis he's right: what difference does it make who
the lawyer is? I start to think: all the lawyers are away on
vacation; it is no fun to try to digest a brand-new and complicated case in two weeks, especially if one takes it on virtually
on the eve of the hearing; and, no matter what the decision, I
would have to cough up dough. So I might as well hang on to
the lawyer I have.

Both of us sighing, both of us pained by the matter, we
settle on the amount and I dictate the address of an ultra-
private banker, counselor writes it down . . . Oof!

Now that he has the dough, he explains to me how he proposes to use it. "I won't take the train back: it takes too much time and it's too tiring."

A good night in a lower berth, an ambulance-cab from the station to his house, hot compresses on his throat until just before he goes into court: it seems to me that this won't tax him too much, even if his vocal cords are as delicate as he professes them to be. But, if he prefers a jet, it's all right with me: after all, it's not my money any more.

Counselor tucks away the address that I've given him and closes his briefcase; his color comes back and he listens attentively. Our conversation grows warm and intimate. Lulled by the distant hum of the radio and the muted sound of the bunches of keys that the guards are playing with at their central post—a tic they have even when there is no locking or unlocking to be done—I allow myself to relax, to offer confidences.

"But, madame, if we do succeed in having the sentences made concurrent, without any increase in either of them . . ."

"Even if the shorter one is increased, it will be absorbed in the other one and the total will be reduced just the same, won't it?"

"Yes, provided that the increase is just the right amount."

(Two plus two makes two, two plus three makes three— —strange!)

"In that case," he goes on, "you'll get out well before your husband. And what would you do then?"

"But what do you expect me to do, counselor? The same as before, I suppose. I always come out lousy with good resolutions; it isn't my fault if being outside spoils them! No, I admit, this time I'm beat, beat and re-beat: I've crossed the last barrier, I've reached indifference. I've been asocial ever since I was born; except that a few years ago I wasn't quite so black, I still could have got you to argue that I could be rehabilitated, I could even have tried to be rehabilitated . . .

Now I can't any more: the years go by, the axe falls too often, and harder every time . . . What have I got to lose now?"

Counselor doesn't answer: he questions. "But why not go back to work? You got yourself various diplomas once . . ."

"But I dropped everything . . ."

"Nevertheless you have them. You know how to type . . ."

"Ha! I learned that in stir, yes. But outside I've never touched a typewriter: my nails . . ."

"You could take it up again: I could ask permission for you to take another typing course, if you . . ."

"No, counselor, don't go to the trouble: I'll *never* work. They've beaten me down, I tell you. Those diplomas that you talk about I got only because it's an extremely good thing to make your brain do a little work in stir on something besides their stupid nonsense. But I've never wanted to study anything except medicine: all the rest was just to kill time. And it would be a bit late to start medicine when I get out of here!"

"But can you turn the opportunity down just like that?"

I smile. "When I still had years ahead of me, and also a full set of illusions, I tried; oh, yes, counselor, believe me, I looked into all those things thoroughly. I was told that there were practical studies, for which it was compulsory to attend the university: there was considerable opposition to the idea of sending me to the university between two cops . . . So, while I was waiting for parole, I started on other studies, to amuse myself, but also to show my good will; and . . . the parole kept on being postponed from one quarter to another: 'That gives you twice the chance of getting it'; 'you're not too badly off here'; and all the rest of it. Actually, I did my work but also a few little things that the guys at the top didn't like. Their heads were too hard for me: I got a bug up my tail and one night I split."

"All the same," counselor says pensively, "healing others is a fine thing . . ."

"You mean altruism?"

"If you want to call it that."

"Perhaps that had something to do with my wanting to be a croaker. I was jailed when I was very young for a really serious job; there was no blood on my hands, you understand, but I was in bad trouble just the same. After my trial I wanted to make some kind of compensation, to redress a balance that I had destroyed . . . I don't know how to explain it: it wasn't that I felt remorse, or shame, I hadn't done anything but nevertheless I was supposed to be guilty, I couldn't say in what way. And besides—oh, counselor! (I burst into laughter)— they pulled that parole shit on me! By now 'healing others' has come down to taking the splinters out of the other girls' feet, they get plenty of them from scrubbing the floors in this joint . . . Besides, I doubt whether the Medical Society would have accepted me . . ."

"After five years you could have applied for a court declaration of rehabilitation."

"That's just it counselor: they reopen the files, they dig up the bodies, and off they go, with the newspapers in on it and all: big advantage!"

"Not at all, not at all: you became discouraged, and I can understand that very well, but you could have brought it off. But what about now? All right, we'll leave medicine aside: you have a good education . . ."

"Which is exactly what they hold against me. But you also know I'm a bastard, no one's child . . ."

"Legally adopted by respectable people."

". . . who, after my hell-raising, had the adoption rescinded. Now the only diplomas I have are in a name that isn't mine any more: just picture what a circus, counselor, if I tried to straighten myself out with the university! Even a normal student has to wait ages for just a transcript. So what about me, who doesn't even have a baptismal name any more? Oh, sure,

I could make a stink with the diocese, but . . . look, the story of my life makes me tired, let's drop it. Incidentally, now we're going to have a Bastille Day mass here! Do you suppose they're going to make it compulsory?"

It was impossible to take another tack, counselor drags me back. "What about your husband, madame? Does it occur to you that when you take this line of thought you run the risk of destroying him? Have you talked to him about all this? What is he figuring on doing? He seems really determined to climb back into society . . ."

"What does he figure on doing? Well, counselor . . . I don't know; it's impossible now to know what we're going to do. The only thing that's certain is that we want to get back together and that we don't have to look any farther than that. That's so much in itself, counselor: just to get back together . . ." And I add defiantly: "I'm happy: here, outside, I'm happy, because always, no matter where, we still have *us*."

"But you quarrel a good deal, don't you?" the lawyer asks.

"We? Who ever told you a thing like that?"

"Why, you did. During the preliminary interrogation."

"Oh, certainly it's none of the court's business if people have a row in the corridor!"

I suddenly remember those terrible silences outside between Zizi and me when one of us was nervous, or exhausted from bar-hopping, or feeling the strain of being together; everything that we threw in each other's faces in our rage, that we wanted to smash together, wounding ourselves without wanting to; the silences of anger, the silences of surrender; but I've never talked to anyone of all that. Whatever we may have told judges and mouthpieces about our "quarrels"—and counselor should understand—was just a way of talking to explain our independence and the freedom that we allowed each other; in short, to make them concede that my man kept me out of his affairs, that he went out where and when he liked, and that I never asked him any questions . . . you build your defenses with the material at hand. In this way I avoided being implicated in thefts and I could argue that any implication in receiving stolen goods was involuntary. Oh, counselor, it's a classic dodge!

In a mental whirlwind I relive other silences, when fatigue itself fell asleep and the drawn curtains separated us from life for a few hours; the tendernesses that Zi could create when he bit the lobes of my ears with his lips, when he hugged me with so much caution lest my happy body cry out too loudly; I think of our games together, the favors and the forgivenesses; and now our letters, our marvelous rationed letters . . .

I look at the lawyer, drumming his fingers on the table in his perplexity.

"I know . . . or anyway I suppose it must be difficult for you to defend girls like me, apparently inaccessible to anything, hard, incapable of arousing pity . . . I have only one vulnerable point, only one open wound—forgive my speaking so badly this evening, but I can't explain myself any better— . . . yes, the wound is this love; and yet you will never be able to find anything in it to justify me . . . And so, counselor, all I ask of you is to help me to play the game. Once, when you were talking about it, you said: 'What a circus!' "

"I said that?"

"Yes, during a jail visit. I rather like that expression: even though to me life seems like a circus at every level; still I prefer that other original expression, *the poker game;* I play, I'm a good or bad player, or simply somebody who plays, but in any case I play a losing game. Oh, these expressions!"

I am beginning to talk bullshit, the way I talk bullshit to myself in my cell, into the mirror. Counselor knows that I'm running scared, and giving up any idea of reaching a conclusion, he gets up.

"Well, madame, I'll have them call your husband. Perhaps

he'll be able to convince you. As for us . . . well, in fifteen days, right?"

"Twelve days, counselor, twelve days! Three days make a difference!"

In the next room two prisoners are talking with a man in civilian clothes, undoubtedly some dick; when I pass by their windows, they look at me, I look at them, at that instant a third prison denim surges out of the depths of the narrow corridor: I find myself trapped between him and the lawyer, everyone begs everyone else's pardon, and I start back again for the harem, walking as gracefully as I possibly can so that my little brothers will find Zizi's wife attractive.

As I pass the central guard post, I hear my lawyer asking the man on duty to send my husband out to him; if only the guard would go get him right away so that I could get a glimpse of him! But the guard passes me and goes to ring the bell of my wing: he won't budge an inch until he's certain I've disappeared.

Meanwhile, counselor starts pacing up and down at the guard post; he paces back and forth in front of me, but now I don't want to look at him anymore: he has squeezed money out of me, he has made me talk about myself, and now I am naked . . .

What is the matron up to? The screw has rung twice for her. My foot taps against the floor as I wait for her, my hands in fists on my buttocks; I'm irritated. My eyes scale the railings of the galleries all the way to the hexagonal window at the top where the gray twilight is filtering in. Finally the door opens, I smile at the lady, and on the threshold I turn my head for another sight of counselor, of his hurt, friendly eyes.

Have I not just told him that I'm happy? What do I want with this compassion of his that is anything but gratuitous?

Holding my shoulders straight under the denim, forcing myself to go up the stairs with dignity—not an easy thing in these skidding soles, Lerouge is obviously not paying for the wax that she spread on them and on those treacherous landings—I yak with my little matron; we praise counselor's broad shoulders, his excellent taste in clothes . . .

"He certainly gave you plenty of his time tonight!"

"Oh, yes indeed, matron, we just talked and talked! What time is . . . oh, no, that's right, you aren't allowed to tell me . . . Well, let me figure it out: the radio's been turned off, I can hear the pots rattling, it must be pretty close to five-thirty."

The lady thrusts her wrist under my nose: on the button.

This is fish night. I am hungry, voraciously hungry. I begin getting my bread and my plate out of the cupboard. Herring or mackerel again, pfui! Suppose I made myself a mayonnaise? That's it: I'll make myself a cup of it, but why a cup? A soup-plate of it, a quart of mayonnaise. Now to set out on the table, in the order of their use, the egg, the mustard, the salt and the oil. I'll add a clove of garlic, a crushed one, so that my tongue will catch fire, my stomach will absorb all my energy, and my imagination will stop working.

"Now he's scrammed with the address and my confidences," I mutter to myself as I stir the yellow mixture. "Oh, to hell with it. If what I told him ever comes out of his treasure vault, it will be totally unrecognizable in the convincing legal arguments he'll dress it in: that's a lawyer's business. I wonder what kind of hash he's cooking up for us this time. Right now he must be drumming his fingers at some post office window, the telegraphic money-order department: the first thing he'll think of is the gas for the plane."

And then it's my turn (watch it, not too fast with the oil) to be overcome with compassion, with hilarious compassion: me take a job? Reach out my fingers for a weekly wage and a rap on the knuckles, when it's so much more exciting to close them on something stolen? Well: the lawyer may get me out of stir, but he'll never be able to save me from my self-chosen doom.

"So perhaps," I say, weeping into my garlic clove, "he'll get our raps run together. What does my runaway mare think about that?"

And, with shame, I find myself hoping that the judges won't be too lenient: a reduction in time, fine: but just enough so that we won't lose the desire to make a break; a break full of unreason and humor, a break that'll be made offhandedly, for nothing, gratuitously, simply to show them that we want no part of their kindness.

Just the same, that mouthpiece has gotten under my skin. Now I recall that he also said that he would come back to represent me "provided that this is the last time." What! I had clung to his knees, so to speak, in that visiting room, and what was more I had paid for my petition, and now he's doing me a favor, and with bad grace at that . . . My case is making him suffer, poor thing!

And I, like a dope, thought counselor was my little brother!

I grab my pen: I must write to him; decorum and my own clumsy tongue in the presence of a Master of the Word shut me up yesterday; but my Bic really knows how to talk. Quick, the writing paper.

"My dear Counselor:

"In the quiet of my cell, on the day after our conversation, I am trying to decipher its meaning . . . without altogether succeeding; perhaps because it doesn't have very much meaning.

"You reminded me of 'my education': true, but my mind is no longer as supple as it was in those days; nothing fertilizes my mind now, I think slowly, painfully; it is only twenty-four hours later that I arrive at the answers! What rust . . . But a stiff mind is a stubborn mind. With sufficient clarity to enable this mind to understand, you informed me of your wish to be relieved of my calls for help henceforth: I promise you this, especially since, as you pointed out, you are not short of colleagues.

(Is he irreplaceable? it will take someone other than him to get me out on appeal by default!)

"I would not have begged: I am a monster of pride, that is common knowledge; it may well be that pride destroys; but I intend to be saved by it, first of all by keeping myself intact. However . . .

(Let's flatter him a bit.)

" . . . until yesterday you were the lawyer who is also a friend, the only worthwhile ally; I dream a great deal, but in the tiny practical part of me you were always welcome . . . That too, alas, was a dream. I know quite well that I judge wrongly, that I confuse and mock everything, that I am a bit off: lack of contact and conflict with reality, no doubt: I don't see people, I construct them . . . Oh, counselor, how much more understanding I had made you!

(He had also said to me . . . now that I had digested the mayonnaise, yesterday's words are rising up on me, making a great clot that it was impossible to swallow back. I warm a coffee and go on writing, glass in hand.)

"I lack experience, I am young, you think; certainly, as far as experiences go, I've had nothing but experiences. Why then, far from succoring me when it is invoked for my defense, should this inexperience become, by some strange process, an aggravating factor? Thus you accuse me of leading my husband into error! But, if I love this man, it is just because I can't influence him, because we have the same motives, because we are each other at the same time; I refuse to separate myself from him, but I likewise refuse to wear the tedious label that says I'm the instigator. I was compelled by force to assume it some years ago, when, since nothing actually criminal could be found in my actions, I was found instead to be endowed with the talent for inciting, or incitation: I am not quite sure how it is put.

"My dear counselor, I ask you neither to understand nor to admit anything; I ask you only to forgive these angry words, which I send you only by chance, because you happen to be at the point of my pen and because my surroundings are too stupid for me to take the trouble to prettify them. I add 'thank you counselor,' and say no more: for yesterday's talk has proved to me once more that there are limits to every intercourse, that dialogues too often end in double monologues. I asked too much of you, more than you needed to do as my lawyer: I had in mind your complicity, in short, whereas, since the accused represents the victim of the shipwreck and the lawyer is delegated to rescue him, they will never be able to swim together. I asked things of you, and what did I give you in return? I had only my trust . . . but I see that, between you and me, that can be only a new ruse: I gave you my trust without reserve; but, since you restrict our relations to those of the lawyer to the client, I must limit my trust in the same fashion. I had thought that trust was rest, exchange . . . I know, counselor: that is a bit thick . . ."

I add that the rupture between us suited me, for it irritates me quite as much to be judged by appearances as to let my inner self become visible; I prefer to see as few people as possible, and thus at the same time dispense with these exhibitions that were regretted as soon as . . . etc. However, counselor has often pulled me out of holes and I am grateful to him for it; my "sincere thanks" are not a mere formula; but I want to drain off all gratitude, every emotion that tends to overflow, I want to cut off everyone.

Aah! What a job, I've spent almost the entire morning

scribbling this letter; but I had finally swallowed the clot. On paper, at a distance, detached, you're less tempted by kindness, by the ease with which you can say what people like to hear; it is easier to give them hell. At bottom, I no more want to raise hell than I want to sing, but it kills time. There is still, however, a tiny corner of my memory that is always ready to answer back, even when I haven't been attacked, that wounded, sullen corner that is always looking for a row; but, with counselor, who has only good and loyal words for me, I have to scrape the bottom of my brain and poke up an odd kind of fire in myself in order to reach the point of really having a grudge against him.

How can I be angry at him? He is doing the compassionate, the human thing, he offers me his cigarette case and at the end his handshake is always a lingering one, his eyes meet mine . . .

I imagine deals between us, bedroom games, I singe my eyebrows at that flame; and the matron, whom I sometimes bring up to date on my moods, says to me: "But you're in love with that lawyer, Damien!"

Come off it! Counselor is my lawyer: a sense of proportion, if you don't mind . . .

I no longer want to play around with either resignation or defiance; I shall withdraw into irony, if not into insolence. In his presence, of course, I'll be at a loss for words, I'll stammer, I'll say "oh, counselor!" with a little pout and out-thrust bosom; but here, at night, I'll fashion complicated, lapidary phrases that I would hurl at the four corners of the cell in the dark; I'll hone my irony in the idleness and the quiet of the nights.

In stir the targets are too huge, and set too close: you must use big missiles, elephant guns, vulgar words; and yet I feel certain that with a tiny cartridge filled with laughter I can pulverize the mammoth targets, the prison, and my punishment with them.

(6)

On the following Sunday I go to the visiting room with a copy of my letter to the lawyer, and, the minute I'm inside, I begin reading it aloud: " 'My dear counselor . . .' "

My dear counselor smiles. "I like it when you call me that . . . But don't you think we might also say hello?"

"Oh, forgive me, darling! But I had to make you swallow a little of my crossness . . . How angry I've been this week." I explain to Zizi, and then I read him the whole letter; immediately he begins to worry about its possible repercussions: "I wonder whether he won't just throw up the case after that."

"Don't worry your head about that, he doesn't want to hand back the fees. On the contrary, you'll see: it'll be a point of honor with him to do the very best he can for us, possibly much more than if we had bogged down in 'anticipated platitudes' . . . He claims to be angry with us, but, if I had taken him at his word and gotten another lawyer, he'd have been really sore. As far as getting back that much money goes, there's nothing to it . . ."

"But what about getting you back as a client! You're talking bullshit, baby."

"And who is it that has too much pride? he or I? Don't you think a little spinal tap might decongest his brain?"

"Nuts!" Zizi says. "The main thing is that he should do his job, and get it over with fast, so we know . . . As far as I can see, this two-week postponement hasn't got us ahead at all."

So there are still no tools available. Oh, shit.

Across the ping-pong table Zizi goes through the motions of laughing; but I am studying this apparent indifference: "I want to bawl like a little kid . . . I can't gnaw through the wall . . ." I know the exact tone, the required words, the others that must not be stupidly fired into his heart; if I repeat to Zizi the unpleasant things that I hear right and left, if I tell him that I'm in the dumps, or that the people around me piss me off, I know his anger will start running on all eight cylinders. Patiently, I poke up his anger and light my own from it once again: one day, certainly, anger will smash everything . . .

After that we'll live a quiet life, far removed from our old rages; I'll light cigarettes that both of us will smoke in cars that eat up the miles at night.

"May I give my wife a piece of candy, sir?" The guard unwraps the candy and gives it to the matron, who gives it to me. We smile, salivating round the thick mints. "The social worker gave me four of them," Zizi says cherubically; "if we're clever, we'll save the other two for our next visit."

So, while counselor lets out all the stops in an impassioned plea for a "last chance" for us, we'll look down at the floor and dream of childish things . . .

"No," I say, "keep them for court." That night we go back to our cells with the wholly temporary social status of prisoners who have been given their final sentence.

The circus is on once again, the judges have come in with a ringing of bells, the orchestra has finished tuning up in the lawyers' stall; the judicial acrobatics are about to begin. Tomorrow there will be an end to "my learned colleague," to trips into the city, to the rights of the accused: we will stop dreaming, or, if we prefer, make the great leap . . .

402

The Runaway

I'm weak in the knees, I feel as if we were back at the preliminary interrogation, almost, except that then, at least, you were allowed to sit down. The honorable clerk of this court reads aloud endlessly, leafing through the various documents that had drawn our portraits in the waxy black of typewriter ribbons; at the end of each paragraph, he takes off his glasses and then puts them back on with graceful little gestures of the wrist and his eternal "the court will understand" . . .

Again, Anick! You leaned on the bar, you gave in. I pull my knees together and my elbows in, I need to pee. The court reporter goes on tirelessly reporting.

Oh, to sit down! I look at our bench: I sigh, there is not the faintest hope yet of our being allowed to go back to it. Our little band of cops is peacefully ruminating there, their bottoms comfortably settled; our brothers too are ruminating: perhaps they envy us our fine lawyers, or they're just plain scared, with a fear that would become plainer and plainer as the clock moves on and their turns draw nearer.

Another girl has been brought out with me this time; she is sitting there, flanked by her two co-defendants; the ages of all three put together probably equal Zizi's plus mine: we're not falling apart, but these three are criminals in the best years of their lives. Three minors who don't know anything, whom no one has ever helped, the mouthpieces will say; no, not even that, Christine's lawyer has never come near the prison, nor does he seem any more likely to turn up today. And yet I know that she has written several times to the bar association.

Her fear-hollowed little face makes me forget the pain in my feet for a second; then I remember that that beaten-down look is a mandatory convention, I give Chris a comforting little gesture below the bar ("cheer-up-it-isn't-anything-at-all"), and I shift the weight of my wretched carcass from the right heel to the left heel, painfully straightening up: beaten but unbowed.

The record goes on with its lullaby: "Burglary . . . burglary . . . The woman (my-maiden-name), the accused (Zizi's-name); Mister So-and-So, Mister Such-and-Such . . ." These were the civil complainants, Messrs. My Balls. Certain accusations are heard again although we were absolved of them during the preliminary investigation; oh, the beauty of an appeal! The more the pages turn, with the meticulous description of the interrogations and the searches, the list of items discovered on me and in my home, the much longer list of items still being sought, the more I feel that the shit is going to hit the fan . . .

What *deus ex machina* could ever open this ceiling and pour down an avalanche of big and little loot on the heads of the men of justice by way of restitution? And what sentence in all this cold heap of red tape can be true enough to make the sluice-gates of our eyes open?

Earlier, on the day before the hearing, I planted myself in front of my mirror, practicing words and facial expressions; the next day I held a dress rehearsal just before leaving for court; I entered the stall with my head full of the speeches I had learned. Then I saw plainly that, beneath the seeming formality of the presiding judge's questions—family name, given name, age, family, status—there was a whole hidden arsenal of verbal traps with subtly hidden springs; in addition, the questions were never precisely what I was expecting; and my prepared responses, through which my memory dug hastily in an attempt to match them to the questions, had a phony and ludicrous ring in the stillness of the courtroom.

I have now given up any thought of forcing the precision locks of legal language with the rubber skeleton keys of my defendant's vocabulary; I tell myself that the bill of particulars will beat us down but that the lawyer's eloquence will raise us up again; moreover, the judges are barely listening to the lawyer, they keep shuffling papers, which are much more important because written documents are enduring.

The Runaway

The presiding judge doesn't give a damn, he has his big clock hanging from the ceiling: he'll look at it more and more often, more and more wearily; the assistant judges, by means of a slight contraction of the oral sphincter, will gulp back their desire to yawn, while a thoughtful hand supports each of their drowsing foreheads.

The only wide awake thing, the tiny chance that frisks on naked invisible feet through the circus—O my good fairy— may take it into her head to take a good look at us and, if she likes our kissers, trace a few arabesques for us.

Chance . . . While counselor, standing behind us, blows tornadoes of eloquence down our necks, I picture the silent entrechats that the good fairy makes for her own pleasure above that floor thick with wax and dust; and suddenly I get the giggles. I hide my mouth in my handkerchief and I move a little closer to my husband, so that the upright of the bar will hide the presiding judge's eyes from me. Theoretically, he can no longer see me either.

Oh!

My maneuvers have brought me into contact with Zizi's hand, which was drumming lightly on the bench: immediately his fingers respond to age-old reflexes and, hidden by my jacket, grope to reach the point where skirt and skin meet.

A night that we had taken off from work to have fun: it is in the days of our glory, and Zizi is watching me undress, to the accompaniment of my play-by-play explanation: "I never wear anything under a tight skirt, otherwise the skirt creeps up . . ."

Zizi must certainly remember, his fingers have found me . . . I catch them in mine and guide them back to the bench. "Wait till they go out to discuss their decision, baby: at the rate they're going today, we're bound to have a record inter-mission."

It's over: the final word of the peroration has fallen like a rock from the lawyer's lips, and now it is re-echoing infinitely in variously affected eardrums. A few seconds, charming ones, go by.

Then the magic vanishes, the woodpecker of a bailiff taps with his beak to call the defendants in the next case: Christine goes forward to the bar, followed by the two boys: her brother and her boy friend, I think. We cross each other between the bar and the bench and I give her the cheer-up sign again, because Justice is harsh toward juveniles, because three together in a job are already considered an organized gang, and because their lawyer still has not come.

And yet in prison I have no particular sympathy with this kid: it annoys me to watch her various asininities, all of them exact replicas of my own imbecilities as a minor—because she is absolutely certain that they're all original with her; I deplore her obvious ignorance, her eyes that spend the day sizing things up after having spent the night weeping; but, when she abandons her graceful hips to the rhythm of her housework and the music from the radio, swaying on the stairs like sea-weed restored to the sea, when through the wall I hear her humming bits of twists and cha-cha-chas that she sings one after the other all day long, I feel that I'm mature, indulgent, ready to be her bosom pal.

But the next day everything is different, the radio is broken, Christine is locked into her cell again, and the slow movement of her hips is succeeded by the quick retorts of her tongue. In the showers the water distribution is badly arranged, so that it is scalding in the front stalls and an ice cold trickle in the rear ones. Christine has *her* stall, in the middle of the row, a nice moderate shower; between those scalded and those frozen, she washes herself with sighs of well-being.

Nevertheless, from time to time, there is some woman who, with the courage of ignorance, decides to emerge dripping and naked from her stall and start yelling for the matron. As a general rule, she opens the faucets and goes off at once to gossip with Lerouge in the laundry, without a thought for the temperature of the water: she is nice enough, but she's also a yakker. And besides, this Turkish bath is no place for some-one who's all dressed and combed .   . She comes back, alerted by the assorted cries:

"What's going on, ladies?"

"Would you be kind enough to let us have a little more hot water?"

"No, cold!" the scalded ones shout.

Or vice versa.

Most of the time I wind up in the cold group: I live at the end of the second tier, I am the last one to be let out to bathe; the first comers take over the best stalls—always making sure, however, not to enter Christine's—and, by the time I arrive, the hot department is posted NO VACANCIES. The other morning it was particularly freezing in my shower: I decided to yell "hot water!" even if half the women on my floor were boiled to death.

Chris, who had been splashing happily about on her tiles, dove out of the shower, slender and glistening with Palmolive; her bath mitt held aloft, she launched into a lecture on the subject of "the salutary effects of cold water on old skins"; I retorted that "Central Prison water had had a major part in destroying my health," that "I knew better than anyone else what was best for my skin," and that from time to time *I myself* felt a certain need to scrape off the dirt with hot water, that "some people should learn to get the crap out of their pussies instead of just playing with their love-buttons," etc. All this was staged amidst the noise of the plumbing and the splashing of the water, as well as the other women's outcries and our matron's "Now, calm down, all of you." Christine allowed herself a small fire dance by way of immunizing her-self and went back to her tepid shower whimpering that it was scalding her; but this time the matron had gone for good.

Rows are Chris' element: she simply has to nag and dig and bitch until someone helps her stir up a big fuss. She has already been trying for some time now to get under my skin, but—aside from the incident in the shower, which was nothing—she hasn't succeeded yet; I hoard my anger and don't waste it.

I answer Chris without haste and without rancor. Now, the neighbor on my left is a real pain in the ass to all her neighbors, as much to those next door as to those below: slamming her cupboard door, nocturnal rumblings in the washstands, bucket lid dropped carelessly on the floor. Christine has the cell beneath hers: although she sleeps like a log, this racket provides her with a pretext. As we are waiting one afternoon to be led out to exercise, she attacks, with an accusing look at the high heels of my mules: someone spends the whole night marching back and forth over her head, it would be a lot better if that one went and learned how to behave . . . If I understand correctly, the poor slob thinks I live above her.

Modestly, I put myself back where I belong. "Say," I add, "I've read that somewhere."

"What do you mean, you've read it?" Christine bawls in a low voice, for it is forbidden to bawl in a loud one, indoors or out.

"I remember now, it's in my catechism: *The Code of Proper Prison Deportment.* Haven't you read it? I'll lend it to you, really good. It says somewhere, I don't remember now which paragraph, that the well-bred jailbird should put on slippers, preferably felt ones, as soon as she's locked in for the night. Unfortunately, all I have is old bathing mules, blue ones: and that's bad, because blue is against the rules. But I promise you, Chris, as soon as I have dough . . ."

I in turn take a look at Christine's feet: she's wearing ragged ballet slippers that she's been dragging about in ever since her arrest because she has nothing else. As Lerouge says, you just have to swallow the kid.

But a cease-fire is proclaimed before we go into court. Since Chris has no coffee, I send her some by Lerouge, through the cell panel, so that she can pull herself together; and I have lent her the twisted barrette that I use for plucking my eyebrows.

Now Christine sags before the bar, and her eyebrows have sagged with the rest of her. Lacking any support, her body-guards rock back and forth beside her. And the poor thing's ballet slippers send a pang through me when I see them motionless on the floor of the court, where she is no longer even thinking of dancing the twist. Going into the chamber, she had whispered to me: "Oh, look, what a wonderful dance floor!"

Counselor is coming toward us; his robe hides the J.D.S. Zizi gets up and speaks to the lawyer; I remain seated, wedged between the knees of the two men, counselor's robe and my husband's trousers. Their words travel high above my head. Oh, there's a spot on the bottom of my jacket: in order to give myself something to do, I try to get rid of it with my fingernail.

Yes, counselor made a fine speech; yes, I was filled with hope; yes, I ought to express, and he would like to hear, my thanks. But they stay blocked in my throat: counselor can't imagine what a world of indifference lies between me and his knees. Let Zizi give out with the gratitude and admiration bit! As for me, I have now got rid of the spot and I am brushing it off.

"We're sure to get a reduction in sentence," Zizi says.

"Let's just wait for the verdict," the lawyer replies; "I remember one evening after a hearing when your wife reproached me for 'always being satisfied.'"

I raise my eyes. "I've probably just got a kick in the teeth that goes all against your predictions."

The lawyer takes off. It's a wise move, because I was about to start talking. When I make forecasts, they're treated as black thoughts, or blue ones; I am being defended with regret, without hope, on the strength of big bundles of money. If everything comes out all right now, does counselor think that I'll consider it my duty to kiss his feet? Was I not the one who had duly signed the petition for an appeal from the sentence that he had advised me to accept? Good lord, he had bitched enough when he found out about it!

In the wagon on the way back to the prison, I squeeze close to Zizi. "Everything's all right, you'll see, everything is logical . . ."

They shaved a few months off my time. Oh, not a great lot, but enough, just the same: enough so that I can rub it in with the lawyer, I can rub his nose in his own omniscience, and I'm smiling when we reach the jail.

But this is not what I'm smiling about: I'm smiling because Zizi's sentence has been upheld. I'm smiling because he's desperate, and because the hope that would very soon surge in him would now have the same name as my own hope.

"Just the same, Zi, if you could have got the two raps run together, you'd be getting out the same time I do. Provided, that is, that my time hadn't been cut . . . "

"We both should have got the cut in time. But their damn heads are just big enough for one of us: so it might as well be you."

Yes: they have sentenced me to something else, that's all. I think of the daily letter, the weekly visit; and the equally daily tears that were held back at the foot of the great wall that will slowly fall to pieces, oh, I flee from it in anger, my fists clenched, at eighty miles an hour, possibly to die and certainly to drink, drink . . . I wake up with a big head, I reach out to find you beside me: no, you are waking up in your prison, and I . . . what shame I feel, being free.

But by contrast there is nothing beside me this evening but Zizi's body: our hands are entwined and our knees cling together, but he's not here; I can feel that he's still in the grip of his old dream, and that he's full of regret.

"Where are you?" I ask.

Turn off, darling. I'll stop for breath on the road where I'm waiting for you, and from time to time I'll turn back, come to me . . .

"We'll get out of it, well out of it, you know that! A soft life for both of us . . . "

I walk slowly, stopping often; catch up with me . . .

"How are your investigations going, really?"

"Bad. The other guys are jerks, by and large, and there's a special watch sign on my door. The other day, coming back from exercise, I managed to tear it off, but they were right there to put up a new one . . . When I have my head under the covers at night, or just lie there without moving, the screw bangs on the door; then I tell him everything I can think of, just to let him know I'm still there . . . Hell, I have to keep my eyes and ears open all the time. This kind of thing can drag us farther and farther, even to a Central, or until I get out . . . Oh, baby, there are days when I just feel all shriveled up . . . "

"Well, we'll stuff ourselves with rest. No more family, no more papers, we'll just skip into complete peace. But I've got to get my arm taken care of, and even now that my sentence is final I doubt whether they'll want to send me to Fresnes: an inflamed scar isn't an emergency, is it? So why not just go have it done right away, outside? It would save time . . . "

"What if our luck doesn't hold and they grab us right away?"

"Are you out of your mind? Us, the birds in the nest? We'll go far, far away . . . "

"Sure, you never think it's going to happen to you."

"All right, so let's suppose it does happen to us: I'll have

411

my convalescence in a prison ward, my paw in a cast, I'll
beat the ninety days in the hole, I'll pile up work . . . And
you! you'll just escape again so you can come and get me
out again. No, seriously, darling, we'll try to be grabbed again
where and when it pleases us, when we've got ourselves into
the right state of mind to expect it. I'll be careful, I swear to
you I'll be a regular watchdog, a walking *Caution* sign. You'll
get so that you'll give me hell for not having any nerve any
more, you like me better when I'm daring . . . "

"That depends," Zizi says, tracing invisible designs on my
thigh.

"Shut up, piggy! As I was saying: let's preserve what little
general health prison has left us; let's make them pick us up
on the edge of the grave, or else later, in top form, if you're
still so anxious for that. But just let me breathe, ah-ah-ah-ah.
Nights when we have nothing to do, we'll plan runaways for
later: that way we can keep them on the road until we die."

"Stop a minute," my man says. "We're almost at the joint
again, and . . . oh, shit. Don't worry about notes, I'm working
on a guy, a kitchen trusty, it should work out O.K. Just keep
a sharp eye on your butts and your canteen stuff . . . "

"But you could talk to him straight, if he's really all right. I
know pretty much what I have to do. I remember the pass-
words, and you'll tell me the day and hour during one of your
visits; the notes are nice enough, but it would be better if you
could get hold of this guy for the tools. If he's a cook, he
must be able to go everywhere."

"There's the prison," Zizi interrupts. "Kiss me, Anick,
kiss me."

A lock of his hair has come loose and fallen over his forehead; I know that lock of hair: even more than what he says,
it reveals his weariness. With a movement of my index
finger I lift it and put it back into place, decently with the
rest, and my hand stays there . . . "Kiss me . . . " In the

412

intimacy of our two salivas, I want my love to feel the excitement that suddenly brings me, all of me, to the point of tears.

The cops have been inconspicuous during the whole journey, but now they're moving about. "We're here, wake up!" they call. "Watch out for a sudden stop, brace yourselves."

We climb out of the paddy wagon in Indian file. Chivalrous hands reach out for Chris and me. I rejoin my man outside the office, a last quick kiss, we still have time. In order not to attract the angels' attention, we go at it as if it were the first: the deputy warden has come out of his lair to get the papers from the sergeant in charge of the detail, he'll certainly ask him whether everyone has behaved properly.

Zizi is all right again, and the lock of hair is staying in place; I see him make a quick movement: he is putting the note into his mouth so that he can pass it through customs.

I could put mine in the same place, as I had done the other day: the lady always does her searching with the same casualness. But one never knows, she might have broken a leg or been called to her old mother's deathbed, and whoever took her place would certainly not give me any breaks. Anyway, it bothered me to con her without going through the traditional forms.

And so, after the hearing, I had asked my angels to take me up one flight.

(7)

Now that I have been finally sentenced, the daily exercise period is mandatory for me. Except on medical exemption. But I wonder whether the croaker would agree to certifying that I was suffering from boredom. So far I have shown the son of Aesculapius only my chilblains (and it's still summer!); I don't dare tell him that I have a hole in my head as well.

If only it were possible to take something outside with which to keep amused! But library books have to be left in the cells, only one's own newspapers can be taken into the exercise yard. They belong to us, so we can take them out at our own risk. I always forget mine: I prefer to drag through the hour without them rather than lend them. The women would do the crosswords wrong, and with pens, they would deface the illustrations, or else they would tear out pages to save the expense of canteening shit paper: that's all!

With Lerouge it was possible to have pleasant talks, sharing the cigarettes like sisters: "Here, take a drag, this is a real ready-made." But Lerouge doesn't go out any more, trusties are not obliged to take exercise: so the only dodge for the cold-blooded is to be either dying or working. Lerouge prefers the companionship of the stove in the work-

414

room to that of a gang of jabbering, frumpy women; and I
would prefer it too: here as elsewhere, the stove is like an old
friend, the warmer of frozen feet and of water for coffee, and
it plays a duet with the sewing machine: the one crackles
while the other hums.

Stoically, I build up a stockpile of oxygen. I'll find a
dodge—neither death nor work: there must certainly be a
third gimmick—when it begins to be a little colder, if that
can be possible: and yet this is just a trivial pre-autumnal
chill. Just wait, my dear first-time ladies, and you'll see what
exercise is like in January! ...

By the second quarter hour I am beginning to dream of my
cell as if it were a lost paradise . . . The conversation in this
courtyard full of sentenced prisoners rarely has any interest
for me. Looking ahead to the warden's return, the lady has
very quietly begun to put the screws on us, separating the
accused but untried, the convicted and sentenced, and the
minors into three separate exercise yards.

Just go on talking, girls: I'm not plugged in, the cold is
putting me to sleep, just talk on and on, but let me keep
my mouth shut.

Among the accused, the conversation deals with business,
lawyers, speculations on verdicts; or else the newcomers are
grilled: "But can't you at least remember the headlines?"
And the new arrivals, if they want their new chums to like
them, have to dredge their brains to try to recall the latest
issue of *France-Soir*.

The convicted and sentenced provide their own news and
commentary: in politics, it is: "If the big shot gets knocked
off, they'll stick somebody else in his place and then maybe
we'll all get a break"; in fashion, it is whatever will be
the style in the year when they will walk: "The very first
thing I'm going to do, before I do anything else, is get everything new from head to foot"; in the area of eternal verities
and lyric threnodies, virtually all they know is cooking

recipes, what will be served that night, and how they've digested what was served at lunch; and, of course, the usual gossip.

Certain girls spend all their time with their ears to the door, just as, on the outside, they must have kept watch behind their curtains; the sound of a key at midnight lifts them right out of bed, their ears pricked up: what's going on?

What could be going on in stir?

I am sick of these nighttime ringings of bells, followed by the quick clink-clink-clink of keys, the clank when the chain of the main door is taken off: another late admission, or the big wheels' car coming back from a night on the town; the headlights glow on my ceiling like a paintbrush, the shadow of the bars circles around the cell and then returns to immobility in the window; I don't stir. But this upsets the others, they ask questions tirelessly, and peddle their gossip; they make me angry because they're greedy, because they're ugly, because their shabby outfits remind me that I'm wearing the same thing and that I too must be ugly.

I'll go on doing my exercise . . . let us say until the middle of October. Until then I won't give in. This solidly fixed milestone makes it possible for me to endure the slow afternoons under the clouds. In good weather the lady allows us to improve our suntans until supper time: our pins stretched out under the pale sun, we play endless card games, Lerouge and I and two partners drawn from the least stupid of our companions: our invitations are eagerly accepted: for the fun of playing, naturally, but especially because it's always good to be in good with the trusty and with the girl who's in good with the trusty. Besides, we always have butts.

But the very last one is gone; playing cards without Lerouge doesn't tempt me; and the lady is still letting us stay outdoors for the same length of time. thinking that we still like it . . . How can you tell her? Especially since those old biddies really do still like it! So I begin preparing a mono-

graph on planned shivering, while my little sisters keep themselves warm chattering and bad-mouthing.

I always sit with my back against the door, on the top step,
which I am careful never to leave: please pass by me, ladies,
after you, please, the wood of the door is less cold on my
poor lousy back than the brick of the wall.

If I feel that I am beginning to waver in the solitude of my
throne, I call one of the less repugnant members of the
troop: she sits down next to me, our four buttocks block
the passage, and the others sit down wherever they can.
There is, it's true, a kind of covered walk, near the cesspool
and opposite the door; if it rains without wind, it's fine, you
can always take refuge under it; but, since the yard is on a
slope and the water floods three-quarters of the shed, you
have to decide whether you prefer a foot bath or a good face
wash, both with cold water, when it's windy.

"It's sure a fucked-up arrangement, they could have made
that shelter a little bigger!"

"It is big, but that doesn't make any difference . . . No,
what they should have done was to make a drain to carry
off the water into the ground behind it, that would suck it
up."

Sitting there on our throne, we laugh half-heartedly.

Anyway, it's every girl for herself, what the hell! No one
gives up her place, there is no priority for expectant mothers,
or for Mrs. So-and-So's varicose veins, or for Granny
Whatsit's advanced age. Unless, of course, it is very politely
requested; but it's a rare woman indeed who ever thinks of
doing that. It does sometimes happen, however, after one
or two hours of being on her feet, that a girl will come over
and ask us to move our pins so that she can sit on one of the
two other steps.

"Well, why not?" I say. "Don't be bashful. Go on, move
our feet yourself."

But you must be nice: I shift my pins, the person finds

417

room, and then the others join her, one by one. Finally the SRO sign goes up on the steps and I find myself hemmed in by the door, its frame, my neighbor, and a sea of backs and heads. In this mass of huddled flesh you can find a bit of warmth; and my comfort increases in direct ratio to the passage of the quarter-hours, because I'll get back that much sooner, in a few minutes now, in another minute, ah! I get back to my cell, my home, my little cube of air impregnated with my smell: it smells in my joint, but it's a good smell: a mixture of soap, of fruit going soft in the cupboard, of ten-times-smoked Gitanes . . . Furthermore, I far prefer john-my-bucket to the mouths of certain ladies who never brush their teeth: you have to have lived in prison, or been a croaker in an emergency ward, to learn just how crummy the majority of people can be. You often arrive unexpectedly in both places.

Gossip sorts out the new arrivals before they've even been seen: "Did she have filthy pants, darling! God, how filthy! But I'd rather not even talk about it, I'll vomit." Or else: "Just seeing her suitcases you can tell that she's no bum: pigskin, my dear. And if only you could have seen her getting straight with the office—so polite, so really distinguished!"

The matron is always at a loss when she bags anything but a bum; it must be admitted that she gets the worst more often than the best. As the saying goes: "In our job you get your hands into everything . . . "

But, when best and worst had been fused into the common product, the jailbird, which has nothing of the superlative about it; when the pigs have resigned themselves to the weekly shower and the clean ones have equally resigned themselves to the absence of deodorants from the canteen list; when the educated have made some attempt to talk like all the others and the illiterate have learned to read old magazines by means of their illustrations; after all this, who could stand

418

these women except themselves? Who doesn't sound off against the good ladies in *petto* or *ex,* depending on the mood and the motive? And which of us could ever be absolutely satisfied anyway? Even outside, in the most divine moments, your eye make-up begins to run or you get the trots . . .

A few minutes ago, though, I was almost contented, I was on my way back to my cell, moving fast past the whole line of the others so that I wouldn't be held up, when the lady caught me in mid-flight and said in a solemn tone: "Wait here, Damien. I have something to say to you."

Oh God! I did a quick run-through of the recent past: nothing had been left in my cell, nothing leaked to anyone, unless Zizi . . . No, in that case I would have been summoned to the office: the sin must be a venial one. I'll know soon enough: I can wait until the lady comes back downstairs.

Leaning on the cold radiator, I study the circus. Normally I am part of the crowd and hence am unaware of it; but, from below, it's quite interesting to watch. These women going back to the cells make me think of those guinea pigs that are trained to enter numbered boxes at fairs and carnivals.

The mechanics of the thing are well organized, the keys turn in the locks, the women unstick themselves from the wall, "excuse me, matron," and are trapped by the sea-green doors. The keys turn again in the opposite direction and move on to the next lock . . .

Somehow revolted—God knows why—I turn away. Above me, along the tiers, doors go on slamming, cold dirty feet shuffle aimlessly in their felt slippers; and the lady, smart and attractive in the smock that Lerouge has starched for her, smiles sweetly at each of these sad cases. She closes the last door, comes down the stairs and walks up to me: "Alone at last!"

I put on my mask of innocence, I swallow, and I repeat:

"Alone at last," with a laugh, in a tone one grade below deference: keeping things in their proper proportions, we're pals.

"Would you mind staying in the workroom a little while with Lerouge—until supper time, say? She needs your counsels on a mending problem . . . "

I smile as broadly as I can and adjust my expression to register "ecstasy."

"Oh, matron, how wonderful of you! Of course . . . "

Five minutes later I am settled on the best stool—not a jiggler, not an ass-cutter, nothing like that, but the stool of my dreams. Lerouge offers me a former coffee tin full of candy, real candy, "hell, it was given to me, take whatever you like best: there're caramels, filled candy . . . " She fusses about in the vicinity of the coffee pot and shoves another tin under my nose: "This was a present too: smell that . . . " Indeed, what I smell is no instant coffee . . . Little Jesus in his velvet pants, as Dufon would have said, is about to descend and enter our little stomachs.

I take a long sniff of the fine brown grains, I grab a healthy pinch of them, I stretch out my toes, and I begin to feel really good.

"What a drag," I say, waving my cigarette package, which has only one butt left in it (I have just stashed the others in my bra). "If I'd known you were going to invite me, I'd have brought down a fresh pack . . . But hell, there's only one here." To whom can I offer it without irritating someone?

For the kid, Christine, is here too; the lady has been unable to find any other way of preventing her from raising hell: with Lerouge, Chris is obedient. But she smokes all Lerouge's cigarettes. She doesn't have a cent for the canteen, any more than Lerouge, but Lerouge manages all the same: what with the girls, the guards . . . Whereas Christine, being under age, has no right either to buy or to accept cigarettes.

420

So here she practices self-service. Similarly, she gobbles down the candy. But what the hell, let them make their own arrangements!

Chris is curled up on Lerouge's bed: completely detached, she is weaving yards of black thread through the holes in her tight-fitting sweater. "We can all smoke it together," she says. "All you have to do is light it and pass it round."

I am puzzled. "Tell me: grown women and minors aren't supposed to mix, what does the office . . . "

Lerouge gives me the answer. "As long as the big shots are on vacation . . . and besides the deputy jerk is off on Saturdays. Even if he did spring one on us and found Christine with me, everything's already been squared with the matron, I'd just say she was helping me. To make it look better, I really do have her sweep a little and scrub the floors: that'll keep the women quiet."

So there are girls who will break their necks to get what I've broken mine to avoid; to have a few yards more to walk up and down, to kill time and not be bored, they are willing to be used as dust rags. It is true, of course, that for Chris the work must not be too tiring, if she always does it the way she's doing it now, and only when the deputy is off on the weekends.

As I sip the lovely coffee, I watch her, and it is hard to recognize the fresh kid, the loudmouth, the terror, not to mention the sorry J.D. in court. All that I knew of her voice was her yelling in the showers and her endless hummed cha-chas; today it's a totally different voice, husky in the lower registers and rounded off into smooth slurrings in the higher. Good lord, she's almost singing: "But have some bread and jam, Anick. Come on, Lerouge, get them for her."

"I don't think Anick likes bread and jam that much," Lerouge says. "I'm sure she'd rather have another cup of coffee; isn't that so, Anick?"

"Fine, why not? Java for everybody, then."

"Absolutely not. You've had enough coffee for one day, young woman. You can have some cider if you like . . . "

"Naa."

"Tea, then?"

"Wait a sec," I say, digging into my bosom with particular care to prevent the butts from emerging. "I heard someone say you wanted to try the canteen cocoa before you ordered any . . . "

"Yes, I'm sure to get some dough any day now, and . . . "

"Well, in the meantime, latch on to this, it's two days now that I've been meaning to give it to you; see whether you like it. Free-sample day."

A fragile little package flies through the air: three spoons of Nesquik in a bit of plastic. My bosom is frequently bigger than nature made it: I pull all kinds of stuff out of it to give away, swap, or just to show. In the afternoon, when it's close to two o'clock, I jump up from the sack where I've been napping, I gather up all the little bundles that I've put in my shoes, near the door, so that I won't forget anything; I quickly fill myself out, left and right, I shove my feet into the shoes, I hide the old blue mules. The matron finds me standing at attention at my door, looking elegant with my hands empty and newly-washed.

I carry letters to be read to Lerouge, songs taken down in shorthand from the radio for the music lovers, recipes for the gluttons, ends of butts for the butt-grabbers: these low-voltage transactions keep my hand in and give pleasure to my little sisters.

I neither like them nor despise them, these little sisters of mine.

Besides, it doesn't cost me much, and it helps to safeguard my peace: I'm a bear, I'm a mule, I'm the whole zoo, but no one talks of me in animal terms, not when I'm present, at least; for I am also audience, maid-of-all-work, public stenographer, decorator of writing paper, and I never refuse a request. All I do is arrange things so that I'm never asked to do too much, either looking at the women with a savage expression or simply not looking at them at all.

You really have to get to know that Anick.

Three spoons of Nesquik, the price of knowing Chris. Wan, her hair hanging over her eyes, dragging her ballet shoes, she moves about the workroom while she stirs the cocoa into the milk. The ones that work get real milk! It's turning sour by the panful, on the cupboard, on the table, everywhere.

"Are you making yogurt?"

"Ah, we can't even drink it all any more," Christine says. "I refused my steak for three weeks, I wanted fruit and milk, and finally the croaker gave it . . . I need a lot of milk and fresh raw food, and their lousy steak, their lousy margarine, their sugar . . ."

"Lousy sugar, you mean," Lerouge corrects her. "Seriously, at your age don't you think it's better to eat steak than to nibble junk all day the way you do?"

"Candy's full of sugar, let me eat what I please."

Tolerant Lerouge goes on with her ironing while she keeps an eye on what the two kids are up to, for mere contact with Chris is enough to set me back ten years . . . I find myself once more on the thorny, foggy road of adolescence, full of impulses both wild and despairing, of words both grandiose and fanciful; and as I sigh, though without regret, Christine's youth is tripping on toward twenty-one.

I make no attempt to inhibit her antics; I let things lie, I let her talk; and I drink my coffee like a lady paying a call, a very old lady: sleep, my once-young heart; don't gambol any more.

"What, me young?" What an insult! We were sincere, and

utterly young in our insistence that we were not young: hunger? astonishment? Over and done with. Life is just meat, and parents are the suppliers of the big steaks. And at the same time we got up in the middle of the night to clean out the refrigerator; and we soiled our fingers with delight on that infinitely distrusted meat and on our own unknown flesh.

What sincere hypocrites we were!

We were forever being betrayed; while we were shouting out how stable and knowledgeable we were, our crafty cells were renewing themselves minute by minute . . . Oh, what a business youth is!

Nevertheless, anyone who labels these years mistakes will get only a smile from me, because these tumultuous years stretch out inside me now like a sorrowful golden road. I offer my hand to this naughty, graceful kid, My Past Self, that darling kid. I mourn that unblemished child; I mourn my fractures, and I cling to them. Thanks to them, I shall never forget that, when you want to lead without knowing how to drive, you have accidents.

But I had been brought back to health by Doctor Love.

Not all my contemporaries had been so lucky, and they were no more whole for all that. Out of everything that was so enticing in the distance, love, wealth, and glory, often all that is left is dull sermons on living-in-a-dungheap and you'll-get-over-that-my-girl.

Love, my youth! Do I really have you safely with me?

I recall the gospels inside myself: I was a wanderer, and I found a tie; I was proud, and I had conceded; I was alone . . . hell, I could say the same things to any God or any friend I might meet. No, love has to be something else, love has to be the exaggeration of ourselves. I'm different, you're different, I can never resign myself to that; I search for you, you search for me, I still miss you.

Hello, my little husband!

We were one for a few seconds: a sob, joy turned topsy-turvy, we were two: "Well, have you finally finished in the bathroom?"

How was the One to be rediscovered here except in loneliness, in cheap caresses?

Christine is talking about the courtroom. "Say, didn't it mean anything to you to see your guy again? I couldn't sleep all night afterward."

"Oh, well, I'm used to it, you know."

"Even so, the way you were necking in the paddy wagon . . ."

Those anemic exchanges! I am far hungrier than that Chris, didn't you know that? Do you think half-pleasures are what I want?

"Anyway, Chris, let me tell you something: I can't take any credit for it, I'm as frigid as an ice-cream cone."

(8)

Bad luck never comes in small doses, and I soon have the proof of that: the warden comes back from his vacation, accompanied by his spouse. She is going to go back to work in the harem, on alternate days: one day of trembling, then one day of recovering from the day before and getting ready for the day after.

The nice little matron is all upset about it. She promises that she'll ask for the keys as often as possible so that she can come and cheer us up, between noon and two o'clock or in the evenings. "I'll say that I need my linens right away, or that I've forgotten something in my little office."

"Please, matron, don't go getting yourself in a jam on our account!"

"But then who's she, will you tell me that? who's *she* to tell me what to do? She has no rank, as far as I know."

Chief matron here, chief matron there: why, indeed? It's a bad habit . . .

"Granted," Christine says, "she's just a plain keeper, but she goes to bed with God the Father . . . "

There are only Christine, nice matron, and I here: the others are all locked outside in the courtyards in the rain. I get up from the sewing machine, where I've been sitting, take the coffee tin, and offer it to my guests: "Have some candy? I've had an inheritance . . . "

Chris won't get candy any more, nor will she go to visit Lerouge any more: nor will I, for the good reason that I am now Lerouge.

The prison authorities changed me into Lerouge after she had been whisked off to Central Prison. I was offered an assistant, I must admit; but, aside from Christine, I don't want anyone here.

And of course Christine has not been assigned to me: the chief matron has an idea that I've taken a liking to the kid, and she knows she's under age: two major reasons.

The chief matron is a big woman, tall and heavy; she comes down on you like a load of bricks—crushing you under three or four layers of linens and starched clothes— but, since I'm small, it's easy for me to duck out from under heavy loads.

I was already hopping mad at having lost Lerouge; when the chief matron came to my cubbyhole to tell me that I had to take the job, "let's get moving," I had really begun to go out of my mind. Later, when I had settled myself and my property in the workroom and the women capable of helping me had been catalogued without my accepting any of them, I finally began to organize my rebellion: whatever had to be done, I was going to refuse to do it all.

"Chief matron, take me to the office, please: I want to see your husband."

"Make a written request for it and I'll take it to him. Don't forget to give your reason."

My reason: to get the order that put me to work rescinded.

It turns out that, every time he comes back after being gone, the warden has the habit of making the whole joint tremble for a few days, just in case the deputy tyrant has let the Rules go slack while he was away. So, as I arrived outside his office, I assumed my "Humble Deference" look, I reminded myself that I no longer had any rights, and I prepared myself to rely on the old left hand.

On the warden's desk blotter I saw a packet of letters addressed to him: probably requests similar to mine. This warden is in great demand here: "Just wait until the warden gets back . . . You'll have to ask the warden about that . . . If that's the way it is, I'm going to write to the warden," etc.

My letter was on the top, covering all the others; it is common knowledge that loud voices and threats don't accomplish much with me: you might as well save your resources for the later supplicants and start out by warming up progressively, methodically.

"So, Damien, it seems you don't want to work. Don't you know that it's compulsory? You've been sentenced now."

"But I'm not refusing to work, sir, I'll be glad to lend a hand, I'll do my very best. All I'm asking you to do is to put someone else in charge in the workroom and leave me in my cell; it's too big a responsibility, sir. How can you expect me to take care of the mending, the ironing, the housework, and everything like that? It just isn't possible! For one thing, I'm handicapped now, it's not the way it was the other time . . ." (Especially because you've had changes made in the workroom transom.)

"Handicapped or not, you're still the best qualified. Besides, I'm not asking you to do everything all alone; just the opposite! You should be delighted, all the others have written to me to ask for the job, but you were the only one I could assign. There's much more than the sewing and the cleaning: a check has to be kept on the linens that get worn out, the clothing-room inventory has to be kept up to date, and so on. The others wouldn't know how, they're not accustomed to . . ."

"But I could teach one of them, it's not that complicated."

"Just what I was saying to you! (Damn, I'm cutting my

own throat with my bullshit arguments.) Naturally, you'll
have an assistant during the day."

"Thank you very much, sir, but your wife already suggested that, and I don't want it. Ever since the new prison
rules for individual cells were put in, the only advantage of
prisons like yours over the dormitory ones, the way I see it,
is that you can really live alone. I'm sick of putting up with
all those women. No matter what, sir, you'll have to punish
me: either you'll put me in with some woman and sooner
or later I'll slug her one, or else I'll just collapse and let everything go, and . . . oh, really, you know, I'd rather just refuse
straight out: write to the regional director and ask him to
send you some 'qualified' people, as you call them: there
must be some in this jurisdiction. As far as I'm concerned,
you can put me in the hole if you want, it's all the same to
me, in fact I'd rather have that than stay in that workroom."

(Oh, my darling little sparrows, who's going to throw you
crumbs now?)

"All right, now, Damien, don't be insolent. I don't want
to punish you. Besides, think of your husband: you won't
have any more visits or any more mail; is that all the same to
you too?"

"Oh, you know, sir, in the end everyone comes out of the
hole." (Whereas, a work detail . . .)

"Come on, give it a try, at least for a little while. I'll see
about having you replaced, if there's any need for that. But
give us some evidence of your good faith. It's going to go all
right, isn't it?"

(Careful, he was getting warm.)

"I'll have to make it go all right," I say. "But I can't
promise you anything."

"That's right, that's right. But you'll see: you'll soon get
into the swing of it: you're intelligent . . ."

"For all the need there is of that!"

". . . and it will help to make the time go by for you."

Period, paragraph. No one offers me any thanks; on the contrary. I leave the office without offering any myself.

Back in the workroom, I throw myself onto the best stool, without thinking that now I had a real chair, a genuine wicker chair, at my disposal, and I begin to get the brain going.

I'm beginning to catch on. They're going to keep me in this prison; otherwise I would have been sent away at the same time as Lerouge: Central Prison centralized.

Apparently this is a favor: I can see plenty of advantages in it, I'll be able to go on receiving just as much dough from outside, canteening within the limits of that dough and limited only by it, whereas in Central only a tiny monthly money order is permitted: I'll see my husband every week, and that . . . for that alone, they knew damned well, I would give in. I had refused, it was true, but that was part of the game: if Damien gave in without first haggling a little, she would no longer be Damien.

My God, the warden knows me better than I know myself. In other words, he knows cons, and . . . Oh, God, am I becoming one of them myself?

All right, what then?

Then, when I am well broken in, when I am well buttered up with heat and with extras—they'll go out of their way to spoil me, to talk nicely to me, to see to it that I never run short of coal—when I am calmed down, have become part of my sewing machine, at once the captive and the champion of St. Duty, my husband will be put down for the next transfer, probably within three months. After his sentencing for the car case, they will allow me to have him back for a few weeks, on the pretext of putting him to work as a clerk or a librarian, or a potato peeler. But then he will be sent off to Central. The warden has plenty of time, because, unhappily, we do too.

430

The Runaway

I can see what you're up to, warden!

Oh, my love, I can see you leaving . . .

I try to recapture the basic savor that I found in the hole during my adolescence; I spent a good part of my time there in those days, but other times have been piled on top, I have to dig through the layers . . . In those days I preferred the cold dry wind of December exercise periods to being marinated in cramped cells with central heating, I had my shoulder to the wheel of hardships, I made frightening bets against myself; I fasted, I burned myself, I pricked myself . . . Illusory comforts annoyed me, after having grown up as an only child: I found more fun in the ugly uniform and the watery soup. Going hungry, my guts shrinking, I was delirious with vague delights, my head went spinning, lights shone . . . There was no connection with the expiatory intention of the hole: I remained alien to my offenses, nor did I give any thought to laying up funds to back the check for future comforts: no, the hole was a vice, as much a vice as being tattooed or masturbating, a vice that I wanted to savor while I had the chance, and, if possible, to learn to like.

But I'm older now: today, in the very act of opting for the hole, I felt weary . . . I now go over my past work assignments, I remember that I'll be able to have clean sheets every week again, that I'll have my bucket of coal every morning, that I'll no longer be cold . . . All right: let's not react, let's just let ourselves be made fools of.

Let's sleep, without tiredness, without thirst, far away from the flood of light.

Let's be just the little dog that follows the matron, the poor little maid who will carry the trays of food from cell to cell, all wrapped up in her butcher's apron. Thus reinforced, the prison costume will encase me in a rigid frame, become a mandatory uniform; and, when I undress myself at night, the denim will retain my outline, swelling at the bosom and the buttocks, pinched in at the waist into great crumpled pleats.

Our punishments and our lives will pass, but the denim dress will never pass. The prisoner does not wear out his clothes: it is the clothes that wear out their prisoner.

The sorrows of the seamstress! I rise, so that I can renew acquaintance with the Temple of the Made-Over.

Heaps of sheets and shirts rise all the way to the ceiling; linens are heaped up in baskets, gigantic baskets in any of which I could easily have made a bed. The dust of lint and straw, the latter of which comes from pallets that the men have not emptied properly and that they washed while still stuffed, clings to every surface, fighting a winning battle against broom and dustcloth.

In my cubbyhole you could have eaten off the floor . . .

At the end, Lerouge let the joint go to hell: I inherited candy, but also a collection of coffee tins filled with old dregs —and not wine dregs—and cartons crammed with layers of fabric: I make a note: lug the tins to the trash barrel, the cartons to the boiler, ask for some bleach. In order to avoid penalties, the men try to repair any damage themselves before they send their things to the laundry: I find darns made with string, buttons put back on shirts with a bit of wire that has rusted and made a hole in the cloth; my tired eyes have a Neronian vision in which ragged shirts twist their shredding sleeves in agony in a vast fire, while trousers rear their scorched flies to heaven in a supreme erection.

A chorus of angry voices brings me back to reality: I run for the chair, I grab a piece of cloth at random from the nearest carton, I thrust it under the foot of the sewing machine, I clack down the foot, *vrrroom* I pedal away, man, have I ever lost my touch! careful of the fingers. False alarm: the voices die out at the threshold of the wing, without coming in.

I go to the door of the workroom on tiptoe and listen. The warden is talking with the male inmate responsible for the showers; I gather that the *casus belli* is a pillow case missing at inspection. The voices bawl at each other, *crescendo,* and then the door slams on the doused douser and the radio floods everything with its sudden tide.

It would be useless for me to disconnect the plug, and equally useless to try to pin my ears to the loudspeaker: the music will help me to know the time of day, since the noise of the sewing machine will drown out the town's bells; but the machine will tear the music to bits at the same time that it's putting the denims together again.

The matrons will turn up frequently; they'll give me lectures on Making Things Over; I'll have to help them wash and settle the new arrivals, "quick, Damien, take two sheets to Cell No. 6, quick, No. 23 has no bread" and Damien will hop to it.

Then, after the first revulsion, everything will fall back again into indifference; without reacting, I'll see, handle, and transport all the shit that anyone decides to unload on me; even the shit will be routine, just like the inexorable regularity of the canteen, the "Come sign for your money order," the light at seven o'clock.

Yes, the women are becoming aware of that, it's the fashionable topic of conversation: "The days are getting a hell of a lot shorter!"

It no longer seems funny.

I weep at having laughed at it.

Perhaps even more than in my cubbyhole, I shall flee into dreams. In order to make it impossible for anything to louse up my dream, or dull it, I'll have to make myself into twins: my hands will deal with the shit and sink into it, while my dream, a gypsy prince, will wander off to peace without end. Peace there undoubtedly will be . . . I am much more afraid of the negative effort than of the quite positive mountains of linens and clothing; as I toil away I'll have to pay attention, keep my ears open, keep my smile on tap, and give nothing . . .

Imperceptibly and then painfully, my time will be stolen from me, it will be made to pass . . . In the beginning, I'll hurry through the work for the inmates, so that then I'll be rid of it, free to spend my leisure time reading or just loafing, then, little by little, they'll start bringing me a few extra jobs: "Naturally there's no rush, let it go until you have nothing to do." As if a prisoner could decently argue that he didn't have time!

Things that will knock me dead.

I saw Lerouge re-stringing a pearl necklace for the lady, arranging them by size; making toys out of denims stolen from the storeroom for the lady's children; and even setting the lady's hair with a crown of bobby-pins. A maid of all work, in fact.

They had really had me; all right: I might as well be "had" with good grace, but let's not accept being thrown onto the ash heap altogether; because now they'll have no further reason to keep alive that Me that is of no use to them.

What the fuck can the warden care if I'm too damn tired to even look at a book in bed after a day spent on my feet ironing his clothes? He'd have his clothes; my skull could crumple and rot.

Jerk that I was! I thought they were interested in me, kind to me, I sized them up in secret, and all the time they were simply getting ready to put me to work . . . Long before Lerouge's departure, I had been chosen to replace her. And I wondered whether nice matron had not had her finger in it, I doubt everything and I believe everything.

She allowed me to pluck my eyebrows and shadow my eyes, she laughed sympathetically at all my little tics, my outbursts, my harmless little infringements of the rules, she humored me . . .

I had imagined that my antics upset them, whereas I was already, without even suspecting it, under the circus tent; the deaf-mute, the deaf-bawling circus of prison. Oh, they must have had a hell of a good laugh! Acceptance! The conquest of my Self through my defeat! The healthy joys of work!

It has been said that no man is a hero to his valet; but I would have preferred to have the warden remain my great man. I'm going to have the honor of taking care of his under-pants, and then what? Whatever I may find in them will not increase the esteem in which I hold him, nor will it diminish it. All these intimacies will simply graft tangible and more or less savory details onto concepts that are already abominable.

I shall console myself with the thought that, among all these uniforms, these formless shirts and trousers, there are cherished garments . . . Zizi has been wearing "regulation" since the end of the appeal, and I figure that he has made a deal with the shower guy so that he has stuff that is more or less his size and is able to get the same stuff back again after it's been laundered. Oh, my love, did you really once exist as I see you here in the photograph, a stranger in your little velvet frame quite as much as my reflection in the narrow mirror?

Our past is as unreal as the smoke of a fire: Truth is the present, the presence of every Sunday, this rusty stove that invites me to be its friend, it is this prison in which we live.

No use trying to stuff myself on details of our past life, I can't believe that it has ever been and that its thread will be knotted together again across this great black rip. Stripped and thrust into the servant's sacking, I wander, I jump, fettered and ridiculous. Have *I* ever been glorious, drunk, passionate?

435

Oh, Anick, put out that lamp! Don't turn back! Come back through the dust of the roads, the roller is coming . . . Not a single hair must be out of place now, I must store my angers and my charms in the cupboard. Let me shut my trap and at the same time work out some formula to keep my rebellion alive. Peace, shining eyelids! I am weary of looking at you.

Visit, letter, official or sneaked: for all that I can give in, even though I know that I ought to refuse; but, with these reasons, I may perhaps elude complete enslavement. I can always tell myself that I yielded in order to get something by it, and not just because I wanted to yield. And yet everything subtly pushed me into it; these weeks in my cell, where I was not made to do anything, where I lived as I pleased, Lerouge's friendship, the lady's kindness . . . I had forgotten the ceiling and I had taken wing, I felt light, moved, almost thankful . . . And bang! I had struck the ceiling, I had cracked my head a nasty one on it. Drop back onto the bed, girl, walk straight into the dark room, because even the dim bulb at the end of the wire in the center of the workroom keeps the denseness of the nights secret.

(9)

Two new logs have been thrown on the fire: Zizi has requested, and got from the court to which the automobile-accident case had been assigned, an order transferring it to this court's jurisdiction. Hence Zizi will be near me until the big day when one or the other of us is moved to Central. Secondly, notes are getting through: Zizi has succeeded in sewing up the character he told me about in court. This costs him a large share of his tobacco ration, but a reliable courier is beyond price.

The system is simple. Zizi canteens tubes of mustard or tomato sauce and cubes of chocolate; he folds his notes very small, seals them in heated plastic and hides them in the edibles; then he very meticulously restores the tubes or other containers to their original shape in aluminum or tin, and gives them to the cook.

At my end, I canteen the same merchandise; the guy, who is also assigned to distribute the canteen orders, goes over the list that comes from our wing and makes sure that I have ordered such and such; he grabs my goods, runs to my husband's cell, opens the serving-door (easy enough, with the end of a penknife, for example), swaps the virgin tube for the treated one that Zizi has all ready for him—in each note, Zizi tells me what to shop for in next week's market—and simply puts the replacement on the women's tray. It's my job to take the girls their canteen supplies with their supper: all I have to do is help myself. Nevertheless, the cook holds back when several of the good ladies have ordered the same things that I have: Zizi always makes a mark on the end of the tube, but, when I have the big shot at my heels . . . It would be foolhardy to look for the secret sign. Fortunately, these ladies seem to have no taste for mustard and seldom order it. In addition, many of them are flat broke, or get very little help from outside: mustard is a dream of luxury. As for tomato sauce . . . the reddish fluid that regulation noodles swim in seems to take its place.

Mother Tomato, Mother Mustard is Damien.

I explain to the chief matron that I come from a long line of mustard makers crossed with papal mules.

Do you think that frightened her? . . .

When I answer the notes, I put my note, likewise wrapped in plastic, into an empty tube, which I then crush and nibble so that it looks like a really empty one; I then drop this into the garbage pail, among the peelings and the fruit cores; the women in the cells do their own dishwashing, and they're supposed to wash the plates on which their pork chops, their fried potatoes, or their eggs were delivered to them: the price includes the cooking but not the cleaning up.

Hell! With all the work that's loaded onto me and my own compulsive cleanliness in all other respects, I can certainly be allowed a dirty mug here and there. One a week, let's say.

This mug contains the conjugal repast.

"You poor woman," the chief matron exclaims when she brings me an unexpected pile of washing just at chow time, "you're really conscientious! Quick, deliver the supper, or else yours will get cold."

"Tst, tst," I say, "don't worry, matron, I'll heat it up
on the stove, or if I don't have time I'll nibble on it tonight
in bed. Business before pleasure . . ."

"But you have to eat Damien, or else you won't be able to
keep going. You're not outside yet, you know . . ."

The chief always knows just what to say to make you feel
good. I look her up and down and also across. "Oh, with a
miserable little carcass like mine, I don't burn up much
fuel . . ."

Zizi has christened her The Rubbish Heap. When The
Rubbish Heap's tour of guard duty coincides with a note day,
I have lots of fun at delivery time. Ever since a "young one"
was put on general service—especially a young one whose
John is on the other side—harsh restrictions have exiled the
cook. In Lerouge's time, he had come right into the women's
wing to leave the tray of food on the table in the entrance
hall; Lerouge, bustling about the tiers of cells or the ground
floor, could see him, and we always made her describe the
guy to whet our appetites.

But it must have occurred to the chief matron—a little late
—that there was always the possibility of monkey business
between my man and me; or else she was afraid that some daring, lustful kitchen worker might try to leap on top of me; in
any case, not only does she shut me into the workroom at
chow time, but she also forbids the cook to set foot inside the
harem: he has to deposit his pots and the tray outside the door
and ring for her, whereupon she opens up, makes certain
that the coast is clear, and makes the final delivery to me with
a triumphant: "Chow's here!"

When she is distracted, or inclined to be chummy with me,
she allows me to pass beyond the entrance door and haul my
load back myself; I put the tray on the table where it has
always been deposited before, The Rubbish Heap takes the
order list, adjusts her glasses, and calls off the names and

orders, while I separate the canteen merchandise into evenly balanced little piles so that I can safely carry them to the girl they belong to. In the meantime, the soup is quietly congealing in the soup tureens.

"Don't you think, matron, that, if the canteen were delivered a little earlier, the women could get their food while it was hot?"

"But that's not possible, Damien, you know I've already asked. Why, with the men's canteen, the sorting out takes almost all morning."

Given the chance, she would tell me that it takes all night as well. Oh, she wasn't going to wear out her legs climbing those stairs! Why make two trips, indeed? Just to please us gripers? For the thanks there would be in it?

What difference does it make to us, after all, if we have to eat cold food? Tonight there will be only one course, and we will eat—in bed, if we like—a nice steaming stew, and forget you until tomorrow morning's so-called coffee . . .

But what gives me even more pleasure is when the chief matron, strongly suspecting me once again, stops me at the door as I am about to dash out of the wing toward the pots, pushes me back inside, and takes it on herself to haul everything in.

Under her three layers of starched apparel the chief matron wears a whalebone corset. I had been in a position to gauge the caliber of its boning when she gave me this armor to wash: I had taken all the stays out first and then put them all back in, all twelve of them, each in its respective scabbard: twelve small scabbards, in other words, in one big one.

With this contraption the chief matron finds it difficult to bend over: in order to see the end of her shoe, she has to lift her leg. So this tray loaded with food and sitting on the floor . . . gets pushed in with the toe of her shoe, laboriously and disdainfully.

The Runaway

I laugh at the sight of her jockeying this big disc, like a giant playing hopscotch without hopping. In a word, my mail is delivered to me by the foot of the warden's wife.

Once this delivery is made and the door is locked again, I make sure, with my ear to the grill, that The Rubbish Heap has really left the wing, slam-slam, and then I go back to my table, where the food is waiting. I set about unpacking the things in the order of their importance.

Chow can wait: Zizi has told me to take the plate at the extreme left of the tray whenever my canteened fried potatoes were next to those given to me free because I'm a trusty: sometimes I find, underneath, a bit of beef or a tiny omelette: the cook has a way with him. But the letter takes precedence.

Today it comes in a mustard envelope. That's fine. I use my knife to unfold the end of the tube, which has been turned up three times; I slide the blade of the knife into the seam of the aluminum and turn it in order to separate the lips of the metal: under slight pressure, the tube eructates little bubbles of mustard and, among them, the string that will pull out the little parcel, to which it is firmly attached by innumerable spirals of heavy thread. With the help of knife and teeth I cut through it all.

The note, including its intestine and peritoneum, is about the size of half my little finger. I unfold it and smooth out the sheets of onionskin paper, I set my plate of potatoes on my pillow, plop down on my belly on the bed, and start to nibble away with eyes and teeth, drying the mustard off my fingers with the potatoes.

One Sunday Zizi spends half our visiting time discussing my diet. No subject could have been more inoffensive, and in such a case The Rubbish Heap simply drowses in her chair. As a matter of fact, Zizi has not notified me what I should buy this week. So I listen.

441

"You've got to get strong, baby, it looks to me as if you're losing weight again. Order some gingerbread . . ."

I am afraid it'll be bad for my teeth, so I timidly express a preference for plain cookies; but Zizi looks at me so sternly that I shut off my *why* and promise to try it.

The slices of gingerbread had been hollowed out and contained a package about the same size as a cigarette pack, which at first I thought I was getting; but it was nothing of the kind . . .

It was a very light metal key, wrapped in a long note, the instruction sheet.

At last!

Since he can't get hold of any tools, Zizi will simply open my door with a key. He's going to make rough key blanks, which he will then notch in accordance with the imprints I send him. The cook has found the raw material for him in the repair shop: the loss of a bit of metal doesn't bring on the same thorough search as the disappearance of a tool . . . the guard, it seems, checks the contents of the tool box almost every evening, the trusty in charge of the shop is a squealer, etc.: in short, we'll have to make do with the materials available.

I am to take two impressions: one of the lock on my cell, the other of the lock on the main door, which is the same as those on the laundry and the wardrobe room. "If there's time," Zizi wrote, "we can make the joke even funnier by taking along your suitcases. In any case, even if it doesn't work . . ."

Yes: we would have fun, that must never be forgotten; let's do everything in a fun way. But nevertheless my smile is beginning to turn a bit wan.

Zi tells me how to get clear impressions, using soap, and how I am to send them to him in an empty box, preferably a camembert box. I'll have to pretend to have become a cheese nut.

The Runaway

While I am waiting for the delivery of the cheese, I spend two evenings cutting pieces of bar soap into hemispheres, the prison-issue soap, which is passed out at the beginning of each month and which I never use but put aside for the benefit of new arrivals. ("Quick, Damien, bring some soap, the new girl's in the shower.") ("And be sure to wash 'down there,' too, you hear? and see that you stick your soap 'in there'!")

These keys are going to exhaust my reserve: the soap crumbles, the hemisphere falls apart, and I have to start all over again.

Yesterday morning I decided to get to work. The little brothers were having their showers, they had to be taken care of, clean towels, mended shirts, quick, Damien, the men's things.

I had begun at dawn to arrange a big basket in neat, careful piles, well stacked and easy to count; but the guards were engaged in a competition to see who could get out of having to check the shipment, and The Rubbish Heap was getting tired of waiting. "Well, if they can't make up their minds, I'll come back later. I'm going to have my breakfast."

The poor thing—aside from three or four cups of coffee when she got up and a few meager slices of bread she'd dunked therein, she had eaten nothing since last night and was beginning to feel the pangs.

"All right, matron. But, if you'll leave the door unlocked, I'll grab the chance to mop up in the drying room: the sheets dripped all night and it's a regular swimming pool. Thanks . . . and have a good breakfast."

The Rubbish Heap gives me an automatic "thanks-same-to-you" and disappears, driven by pangs of hunger.

I run to the drying room, I sweep all the water into the drain in great back-handed swipes, I open all the transoms so that the fresh air can finish the job; then, my soap and my key in my pocket, I go upstairs. The first item on my agenda is the cell lock; since they're all the same, I prefer to work on the lock of an empty cell.

Out of superstition, I opt for No. 7.

I slide the key into the lock, but it is much too small and wiggles horribly; nevertheless I go on trying, and finally I catch it in a tumbler, I turn it slowly . . . good, I've got it through half a turn, and I begin to rejoice, because I can feel the bolt going slowly back . . .

Suddenly the key sticks half way around.

Take it easy, girl, I turn the key in the reverse direction, forcing it slightly; and crack! the key slips out as easily as if it had been in butter. The only trouble is that not all of it has come out.

I get back the handle, but the business end has broken off and is still inside the lock; and there I stand like a j-e-r-k staring at that flat, soft hunk of metal with its bright new evil shine at the place where it had broken off.

I shove the handle back into my marsupial pouch, where my fingers find the hemispheres of soap . . . if only I had started with those . . . I light a butt and feel a wave of nausea come up into my throat, God this Gitane tastes foul. It's just my luck . . . Angrily I crush it out against the railing. I could see the whole scene: the matron would not be able to open No. 7, the carpenter would come on the run and find the end of the key in the lock, everyone would be put on the griddle . . . If the cook's O.K., Zizi will still come out of it clear. But what about me?

Then I pull myself together, I tell myself that there is no reason why No. 7 should be opened for a while: I gave it a thorough cleaning after its latest inmate left, about a week ago, I figure; there is no bed linen left in it; if I'm not mistaken, I even swiped the chamber pot to make myself a waste basket for my palace.

There are still two possible dangers: an inventory or a new

arrival. Sooner or later someone was bound to try to get into that lock. Might as well begin right away. The Rubbish Heap will not have finished eating yet: I run down the stairs to the workroom, which has fortunately been left open, and I grab up a whole arsenal: scissors, an old bent spoon, pieces of wire; I roll the lot into a dust rag—if she comes, I'll start polishing zealously—and return to the scene of the crime.

But it is useless to fish, to pry, to twist my wrist and the scissors at the same time; I gather my tools up again and the matron gets up from the table and will be back with the guard for the laundry.

Too bad. I give up and go back home.

I sit down at the sewing machine. Just in time: I haven't pedaled three times when the chief matron appears, absolutely glowing from her breakfast. Seeing me going at top speed, she begins to bask in her own glory: "Good, I see you're not wasting any time. Oh, I picked up the laundry list on my way back, I don't know what's happened to those guards. We can count it together: you call off and I'll write down."

As I sing out the items I am thinking desperately. Once I am alone again, I obviously go right on doing so. Of all the senseless clumsy projects that I imagine one after another, not one seems to have a hope of working. In this misery there is just one chance: it's the day for the secret letter. Tonight Zizi will have whatever I slip into the noon trash. If only I can find a solution by then! But what solution?

My man will simply have to con the carpenter, make him stick his neck out in such a way that he can't pull it back in, perhaps by getting him to write a note that will simply be kept in reserve for blackmail; of course no man of mine would turn in a note, but you can be absolutely confident of making yourself clear if you threaten a stool pigeon this way . . .

No, it's too complicated. And, if he manages to send me

the means of taking the lock apart myself, how can I do the job and send the tools back on the same day so that they won't be missing?

There is not too much time, especially since Zizi can't rely on any other legs except the cook's, the cook might just say no or get caught, the special watch notice is still on the door . . .

That lousy broken key!

I would gladly have given myself a first-class beating. So often everything seems to dovetail and mesh, naturally and logically, to guarantee that we have bad luck. There seems to be some implacable evil force, which, furthermore, we never try to resist: we allow ourselves to be pushed toward accidents, we can see what stupidities we're committing, we're numb, submissive, and yet completely clear-sighted . . .

And then, when it happens, we feel almost good, like an injured man waking up in a strange bed after an accident.

I am not at all frightened when, a little before supper time, I hear a guard crossing the gravel in the courtyard and his voice shouting under the chief matron's window: "New prisoner coming!"

Where will this woman be put? Into No. 7, of course: it's the only empty cell on the first tier. There are a few others on the second—as a matter of fact, no one has taken over my old cubbyhole—but the more The Rubbish Heap can save her feet . . . A new prisoner will have to be taken to the office, to the lawyer, to the statistical department, to the social worker, to the croaker . . . Even if it's only a matter of one floor, this means a tremendous amount of going up and down the stairs.

I take up sentry duty at my grill. I'll wind up doing everything in this place, even peeping through keyholes. Damien, my girl, you're going down in your own estimation.

Quiet, the search has begun.

The Runaway

I heard the door of the wing, the door of the wardrobe room, and now the door of the linen room: I put six pairs of clean sheets in there this morning, so the chief matron won't come into the workroom for any; it's a pity, I would have liked, just once more before the storm, to hear her call me "Damien" so kindly . . . oh, my beloved chief!

Four feet tak-tak-tak along the hall: the new girl must be trying to keep her balance under her load of sheets and blankets, her cooking things, her messed-up luggage, her clothes; and behind her The Rubbish Heap, carrying nothing but the keys.

The footsteps pause at the landing of the first tier . . . Would you be so kind, madame, as to be willing to climb a little higher and put this miserable girl on the second tier? I'll behave myself, I won't make any more trouble for you, I'll be your servant. Later, when I'm free, I'll tell you that I haven't forgotten you, on the kind of postcards that I know you like, the ones with glaring orange sunsets and oceans on fire.

You won't? You're opening No. 7? All right, I'll remember that too. I . . .

But oh God, SHE GOT THE DOOR OPEN!

Yes: meekly, piteously, without resistance, my amputated key allowed itself to be pushed inside by her key, and undoubtedly it has fallen to the very bottom of the lock; the jailbirds' God has looked kindly on us, and I dance around the workroom like a mad thing, the key is dead long live the key, we'll make new ones, stronger ones, and, if they break, what of it, there is more room in the bowels of the lock.

I stop in front of Zizi smiling in his little red velvet frame. "No, darling, seriously, I don't mind playing Louis XVI, but the next time dig me up something a little stronger for the job."

(10)

My two half-balls of soap seem to be all right, I'm sending them off by the next tray. But, after the business of the broken key, I am no longer in such a hurry to X-ray the inside of the lock; a sketch of the outside and some approximate measurement will do the job. To compensate, I'll make a very detailed drawing of the keys. I go about with a pencil and paper in my marsupial pouch, waiting for my opportunity.

The silhouette of the key to the cell is childishly easy to remember: I had sized it up in a couple of glances, and in a couple of pencil strokes I sketched it. But the other one!

Key No. 2 is a direct descendant of Greek friezes, the swastika. and a Cubist painting. And to think that during the summer, when nice matron had been on duty every day, the keys were always left lying all over the place! Lerouge used to pick them up and have fun locking the wardrobe room with the lady inside, shouting with laughter until her prisoner, who was also laughing—though with a certain undertone of anxiety—begged her through the door, keeping her voice down, to be let out . . .

Now the lady no longer plays games with the keys: she

must still be hearing in her mind what was said to her when the warden came back, she has become much more strict, and she rations her smiles in proportion to the character and the seniority of her prisoners. I am still her favorite, but that doesn't get me what I want.

The Rubbish Heap carries a regular bouquet: a bouquet of key rings. The important part, the actual keys that do the opening, she always keeps hidden in her fat fist; and when at times she gets sleepy and opens that fist a little, at mass or during a visiting hour, her lap with the keys resting in it seldom comes into my view when there is adequate light as well. Or else Key No. 2 is hidden among the others, which are of no interest to me . . .

The Rubbish Heap never lets go of her keys, even when she is rinsing her laundry, a task in which I have been eagerly assisting her for some weeks, and with good reason. The keys are almost always in the pocket of her smock, and the flap of the pocket is turned down and buttoned; but sometimes the chief matron hooks the keys into her belt: if only they would slip out!

The laundry is rinsed in the bathtub: there is a bathroom next to the laundry room, for those who are entitled to use it: the ailing, the pregnant, the I'll-choke-to-death-in-those-showers asthmatics. But since the chief is neither pregnant nor short-winded (or not very), she showers in her own quarters and washes her laundry here. She feels she has to have the benefit of the bathtub too.

But that belt of hers is tightly fastened, and, no matter how she gesticulates, twists her body, wrings out the clothes, raises her arms, nothing ever falls out. The keys are just not washable. Ah, you bitch, I'll get you yet, one day or another.

I am constantly on the alert, my sharp eye concealed under a blank lid; more than ever, I follow the matrons like their shadow: I am indeed their shadow.

But my situation hardly improves. Nor does the weather: as a prelude to the endless winter fog, rain, and clearings in the clouds alternate without advance notice.

Instead of having me hang the wash over the railings and letting it dry in peace, the chief matron, obsessed with the good smell of cleanliness, insists on making me hang it out in the courtyard. This means: out of the drying room into the courtyard, to get the fresh air; out of the courtyard on to the railings, to escape the drizzle; off the railings out into the courtyard, to catch the sunshine; and so on until everything is finally dry. It seems to me I'm back in Jane Dufon's joint. Except that here I don't help anyone and no one helps me: the unending trundling of these heavy wet sheets, which I carry in huge bundles held to my bosom in order to go easy on my legs, saws my arms and breaks my back. But the chief matron is even more tired than I: how could she rush out of her quarters at every shower, open all these doors for me, close them again after me, spend all her time keeping an eye on the sky, and at the same time keep her other eye on her staff, the maintenance of the dump, the buying, etc? No, you have to be understanding.

I am understanding, and, since I can't ease her burdens, either personal or professional, I offered to take over the custody of the weather. As if, through the filthy panes of my narrow transom, I could do more than guess what the sky looked like!

"Well, Damien, can't you see it's raining?"

"Oh, I'm sorry! But anyway I couldn't have gotten out because of the door. And it's too far to try to yell to you through the window . . ."

All right, then, there's one way to get around that: hereafter, on drying days, she'll leave the doors unlocked: that way I can run out at the first sprinkle and she won't have to bother.

The Runaway

What a palace my prison is with all this space, these doors that yield at the touch of a finger, this solitude in the labyrinth!

Of course, it never goes quite as you like; no matter how fast I operate, I can never finish all the chores, get the sheets in soon enough; and, if it's not rain, it's soot from the chimneys dirtying the wash; as far as the prisoners' laundry is concerned, who cares? but when the dirt falls on the bosses' things, it's a tragedy, *fortissimo,* and the fault is always Damien's.

I dream that if in some future life I become the goddess of bad weather, I'll cause downpours of shit whenever it's the day for the bosses' washing, and follow those with showers of piss by way of rinsing.

In the meantime, however, if I don't want to be shut in myself, I have to keep my mouth shut.

When the sun is shining again, I abandon my mending and go out into the courtyard, dragging an old blanket, which, folded into eighths under my ass, is used in the workroom to raise me on my chair; but in the sunshine it's my beach towel. I stretch out; when autumn is occasionally broken by a hot spell, I disrobe. But I take no chances of being caught with my pants literally down: I always keep my dress handy and my ears open: over the wall I can catch the sound of the chief matron leaving her apartment, a familiar double sound: clack of high heels and clink of keys.

In addition to the two main keys that are the objects of my desire, the bunch also includes, God knows why, a vast number of old keys that seem to have nothing to do with anything on the premises and that even The Rubbish Heap must not know the use of. The whole collection is strung on a most impressive chain, not unlike the sprocket chain of a bicycle; and the matron seems so deeply attached to this chain that she will surely take it with her to heaven.

451

I picture The Rubbish Heap, turned into a ghost, dragging her chain all night long through the prison corridors.

This iron carillon, then, always warns me of the approach of the enemy and makes it possible for me to wander everywhere, even when I'm playing Eve, with my dress over my arm. Hence I have been able to obtain, without being surprised while I'm at it, the two excellent, clear lock outlines that I'll put into the mail in a little while. Good enough to get the keys accurate to a fiftieth of a millimeter. This will go a long way toward making up for my clumsiness the other day. Zizi, to whom I told the story, managed to console me: "*I* break locks, but you're more delicate: *you* break keys."

But he hasn't sent any more hardware. That's what gave me the idea of making drawings of the keys.

To accomplish this, I do embroidery work in my leisure time. I am Penelope in every sense of the word: I begin to make an embroidery reproduction of a Dali watercolor that I have seen in *Paris-Match:* Dante and Beatrice in a kiss at the eternal gates. I talk about my work to whomever will listen, but I never offer to show it.

The Rubbish Heap, like all chief matrons, has a high opinion of women who can embroider: using the pretext of keeping them from being bored, she brings them a million things to do, decorations for her mantelpiece, bibs for her children's children, doilies for her liqueur glasses. So much the worse if she puts me to work: I talk nothing else but embroidery, and even Zizi, in his letters and in our visits, always asks me how Beatrice is coming along.

When I close my eyes at night, I practice voodoo: the chief matron must ask me to let her have a look at Beatrice. This is the only way to get her to forget about her damned keys for three seconds.

One night, instead of replying: "Thanks, same to you," when she wishes me a good night, and then turning my back on her, as I generally do, I subtly poke the toe of my shoe between the door and its jamb, thus giving a signal that I'm willing to indulge in a little pre-bedtime chat. I don't often spoil her, poor woman, when it comes to jabbering; "surprised and delighted," she snaps up the invitation.

We begin with small talk: household matters, recipes, the health of her elder daughter's newest child; from the art of cooking we moved on to just plain art, and from that to my own art, or it would be better to call it my handiwork, matron.

"Oh, yes, that's right! You do embroidery, don't you? Yes, I overheard during the visiting hour, when you were talking to your husband about it . . . You know, we have to listen, and so we remember things like that without even wanting to . . ."

Like me ever since I took the memory course!

"Oh, you remembered? I'm really flattered, matron. But it's such a trivial thing . . . I don't think I'd dare try something beautiful, something for you, for instance; but with what I'm working on it doesn't matter whether it's first-class: it's more as a symbol."

"What? . . . Oh, of course. What does it represent? Would you show it to me? I'm very fond of embroidery. Even if, as you say, it's nothing remarkable; but I'm sure what you're doing is very good. I can tell that just by looking at your mending . . ."

"It isn't quite the same . . . You know how it is, I'd like to finish it before I show it, I . . . and . . . of course I know you aren't going to run and tell him about it: my husband knows, but he doesn't know it's for him that I'm doing it. As long as it'll be another year pretty soon . . ."

"Oh, has he still got another case?"

"Yes, but that's more likely to be another month. No, what I meant to say was that it's going to be his birthday soon and this embroidery will be his present. That is, of course, if you'll allow me to give it to him . . ."

"Let me see it, and I'll arrange things with the warden." She always says "the warden" when she speaks of her John. It's as if I said "the prisoner" when I'm talking about Zizi.

"Gladly. Can I rely on you then, matron?"

"Oh, Damien!" The Rubbish Heap said reproachfully, as I went over to my table to go through my sewing box, which stood there as if purely accidentally. But I turned over the skeins of thread in vain: I could not lay hands on Beatrice before the matron, driven by curiosity, had come all the way into the room and taken the key out of the lock, putting it with the others in her fat fist. I thereupon pulled my handiwork out of the bottom of the box and offered it as charmingly as I knew how, coming forward midway between the table and the door.

There I halted and displayed the marvel, waving it like a muleta just out of the matron's range of vision; then I began moving back imperceptibly, step by step, toward the table; and The Rubbish Heap, step by step, moved forward toward me.

And at last it happened! She laid the keys down on the table, among the skeins of thread, in order to dig into her pockets for her glasses. Immediately I elevated Beatrice to the level of her chin, holding the fabric flat on my palm: the matron is a good-sized woman, easily five feet eight or ten inches tall; so a floor-scraper like me was literally "under" her: sheltered by the roof provided by my tapestry, I was easily able to let my eyes wander to the keys and print their images indelibly on my retinas.

After that I didn't want to "take advantage of her any longer," I put the old dame out and went right to work to get what I had seen down on paper.

Then, without a word of thanks, I set to work to finish off

Beatrice with a diligent needle: after that, I had to get her done in time for Zizi's birthday.

All day long I work away at the machine, stitching the Dantean lovers, stitching my fingers; I stitch myself into a drunken orgy of waiting and imagining. I call it fixed imagination.

As others teach themselves patience by observing the movements of flies, I concentrate on the point where chance takes over. It is a tiny speck, more minuscule even than the pores of my Beatrice; but this point would be *my* chance, I must never lose sight of it for a moment, even a second.

If I look at any other firefly, if I stop staring and start thinking, my brain at once refuses to start up and drowsiness overcomes me: the minute I open my mind, it is infiltrated by shooting pains that spread all through it, twisting every thread of thought and draining them all in an irresistible, inextricable whirl.

My brain is even more of a mess than the skeins of thread in my sewing box: I get to such a point that I'm not sure I can get everything back in place, make thought keep its distance, and I simply dope myself. I drug myself with all the details of my job, with the unchanging movement of the needle guiding the thread, with the radio—it doesn't matter what comes out of it, the main thing is for it to go on blaring —I would like to be constantly drunk . . . And, because I'm ashamed of being so doped up, I long loudly for Sunday, "I'll finally be able to do a little reading," and I politely curse the work that is being loaded on me, "there's no end to this fucking laundry."

I know very well that on Sunday I won't read, that I'll dash off my official mail, which, now that the note system is working, is doing a double job; and that the sum of my progress, on the evening of this Sunday that I pretend to make so studious by strewing a whole collection of books and stationery round me, will be to be able to sigh: "Ah! another day killed."

I want to split, because I've got out of jail all there is to be gotten out of it.

By dint of trying to exhaust its resources, it is my own that I have drained: it is one of those subjects that you think you've covered from beginning to end and that turn out to be circular: at the end I'm back at the beginning, right where others are starting out on their own and questioning everything.

I'm like those school kids, who aren't grinds but just have a gift, who always hand in their papers before the bell rings for recess.

Fixating helps me to keep from imagining things, but it's making me risk becoming a mere animal.

That's all right with me: what state I'm in when I get there doesn't matter, as long as I get there fast: at the end of the road, out of the circle, fast, fast. To get there. So much the worse if I lose weight, become exhausted, get rusty: all of that will pass, the main thing is to hold out; to save what's left of my carcass and my mind if possible, but above all to get through the hours. Stuffing them with a drug, with stupidity, with no matter what, doesn't mean a fucking thing to me as long as they kick off and kick off fast so that out of that dead mass of them, that infusorial life in the elementary depths of myself, I can finally rise again to resurrection.

(11)

"Now why in hell did I make that circle there?"

Today's date is surrounded by a red ring on the calendar, like a bump that I can't understand.

It must be six o'clock: I spring out of bed to make my first coffee. I like to drink that coffee in comfort, with a blanket folded behind my head as an extra pillow and my biscuits on the stool that is also my night table: this is my free-woman breakfast, which makes it possible for me to throw the jail-house slop down the washstand, and even, when I have eaten too many biscuits, to give the chamber pot the pleasure of swallowing the eleven-thirty meal.

A good breakfast gives me guts for a whole day.

Waiting to hear the song of the water being heated on the hot plate, I was dragging my slippers around the cell—my own misery providing the scenery for this healthful stroll—when the calendar hit me in the eye.

And yet I look at it every day, I mark it up, I write code on it, I embrace it, I curse it; I renew the four pinches of cooked rice that paste it onto the closet, and which never cling long to the painted metal. But I can't remember why I made that ulcer there. A holiday? A birthday? Hell, it will eventually come to mind. The water is singing, it is time for me to officiate: coffee powder piled in the spoon, handkerchief-filter over the glass, butter on the little cookies.

How can I manufacture repentance and good resolutions under such conditions? Modern prisons soften instead of punishing; where whips should have been employed, there are comforts; people are locked up instead of being given a good clout and then shoved out on their own, free to die of it or recover from it. The kindness tactic warms the blood in the beginning: you expect much worse, you're touched, at bottom jail is not too awful . . . Then you grow used to this gentleness, you no longer limit your demands: you grab the guards by the arm, you yell, you wheedle, or you sneer.

I think I would have liked the jails of other times, prisoners arrayed against keepers, wooden shoes and rough hoods, severity and shit; all the things to which it was impossible to grow accustomed, to submit, unless you had been born in jail. Nowadays the can makes a hard life impossible . . . ("say, Anick, how about a little more butter?"). I loll back with pleasure on my gray pillow and sniff the last of the glass, which still warms my hands a little: St. Java. Saint, saint, saint. What saint's day is this with the circle round it? It is not St. Expédite . . . Now I have it: Nicole wrote to the social worker here so that she could tell me the date she's being released; and now I remember that lazy afternoon when I whispered: "Take a good look in every direction, Nicole: if I know and if I'm able (and, if I know the date, I will be able), I can assure you that I'll be there . . ."

In two hours Nicole will be free. I picture her silhouette, at the threshold of the smaller door, under the trees of the sidewalk, the door through which I had walked to climb into the paddy wagon for my transfer.

Nicole would have her slacks back, her hair would glint with the autumn sunshine, Nicole would stand at the entrance of that lonely avenue on the outskirts of the town.

And I loll here, far from the grass of our walks, sipping coffee, I who was not supposed to forget.

Clink!

I was a good shot: I hit the bull's-eye in the sink with the glass; when it shattered, it spattered the blue enamel with little brown spots of coffee that ran down slowly, hell, I had just scrubbed yesterday. Now I will also have to drink out of the penal mug until the next incidentals day in the canteen: Nicole has just cost me thirty-five centimes.

Well, I'll try to take my mind off that by going to work on the conjugal letter: but it will have to absorb all my attention.

From breakfast until lunch I spend the whole time decorating the upper left-hand corner, using my cheap watercolor equipment for a splendid miniature orchid. My letter will be discreetly perfumed: I open the black ink, leaving the embittered ball-point in its sheath, so that I won't be tempted into exuberance when, arriving at the other side of the paper, I can no longer see the warning of the flower: it tells me that this is "a perfumed letter, and don't forget"; and the pen that must forever be dipped into the ink, the blots that must be avoided, all these force me to pay attention. I murmur the words before I write them, I trace them slowly, as laboriously as a court clerk. For the first time since our arrest, I speak of leniency, of asking for clemency, of chance—loathsome chance!—"that it might be advisable to take into consideration"; immediately I add, in order to cancel that: "It is not that I am losing sight of what I want, what we want . . . I have always thought that my sentences would be made concurrent, but, when I thought *I,* I was also thinking *we* (damned old liar!) . . . but what's the difference? This clemency can't change the plans in which it has been a factor since the very beginning, even if as an insignificant detail. I am talking to you about other blessings today, because it is essential to find something else to take the place of that in order to keep hope complete, in order always to have the same number of streets running out of the crossroads of the chimeras . . ."

We girls, who are supposed to be so crafty and bewitching, have the gift for reconciling two mutually exclusive solutions without difficulty; we can take two different directions at the same time without tearing ourselves in half.

My letter is finished; to support what I have said about parole, petitions to the Place Vendôme, and probation boards, I then write to the prosecutor; finding invention difficult now, I recopy the letter to the prosecutor, changing only the salutation and the concluding compliments—*my profound respect* becomes *my most profound respect*—and address it to the Minister of Justice; finally, I go over the list of all my lawyers and write to one of those whom I have used least to come and see me: he'll stand behind me here.

Undoubtedly the wait for the answers will kill the rest of the year; but . . . it seems to me that I too am undergoing a change of season; that I am discovering new energy within myself. Zizi has perhaps given me a subtle transfusion. In our recent conversations, both at court and in the visiting room, beneath the words caught and peeled bare by our guards, even beneath the letters, I have sensed the growth of a grim shadow of hopelessness. Zizi sets his jaw and says again and again: "All I have is my teeth . . ."

I know that he is neither a weakling nor a fool, and that it is possible to mount and ride a runaway with nothing more than a broken kitchen knife: if he had been alone, Zizi would have been far away by now. But there is me: he has to get into the women's wing, fetch me out of my hole, get me over the wall and the broken glass.

Try it alone? I have no more desire than he to do that: the failure at Christmas was enough for me, and this time I won't get married . . . if I fail on my own, how can even Zizi console me for it?

I want to wait and hope, without wearying . . . Keep your spirits up, Zi, we'll be back together again. Don't be sad: escapes are not built on sadness. Hate, suffering, that's what drives, what lights the fire; there is nothing dynamic in sadness. I know, we have no one to hate, no reason to feel bad: it's a good hotel, we're well taken care of, the worries of the Palace of Justice are over.

So it has to happen that, just when Zizi seems to be weakening, I seem to be collapsing. Falling precipitately into the old ways, help, gentlemen, be merciful, put me back on my feet. I am half sincere: if the runaway mare has to die, or if it goes mad so that we have to strangle it to prevent it from screaming from the rooftops, well, I'll always have my little favors to ask . . .

Don't get confused, little noodle of mine, in this vast mass of dream.

This very afternoon, when I sign the register for official letters, I am sure that mine are on their way to high places. The progress of a plea for clemency is rapid enough, all things considered, and, compared to that of an escape, it's a piece of cake. All that it requires is a petition written with proper spelling and proper humility, bootlicking and good resolutions; the index finger timidly extended to tap on the sacred doors, instead of cutting tools; in place of little double-crossers, relatives and friends to raise a chorus at the Ministry, and, finally, an onion hidden in your handkerchief.

And, if it flops, no bullets in the ass, no pals bitching at you because you brought on a rash of searches and stricter surveillance for everyone else.

If, after the three months of waiting, my letters haven't decided to come down from their lofty heights, I'll pick up my pen and start the whole thing over again: "I take the liberty of presenting a new petition." It is the only liberty you can take, once you've decided to stay in stir.

One morning, finally, the matron will take me to the office, unless the office has too much to do and sends the matron to my cell with the thing; either way, I'll be presented with a piece of paper headed *Ministry of Justice,* on which, among all the fly tracks in small print, three big words will splash in my face, three thick, shining cockroach tracks: PETITION IS REFUSED. I'll be offered a pen, I'll take my own out of my pocket, and I'll initial the refusal, without opening my mouth, because in such cases it is not the interested party but the messenger who does the talking: as a rule, the clerk or the matron suggests that you prepare a new petition right away: "it isn't very often that an appeal for clemency succeeds the first time, y'know," but "you can appeal as often as you want to . . ."

Oh, no! I've done enough of that kind of thing before, when I still believed that it was as simple as self-service places: I got back the money I put in, I must admit, but I never have been able to get anything to eat . . .

Oh, my runaway mare! You could abandon me so easily, I give you so little to keep you alive! Even though I never wanted to hurt you, I've grabbed you by the bridle a hundred times to haul you back to the stable . . . I thought that you would start to buck and whinny, that you would paw my plates and my bed, keeping me from eating and sleeping until I paid attention to you again . . .

On the contrary: the runaway mare has quietly stretched out on its misty bed: am I not its master, have I not created it, do I not possess the right of life and death over it? The mare will wait for me another season.

As for my husband, he admired and smelled my orchid without perceiving its meaning: at our next visit he was smiling . . . He must have thought that I'm getting ready to tune up the violins, and . . . has he ever doubted it?

I am a girl and I'm dark-haired, and Zizi, a guy and blond,

lacks my impulsiveness. Whenever I'm ready to kick up a fuss, he counters with his famous "mind over matter" . . . and I am on the alert: there have been many times when I have experienced this power, this silent, gentle persuasion that insinuates its velvet augers into the flesh without ever giving the advance warning of an unexpected or painful prick. It was thus that Zizi overcame my refusal to love, taught me the arpeggios and the harmonies of joy; and love, which pursued me for years without ever succeeding in seducing me, was able to prove itself a tender victor; with the utmost gentleness he persuaded me to accept its disturbing presence; to cultivate, somewhat coyly, its apparent fragility in order to seem to be forcing me when it was I who yielded . . .

Through love I have discovered the side of life that is all abandon, all feelings and sentiments, without lunatic rituals, without thought, without error. Oh, yes, Zi, I am on the alert!

You think that our property is private, that its paths cross time and punishment, that it makes no difference where we seem to be . . . oh, darling, how I would like just the opposite, how I want love to be all round me, to enter me and find the love concealed within me. But there is no love in a prison. Nothing and no one here can make me want to sing: how can you sing here?

If I am unlucky enough to misinterpret some noise as a door slamming and, thinking that the matron has gone out of the wing, raise my voice in song, she runs to my door and tells me to shut up.

I laugh at her muzzle, my mind is on other harmonies. Prison is a perpetual, a frightful disharmony: between heart and words; between the broad morning smile for the new-born day and the dull routine, with its dirt and its burdens; between the trust that constantly is on the point of being offered and the deceits, the indifference, the callousness of others.

I've had enough of it, I want to sing.

I love you, Zi, but my love needs air. I put this idea of an escape into your head; you didn't discard it because it is an aspect of me, but you would be well pleased if I took back this idea of mine!

Zizi has lammed too, long before me, long before he met me; he is familiar with the sudden furies of that crazy steed, and, if he has agreed to try again, it's because he wants to save me, if he can, from a fatal accident, since I insist that I am going to mount the beast. But how much it would please him if I said: "Let's forget about it!"

That can't not be true, we're just acting like old fools. Since I've been alone I've seen for myself how decisions can lose their reality, how difficult it is to keep rage alive, when there are no more promises to keep or fronts to maintain, when you can no longer make yourself drunk with stupid talk, when there is no kind of drug left.

I am confined in a cell. Forcibly sobered up. A hand is stretched out to me in good faith, I am invited to cross the gangplank of human kindness . . .

I vainly tell myself that this commits me to nothing . . . Bah!

(12)

These lawyers are real geniuses.

They talk much and write little. They play hard to get.

Perhaps that is why three sentences from a lawyer are worth three double sheets from any non-lawyer.

Whenever a letter comes from counselor, you feel as if you've been a little nutty, just the same, to have had such nasty thoughts about him: No, he had not forgotten me, it was just that he doesn't waste words, he waits until he has something concrete to tell me, but it takes time for that to happen, etc. And so you defend your defender.

If the letter is only a notice of a hearing, preliminary or other, it is usually typed by his secretary, short and to the point; only the signature can offer a bit of comfort, unless it is quick and casual and in effect an anonymous signature.

What is preferable is a handwritten letter: even if it consists of only a few square inches of words, you read it over and over again.

Gone with the wind.

But the indention of each new paragraph opens an abyss, each period is a little planet; you interpret the words in every possible sense, until they no longer have any sense at all and become little piles of inky coal in front of your eyes, giving off a friendly warmth.

The lawyer whom I got in touch with for my appeal for clemency answered me by return mail: "I will come to visit you at once in order to discuss the entire matter with you."

As a result of this I have been playing Penelope for a week; a Penelope who, instead of doing embroidery, mends the seats of Ulysses' trousers. Often I abandon the seats, the collars and all the rest of it, now that I have my observation post. The transom of the workroom can now be opened like those of the cells, but, since it looks out on the main court-yard, there is much more to be seen than from my cubby-hole. The workroom is situated in a corner, but by twisting my collar bones I can see beyond the block of brick that cuts off my horizon and capture half the main gate in my field of vision.

It is the good half, the side with the postern door through which pedestrians, motor bikes, clerks, etc. come and go.

Throughout the whole week, every ring at the bell is like an irresistible lever pushing me upward, as I climb onto the stool and then onto the table for a good look.

Opening the door of a prison is a ritual in itself. First the guard on duty selects the key: sometimes he walks to the gate and stops in order to go through his collection; sometimes he chooses the key before he goes out and then advances with it trained on the lock as if he were holding a gun.

But, before he brings key to lock, he looks through the peephole.

If he doesn't like the visitor's mug, he asks questions, gesticulates, protests, or even brutally slams the cover of the peephole shut.

(In such cases I climb down without wasting time: the screw opens up for lawyers without any argument.)

The lawyer has pointed out to me, in a postscript, that he

will have to have an authorization from the prefect for his visit, in view of the fact that I am now serving a sentence; but his *at once* made me forget what I knew about prefectural delays, and I never missed a ring, all I did all day long was climb until meal time, a barrier that even lawyers are not allowed to breach. Then I would be reminded of the grim realities of my aching legs and the piles of mending left to do. I rushed through dinner and personal hygiene, and I did everything on the double, pedaling furiously until I had caught up.

Last night, therefore, I stayed at the machine long after the matron made her round—I have the right to turn out my own light—and I didn't stop until the thread was starting to dance in front of my eyes and I was putting patches on backward. I had just about finished brushing my teeth again (I had been keeping myself going with plenty of candy) when I fell into a coma full of ringing bells and whirring sewing machines.

So I made up my mind this morning to stop climbing up to the transom . . . beginning tomorrow. I won't have to go back on my word: the lawyer came this afternoon.

When the screw brought in my caller, I didn't "almost swoon with emotion," I didn't "go mad with joy"; I felt absolutely nothing. He was there, it was perfectly natural; my week of waiting suddenly seemed ridiculous: how had all my climbing been able to accelerate by even one second the arrival of this minute, this minute suspended in time as I was suspended in space, clinging to my transom, out of touch with reality, my mind not functioning?

When counselor had disappeared behind the brick, at the extreme left of my field of vision, I got back the use of my head and legs and jumped down from the table without even thinking of using the stool. The shock of the concrete under my feet completed the job of bringing me back to reality: in two steps I was at the mirror, making myself into a lady: I reached my hand gracefully toward the faucet; I bit my lips to make them look enticing, and I rubbed saliva over my lashes and pressed them vigorously back on the eyelids so that they would seem naturally curved; all to such good effect that, when the chief matron came to get me in a rush and found me with my eyes shining and full of water, she thought it necessary to say kindly: "Don't cry any more, now, you're going to have a wonderful visit . . ."

"A visit?" I repeated, stunned. "But who can it be?"

Apparently the chief matron didn't have the faintest idea.

Completely lost in my own speculations, I forgot to trot docilely behind her and branched off automatically toward the central guard post, where the lawyers' conference cubicles were, so the chief brought me back on her beam. "Where are you going?" she demanded. "I didn't say we were going to the office, I said you had a visitor."

I change course without protest; I know a thing or two about my friend the lawyer. As soon as he came into the visiting room, I rose and put out my hand across the ping-pong table without even thinking of the angel at my shoulder, who showed clear signs of uneasiness.

"How do you do, counselor? . . . Before we do anything else, would you ask the office to move us to a better room?"

"But I don't understand," the lawyer says. He had never been in this prison and kept looking around.

"This is just an ordinary visiting room, counselor . . . The ones for lawyers are in the rotunda, behind you . . . Someone probably made a mistake."

The chief matron was trembling. "I was ORDERED to put you here. Don't forget that you're under sentence."

"Granted, but this gentleman is a lawyer. Either you take me to the proper place or you take me back to the workroom. I . . ."

468

"One moment, please, madame," the lawyer says, addressing both of us. "Let me go and see what can be done."

He went out. A few minutes went by in complete silence. Finally a compromise was reached: we were transferred to the office.

The embryonic file prepared by the lawyer lay spread out on a narrow table between us; it was comfortable here, as in the workroom; and my head began to warm a little too, it felt full of bubbling, fleeting thoughts, as it always did in the company of a mouthpiece; I felt like bursting into laughter, restrained and subtle laughter; I wanted to be clever and civilized, to belie my wretched clothes and to wipe out for my guest the reality of the dreary room that surrounded us.

Right at the start he made the matron go away; she had planted herself right next to the table and was watching each word come to life on our lips. I knew that, under the Rules, we could be made to submit to the presence of hostile ears; but I engaged in such doubletalk, I led the lawyer into such dizzily abstract discussions, I made such badly disguised threats that the matron, being both bored and cautious, finally left us and went to sit at a table nearby and gossip with one or another of her husband's menials. For form's sake, now and then, she threw us a stern and omniscient glance.

Our chairs drawn close together, we whispered like two lawyers in a corridor or two convicts in two corridors: we were fraternally sly. There was no danger that they would interfere! I had shifted my chair in such a way that I had my back to them; through the window at the lawyer's back I could see a heap of coal, the familiar pile of every prison courtyard, which from summer on stands as a reminder of the frozen feet to come, of the haste in which we'll go back into our winter cocoons. The sight of this little mountain of evil omen gave me new strength: do something, counselor, catch my prayer on the wing, find its best side and spread it before the eyes of the High and Mighty.

I had dreamed of this man so much that I was devouring him with my eyes to prevent him from evaporating, to be able to believe in him . . .

Yes, it was really true: the lawyer made me recapitulate the story of my life while he made notes on a huge sheet of pink paper; when I paused, groping for what to say next, he helped me along with gentle but precise little queries.

An old-model Remington, the bureaucrat's organ, with a moleskin cover, shared the table with our papers and provided a rampart for our hands and our voices. The chief matron, absorbed in her chatter, seemed to have forgotten us; and I was hoping that our conversation would go on forever so that she could eternally pursue her own.

Counselor was giving me instruction. At this point, to assure the progress of a petition for clemency, it was advisable to get in touch with the local judge assigned to the Application of Penalties. I knew in a vague sort of way that there existed other judges besides those who sat in courts, but I didn't know their exact functions. Was it really possible to "apply the penalty" otherwise than in pronouncing judgment, which was slapped on you with a heavy, uncaring trowel, plop! without a thought to what might be thus walled in?

The A.P. judge had the job of delicately peeling off the plaster, and, like a good croaker, observing how we had progressed beneath it: we, the sentenced, the living scars, with the pink buds of our hopes, our potentials, our necrosis, and the areas of undamaged skin. The A.P. judge studies all of that. If in his opinion the cure is making good progress, he has the power to facilitate the patient's discharge . . .

As the lawyer went on talking, I felt as if I were becoming a scar, I turned pink and pearly, then I began to close, I shrank . . . It was not worth the trouble of going over the wall of the joint, the J.A.P. was going to turn me loose! The lawyer put me back into the cell: you must not forget, madame, that the J.A.P. is only one wheel in the machine, that the controls are handled at Central in the Place Vendôme, where hundreds of requests of this kind are received and filed every day. The lawyer added: ". . . in addition, during this holiday period, the J.A.P. may very well be away: I am not at all sure that I can get in touch with him immediately. I shall have to ask for an appointment; after the eleventh of November . . ."

I sniffed at these words with distrust, afraid that they had a smell that I knew only too well: in my haste to strike while the iron is hot I too often set the place on fire, at the smell of burning everyone flees . . . Was the lawyer easing himself out? Was he going to advise me to let the forge cool down a little? Too bad for him, I just stirred up the fire all the harder: "But why not make sure right away whether he's available? The Palace of Justice could tell you: telephone from here . . ." Since the mouthpiece seemed to be hesitating, I tossed my live coal right into his face. ". . . if, that is, they'll let you use their phone."

The lawyer seemed to swell up immediately. "If they'll let me? Why, the warden will be delighted!"

In this way the lawyer, who is not my superior, after all, made it plain to me that the warden, who is my superior, was ready to obey him. While I was pondering over the mysteries of the hierarchy, counselor had gotten to his feet and gone over to talk to the guards. There was no need for him to go to the warden's office: in a confident tone he wove an intricately complimentary wreath of words, the guards' feet got all tangled up in it, and they handed the lawyer the office telephone obsequiously. The Palace answered with a busy signal, and that sound had in it all the agony of the desert.

Then counselor was connected with the front desk, which transferred him to the main office, which launched into an interminable crackling sound; I tried to keep track of the calls, in case the lawyer should forget to leave the money for them and the clerk should take it out of my account; finally someone unearthed the judge's private telephone number and address; the lawyer wrote the address down on a piece of paper that I immediately tucked into my sleeve, and urged me to write my letter that very evening, in such a way as to lay the groundwork for the appointment that he would immediately request.

I said: "I also have a few little things that I've written here in stir: short stories, poems . . . Do you think they'd help to fill out the picture?"

"Oh, that's extremely interesting! Send them to me."

"I . . . well . . . you see, I'm not supposed to write anything but unsealed letters to you, and I'd just as soon not let the censors in on it."

Counselor thought a moment, playing with the spring of his ball-point: "All right, send them directly to the J.A.P. And don't worry, I'm going to do everything in my power to get him interested in your case."

I remembered a recent trial, when the mouthpiece of the moment had tried to draw attention to my "capacities for intellectual rehabilitation"; and suddenly I was ashamed . . . since I had been put to work, I had written nothing but the usual letters—and the laundry lists.

When I returned to the workroom, I went right to work on this new request, recapitulating my life story, outlining my potentials and prospects for the future; I spoke of my married life, which was still only a pretty dream born in prison; I made new copies of some of my work, those most suited, in my opinion, to the purpose of my letter. And, long after I had licked the envelope, I went on writing still, but this time for myself alone.

Two months . . . Without my having been aware of the fact, my mind is beginning to die of boredom; or, to be more accurate, I am aware of it, but I cheat. The work is a good excuse; I don't have the time, I am pooped, I have no gift for writing, I can't take on brain work "in addition." To justify myself, and while the pile of denims under the incessantly whirring machine mounts higher, I say to myself that I'll get back to all that whenever I want to, because I'll always be able to write and to remember: so why force it? I am saving myself, I am ringed round with the inexpressible, etc.

Now I am using only the indispensable words; to me the others seem old and demanding. I forget the words that the beloved voice set, one by one, like jewels, into caresses; words, those silken outlets for the radiations of the heart, little words, big words, coarse words; for two months I have had a vocabulary composed entirely of formulae, of conventional phrases that I cling to to express sincerity, of shabby, run-down platitudes . . . The slightest obstacle creates a hiding place for my words from which they refuse to come out: I forget them there, deliberately, on the pretext of creating new ones, later, somewhere else; I say that the intensity of my feelings and my impressions is such as to engrave them forever . . . Oh, in other days I was not so spendthrift . . . I had only my ball-point to pull me out of the shit and the despair; with it I could distill the bad so that only the truth was preserved. Now I am waiting: instead of looking forward to everything, or no longer looking forward to anything. A passive hope, more passive than despair.

The landslide of clemencies, amnesty, the return of the tools, the escape, all the things that may never come.

I tried tonight to capture my lightness of heart after the visit, my complacency of conscience after the begging letter, the sly hope that deceives and distorts . . . I am quite aware that by tomorrow I will have got rid of all of this again. Tomorrow I'll be conscious of my cell again, just as later

473

I would lose that cell again, like the thousands of dead cells thrown off by my skin.

I am making progress: the proof of that is the mercury falling as the months go by: and I am satisfied with this proof. I have gained nothing out of my day, but I have gained the day, and another stroke through the calendar is not so bad. Slowly the mercury is getting down to zero, and from zero you make a fresh start. I have not yet, however, reached inertia; I will never resign myself to accepting the props sanctified by tradition, to counting the days backward until I reach the end, in the fashion of every conscript private in the world and of some of my companions: I constantly envisage the possibility that the mercury can hit bottom in a single plunge, that some cataclysm may destroy the jail, or quite simply that somehow I may find a way to split. Oh, these momentary, unpredictable, total rages! Then the bulk of the anger outweighs the bulk of the torpor: since these two bulks no longer neutralize each other, I am threatened with being crushed to death. Beneath the appearance of submission the storm forever gathers, bursts, and gathers again.

But each explosion makes me a little more clear-sighted, a little more corrosive: the cocoon of toughness will not be dissolved by the first interval of happiness, I will not be a better person that easily . . .

And yet all these murdered days have had a reason behind them. I squandered them, true; but, in spite of my constant vague feeling of having let something get away from me, the waste is slight and devoid of bitterness.

Zizi loves me: that is the golden thread. What does it matter if for a moment the golden thread and the black rope stretched out together?

When we are together again, at the very moment of entering again into delight, the dream will naturally branch off from this moment; and yesterday's sufferings, now left behind, will flee into the garret, into oblivion. Go forward, Anick, and look at these petitions and appeals as nothing more than a somewhat different means of making the time pass.

The passage of time. This miraculous sterile time too will pass.

The matron passes on her round.

Damien is out like a light, as a glance through the peephole shows.

Wide awake, I stretch out my pins under the covers.

I feel tired and sated, too quiet . . . I don't want to be quiet! Let my fury never abate. Let me always keep intact my wrong, my hurtful ways.

$\left(13\right)$

. . . and Christmas is over.

After these holidays that to me were an incessant hum, the single note of silence has returned to the prison.

Nauseated with chocolate and chicken, the girls emptied the medicine cabinet's entire stock of laxatives and resolved to go on a permanent diet of vegetable broth: as soon as they get rid of the last crumbs of sticky English candies that they mechanically share among themselves on their walks, as soon as there is not a single shred of chocolate left in their cupboards.

I still have enough for a little while longer; I saw to it that my Christmas packages were filled with things that took a long time to go bad: bacon, smoked pork sausages that can be hung up and from which a slice can be cut from time to time, and, in the sweets department, nougat and fruit in jars.

On Christmas Eve I managed to get stoned.

My solitary evening with the photograph of my husband had been irrigated with warm, sweet beer. Pfui! It was revolting to swallow; but, once it had got down, a pleasant knot of heat invaded my spinal column and kept me balanced on my coccyx, all my fibres in that area taut and slightly tingling,

476

while my head seemed to disperse itself into little splashes on the walls of the cell, which had become a real room.

I had covered the electric light with a pink paper bag, and its glow spread over the table like the music from the radio, everything just right for a civilized evening of nibbling and picking and pecking: the mayonnaise was decorated with black and green olives, the chicken was cut in cubes and slices and there was custard with cookies.

I wanted to eat and doze without any problems, never losing the quivering little hollow of well-being in my stomach, the hollow in the full belly.

We were allowed to have the radio until lights out: Mozart came on fleecy wings; I thought of Mary, you had to think of her a bit, forgotten as she was in all the holiday-making; a splendid, dark Mary looking down.

In the whole array of my Christmases in prison, this one would stand out like a smooth stone.

Tomorrow too there will be a feast, the last before the advent of the perpetual broth: the mouth and the year are about to change. Bring us back to life, O St. Sylvester.

Perhaps we are still in the old year, perhaps we are already in the new one: I don't know how long I've lain here under the dark ceiling, chain-smoking the cigarettes that were given to us by the various official visitors. One by one I glimpse the facets of this new year, some dark, some fake, the kaleidoscope turns and I grow dizzy . . .

Three hundred sixty-five days!

No. I am ready to howl at the impossibility of it. I can't get this great hard lump down in one swallow: as well try to finish the year's bread ration in a single meal.

This impossibility must be made to yield the possibilities of each second; the key word is perhaps, perhaps manufacture an existence . . .

Happy New Year! Rain pours down the window, rivulets

glow on the panes. I would like . . . Oh, I would like to re-
examine everything, to halt this passage of time that is
resolving everything in spite of me; I would like not to know
the schedule of the days that lie ahead, to reconstruct dreams
and fantasies so that they resemble last year's, to believe in
them, to wait for them to come true, without posing heathen
questions, without doubting, without giving up.

But I can't believe any longer.

All right, carcass, make a great cross over the sun, forget
that spring can be born only out of winter; make yourself
nothing but frozen feet, a shivering, bundled-up body seeking
only the fleeting pearl of warmth of the coffee water or the
shower.

Tomorrow, laundry: it is a day of rest, but the men don't
want to rest. The cook is working, the laundry man is working, the guard is working. You'll work too, Anick: you'll
breathe in—and without displeasure, right?—the aroma that
comes up from the cellars, the stream, the acridness of wood
that does not want to catch fire. Smell, my girl, take a good
sniff: it is a barbecue, it is a cake baking, rich living after
days of stew; it is curling up in a comfortable ball, the
downiness of the life that you rejected. I sigh: what difference
does it make, it is all right the way it is, I will stay here.

There has been no miracle, only a bit of luck, the luck of
being alive. I still have a strong devotion to luck and miracle,
as I have toward everything in my past; I am thankful for
having been so often, so persistently comforted, inveigled,
coddled, angered. You were all lovely children whom some
unknown power of good has called back into itself.

And we stay where we are.

We will be transferred to Central, we will be forgotten in
this provincial jail, but either way we will be *here*. When it is
time for the others to go and talk to their visitors, we will

remember our little talks, our crazy little notes, and the strange pang when we are brought face to face like two packages carried to the right address, with a half hour to look at each other; we will remember these cocoons of hateful denim that we wanted so much to push away with delicate, pitying hands so that our fingers could feel out the sleeping sources of love.

But I am dreaming and we are here, we will see each other again on Sunday.

We will speak: that was what the visit is for, isn't it?

We will speak of the planets, the unexplored planets and the vanished planets; yesterday is taboo: "Your stupidities are too well known"; tomorrow is a mystery: "Well, my poor Damien, haven't you heard yet about your petition?" Today . . .

"One day at a time, baby," Zizi will say.

Zi, my love, one day the cycle of days and nights will stop torturing us and turn kind to us again, as it used to be; but there is no kind of change that has the power of accelerating the passage of time, I know. The cold is maddening tonight; and yet the hateful blanket in which I roll myself up will vanish like the cold, and I will gorge myself on sun.

And the sun will melt the dripping candles that want to burn, that think they can give light. I love you, you lousy old prison blanket, I wrap myself up in you and I let everything dig into me through you: the eternal archer, the lack, the pincushion in the guts, the throat locked tight on the need to weep.

And little by little the sparks fade and vanish, as the ashes of my cigarette die on the stone floor of my cell.

Good God, I'm bawling!

Weep weep, for everything and for nothing, flood away on the tide of those silent tears all the old lodes of anger, the vast, absurd, sweet problem of my existence.

The year is beginning. Weep, my girl: you won't have to piss so much.

I must sleep . . . Why, really? Time passing at night is good. I would like to get through all the nights of this year in this way; and each morning to be only a girl who jumps up and runs about all day, waiting for night to come.

A girl in a coma, in this golden coma of prison where nothing makes a mark, where anything at all can dazzle, caprice, a gay, rich display put on for me alone, my secret break.

I hear midnight strike: I dry my eyes on the blanket; up into the saddle. The bells of the city mingle their arabesques, like the bells at a wedding; and long before the sky grows light I will begin to imagine the New Year's presents that I'll be getting.

April 1961–June 1962